DEVIL'S ISLAND

C R DEMPSEY

CRMPD Media

CRMPD MEDIA LIMITED

CONTENTS

For Mena and Poppy

CHAPTER I
THE CAULDRON OF HELL

T he wood of the ship's hull was coated in a layer of slime as if dredged from the depths of a putrid and forsaken cavern, a stopover on the descent to hell. The dampness clung to the walls like a thick mucus, remnants of wicked creatures slithering back into the underworld, figments of an overstimulated imagination. Francisco Butero found himself trapped in this cursed pit, impervious to prayer, clean air, daylight, or even hope.

The voices inside his head echoed the accusations that had led to his plight, reminding him that he had brought this upon himself. He felt his skull bounce off the grimy walls of the tiny cell, the sharp sting of pain radiating through his head. He tried to move, only to find himself bound by cold, unwavering iron manacles on his wrists and ankles. The stench of his own waste permeated the small space, mixing with the putrid odour of the cramped quarters. But he was the lucky one. The one privilege he had been granted was a cell to himself, a privilege he was not allowed to forget by his neighbours.

Struggling to find some semblance of comfort, Francisco lifted his feet off the filthy floor and collapsed onto a rusted bench attached to the wall by a single hinge and chain. But even in this momentary respite, he could only cry out in despair. "What infernal cauldron have I been cast into?" he bellowed at the bars of his cell, hoping for some sort of answer or reprieve. Instead, all he received were taunts from other prisoners, their words laced with bitterness and resentment. "Now you know what it feels like," they goaded, "there's no one to make your meals and wash your clothes here, your lordship." To which Francisco could only curse and swear revenge towards his tormentors and the cruel world that had cast him into this wretched place. But at least he had finally got some attention from those who controlled the keys.

The jailer sauntered in, his heavy footsteps echoing like a death knell. His face twisted in resentment at being disturbed by the noise and activity that demanded his attention, tearing him away from more enjoyable pursuits. Sickly pale skin clung to his gaunt face, a reflection of his neglectful care for himself, the prisoner and guard duties.

His scruff matched the unkempt appearance of the man behind bars, but unlike the tattered rags adorning the prisoner's body, the jailer boasted a pair of sturdy boots and a filthy breastplate as symbols of his authority. While the imprisoned man had no protection for his head against the violent thrashing of the ship, the guard wore a morion to shield himself. While the prisoner clung to a simple chain for support, the jailer held onto his freedom and authority with a wooden club and sword.

"Release me from this hellhole!" Francisco's hands gripped the cold metal bars of his cage with trembling fingers as he pleaded, his voice hoarse from weeks of neglect, making him sound pitiful.

A flicker of desperate hope burned in Francisco's eyes.

"Surely I could better serve my admiral, fleet, and king if I were up on deck using my skills? If God were truly judging my supposed crimes, then I should have been thrown overboard to suffer at the mercy of sea serpents and monstrous creatures. But God, in His boundless wisdom, would surely command those beasts to spit me back out onto the deck so that I may continue to serve Him and our fleet all the way back to Spain. There, I would stand trial for my alleged crimes and let God be the ultimate judge. He would see that any perceived wrongdoing has been more than redeemed by the countless souls I have saved through my service."

The desperation in his voice was almost palpable as he begged for mercy from both God and his captors.

The jailer threw his head back and let out a deep, bellowing laugh. He was accustomed to grasping hands protruding from the cell bars and the eloquent pleas generated by the fear of meeting one's maker or one of the implements of discipline the jailer may bring with him. With a sarcastic sigh, he pulled up a small stool and settled down, revelling in the entertainment that would surely come from this afternoon's interrogation. As the jailer, he held respect and power in only one area of the ship and at only one time in his life. It was over these prisoners, and he would make them pay for all those who had mocked and taunted him all his life for his lowly standing, portly body and distorted face, and take pleasure in their suffering.

He tilted his head and sneered at Francisco, who now sat humbled and cowed in his cell. "Oh, Francisco, how the mighty have fallen. Can I now refer to you by your first name since you share the stench of this jail with me?" The jailer's smirk widened as he continued to mock his prisoner. "Were you too much of a coward to face our enemy, or perhaps you were in league with them and the devil himself? How do we know it was not your actions that brought us to this cauldron of hell as punishment for your sins?"

The jailer paused, savouring the torment he inflicted on Francisco. He leaned in close, his breath hot on Francisco's face as he whispered cruel accusations.

"How do we know you're not a secret heretic, seduced by the heathen queen's beauty and lured by the hope of gaining her favour? You could have conspired to overthrow the admiral and claim the kingdom for yourself. Who knows what dark fantasies linger beneath that stern exterior of yours?" The jailer scoffed, relishing his own twisted words. "No, no one can trust a man like you. That's why the admiral has ordered your trial as soon as this storm passes, hoping your sacrifice will appease any further occurrence of the raging tempest."

Francisco could no longer bear to sweeten his words for this cruel man. He fell to his knees, clasping his hands together in desperate prayer.

"I swear, I am not a vessel for the devil's work," he pleaded. "I will only speak of breaking ranks when my words are heard by those who truly matter. I implore you not to reduce my case, which could decide whether I live or die, into mere entertainment and idle chatter for your own amusement."

The jailer's face cracked with laughter, and what was left of his crooked brown teeth was on rare display for Francisco's benefit.

"You may have been a captain of the fleet once, but you are no more. Now you are the lowest of the low, a mere prisoner and I have your life in my hands. The more you respect me, the less I piss in your food."

"Don't debase yourself," Francisco retorted through gritted teeth.

The jailer let out another harsh laugh. "Captains like you always rely on people like me to do their dirty work. But when your own mess is staring back at you, suddenly you're not so brave."

Francisco withdrew his begging hands and shifted off his sore knees onto the bench, curling up into himself with his arms wrapped tightly around his legs. It was a feeble attempt to protect what little dignity he had left.

"Can't even give me a blanket? Don't let your admiral put a corpse on trial."

With a smirk, the jailer left and returned with a threadbare and ragged blanket. He shoved it through the bars, and to Francisco's horror, it landed directly in the foul contents of the water bowl and latrine.

"Any lice are from the last prisoner, not me." The jailer snickered.

Francisco sighed and lowered himself back to the ground, examining the blanket for any dry spots or holes that could provide some warmth. But as he lifted it to cover himself, he couldn't help but recoil at the overwhelming stench that wafted from it. He resigned himself to the fact that there would be no comfort in this blanket, only repulsion.

"And I haven't even been put on trial yet, let alone found guilty," Francisco muttered bitterly.

The jailer sneered at his dirty and beaten appearance. "Make good use of this time before your trial. I could send for a priest if you wish."

Francisco's mind drifted towards his own ship, where he was master and commander. There, he had the protection of the crew, who vigorously protested when the admiral came to take him. If he could get back to his ship, he would have their protection, which would grant him the time to prove his innocence.

"If you're granting requests, send for Father Pedro from my own ship," he said with a flicker of hope.

"I'm sure for your past services, no one would deny you access to your own priest. If the weather allows, I will send a boat to your ship," the jailer replied callously.

"God bless your kindness," Francisco said sarcastically.

The jailer chuckled. "And so he should. He sees it so rarely."

CHAPTER 2
THE DOWNWARD SPIRAL

L ike a ship caught in a whirlpool, Francisco was pulled deeper and deeper into a descending spiral of ill health and melancholy. His once luscious locks now clung to his pallid scalp like seaweed on a drowning man. The disorderly state of his usually well-groomed beard mirrored the disarray of his thoughts and emotions. With each passing day, the shadows under his eyes seemed to darken, revealing the true depth of his inner turmoil. In a frenzy, he clawed at his own head, desperate to break free from the suffocating grip of his inner demons.

He repeatedly mulled over the events that precipitated his downfall, clinging to the faint hope that one more meticulous examination might yet unearth an elusive answer. His last glimpse of his beloved family on the dock was bittersweet as he eagerly boarded the ship, filled with anticipation for the voyage ahead. It was a sight unlike any other, with the grandest armada ever assembled setting sail from the port. Once out to sea, the devil seemed to force his hands up through the roof of hell, through the ocean bed and whip up the seas into the worst tempest ever seen by man. The ships of the most powerful man on earth, the king of Spain, were tossed around like a child would toss his toys around in the bath. When they were out of the storm, they got to the English Channel, where the more nimble English ships harassed them. The English sent their demonic fireships brim-full of burning tar to break up the Spanish fleet, and the heretics then attacked and defeated the forces of the Spanish crown. Their only escape route was into the North Sea. Little did they know that they sailed straight into more of the devil's storms. The devil tossed them around so much that all they could do was huddle below deck and pray. So battered was Francisco's ship by the time the devil released it from his grip he could not join the formation the next time the English attacked, and so began his journey to the cell. Francisco stared blankly at the ceiling, trying to order his muddled thoughts. No, nothing. Francisco slammed his fist against the wall for another retelling that did not reveal a solution.

The unyielding storm continued to rage, pummelling the ship with its relentless fury. Francisco's thoughts tumbled in his head, mirroring the relentless ebb and flow of the waves. The despair induced by the ceaseless motion of the sea ruthlessly stripped away what little courage and hope remained within him. His stomach churned, and his soul felt weighed down by the never-ending turmoil.

Amidst his unbearable suffering, he held onto two flickering candles – his family and his faith. He could envision the radiant smile of his wife, her curls framing her face like a halo. His heart ached for his young children, chasing each other around the sunlit garden.

But the images in his mind were slowly fading, replaced by the grim reality of his jail cell. The faces of his wife and children became hazy. Their smiles turned into frowns as their garden was engulfed by darkness. He desperately clasped his hands, praying for an escape from this never-ending nightmare, longing to be back in that peaceful dreamland where his children's laughter awoke him. But as a cold drop of water hit his face, he came to the harsh realisation that it was all just a cruel mirage.

The cramped hold was filled with the scum and filth of the fleet – petty thieves, ill-tempered sailors, rapists, cowards, and other assorted low-lives. The stench of sweat and fear hung heavy in the air, mingling with the occasional outburst or whispered plotting. The dim light filtering through the small portholes cast eerie shadows on the haggard faces of the prisoners, adding to the tense atmosphere in the hold.

The other prisoners either jeered at him, revelling in the downfall of an authority figure, or attempted to win his favour, hoping he would speak on their behalf in their case if he was found innocent in his. Francisco tried to pacify them, but he mostly kept to himself, tuning out their constant murmurs and schemes. But the main source of his torment was the jailer.

The jailer brought him a bowl of what he told him was salty soup, but it was more like a murky brew with occasional solid objects floating within. Francisco could only hope they were vegetables, but he could not be sure as the sadistic grin on the jailer's face never wavered. "Rat or vegetable?" he would ask, holding the soup just out of reach through the bars. Francisco always answered with vegetable, hoping against hope that it was true. But the jailer would always laugh and hand over the soup while taunting him again for being wrong. If Francisco dared show any disrespect, the jailer would tip the soup onto the filthy floor of his cell and blame it on the rocking of the ship. Therefore, many a night ended in hunger until another bowl of questionable soup arrived the next day.

Francisco found himself alone once again, the creaking of the ship his constant companion. The sound reverberated through the dank jail cell as the heavy door slammed shut, sealing out all light except a mere sliver peeking through a crack. This small sliver of brightness offered little comfort to Francisco, for he knew what would come with the darkness – the rats. They would scurry and scamper around the perimeter of his cell, their sharp claws scraping against the rough floorboards. He would huddle in the corner, lifting his legs to avoid their gnawing teeth.

The rats seemed to be conspiring with each other, squeaking and chattering in their own twisted language. Francisco could not help but imagine them plotting his demise, ready to pounce and devour him like helpless prey. With so many of them infesting the ship, it wouldn't take long for them to swarm and overwhelm him. His frail body would offer little resistance against their insatiable hunger. Each minute felt like an eternity as he waited for dawn, praying for salvation from his disease-ridden, vicious cellmates.

But the light would return eventually, and Francisco would call out for his one beacon of hope.

"Is the priest coming?"

The jailer paid no attention to him as if to display his disdain for Francisco. He vigorously mopped the constantly dirty prison floor in a rare show of diligence, perhaps to further emphasize his contempt for Francisco.

"Is the priest coming?"

The jailer spat where he had just cleaned.

"A priest is certainly coming, but I'm not sure he is the one you want to see."

Francisco could see the jailer did not want to talk to him, but his opportunities to gain the jailer's ear were rare, so he persisted.

"I can feel the boat's rocking has eased these past few days. Surely it should be calm enough for the captain to send someone to fetch him?"

The jailer smirked.

"When the ship settles, your trial begins. I would pray for storms if I were you."

"So they leave a faithful servant of the king once more to starve and rot."

"Save your dramatics for the trial," said the jailer. "I hear the admiral's mood grows worse by the day. You will need all your luck and charm not to leave that room a condemned man."

Francisco sighed and sat back on his bench once more. He decided to make the most of the light he was granted and looked back over his right shoulder to his tiny window to imagine what was happening on the deck of his ship. He only hoped his mind would remain his friend long enough to imagine some pleasant thoughts upon which he could get some sleep.

Francisco's days merged into an endless blur. His life was reduced to a mere tortured existence in the dark and dismal confines of his cage. But then, the deafening clang of metal on metal shattered the tranquillity of his slumber, ripping him from unconsciousness as if by force.

His eyes snapped open as he frantically tried to orient himself in the dark and cramped space. The musty stench of rotting wood and rusted metal attacked his senses, enveloping him in its claustrophobic embrace. He could feel every inch of his body cramping from confinement, begging for release that would never come. As he steeled himself for what awaited him beyond the bars, his heart pounded against his ribcage like a wild animal desperate for freedom.

"Get up," the jailer snarled. "Your favourite priest is here. Maybe he should read you your last rites at the same time. Then we could go straight from trial to execution."

Francisco's head throbbed painfully as he violently shook it, desperate to clear his foggy mind and numb his ears from the persistent ringing. The sudden news of the priest's imminent arrival jolted him back to reality, causing him to struggle against the weight of exhaustion that had settled upon him like a heavy cloak. Finally, he managed to stand up from the hard bench he had been slumped upon.

The priest appeared in his traditional monk's habit, shrouded in darkness as if cloaked in mystery. His hood shadowed his face, adding an air of ominous authority to his presence. As he set his eyes on Francisco, he turned to the jailer and extended his finger to point at Francisco.

"This man is still a ship's captain in the king's fleet," he declared. "He awaits trial and should be treated with the dignity and respect his position demands. Clean him up and dress him in a captain's uniform so he may face his trial as a proper gentleman."

The jailer paused and furrowed his brow.

"But if he is sentenced to drowning, we'll lose the uniform. And if they choose to shoot him, it will be riddled with holes."

The priest remained resolute.

"Do as I say or face eternal damnation."

A defiant smirk crossed the jailer's face.

"What more damnation could I face than what I already endure? My life is nothing but misery on this cursed ship."

The priest's stern voice cut through the air.

"I assure you, it will only worsen if you continue to defy a holy man. Now do as I say!"

Grumbling under his breath, the jailer trudged off to search among the meagre possessions on board for a suitable captain's uniform.

The priest dragged a rickety stool from beside the jail door and positioned it before Francisco's cell. The other men trapped in nearby cells moaned and called out to him, but he gave them no attention. With a slow, gracious arch of his hands, he removed his hood to reveal the face of a handsome, fair-haired young man. His well-groomed beard was little more than a wispy gathering atop his small chin. Despite the faint lines etched into his features, he exuded an air of youthfulness that contrasted with the harshness of his surroundings. His complexion bore the telltale signs of a seasoned sailor – sun-burnt skin and a tinge of green around the edges. But something in his piercing blue eyes betrayed his true profession – he was no holy man but Francisco's trusted lieutenant on their ship. They often referred to him as "Pedro of the *San Pedro*" in jest, and "go get the priest" actually meant "go get Pedro". It wasn't for any priestly qualities that Francisco had summoned his friend now but for his cunning and guile in times of trouble.

"What news do you have for your poor captain, Pedro? Can you work your magic and get me back to our ship? I fear if I am put on trial here on the admiral's ship, I am doomed."

Pedro's head sagged.

"I wish I could bring you good news, but such was the scale of the disaster that all glints of hope were swallowed up. They hunt for scapegoats everywhere and have found a large one in you. For the storm that wrecked the Armada in the English Channel, they could say it was the devil and his work alone that cursed us. But once we were driven around the British Isles, the storms didn't relent. It was the devil through men's hands, and the devil reduced men to cowards. It is not the king's or his admirals' fault anymore once the devil made cowards of ship captains."

Dejection once more smothered Francisco's mind and complexion.

"But we stopped for repairs. I have told them repeatedly. I noted such in the ship's log, for we needed supplies to complete the repairs," Francisco said.

He stopped to breathe, his overexcitement costing him dearly in gruel-fuelled energy.

"They took all your papers when they boarded the ship. We can prove nothing. All we have left are ill-informed eyewitnesses on the other ships who only saw you breaking formation."

Francisco stared at the ceiling. He had been oppressed by brain fog while trapped in this dark, dank cell. He needed to think clearly if he was to win his trial.

"How long have I been here?" Francisco said.

Pedro scratched his head.

"About five weeks, give or take. Things have got much worse on the ship since you have been gone. She is a shadow of her former self. Many of the crew drowned in the storms, and the rest are either sick or injured from the battering we have taken."

Francisco's whole body tensed.

"Can you break me out of here? Then, we can storm the ship with the remainder of the crew. I will die in this cell the way I am treated, long before they get me to any trial."

Pedro bowed his head.

"Unfortunately, I have been sent to tell you that your trial is supposed to be this afternoon, and I am here to prepare you for it."

"Can you get up and speak on my behalf?" pleaded Francisco.

"Unfortunately not, for they may discover I am not a priest and then there would be two of us condemned to your fate. No, they will send someone, probably an officer, to make your case. They want to get it done quickly, for we are in the relatively sheltered waters off Scotland, whereas we will travel to the coasts of Ireland over the next couple of days, where the storms are expected to continue. I will help you run a blade across your face and button up your uniform, and then all I can offer are the blasphemous prayers of a priest impersonator. Now get to your feet. We don't have long."

As Pedro ran the blade across Francisco's face, he felt elation at the kind touch of another human being. Pedro paused and looked upon his captain's face, which creased into contentment where there had once been pain.

"Oh, I almost forgot." Pedro fumbled in his pocket, searching in every corner, then emptying it and searching within its contents. Francisco scowled, for his dream had been rudely interrupted.

"There it is." Something shiny protruded from the grip of Pedro's fingers.

"Is that...?" Francisco said, his face turning to fascination.

"It is," Pedro said. "Take it."

Francisco focused on the shiny piece of metal between Pedro's fingers.

"How did you know?"

Pedro smiled at the joy his gift brought to Francisco.

"I was searching through your papers in your cabin on the ship, and they were in one of the drawers. I wondered why you left the St. Christopher medal your wife gave you behind. You always treasured that, so I brought it to you."

Francisco took it and sheltered it in the palm of his hand.

"She gave this to me on the dock before I left with the Armada. It was supposed to protect me and give me luck."

"Luck appeared to have deserted you once you lost the medal."

Francisco closed his hand and smiled at Pedro.

"No matter, I have it now. I go to the trial with a heart full of hope and St. Christopher hovering over me. How can I lose?"

Pedro thought hope was a double-edged sword but did not articulate it. He saw Francisco's elation and decided to leave his friend with what little joy he had.

Francisco sat and felt the razor on his face as each bristle succumbed to the blade. He saw his wife in his mind's eye as if he was there with her, the sun blazing overhead, his children laughing. Her every freckle was visible to him as she bent in to kiss him. The blade gently caressed his face, and he revelled in his dream.

CHAPTER 3
BETWEEN TWO ROCKS

F rancisco was dressed in a drab, scratchy captain's uniform two sizes too big for his now lean frame. His weeks spent in jail and his diet of gruel had stripped him of both physical and mental strength and his body bulk. He was wedged between two bulging guards, their rough hands still lingering on his body as blood dripped from his nose where they had been too heavy-handed with their fists.

His shaggy beard had been somewhat tamed, but there was no saving his wild, tangled hair that stuck out at odd angles. The most generous observation that could be made was that he looked marginally better than he did when he was confined in his cramped cell.

But Francisco had little concern for appearances, never mind his dignity. He would gladly grovel and beg anyone, be it man or deity, if it meant obtaining clemency and avoiding further punishment. His only goal was to escape from this oppressive prison.

His head still spun from the weeks of confinement. The constant noise and chaos of the jail rattled his mind. His nerves played him like a harpsichord, and he flinched at every loud noise or when his name was mentioned. "I am a captain of the fleet," he repeated like a mantra, hoping the familiar words would bring back memories of his glory days, raising the sail of confidence up his mast of resilience before the judge began the proceedings. But there was plenty around him to suck the wind from his sails.

All around him were faces to impress, a sea of officers and priests who represented the fleet's glory and decay. The room was tense as officers of different ranks stood on one side, their tattered uniforms and hats showing the fleet's faded glory. Each face was stoic, carefully avoiding any display of emotion that could potentially label them as another scapegoat for the admiral's failures.

On the other side stood the priests, their long habits equally worn from the journey but appearing more at ease with their humble circumstances. Rosary beads dangled from their hands as they prayed for all who would face trial that day, their eyes fixated on the ceiling as if seeking guidance from above. The murmurs of their prayers echoed softly throughout the room, adding a sense of reverence and balance amidst the heavy atmosphere. For these men of God, their concerns lay in heavenly matters, fervently hoping to discern any evils that may be revealed during the trial. Inquisition burned strongly in their native country, and they remained vigilant for any signs of blasphemy or possession by the devil. Yet, amidst their duty to uphold the teachings of the one true faith, they also sought clemency for good Catholics who may have been led astray or were victims of circumstance. With bowed heads and fervent pleas, they prayed for divine guidance in discerning between guilt and innocence.

Francisco's chest constricted as he inhaled the damp, heavy air of the cramped room. The heat and humidity enveloped him, bringing his senses back to life after weeks of numbness from the cold of the cell. His skin prickled and tingled, overstimulated by every touch, causing him to twist and squirm. Claustrophobia clawed at him, making it difficult to focus on the imminent events unfolding before him. He wriggled between the two guards, desperately seeking a more comfortable position but finding none. Each breath felt heavy and laboured in his chest as if he were drowning in the thick air. Every inch of his being was on edge, ready for what was about to transpire.

With a sharp, crisp stride, a young man in a pressed military uniform approached and stood before Francisco. His posture was rigid, and his expression stern. A guard leaned in close and whispered in Francisco's ear that his legal counsel had arrived. Feeling a wave of desperation wash over him, Francisco turned with pleading eyes to face the unfamiliar man. He knew it was beneath him to beg, but he hoped it would evoke some compassion from the young counsel and motivate him to fight for justice on this crucial day.

The young officer turned his head to acknowledge Francisco, but his expression was strained and tense. He rubbed the back of his neck as if trying to soothe an invisible rash and could barely manage a forced smile. He was a young officer bearing the weight of defending someone facing a court martial. He wanted to make a good impression, albeit on the admiral and the officers rather than the defendant. However, with so many seeking someone to blame for the calamity that befell the great fleet, fulfilling his duty and not causing any trouble was the best way to do so. Deep down, he knew he would rather not be involved in such a messy and high-stakes case.

At the end of the winding path of priests and officers, the major general of the fleet, Francisco Arias de Bobadilla, sat behind his imposing desk. It was adorned with intricate carvings of sea creatures and gilded with gold leaf. It was his cabin, his ship, his fleet, and every element of the room impressed that onto Francisco.

The admiral's head was in his books. The rich smell of leather-bound books barely penetrated the musty smell of sweat and sea. There was the faint sound of quills scratching against parchment as he meticulously combed through the logs of the *San Pedro*, one of the most prized ships in his fleet. Each page held a piece of history, a story waiting to be uncovered. As de Bobadilla leaned forward, his brow furrowed in concentration. It was clear that he would not rest until every detail was accounted for. Francisco could only stand and wait.

But Francisco's anxiousness proved a cruel mistress and banged her demands off the inside of his skull.

"Tell him to look at the entries around the beginning of August," Francisco whispered in the ear of his legal counsel. "That will catalogue the repairs I had to make and why I had to break the line and could not continue."

The young man looked agitated and brushed him away. "Shh, not now. We have to see which angle the admiral will approach it from."

"I know what he is going to say!" Francisco said. "It is not like he has tried to hide his opinion of me."

"Please control your client," said de Bobadilla. "The captain can flaunt his disrespect for God, king, army and country, but he will respect this court."

"Rebut him!" said Francisco.

"Please be quiet and leave me to sort this out," the counsel told Francisco. He turned to address the admiral. "The accused will wait his turn to speak, lord."

"Good. See that he is at least remorseful for his actions and expresses that through his silence."

Francisco grabbed the shoulder of his counsel.

"I am not supposed to be guilty before the trial starts!"

The counsel wrenched his shoulder back.

"Control yourself, Captain Butero, or I will add assaulting an officer of the court to your charges," said de Bobadilla. "If I do that, you will never see your jail cell again."

Francisco juddered at this, for he knew the admiral did not mean he would set him free.

"I apologise to the counsel and the court," Francisco blurted out. His counsel turned and scowled at him. De Bobadilla glanced over his glasses and then flicked through the diaries.

When sitting alone in his cell, Francisco's mind had raced through endless permutations of how the trial would go. Each thought was more harrowing than the last. He imagined himself being hanged or thrown overboard, but in every scenario, he managed to put up some form of a fight. But now, standing impotently by, unable to defend himself, it felt like all his mental preparations had been for nought. His representative seemed just as eager as anyone else in the court to see him declared guilty, perhaps hoping to quickly resolve the case and preserve his reputation. Francisco's counsel avoided eye contact with him, instead fixating on the top of de Bobadilla's head, a symbol of power and authority that Francisco could only dream of reclaiming after this ordeal.

Time seemed to stand still as he waited for the verdict to be delivered, his heart pounding and his palms slick with sweat.

The priests in the surrounding silence took to their knees, their faces serene and unreadable, their voices blending in a solemn prayer. But the officers standing behind them struggled to hide their emotions, their brows furrowed with conflicted thoughts. Some were for the captain, as they had all made mistakes for which they did not want to be held accountable. Some hoped Francisco would be a sufficient scapegoat and all their errors and misdemeanours would be swept off the deck. While the rest tried to keep their faces as steady as stone, ready to fall behind whatever judgement the admiral may make.

Francisco surveyed the faces and decided the most sympathetic were those of the priests. He tried to join in the prayers, but his bitterness at his unjust circumstances made speaking difficult. He tried to focus on the trial, but his thoughts were scattered and unfocused. Instead, he fought to control the violent twitch that overtook his right thigh.

Finally, de Bobadilla lifted his head from behind his notes and motioned for Francisco to approach. The two guards stepped forward in unison, their hands reaching back to grip a struggling Francisco. De Bobadilla's cold gaze pierced Francisco as he stood before him, awaiting judgment.

"So what excuse do you have for placing the fleet in such jeopardy?"

Francisco's muscles tightened and strained as he focused all his attention on his diary, searching his memory for the specific page where the details of why he had to break ranks were written. The memory of his time in jail flooded back, rendering him powerless, like a hole had been drilled into his heel, and all of his energy was seeping out. A deep flush spread across his cheeks as he blurted out, "I had to—"

"Not you, him," said de Bobadilla as he calmly pointed his finger at Francisco's counsel.

"He had to stop for repairs, lord. He says it is all itemised in his diary."

De Bobadilla sighed. "I could show you the list of repairs needed on my ship, which would be almost identical. All the ships needed repairs after a storm of that ferocity. But we still had to pull into battle formation, for we were still in hostile territory. I could manage it. Why couldn't you?"

Francisco swallowed hard. Was the question addressed to him or his counsel? The weeks of degradation in his cell robbed his mind of his sharpness. His counsel did not look back at him. Francisco opened his mouth to speak, but de Bobadilla's head was back in his books. The moment had passed.

De Bobadilla glanced at the charges and turned his head to the counsel.

"So what took him so long to surrender when we informed him that charges would be brought against him? The report says that the captain had to fetch him from his own ship, place him under arrest, and throw him in the cells of this very ship to ensure he would turn up in this court today."

The counsel leaned over, and Francisco whispered in his ear. The counsel pulled his face away in haste for he was unimpressed with the amount of saliva Francisco had showered upon it.

"The captain said he received your message but was caught up in the storms off Scotland. He was going to send a message asking who would take over in command in his temporary absence."

De Bobadilla gave Francisco a hard stare and then returned to his notes.

"That says much about his attitude and state of mind, that leaving his comrades in the lurch means so little to him."

Francisco's face turned a deep shade of crimson as he flailed his arms furiously, desperately urging his counsel to come up with a response.

"Control your client, please," said de Bobadilla calmly but firmly. It seems he does not realise why we are here."

De Bobadilla heaved as he flicked through his notes, the leather-bound book worn and dog-eared from constant use. His weary eyes scanned the pages, filled with reports of battles and losses. Despite all they had been through, it was still necessary to hold these trials to maintain morale among the fleet.

His hand trembled as he read over the sentence he already knew, and he could see the weariness mirrored in the eyes of those gathered before him. The constant cycle of death had taken its toll on everyone. With a frustrated gesture, he threw down his pen with a loud clatter, the sound reverberating off the wooden walls. The atmosphere was heavy, like a storm brewing just beyond their reach. De Bobadilla longed for peace and an end to this endless battle.

"I have no time to waste on niceties nor ceremony, for this gives me no pleasure as you have served the king well in the past, and it shows because you rose through the ranks to lead a fine ship. But because of your conduct in abandoning the line at such a crucial time, I sentence you to death by hanging. The sentence will be carried out on your own ship in front of your own men at the earliest opportunity, weather permitting. I suggest you use your remaining time wisely and make your peace with God. I bid you a good day."

"What!?" cried Francisco. "Have you not read my diaries? It is all there in front of you. How can you do this to me?"

De Bobadilla slammed the diary shut. "There is no evidence that you wrote this diary at the time or made it up later as a defence for your cowardice," the Admiral replied. "Given our positions, you and I must set an example. But make no mistake, your actions have forced me to set this example. Who knows, I may attend your execution but try to use your last days to set an example for your men. Now take him away."

The guards grabbed Francisco by the arms and shoulders, held him down, and marched him out.

CHAPTER 4

THE LAST DAYS OF A CONDEMNED MAN

F rancisco sank to his knees, the rough ground scraping against his sallow skin, leaving raw, red indents behind. He clasped his hands together in prayer, seeking forgiveness from heaven and hoping it would trickle down into some mercy on earth. Memories flooded his mind, each a reminder of the lives he had taken in service to the king. Did God hold him accountable for these deaths? Is that why he was being punished? Why would he do so if they were killed under the king's orders, and most of them were heathens anyway? How could God be punishing him for doing repairs to his ship? He was protecting his men, for to go to battle in that condition would have meant doom for them all and hell for him. The thoughts weighed heavily on Francisco's soul, even though he could barely think because of the pain in his knees.

The only response was a deafening silence that seemed to deepen the void within his soul. Should God not right any wrongs he had suffered? Francisco closed his eyes and prayed for guidance, desperate for some semblance of peace amidst the turmoil within him. But his mind just spiralled with doubt and confusion. Why would God allow such suffering and injustice?

The old, worn floorboards creaked under Francisco's weight as he paced back and forth in his cell. The constant drip of water from the leaky ceiling echoed through the cramped space, a counterpoint to his thoughts. He squeezed the St. Christopher medal in his palm, which immediately flooded his heart with hope.

Despite his best efforts, Francisco couldn't shake off the unease in his gut. He strained his ears, hoping for any sound that would offer a sign of hope or escape, but all he heard were the familiar sounds of the ship: the creaking boards and the distant shouts of sailors. But Francisco thought about how he served his men on his last mission and thought there was nothing wrong with his actions and that they were just making him a scapegoat for the failure of the mission. The ship remained relatively still and Francisco wrapped himself up in his blanket so illness would not take him and save the executioner a job.

The jailer returned to give Francisco his supper.

"Drip, drip, drip goes the rain, and when it stops…" The jailer held his right hand as if holding the supporting rope as the noose tightened around his neck. One last choke became peals of laughter as the jailer enjoyed his own joke. Francisco gave him a withered look. The jailer shook his head. "I'd swap a sense of humour for piety if I was in your position too. But look."

The jailer held forth Francisco's bowl of gruel. Francisco peered over the edge of the bowl, convinced it was a trick. But amidst the beige murkiness were three lumps. Francisco raised his eyebrow.

"Are those three lumps edible, or is this another one of your tricks?"

"Oh, good captain, am I that bad? These are placed in your lovingly prepared gruel by the admiral's order. I think, why waste good food on a dead man? But the admiral does not want to hang a skeleton. It's bad for morale, apparently. But if you ask me, if you gave the turnips to me, I'd be just fine watching a skeleton hang."

Francisco fantasised about tearing the jailer limb from limb, but the vivid dream soon faded as it became too exhausting. He put out his hands to take the bowl and utensil.

"What are you doing?" the jailer asked. "They will never fit through the bars. Get back while I open the doors."

Francisco stood at the back of the cell as the jailer, who never took his eyes off him, placed the bowl out of the range of the cage door and shut it quickly after himself. Francisco pounced on the food and devoured it.

"If you eat that quickly, you'll make yourself ill," said the jailer as he laughed and locked the cell door.

The jailer stood and watched Francisco while he ate. The ship stopped lurching from side to side, and the dripping from the ceiling of the cells somewhat dissipated. Francisco looked up from his bowl. The more settled the weather, the more unsettled Francisco became.

"When the ship goes steady, the hangman's noose is ready," said the jailer.

He grinned as Francisco stood by the rear wall. He stuck his face between the two bars.

"Look, you had three lumps today. I wonder what the special occasion is? Do you know?"

Francisco glared at him and sat so his food could digest properly.

"Maybe it has to do with this letter I have here?" The jailer reached into his pocket and pulled out a piece of paper. "I wonder what it says?"

Francisco smirked.

"Sorry to spoil your fun, but all men locked in a cell all day have to do is talk. You can't read. The paper is blank. You need to expand your repertoire."

The jailer slammed his fist on the bars. "The admiral is coming for you, and you'll hang from the masts of your ship before the week is out. Now, stand back against the wall so I can collect your bowl."

Francisco turned and smiled to himself, for rarely could he spoil the jailer's fun.

After a restless night of tossing and turning, Francisco finally drifted into a fitful slumber. However, his peaceful rest was abruptly interrupted when the jailer appeared with all the subtlety of a raging bull. The loud slam of the door against the wall jolted Francisco awake, causing his heart to race and his body to tense in fear.

"I have another letter, good captain, and the joke is upon you this time!"

He pressed his face between the bars and grinned, exposing every yellow tooth and the gaps in between. Francisco glared at him until the captain of the ship and several guards came after the jailer. This time, the captain produced a letter from his pocket.

"On behalf of the king of Spain, Admiral de Bobadilla found you guilty of cowardice and disobeying orders, endangering your men and the king's fleet. For those crimes, they sentenced you to death by hanging. They will carry this sentence out tomorrow morning. Do you have any last requests?"

Francisco turned to face the wall. He clasped his hands together to stop them from shaking. He was determined not to reward the jailer by showing his fear. Once composed, Francisco turned to face his executioners. He fixated on the captain, for he was the one who wielded authority.

"I wish you to summon my priest, Father Pedro. I need to settle my affairs with God upon this earth before I face him at the gates of heaven for my judgement."

The Luciferian fury of the jailer turned on the captain of the ship.

"This is just a delaying tactic. His men will sail the ship further away to buy their master time, and they will pray to their demons for another storm. Hang him now and be done with it!"

The captain stuffed the letter in his inside jacket pocket and turned to leave.

"They will deny no man his opportunity to settle with God, especially a ship's captain. If we denied him this right, what sort of example would this give to the men? No matter how valiant our further efforts, the heretics would have won. Give that man whatever he wishes for as long as he continues to pray to God. He hangs when his priest arrives."

The jailer shook his fists and roared. Francisco took to his knees and prayed.

After a few days of surprisingly calm weather, the admiral's impatience intensified, eager to swiftly carry out the sentence. Francisco's courage faltered at the thought of Pedro not arriving. Despite the discomfort and pain in his knees from kneeling for so long, he remained on the cold, hard ground during each visit from the jailer. The jailer pulled up a small stool and peered intently through the rusted iron bars, his eyes calculating and cold. A big smirk covered his face.

"So, I reckon, from what the captain says, if you stop praying, no matter if you are still waiting for the priest, then you have made your peace with God. If you have made your peace, then we can execute you."

"How can you tell if you cannot see me?" Francisco said without lifting his head from prayer.

"You know what? You're right." The jailer stood up to address the remaining inmates in the cells further into the jail. "Double rations for any man who spots this wretch not praying."

The inmates rattled their cage doors in appreciation. Francisco laughed.

"You know what will happen, and I don't have to be a soothsayer to predict this. They will all see me not praying and rattle their bowls for seconds. Then, you will have to approach the captain and ask him for more rations, which he will have to take from the fighting men. Then, do you know what I will do?"

"What?"

"Accuse you of trying to prevent a condemned man from settling his score with God. Do you think the captain will give you double rations when you are behind these bars?"

The jailer picked up his stool to the jeers of the prisoners and threw it at the bars of Francisco's cage. He slammed the jail door shut after himself.

Francisco's knees burned with the intensity of a thousand blazing fires in hell. They ached as if he had crawled all the way from heaven to hell and through purgatory in between. With each passing moment, Francisco had to make a choice – use his blanket to cushion his knees or wrap it around his shoulders for some meagre protection against the frigid air. But he knew that if the jailer caught him not praying, he would surely report him to the captain, and they would hang him faster than he could succumb to the bitter cold. So he continued to mutter prayers, the words becoming a dull hum as he focused all his mental energy on devising a way to escape this torturous place.

After what seemed an age, the jailer gently opened the door. Francisco sat on the floor with his hands clasped, but he had to rest his knees.

"I am still praying," Francisco said. "I thought our Lord would like more variety in my poses."

"You still have it, you crafty beast," said the jailer as he grinned and shook his finger at Francisco. "They postponed your execution by a day so you could see your priest."

Francisco raised his head from between his knees.

"At least I've been shown some mercy," said Francisco. He tried to look more pathetic than he was, but he could not elicit a single ounce of sympathy from the jailer.

"When the priest finishes with you, they will set the time of your execution. What do you want for your last meal or is it my choice?"

Francisco remembered his life in Spain and what he enjoyed eating with his wife and family.

"I would love some beef and maybe some wine. But my lips are dry, and I could kill for some water."

The jailer grinned. "I can do some water and am afraid with those types of requests the choice of dinner is mine."

The ship suddenly juddered from side to side.

"You may have done a deal with the devil for your withered soul," said the jailer. "He might just save you once more."

Francisco looked around his cell to see if he could measure the ferocity of the coming storm by the shaking of his cage.

"This expedition seems to have been cursed from the start," said Francisco. "The devil be in the wind, the waves and the sails of our enemies."

"Your talk of your true master does not frighten me," said the jailer. "I'll ensure your last supper of gruel is extra watery so you don't shit yourself on the deck before you die."

"And here was I sitting in my rags and vomit, thinking I was at last shorn of dignity."

"It'll all be over soon," said the jailer. "They'll dispose of you quickly, for they won't want a ship's captain to embarrass them by begging for his life."

"I would not give you the pleasure," Francisco said, turning his back on the jailer. He took to his knees once more to pray for redemption.

CHAPTER 5

THE DEVIL'S SOUP

As the sun began to set, Francisco clasped his hands in despair, praying for a miracle. His heart raced as he anxiously awaited Pedro's arrival, who was his best hope of answering his prayers. The ship rocked violently, tossing Francisco from side to side like a rag doll. Francisco closed his eyes and breathed deeply, trying to steady himself amidst the rocking chaos of the sea.

"Jailer, come tell me what is happening. Am I to die in the bowels of an English sea creature?"

But there was no response except the moans of his fellow prisoners. The ship's lurching became increasingly violent.

"Am I in another of these cursed English storms? Does the heretic queen have the ear of God or some otherworldly being? If she does, they have blessed her with the weather."

Francisco could now clearly hear the rumbling thunder above him, and water seeped in under the jail's entrance door.

"Jailer, are you going to let me drown in here? Surely it would spoil the pleasure you would get from seeing me hang?"

Still, no one came to the door of the jail. The violence that possessed the ship was growing and threw him from wall to wall in his cell.

"Help me! Help me! I am going to drown."

But nobody came. The relentless rush of water pounded against the prison door, shaking it in its frame and causing Francisco to grip the bars of his cell tightly. He could see the strain on the door's hinges, each fighting to hold back the force of the wave while the water forced itself under the door. The water was now up to his knees and rising quickly. With a sinking feeling in his stomach, he resigned himself to the thought that he would die here, alone and without absolution for his sins. In desperation, he recanted all the wrongs he could remember, pleading with God for mercy even without a priest present.

Suddenly, the ship jolted to a violent halt, throwing Francisco against the iron bars of his cell. His forehead split open, blood trickling down his face as his head went numb from the impact. The ship had stopped moving, but the water continued to rise. And then, with a deafening roar, the jail door collapsed under the immense weight of the water.

As Francisco struggled to stand, he saw the hazy figure of a man approaching him through blurred vision. Was this death coming for him? His head slammed upon the bars once more, and there was blackness.

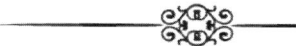

As consciousness slowly returned to Francisco's body, he was met with a parched throat and the overwhelming taste of salt on his tongue. Grogginess gave way to the realisation that he was lying on sand, with waves gently lapping at his midriff. His chest and face were damp, while his back was chilled by the cold wind that howled past. He pushed himself up onto his elbows and surveyed his surroundings.

His eyes stung as grains of sand fell from them. The daylight temporarily blinded him. But as his sight returned, it revealed a cove beach littered with his comrades' bodies. Some were still, either face up or face down, while others groaned and struggled to move, pleading for help. The relentless tide carried some in and out, their fate uncertain.

A sharp pain erupted at the back of Francisco's head as something collided with it, causing him to cry out in agony.

"Come on, we've got to get out of here."

Francisco turned to see who it was.

Pedro was crouched behind him, his knees pressed firmly into the ground. He looked like a half-drowned version of himself, his usually tanned skin now a sickly pale. Francisco couldn't help but shudder at the thought of his own appearance. He examined the surrounding area, taking in the desolate landscape and the chill in the wind. He felt a sense of unease in his stomach.

"Where do we go?" he said.

"Anywhere but here," said Pedro. "We need to get off this beach, or we are dead men."

Francisco looked around again and saw his fallen comrades.

"What about all of them?"

"They're already dead," said Pedro. "Trust me, for if you don't, we'll die too. Now come on."

Francisco rose to leave but froze when he saw the body of the jailer lying face up on the shore, the waves lapping around him.

Pedro grabbed him by the underarm and hauled him up. Francisco struggled to his feet, and as he did, he realised how much of his body ached. The energy drained from his legs when Pedro let him stand free.

"Get up," said Pedro. "If you can't stand, you can't run. If you can't run, you're dead. Now stand up."

Pedro grabbed him once again and hauled him to his feet. He pointed to the dunes at the top of the beach.

"We'll run over there, hide somewhere, and observe the beach," said Pedro. "Then, we can devise a plan once we've sufficiently rested."

Francisco coughed and nodded. "Tell me where and when."

Pedro looked around the beach. "Now!"

They ran across the beach, or rather, Pedro ran, and Francisco stumbled after him. Francisco fell and picked himself up several times before his feet could find a firmer foothold in the sand.

"Come on, come on," said Pedro. He tried to wave his friend onwards.

They reached the golden sands of the dunes dotted with tufts of long green grass where once more Francisco fell foul of the precarious footing. Pedro reached out from behind a bush and hauled his friend in to join him. Francisco's heart beat so fast he thought it might beat out of his chest.

"Are you all right?" said Pedro. "I don't want you to die on me now we have found a modicum of safety."

"If I am going to die, then it will be in Spain rather than this godforsaken place," said Francisco. He rested his hand on Pedro's shoulder. "Where did you come from? God granted me an angel to look after me when I found myself on the beach."

"I am no angel," Pedro said. "I arrived on your ship just before the storm broke. I was arguing with the captain about the terms of your execution. Then I went to the cells to see if you were all right, but the storm ripped the ship in half."

Francisco glanced over Pedro's shoulder to glimpse the broken ship. He gasped and stumbled back, his eyes wide with shock and disbelief. He waved to Pedro, beckoning him over to the edge of the dune. Together, they took in the sweeping view of the bay, their once proud ship now a twisted mass of wreckage on the horizon.

Its hull had been ripped open by jagged rocks, and now it lay sprawled out like a wounded beast, spilling its guts into the ocean below. Bodies, barrels, and wood and metal fragments littered the water, creating a macabre scene. Bodies floated alongside wreckage, splintered decking, and tangled rigging in a chaotic and gruesome display. On the beach, bodies lay strewn about, some being picked over by gangs of locals who descended upon them like vultures. The air was thick with the smell of blood and death, but that did not stop the looters from rifling through pockets and bags, killing any wounded survivors they came across, and taking prisoners from those still able to walk. It was a scene straight from hell itself.

"We need to get off this beach now," said Pedro.

They both turned to run but were met by four sword points.

CHAPTER 6
A BARGAIN WITH WHAT YOU DO NOT POSSESS

Francisco and Pedro slowly raised their heads. From the four glinting sword points pointed at their chests, their eyes climbed up four imposing figures. Standing before them were four rugged men, their beards unkempt and their hair long and wild. Layers of dirt seemed to be ingrained in their skin, making them appear as if they had been born from the earth itself. Pedro subtly gestured to his empty pockets, signalling that he held no valuables worth stealing.

"We'll be the judge of that," said one of their captors. Francisco and Pedro stood barefoot in the soggy sand as their captors stripped them of anything of value. They pushed Francisco to the ground when his pockets yielded nothing but sand, shells, and a worn St. Christopher medal, all of which they cast in a puddle. Such was his manhandling that Francisco had not had the chance to feel his pockets to notice his loss. They left Pedro to stand after relieving him of a few Spanish coins.

"Where's the ship's gold?" the man barked.

Pedro looked confused at the man shouting but turned to help Francisco. Francisco steadied himself as he held his friend's hand for balance, for he was still reeling from the effects of his imprisonment and being half-drowned. Once fully upright, he raised his hand to signal to Pedro that he would take care of this.

"We were prisoners on board the ship," Francisco said in broken Irish. "We never saw the sunlight, never mind the gold."

The Irishmen looked confused at such a fluent reply from a half-drowned foreigner. But one of them was so consumed by greed he failed to notice.

"Liar!" cried the man as he slapped Francisco with the back of his hand. "We're going down to the beach, and if you don't show me where the gold is, it's a watery grave for you and your friend."

The Irishmen waved their swords towards the beach, and the Spaniards' hearts sank as they trudged back down the dune.

They marched Francisco and Pedro through the bodies of their drowned comrades and to the seashore. The waves lapped around their feet as they watched the water clean off the sand. They stood mesmerised, relishing the last moment of pleasure they thought they might ever have if they could not compose a believable lie, or if not, then to side with the devil and invoke some hellish intervention. Francisco snapped to after a punch on the shoulder.

"Your ship is sinking fast. Where did you bury the gold?" the lead captor said.

The two Spaniards looked at each other. Francisco winked at his friend and turned to their captors.

"The gold is still on the ship," he said. "We were sent ashore to get small boats to transport it off. If you help us, the king of Spain will treat you with the utmost generosity. He has more gold than he knows what to do with, coming back from the new lands across the ocean."

The Irish looked confused.

"How do you know our tongue?"

Francisco smiled at memories from his youth.

"My father became a tutor in theology in Bilbao after he left the navy," he said in Irish. "He was a very learned man. He used to train the Irish Jesuit priests to be sent back to Ireland to ensure the one true religion lived on. He learned Irish to speak to the priests, and I picked it up as many Irish priests stayed in our home. They told me many tales of their homeland but forgot the ones about it being so cold."

The Irishmen looked at each other perplexed until their greed returned.

"Well, we'll thank your father for the priests, but thank you even more for the gold. Now, we only have small fishing boats. Will they do to get the gold?" Their captors were becoming agitated, as if a lifetime opportunity may pass them by. Pedro looked flabbergasted at his friend, for he never knew of his linguistic dexterity. Francisco signalled for him to play along.

"What size of boats do you have?" Francisco said. "These chests of gold are large. We stole them from the heretic queen as we sailed around her country. We don't want the devil to try and take his bitch's gold back and drag you to the depths of the sea along with it."

Their captors' faces dropped. They turned to hide their mouths as they whispered to each other. They knew they had to get the gold and get off the beach before the other clans came. Once their confidence had returned, they turned to their prisoners.

"They can fit two men, one if we fill them with gold," said one captor as he scratched the back of his head. "Surely we can crack open these chests and go to and from ship to shore?"

Francisco stroked his chin, partly to hide his grin, which indicated that his captors were now well and truly invested in his lie. "I suppose we could. But surely others of your kind would notice all your trips to the ship. They may then steal it from you."

Their captors danced as panic became masters of their limbs. They looked frantically at themselves, to the boat, at their prisoners and back to themselves again.

"Calum," said one man, "my cousin has a large boat that could carry a chest." He was sweating despite the biting wind.

"How soon can he get here?" Calum said.

"By the end of the day. He wouldn't want a large cut, as he owes me a few favours."

Calum paused for thought. The more people who knew about the gold, the more likely it was to be stolen. The more people involved, the smaller his cut. But he could not pass this chance up.

"We shall all go," he said. "Pick up your things, Spaniards."

Francisco folded his arms and stuck out his chin.

"If my friend and I leave the beach, the gold will be gone," Francisco said.

Calum gritted his teeth. He did not have time for this. "And why's that?"

"Because some other comrade of ours will plead for his life and promise the gold to someone else, and they will steal it from you."

Calum's face flamed red, and his nostrils flared. He raised the point of his sword to Francisco's face.

"How do I know I can trust you to know where it is? Why can't I just kill you and take some other half-drowned rat who is more agreeable to lead me to the gold?"

"Because I am the ship's captain, and he is his first mate," Francisco said.

"Dressed like that?" Calum said.

Francisco raised his arms and extended his palms in confusion.

"We've just been washed ashore from a violent storm and almost drowned. What do you expect us to look like?"

Calum growled and turned to his companions.

"I will stay here and guard them, and you three will get the boat."

His comrades muttered but obeyed.

"Now we are going to sit here behind this dune until they come back," said Calum to Francisco and Pedro. "If you call for help or try to escape, I'll slit your throats." Calum pointed to the ground with his sword. "Sit down with your backs to the beach."

"Can we get some water or something to drink?" said Francisco. "We're dying of thirst."

Calum threw them a bottle from his belt. Francisco took a swig and spat it straight out. Calum laughed.

"Are you not used to the hard stuff? When we get our gold, you can eat and drink all you want. Now sit there and be quiet. They'll be back soon enough."

The two Spaniards sat and watched the sun move through the sky when the thick grey clouds allowed it. The wind picked up, and they shivered in their rags. They heard shouts and screams from over the dune.

"Stay here," Calum said. He peered over the dune and returned, looking like a frightened rabbit. He waved his sword in front of his prisoners' faces.

"Get up. We're leaving now."

Francisco signalled for Pedro to stay put.

"What about the gold?" Francisco said. "Your friends have only just left to get the boats, and now you want us to leave?"

"You either move now, or I kill you where you stand."

Francisco grimaced as Calum once more pointed his sword at him.

CHAPTER 7
A GLITTERING PRIZE

E merging over the crest of the dune, a band of formidable men appeared, clad in Spanish morions and wielding axes welded to six-foot-long staffs. Their faces were hardened and determined, ready for battle. Following closely behind them was an older, stocky man with a thick beard and piercing eyes, his youthful companion trailing behind. The group encircled Calum and his two Spanish prisoners, their weapons at the ready and their expressions unreadable. The older man stepped forward.

"I'm Desmond MacCabe, here to claim all Spaniards for the Maguire. Don't stand in our way."

"The O'Rourkes got here first, and I claim these men for us," said Calum as he stood in front of his prizes.

"These men are MacCabes, and I am their leader," said Desmond, pointing to the armed men. "Stand aside or be made mincemeat by our axes."

Calum still did not move. The stocky man took a coin from his pocket and flicked it at him.

"That, plus your life for these men. Take it. It's the best deal you'll get."

Calum bent over and picked up the coin while not taking his eyes off the MacCabes. He saw the resolve in their faces.

"This isn't over," he said. "That's O'Rourke gold in that ship, and we're going to claim it."

Desmond laughed.

"Well, if you're fool enough to fall for that story, you can fish out what you can find when the ship gets pulled out with the next tide. Now be off with you."

Calum scowled at his prize being stolen but turned and ran.

Desmond turned to his prisoners. He grinned as he sized them up.

"I own this beach, and now I own you," he said in Spanish. "What are you worth to the Maguire? Be quick about telling me, or I'll leave you here to come up with a pot of gold for that lot." He smirked as he pointed to where Calum had just disappeared.

Francisco was so dumbfounded by what just happened that he blurted it straight out.

"I'm a ship's captain, and he is my first officer. We are excellent trainers of men and know ships, guns and warfare like the backs of our hands. I'm sure we can be of enough service to find favour with your master while he names our ransom price to the king of Spain. The king will pay handsomely for his men. The more you keep alive, the more gold you get."

Desmond smirked, for he knew he had to sieve out the truth from another 'pot of gold' story.

"The Maguire's a fickle man, hard to please, but I'm sure you're used to that, dealing with kings. Where have you served your master to gain such skills?"

"All over the high seas, the Netherlands, Portugal, the Atlantic islands. I have had a long and distinguished career that is easily provable on the training ground if doubt still clouds your mind."

Desmond stroked his chin as he decided whether he should keep these prisoners.

"I also served in the Netherlands, in the Irish mercenary units of the king's army. Many an experienced Irish soldier will have done the same and have a similar command of Spanish to me."

He pointed over the dune.

"My men will escort you to our party of the survivors. They'll give you food and drink, but be prepared to march, for we could leave anytime."

Pedro clasped his hands together, almost grovelling. "Thank you, señor, for your kindness. We will repay it many times over."

Desmond smiled in smug satisfaction as he walked away. "That is good to hear. Now go join your other men."

The pounding of the waves echoed in their ears as they were escorted down the sandy beach. They tried to ignore reality as they picked their way through debris and dead bodies for they could not afford to fall into melancholy if they were to save themselves. Ahead, a group of Spaniards huddled together in an inward circle, surrounded by scruffy, poorly armed Irishmen. As they approached, one man barked orders and Francisco and Pedro were forced to sit on the damp sand. A canister of water and a small piece of hard bread were shoved into their hands, along with a harsh command to stay quiet. The other Spaniards looked worn out and defeated, their faces etched with exhaustion and despair. Francisco leaned over to one of them, seeking any signs of hope or a way out of this dire situation.

"Are they going to kill us?" he asked.

"They are no better than savages," said the man. "They will kill us the next time they feel afraid."

"Be quiet," said one guard.

The stale bread had done nothing for Francisco except inflate his hunger.

"May we have some more food?" he said to the nearby guard.

"Wait until my leader returns," said the guard. "He will tell you what will happen to you next."

They sat there for what seemed like an age until Desmond returned, huffing and puffing from down the beach.

"Move!" he said. "Everyone move."

He picked up a couple of prisoners and herded them forward as an example to the rest.

"We leave for Fermanagh now."

Francisco looked around him. The panic seared through the air. He tugged on Pedro's sleeve and winked at him to signal that he should stay alert. He did not trust his new set of captors and meant to make his escape at the first opportunity.

CHAPTER 8
A LEAP IN THE DARK

The Maguires mercilessly drove them forward, their heavy boots pounding on the damp sand with a deafening crunch. Bruised and battered by the storm, the Spaniards stumbled and struggled to keep up, their bodies crying out for rest. The unforgiving chill of the wind whipped through their threadbare rags, gnawing at their exposed skin and fuelling their desperate desire to escape this desolate beach.

For what felt like hours, they were pushed deeper into the heart of a forest, their feet sinking into the muddy ground as they followed the winding path. When they thought they might find some respite from their gruelling journey, they emerged again into open terrain. Their spirits lifted momentarily until they realised their feet were sinking into waterlogged earth, causing them to howl in frustration at yet another cruel twist of fate in this treacherous land.

Francisco noticed how the Irish constantly pumped themselves up to keep moving forward, with their attention always over their shoulder. He leant over to Pedro.

"These men are afraid of something. Do they work for or against the English? We were told before we departed Spain that the Catholics of England and Ireland would be our friends, yet here we sit, their prisoners."

A guard scowled at them. "Be quiet, or you'll force me to come over there and shut you up."

The Irish seemed to quiver like rabbits at something in the distance. Francisco and Pedro edged towards the rim of the forest to investigate. Horsemen were in the distance. The glint of their steel armour and swords indicated they were better armed and equipped than their captors.

"They must be the English," said Francisco, who unwisely pointed to the objects of his attention.

Francisco felt a whack to the back of his head.

He awoke in excruciating pain. He rubbed his head and saw that he was back in the forest in the middle of a circle of his captured comrades. He saw Pedro's concerned face lean towards him, then get overcome with fear, then he looked to the ground and refused to make eye contact.

"Get up! Move!" A guard came and threatened them with the butt of his axe, and the prisoners forced themselves to get up, a bundle of moans and groans.

The pain in Francisco's head intensified at the build-up of anger when he saw Desmond pass alongside him.

"We are officers of the king of Spain," Francisco protested. "The same king your leaders spend so much time writing to, pleading for help. Yet, when we arrive, why do you treat us so?"

Desmond turned in a hunched posture as if to reassure Francisco. "We need to get you out of here. I know your predicament. I served in the Netherlands. Many others would rob you, sell you to the English, or worse. This is the best way. Trust me."

"The best way?!" said Francisco. "The only way it could be worse is if we were bound hand and foot."

"Not so many of my brethren yet appreciate the Spanish as our allies and only see your huge hulking ships as something they steal from. Trust me, you are far better off with us."

Desmond reached into his bag and pulled out a hunk of bread. "Consider this a peace offering, and I hope it will earn your trust."

Francisco's rampant stomach acid also dissolved his pride, and he snatched the bread from Desmond's hand. He stuffed his mouth so full he could not speak. His eyes could still stare daggers, but Desmond had long since turned his back.

"We should escape."

A faint whisper danced in the air and slithered into Francisco's ear. Francisco froze, for he was unsure of whether it was a demon or an Irishman pretending to be one, albeit experience told him there was little difference. Suspicion and fear swept over him as if he were again drowning in a wave, and he spun around. He saw no one behind him to claim the utterance. The words were like fiery arrows aimed at his soul, meant to ignite anger and violence within him.

With a shiver down his spine, Francisco concluded it was a demon wreaking havoc with its deceptive urging. He swiftly began reciting prayers, hoping they would be enough to banish the malevolent entity from his presence.

A stick hit his back. He turned, and this time, a pair of eyes claimed the deed. Francisco edged over to the man when the guards were not looking.

"You sought to disturb me with your stick?" said Francisco.

"We should make a break for it at our next opportunity," said the man. "I overheard them talking. They are at least a day from their homes. They would never catch us all if we ran in different directions."

"Where would we go?" Francisco asked. "None of us know anything about these lands. Wherever we may go, we may end up dead."

"Where are we going now? Probably to be sold to the English and then to decorate a spike somewhere."

Francisco edged away as he saw they attracted the attention of at least one guard.

"We'll see when the time comes. We shall speak again."

Francisco turned away.

The Irish patrols returned sometime later. The scouts covered their mouths and whispered in Desmond's ear. Desmond looked hot and bothered.

"Get them all up. We've got to leave now."

The soldiers dragged the Spanish to their feet and set them off on another forced march. They came out in the open and saw the English cavalry in the distance. The Irish panicked and turned to Desmond for guidance. The Spanish saw their chance.

"RUN!"

The man who had shouted suddenly took off, his feet pounding against the ground as he bolted towards the safety of the dense woods. His comrades also made a break for it, some limping and others stumbling in various directions, desperately attempting to escape. But Francisco remained calm, holding a hand to signal Pedro to stay put. With a fierce determination in their eyes, the Irish guards gave chase to the fleeing fugitives.

Francisco shifted his weight, crouching like a cunning fox ready to pounce on its prey. He surveyed the scene with calculating eyes, waiting for just the right moment to make his move.

Desmond saw his men get frustrated at having to run after motivated prey and reaching for their weapons as an easy way to end their exertions.

"Don't injure anyone," he cried over the developing melee.

With a loud slap on Pedro's shoulders, Francisco burst forward and flung his arms wide to steady himself as he leapt off his heels. Surprised but determined, Pedro quickened his pace to catch up, their feet pounding against the treacherous ground. Overhead, the sky was a deep shade of blue, marred only by wispy clouds that drifted lazily by, not knowing what went on beneath it. The distant sounds of angry Irish voices chased after them like a pack of hounds, urging them to run faster. They held their heads high, but their eyes stayed fixed on the uneven terrain beneath them, not trusting the treacherous bog. Each breath rasped in and out of their lungs as they pushed themselves to keep going. Behind them, they could feel the weight of danger looming, a constant threat that spurred them onward.

The trepidation coursed through their veins as they ran towards a distant wood, hoping to find safety and escape their enemies' relentless pursuit. But as they reached the edge of the woods, their bare feet were met with sharp sticks and rocks, forcing them to slow down and tread carefully. Despite the pain, they pressed on until they reached the shelter of a fallen tree, where they finally allowed themselves a moment to look back. They saw the trees close behind them, hiding them from potential pursuers. They exhaled and breathed deeply. Now, they had a temporary respite.

"So what now? said Pedro, his heart almost pounding out of his chest.

Francisco shrugged his shoulders and regained his breath. He raised his head to the sky and smiled, wanting to take in his newly found freedom.

"Let God guide us," and he made the sign of the cross.

CHAPTER 9
THE WANDERINGS OF WEARY MINDS

"Where shall we go now?" Pedro asked, his words buttressed with insistence. The sea could rip his clothes to shreds and strip him of everything except his yearning for a map.

Francisco looked to the sky to see where the sun was. He pondered a moment and thought back to himself as the captain of his ship making a decision that his entire crew relied upon. "Let us follow the woods, for as far as I can tell from above, the edge of the woods is pointing south and to the south lies Spain."

He smiled at Pedro, hoping to exude confidence. But Pedro was too exhausted for confidence, so he just shrugged and walked after him.

"Will there be any sun today in this godforsaken place?"

Pedro shielded his eyes in mockery of the multiple shades of grey cloud formations. Francisco forced himself to rise above such sarcasm and concentrated on what he could practically do about their predicament. Responsibility had shaken him back to being a captain, albeit still a shrinking shadow of his former self. It was time for a different approach.

"Last night, I spent my waking hours in prayer and contemplation, praying for forgiveness for sins known and unknown. Even though my penance is not over, the Lord will grant us a better day today."

The prospect of potentially enough prayers being said to warrant some divine intervention did not brighten Pedro's face.

"I hope my deference to friendship rather than sense will be rewarded some-where along this godforsaken march, and I'm not lumbered with a cursed man."

Francisco shook his head from such notions that he was a burden and their predicament was not some penance. His weakened mind and limbs made him succumb to anger and irritability, but his rational mind said he should not flay the bond between himself and Pedro. He should be a ship's captain once more and lead. Francisco ignored Pedro's miserable pondering and pointed to the sound of water.

"Since fate has tossed us from our ship, I think it is back to the water we should go."

They walked for a while, and Francisco, considering they may be trapped here for a while, pondered what they must do to survive. He decided to broach the subject with Pedro but paint it in a positive tone, for his own confidence had not yet returned, and his will was fragile.

"We must become men of many tongues to survive in this land," he told Pedro.

"I hope I won't be here long enough to become the master of any," Pedro muttered, his tone laced with bitterness.

"Nevertheless, I will teach you Irish as we travel. At worst, it will help pass the time. In return, you can teach me some of the English you know."

"I suppose it will distract me from my rumbling stomach," Pedro replied. "You go first."

As they walked, Francisco pointed to all he could see and could recall the word for in Irish. He also got Pedro to repeat after him what they were so he could commit them to memory. After some initial difficulties, Pedro proved to be a quick learner.

As they followed the sound of the water, they found an oasis of bushes laden with berries, an island in a green sea. They went to fill their pockets, and suddenly, something struck Francisco. He jammed his hands in his pockets and found holes, or if there were no holes, sand. He cursed and looked to the skies so Pedro could not witness the formation of tears. Pedro reached his hand out.

"What's wrong?"

"It is gone," Francisco said, his voice a-quiver.

"What is gone?"

"The St. Christopher medal from my wife. It was the only thing I had left to remind me of her. My memory of her will ,fade if I cannot press it between my fingers."

Pedro wrapped his arm around Francisco's shoulders.

"You will remember her for you will see her soon when the king sends a ship for us to bring us home."

Francisco threw his arm off.

"That ship will bring a noose for me from Admiral de Bobadilla."

"I'm sure the king, in his mercy, will declare an amnesty for all those who showed bravery on the shores of Ireland."

"You don't know that."

"I don't, but I know that you have just got out of prison and been half drowned. That would leave emotional scars on any man. What I do know is we must gather food and continue our journey towards the sea before the natives capture us once more and use us for ransom."

Francisco nodded, and they filled the pockets whose holes had not been ruined with as many berries as they could hold.

"We must at least wash these before we attempt to eat them," Pedro said. "Your stomach must be very delicate after your time in prison. We cannot afford for you to be ill and slow us down."

Francisco smiled at Pedro, for he wished at least one of them had an optimistic disposition. Pedro was in no mood for Francisco to reassert his captaincy over him, so Francisco strode past him.

They walked further until they found a stream, the source of the noise of running water. They followed the stream through wood and pasture, believing it would eventually meet the sea, where they might hail a Spanish ship that could rescue them. But they did not get far before their weariness caught up with them.

"Can we see if there's a local farm?" Pedro said. He cradled his stomach like an empty basket waiting to be filled.

"Let's follow the stream," Francisco said as he could empathise with him as his stomach also rumbled. "As soon as we see a farm, we will veer off, and once we have had our fill, return to the stream again."

Pedro nodded and stumbled on.

The stream continued onwards, with no sign of the sea. The land became boggy and unpleasant under their bare feet. Their once swift pace descended into a slog, and Francisco saw they needed to rest. He looked for a dry patch in the grass while Pedro studied the horizon.

"Look yonder," said Pedro, his voice striking a rare note of optimism. "That building over there must be a farm. Look below that hill."

Francisco strained his eyes and could make out a circular mud hut. He had seen similar buildings before, but only in the poorest parts of Spain. "It certainly looks man-made, but it does not look occupied. There does not seem to be any crops or food around it."

Pedro shook his head. His dreams of food would not be dislodged. "You cannot tell from here. We need to go there, for I cannot go any further. It is the only farm around here."

Francisco saw his friend was not for persuading. "We can go as long as we do not lose sight of the stream."

Pedro looked happy for the first time that day.

When they arrived, the hut was deserted, and there was no sign of any food.

"This is a cattle herder's hut," said Francisco. His rumbling stomach and their lack of success dulled his mood.

Pedro looked distraught. "How do you know?"

"The grass in the pastures is lower than the rest, and the cows have cleared themselves a path in that direction," Francisco pointed out. "It is probably part of a set route followed by nomadic herders. There is little chance of them returning soon."

Pedro collapsed on the floor and cast his head into his hands.

"Come on," said Francisco. He saw his friend was faltering, and he needed his captain again. "We should return to the stream and follow our original plan."

Francisco extended his hand to help his friend up. Pedro peeled himself off the floor and gave his friend the limpest of hands to pull him up.

"We'll get to the coast soon, and the fleet will not have passed us by yet."

"But what about you?" said Pedro, surprised he was on the reverse side of previous arguments. "If you surrender back to the authorities, surely they will hang you?"

"I'll take my chances. Better to be hung on a Spanish ship than die in an Irish bog."

Francisco heard a cracking twig outside. He looked to his friend and signalled that they should sneak out the back of the hut. Francisco parted the cloth door at the rear of the hut, and three Irishmen stood in front of them.

"We've been looking for you."

Calum stood in the doorway, flanked by two of his men who brandished glinting daggers. Francisco's heart pounded in his chest. Fear coursed through his veins. His throat tightened, and his hands shook as he anticipated Calum's blade piercing his flesh and entering his heart from below. He wanted to cry out, to beg for mercy, but he knew it would only bring him closer to his impending death. He had to put all that behind him and use his wit and charm if not to save himself, but to save Pedro, who by this time lay ill on the floor.

"You owe us some gold," Calum said. "If you can't give us what you owe, then we will slit your throats here and now rather than you be a burden to us."

Francisco steeled himself, determined not to show any fear.

"The gold was in the sea and was not ours to give but was there for the taking."

"An excuse won't save your life," Calum said. "Only gold will."

He drew back his dagger as if he would shove it through Francisco's face. Francisco put up his hands to appease him.

"We are worth far more to you alive than dead. Who is your master so we can arrange our price?" Francisco asked. His eyes rolled upwards as he contemplated moving his raised hands to wipe off the telltale droplets of sweat on his forehead.

"My dagger and I are my only masters," Calum said as he curled his lip.

Francisco panicked, and his forehead became sweaty as memories of the Irish priests' teachings on Irish social structure flooded back to him.

"Sorry, sorry, who is your clan?"

"The O'Rourkes are my clan. Calum O'Rourke is the name my father gave me until he died, and I went to the woods to fend for myself."

Francisco summoned all his confidence and extended his arms.

"Calum, if I may call you that, don't risk your lives on a fool's errand rowing out to get the gold. Sell us to your master, for I can either train his men since I am a Spanish captain, or he can ransom us back to the Spanish king for a handsome price."

"Or I could just kill you now and be done with it," Calum said.

Francisco saw the point of the man's blade and thought, this may finally be it. The priests reached through time once more.

"A wise man always recognises a chance to better himself," said Francisco, "and ingratiate himself with his master. I see in you such a wise man."

He saw a flicker of interest in Calum's eye.

"To achieve anything in life involves a risk," he continued, "and smuggling us back to your master would be amply rewarded."

Calum lowered his dagger.

"I suppose for all the trouble we've been through today, there's no point in returning empty-handed."

"I knew from the moment I saw you, you were an astute man," said Francisco.

The dagger shot up again.

"And if I bring you back, you'll cause me no trouble?"

Francisco shrugged.

"Where are we going to go? We're glad someone we knew came along to rescue us."

"Good," said Calum. "Here's a hunk of bread for your good behaviour."

Both Francisco and Pedro devoured the stale bread.

They crouched in the shadows for what felt like an eternity, waiting for the golden light of day to fade into a deep, velvety darkness. The air was thick with droplets of tension and the scent of damp earth, hinting at the coming nightfall. The giveaway came when the air began to chill rapidly, and soon after, the light faded.

As the sun finally set and the shadows grew long, they quietly emerged and began their journey. The dim light of dawn slowly illuminated the landscape as they trekked through dense fog, with Calum leading the way. Just as the mist began to lift, he pointed out a cluster of circular huts nestled between two rolling hills on the edge of a tranquil lake. Wispy tendrils of fog danced around the structures, adding an eerie but captivating ambience to the scene.

"Here we are. It may be modest, but it is home, and I like it."

Calum glared at Francisco and Pedro, hoping looks alone would suppress any expressions of discontent. But the Spaniards were too hungry and exhausted to express their disgust and were glad of anywhere to eat and rest. Francisco and Pedro were given their own hut, for Calum's fears of them running away had dissipated.

"You can wash in the lake, and my wife will make some fresh bread, so don't despair. You'll have eaten before the sun is on top of the sky."

Both Spaniards were too exhausted to look grateful and could only concentrate on pleading for a list of essentials.

"We need fresh clothes," said Francisco, "and my friend here is in a bad way. He needs to see a physician."

Calum bent down to look at Pedro, who had lain down on the ground as soon as they arrived in the village.

"He has the fever," said Calum. "It is a common ailment for outsiders to these parts. The English soldiers catch it all the time when they first arrive. It can be fatal, but he should be all right in a week. We'll have him better before we see the O'Rourke."

Calum rose back up.

"This O'Rourke fellow you mention. He is your leader?" Francisco said.

A certain pride swelled in Calum's chest, and his eyes lit up. "He is our leader and the greatest O'Rourke since we were the kings of Ireland. Never a man inspired so much fear when he wields his broad sword. He is the bane of the English and will reward me handsomely for rescuing you ."

Francisco flashed a forced smile at Calum, hoping to convey a sense of admiration. After his recent encounters on this island, he couldn't shake the feeling that this imposing figure may be nothing more than a common thief lurking in the woods. Despite his exhaustion, Francisco mustered all his remaining energy to charm their hosts and win them over.

"I look forward to offering my services to your leader, but in the meantime, I would appreciate it if my friend and I could rest and recuperate before I have the honour of meeting him."

"Aye, but I'd need to hide you and put you to work. No one eats for free in a land like this."

"If you give me a day or so, I'll do the work of two, for my friend will need to be excused."

"We'll see. There'll be no baggage here," Calum said, turning to leave. "Wait here, and I'll fetch you some clothes, blankets, and food."

Calum returned, and Francisco gave a grateful smile for the kindness. Calum smiled back, and Francisco felt like a bridge had been built between them. His mind wandered to his wife, his light when he needed solace.

"What's wrong?" Calum said after noticing Francisco's change of expression.

"I hate to ask you, but you may have stolen something from me. It would be of no value to you but a sentimental treasure to me."

Calum shook his head.

"We were most disappointed only to find sand in your pockets. Surely, there must have been a greater bounty in the pockets of a ship's captain? That's why we did not believe you were who you said you were."

Francisco's head dropped.

"There was. As I departed, my wife gave me a St. Christopher medal on the docks. Was that amongst the sand?"

Calum scratched his face.

"No, I would have remembered that, for I would have asked if it had any value. No, but I will get you a new one. I have no interest in a fellow Catholic's soul passing to the devil because he lost his saint's protection through no fault of his own. I will bring you a medal when you have earned your keep and I can present you to the O'Rourke."

Francisco placed his hand upon Calum's shoulder.

"Thank you for your kindness to a fellow Catholic."

Calum smiled back, genuinely touched.

"Think nothing of it. However, you may need to hide for a long time before meeting the O'Rourke. Now get some sleep in the knowledge for the time being you are safe."

CHAPTER 10
THE SEEDS OF REDEMPTION

Six long months passed. Among those months was the passing of the new year, which Francisco and Pedro missed, having succumbed to illness. It was a blessing in disguise for English soldiers came searching for survivors of the armada. Calum opened the door of their hut to the soldiers and pointed to the two Spaniards shivering in thick blankets with their heads covered. The soldiers declined to check who they were when told they had a contagious illness from which they would soon die and had to be isolated from the rest of the village.

When spring came, they recovered somewhat and were able to help with the sowing of the crops, a down payment to Calum for saving their lives. No one could tell them apart from the natives as all wore heavy clothing in the biting wind, and they had not lost their sickly paleness. But now spring was in full bloom, the O'Rourke felt confident enough to summon the survivors of the armada to his castle.

A sharp knock sounded on the Spaniards' door as the sun rose over the horizon, casting a soft golden glow through the crisp morning air.

With a furrowed brow, Francisco rose from his bed and shook off the lingering tiredness of the night. He had languished in the village for months of relative peace, so he wondered who could be assaulting his door in such a manner so early in the morning. He opened it slowly to see a grumpy-looking Calum standing before him.

"We're going to see the O'Rourke today. Make yourselves presentable, for the more you impress the O'Rourke, the better for both of us," said Calum.

But before Francisco could respond, Calum had already returned to his cart to load it up for the market by the O'Rourke's castle.

Francisco's arm trembled uncontrollably as he stood in the shadow of the doorway, a heady concoction of the remnants of his fever he had subsequently caught from Pedro and the nerves that consumed him. He had high hopes for this meeting – one that he hoped would finally provide him with answers about his time on this island. But he could not shake off the feeling of unease. Was he being brought here to be smuggled back to Spain? Or perhaps used as a bargaining chip in some sort of deal with the English? Worst of all, he feared being forced into a life of indentured servitude. The swirl of pessimism sent shivers down his spine. His mind clouded with doubts.

Everything about Ireland seemed backwards and foreign to him. Even the accommodation was barely suitable for pigs, and the meals, even when fresh, were scarcely fit for swine to consume. As Calum had paraded him around, Francisco couldn't help but feel like nothing more than a prize pig brought to auction. Surely the O'Rourke, judging by all the efforts Calum made to talk him up, had to be more civilised than this?

Francisco and Pedro trudged towards the cart, the remainder of their slumbers clinging to them like wet blankets. Calum tutted, for he was not impressed by his guests' state. He pointed to where they should mount the cart.

"Oh wait, Francisco," Calum said, his face lit up, having remembered something important. "I have a gift for you."

Calum reached into his pocket, took something out and gestured for Francisco to open his hand. Francisco did so but did not take his eyes off Calum, for it was easy for him to succumb to suspicion. Calum placed a medal in the palm of Francisco's hand.

"I could not find your old medal, but hopefully, that is the next best thing. Let an Irish St. Christopher medal remind you of your wife since you have lost her gift."

Francisco looked at the oblong medal in his hand. His lip trembled as memories came flooding back. A wave of disappointment surged. It was not the same. The colouring was different, and St. Christopher's beard was much longer. It was like he was modelled on an Irish man instead of the majestic figure on his wife's medal. A rush of feelings came from the pit of his stomach, the primary one being guilt at losing his wife's gift. But he should make do, for St. Christopher looked down on all travellers, not just ships' captains. He closed his hand.

"Thank you. Now let us go and see Señor O'Rourke."

Calum took great care in preparing his rickety old cart for his guests, Francisco and Pedro. He stacked heaps of dry straw on the back, cushioning them as best he could for their journey to market. Amid his convoy of carts headed for the market, he strategically placed their cart in the middle to avoid attracting attention from passing English raiders.

The bumpy terrain made for an uncomfortable ride, with the cartwheels struggling against the rough ground. As they trudged along, they whispered prayers under their breaths, both in the hope of survival and that time would pass quickly.

Francisco grasped for the medal in his pocket and caressed its sides. He squeezed his eyes shut and thought of his wife. Her image was faded, like the yellowing pages in a book that had become worn, stained and hard to read. He squeezed until the medal left an indent in his hand, but the image of his wife refused to become more vibrant. He began to panic, and thoughts flooded through his mind. What if God has forsaken me? What if St. Christopher is punishing me for making demands of him? Will I ever leave this hellhole and see my wife again? Pedro elbowed him in the ribs.

"Shh. Now is not the time to have a panic attack. We need you to be at your best when we meet Señor O'Rourke."

"Yes, of course, of course," Francisco blurted out.

The image of his wife faded, and Francisco gulped, hoping he could swallow the surge of negative emotions. He cleared his throat and focused his mind on meeting Señor O'Rourke. Now was not the time to think about his wife.

The journey seemed to go on forever, but relief came after what seemed an age.

"You can come and bask in the glory of our castle now," said Calum, his voice bouncing on the melody of pride. "It is safe, so you can come and see the crown jewel of the O'Rourkes."

The affliction of cynicism had welded itself onto the Spaniards' other ailments, but the delight in Calum's voice pricked their curiosity. They poked their heads out from amongst the hay and witnessed the castle in all its glory, backed by the pale blue sky. Irish eyes saw imposing walls, towering high and impenetrable. Spanish eyes saw short work for several of the king's cannon crews. Irish eyes saw a mighty keep symbolising their clan's long-standing pride and strength. Spanish eyes saw a lone tower that would barely make one-half of the gateway to the king's castle. Irish eyes saw the proud and stout galloglass that guarded the gates. Spanish eyes saw antiquated axemen more likely to repel with their putrid stench than their rusty blades.

As good sailors, they preferred their melancholy undercover and in darkness, so they retracted their heads and buried themselves in the hay again.

"A hut for a pig herder," Francisco said to Pedro. Our king would barely use this place for stables." All their ill feelings about being traded with the English returned.

They heard the castle gate open and braced themselves for the points of English swords penetrating the hay and piercing their bodies.

"We're here," said Calum. "You can get out now."

Francisco reached out to Pedro, who was buried beneath the hay, found his forearm and gave it a reassuring squeeze.

"It is time to meet our fate."

With a collective groan, they rose and shook the hay off their clothing, eager to get out of the cramped cart. As they leapt out, grateful that their route was not obstructed by any weaponry wielded by a previously unforeseen foe, they found themselves in a grand courtyard. It was filled with bedraggled Spanish sailors, about sixty in all. They all looked exhausted and relieved to be on solid ground once more.

Pedro eagerly reunited with his comrades, pulling them into strong embraces as Francisco hung back cautiously. He couldn't help but feel nervous about how he would be received after his well-publicised trial.

But to his surprise, there was no hostility or resentment towards him. Instead, everyone welcomed him with open arms. As they caught up with each other and shared tales of survival and joy at being alive, there were also sombre accounts of mistreatment endured during their stay.

The reunion was cut short as the O'Rourkes called for them to enter the castle and rounded them up, and funnelled them into the tower. They were ushered into a grand hall, the walls adorned with intricate tapestries depicting ancient legends of burly bearded heroes brandishing broadswords, their heads adorned with shiny crowns.

As they stood in the centre of the room, their voices filled the space with excited chatter until a loud thud echoed through the air, silencing them all.

At the head of the room stood a towering figure draped in a cloak made of wolf fur. His steely gaze scanned the gathered crowd. The flickering torches cast shadows across his stern face, giving him an almost mystical aura in the dimly lit hall. With a commanding voice, he addressed them, his words thundering across the air with authority and wisdom.

"I am the O'Rourke," the man said, opening his arms to show his bulk. "And I have saved you." The O'Rourke gave a benevolent smile as he observed the puzzled faces.

"No doubt you are surprised I address you in Spanish. I served your king in the Netherlands in my youth in his Irish mercenaries. His officers commended me and begged me to stay. But alas, I had to leave to complete my mission – removing the tyrannical English yoke from the sweet neck of Ireland."

He paused, his arms aloft to gather in the applause and praise. But his arms fell to his sides, disappointed to only attract a ripple of clapping.

"I also picked up a few words of your beautiful language." The O'Rourke paused as he reconsidered his approach to his speech. "Do not think us savages. We are well acquainted with what goes on on the continent. When you eventually return to your king, you will tell him of the greatness and benevolence of the O'Rourke, so your king will one day return with his armies to repay my kindness and free us from the heretic queen. When you return, you'll see that you were the lucky ones that the O'Rourke stuck his neck out to protect, and you will witness the graves of your comrades the English left behind."

"The pig master is full of himself," said Francisco. Pedro nodded and gave him a knowing look.

"I am the greatest rebel in Ireland," the O'Rourke declared, disappointed the faces did not turn any the less blank. "Breifne, the land upon which you stand, is on the front line of resistance against the English. Ask anyone you meet on these shores, if anyone fights the English, no matter if he is alone, it is the O'Rourke. He who is a descendant of the high kings of Ireland of old. He who spits on any English claim to his lands. He who is rebellion in Ireland and your king's greatest ally on these shores."

The O'Rourke looked down for applause, only for a polite ripple to break out amongst his guests. He put their misunderstanding down to ignorance and carried on.

"However, only a handful of you need to sacrifice yourselves for the sake of your comrades and stay and help me train my men. But they must be your best men, capable of training raw recruits to the standard of your fine armies on the continent. Then, together, we'll create an escape corridor for the rest of your king's men."

At this turn of events, the men murmured amongst themselves and debated who would go and who would stay.

"I have prepared a feast for you," said the O'Rourke. "Then we must go our separate ways until it is safe. But first, you must decide who will go and who will stay."

The O'Rourke paced up and down the top of the hall until he had granted his guests enough time. Then he turned to them and smiled.

"Now, who amongst you will make the sacrifice, stay, train my men, and allow his comrades to escape?"

He looked around for signs of any volunteers.

"Did you all understand what I said?" he asked the mass of blank faces. "Most can go, but some must stay. I can give you a letter to give to your king so we can arrange safe passage for those who remain. But remember," and the O'Rourke's index finger took to the air, "we are bartering here for, as much as I would like to release you out of the goodness of my heart, having you here places me and my clan in great danger. I must have something to show my people it was worth it, placing them in such peril."

Again, he was met with blank faces and silence. He began to pace up and down because he wanted to use up his agitational energy rather than direct it at his guests.

"I am assuming you can understand me and are not cooperating on purpose. If this continues, I will have to select those who I want to stay, and I may have to reassess how many I can offer safe passage to. I will also have to hand over some to the English as a token gesture to protect my people."

"Lord?" called a man from the middle of the mass of faces.

"Yes?" said the O'Rourke as he stopped pacing.

The man made his way through the crowd and stood behind Francisco. "This man here is the captain of a great galley and an able trainer of men. He will help you."

Francisco turned, and he could have ripped the tongue out of the man's mouth, such was his fury. Then he recognised him from his trial, which sent a shiver down his spine.

"Why doesn't this man volunteer himself? Are captains not supposed to sacrifice themselves for their men?"

"I think he should," said the man. "He is a dead man walking in Spain."

The O'Rourke signalled to his men, and the guards fished Francisco out from the crowd and stood him beside the O'Rourke.

"Why did he say that you are a dead man?" said the O'Rourke as he looked Francisco up and down. "You look very much alive standing beside me."

Francisco looked at the ground. "The man must have me mixed up with someone else. I have a wife and young children. I very much hope to go home like everyone else."

The man worked his way to the front of the crowd.

"It is you who are mistaken, Captain Butero. I was at your trial. You may be a fine sailor, but as soon as you set foot in Spain, the only thing waiting for you is your family's shame for your cowardice and the hangman's noose. If you stay here, we can tell the king of your sacrifice and try to get your conviction annulled. Then you can return a hero, the saviour of your men."

The room went silent. The next to speak was the O'Rourke.

"So all you offer me in reward for putting my people in danger is a coward who will only help me so he can avoid the noose?"

Francisco stood between the O'Rourke and his mix of fellow Spanish soldiers and sailors, feeling the weight of shame bearing down on him. The recent storms, the trial, nearly drowning, and being held captive by "savages" had chipped away at his sense of self-worth. He knew he needed to redeem himself somehow, even if it meant sacrificing his own life for the few remaining men under his command. He wrestled with conflicting emotions – the desire to redeem himself for his failures and his overwhelming fear of sacrificing his own life for the safety of his men. Yet, deep down, he knew that sacrificing himself was the only way to make up for his mistakes and protect what was left of his comrades.

Pedro struggled to his feet and raised his hand to speak.

"Lord, my comrade is indeed a great captain and a fine trainer of men. He may not come to you in the most conventional of circumstances, nor have he volunteered himself, but you will not regret having him in your employment. I volunteer myself to assist him should he wish to redeem himself in his own eyes and in those of God, his comrades, your clan, and his king. I was his first officer on the San Pedro, and it was an honour to serve under him."

The O'Rourke waved him forward, and Pedro stood beside Francisco.

"Well, captain," said the O'Rourke as he circled before Francisco. "What is it to be? We all await your answer."

Francisco raised his head and looked at his comrades' expectant faces.

"If my men can go home as soon as it is practical, then you have my services for as long as you require them."

The hall erupted in cheering. The O'Rourke gave him a hearty slap on the shoulder.

"Then let us eat since we have a bargain to celebrate," he said.

The O'Rourke laid out a modest spread of food and drink for his Spanish guests. Yet, in the eyes of the Spaniards, it was fit for a king. They feasted eagerly, savouring every bite and sip as if it were a rare delicacy. Raised goblets clinked together in toasts, and melodic Spanish songs rose into the air, filling their host's heart with warmth and gratitude. But as the evening wore on, it came time for the visitors to depart to their secret hiding places, accompanied by their Irish hosts. Only Francisco and Pedro remained.

"Don't think me rude," said the O'Rourke, "but I must see your skills on the training ground before I release your comrades. Despite my show of enthusiasm, they did not exactly sell either your capability or reliability to me."

Francisco was tired but was in little mood to spoil the pleasure of having a full stomach on the best food he had eaten in months.

"So what is to be done with us?"

"You can stay here and lodge with the servants in the castle. It is the least conspicuous place I can hide you."

Francisco bowed his head.

"Thank you, Lord. I'm sure it will be our most comfortable lodgings since we came to this island."

"Get some rest, for you will need it. Tomorrow, I will introduce you to my sons Eoghan and Brian Óg, and the fun will begin."

Francisco bowed again and returned the O'Rourke's smile. A servant came to show them to their quarters.

CHAPTER II
A LESSON IN IRISH WARFARE

The sun rose, its warm rays struggling to penetrate the narrow, dirt-encrusted windows of the servants' quarters. Inside, the open square rooms were filled with sleeping bodies, their slumber peaceful and deep despite the cramped conditions. In one corner, Francisco and Pedro lay intertwined with their fellow servants, oblivious to the occasional stray arm or elbow that would have annoyed them in their waking moments. Even the persistent crowing of a rooster could barely rouse them from their dreams of shipwrecks and prisons without windows, both the world of sleep and reality dank and musty. But amid the gloom, a burst of youthful energy bound through the door. Said youth, who may have just left his teens, swung a foundling stick around like a soldier preparing for battle, his enthusiasm contagious as he imagined himself an officer of the king of Spain engaged in a duel for the honour of his country. When he saw the mass of servants, some still in slumber and some rising for their first piss of the day, he put down his stick and towered above them.

"I hear you have two Spaniards amongst your ranks today. Yield them to me, and I will cease to disturb your morning."

A hand rose from its slumber and limply pointed to the far wall beneath which the Spanish lay. The young man picked his way through the rising bodies. Soon, he towered above the men he sought, picking out their sun-and-windswept skins from that of the sallow Irish servants. He shook Francisco by the shoulder.

"Come, teach me to fight. Teach me to fight like a captain of the greatest Catholic king on earth."

He picked up his stick again and duelled with invisible enemies, berating them in a mock Spanish accent.

Francisco lifted his head from his slumbers. His parched mouth prevented him from cursing what he thought was one of his rogue Spanish comrades ridiculing his martial skills.

"Water," Francisco cried.

The young man reached for his belt and passed over a water flask.

"I think I like you already," he said. "Drinking and fighting are amongst the noblest of pastimes."

All this boisterousness was merely an aural assault on Francisco in his groggy state. He dragged himself to his feet, much to the annoyance of those around him. He settled his gaze on the source of his irritation.

"Who are you, and why do you bother us so?"

The young man bent down, smiled and rested his arm upon his knee. "I am Eoghan, son of the O'Rourke, and I forgive you for not recognising me, for you have only just arrived. We are going to get to know each other very well."

Francisco threw his eyes to the heavens. He had already had enough of holding his tongue, but he still did not desire to have it removed from his body. It was time to pretend he was on trial before the Spanish admiralty and sit as silently as a rock in a stormy sea of temptation. But Eoghan still grinned beside him, and Francisco knew he had to deflect such eagerness away from him.

"May I trouble you for some ale and bread for my friend and me? Once I have eaten, I can tell you tales of the Spanish military school."

Eoghan beamed with delight and cast his sword stick prop behind him, not looking or caring to see that he threw it into a mass of sleeping bodies.

"I can give you freshly baked bread today, and any other day my father still deems you an asset."

Eoghan reached his hand across and helped Francisco navigate the tangle of sleeping bodies to a clear path to the door.

"If we could have some better accommodation—"

But Eoghan cut across him.

'Whoa, hold on there, brother. First, you need to prove yourself before you make demands."

Eoghan pointed to some stools in the courtyard, and Francisco and Pedro sat and made themselves as comfortable as possible. Eoghan handed them some bread from his pouch.

"What next?" Francisco asked after he had finished eating. "Are you going to parade the men in front of me?"

Eoghan laughed.

"We're not that kind of army. I'll fetch my men, and we'll raid Connacht. We can see if you prove yourself in the bogs and forests."

A chill went down the spines of Francisco and Pedro, for all the bogs meant to them were cold and illness, whilst the light in Eoghan's face showed to him they meant glory and plunder. They sat silently while Eoghan energetically prepared for the raid, resembling a child eagerly awaiting Christmas. They brought out horses and set them in front of Francisco and Pedro.

"In your own time," said Eoghan. He extended his hand in invitation.

Francisco and Pedro looked at each other, unsure if they were victims of a prank.

"Anything wrong?" asked Eoghan.

Pedro egged Francisco on to give a proper answer.

"Are your men going to get our saddles?" Francisco said, his voice quivering, for he was unsure of the reaction his question would provoke.

Eoghan laughed again.

"Sorry, boys. We have none of your luxuries here. We ride bareback. Look."

Eoghan was on top of the horse with a hop, skip and a jump. "Look," he said as he sat perched on the horse and extended his arms to show off. "It's easy when you know how. Now mount up, for we have to go before the day wears on."

Francisco and Pedro looked at each other, inviting the other to try first, but in his attempts to reassert himself as the captain, he elected to go first. With a hop, skip, and jump, he was face down in the mud, surrounded by laughing Irish.

"You next," said Eoghan to Pedro as he tried to hold back the laughter. Pedro's fate was similar to his captain's, much to the amusement of their hosts. They tried several more times, if only to be good sports and build a bond with their hosts. Eventually, Eoghan called time.

"Men, help them onto their horses and hold them in place until they are steady. Try not to do it with a smile on your face, for they may not know how to ride like Irishmen, but they are our guests. Extend to them the legendary O'Rourke hospitality. I will ride alongside them to ensure they remain aloft, for it seems old habits will take a long time to break."

After the conclusion of making fun of their Spanish guests, fifty men eventually set off for Connacht in high spirits with Eoghan and their guests at their head.

Francisco and Pedro whispered together at every opportunity they got. They saw this raid as an excellent opportunity to find out how things worked here and how they could use it to their own advantage. Once they had a library of knowledge and some experience, it should be easy for two Spanish officers to find an escape route. Once home, Francisco could negotiate away his previous sentence because of his knowledge of the native Irish and become an advisor to the king. They started with their observations of the gentry.

With his broad shoulders and fierce countenance, Eoghan was the son of the notorious O'Rourke – a local warlord feared by the English and revered by his own people. Despite his jovial facade, Eoghan was a serious warrior at heart – trained from birth to wield a sword and defend their territory. He was also known as his father's favoured son, destined to inherit his title and the kingdom his father had built in this part of the country.

The pride of their army resembled the little toy soldiers Francisco used to play with in his childhood. The Galloglass's chain mail glinting in the sunlight brandished broadswords and axes that seemed more suited for medieval times than this era of muskets and pikes. Despite their mercenary status and questionable loyalty, they were still considered elite soldiers, hired by clan leaders who would gift them land and build allegiance through generations. But compared to what else was available, they were the cream of the crop.

The rest of them were a ragbag of vagabonds referred to as Kern. They were armed with javelins, swords, bows, and arrows. Francisco considered them no more than disagreeable peasants.

But Francisco had to bite his tongue. They may have been from a different age, but their blades were still sharp, and their arrows were enough to kill him. He had to pray that they were backward enough to be easily impressed, and himself and Pedro would have to do little to satisfy them before they were sent on their way back to Spain.

Eoghan O'Rourke returned from his scouting mission and went straight to his Spanish guests.

'We're almost at the flatlands of the Earl of Clanricard. Then you'll see how to do an ambush and how an Irishman gets rich. We can discuss how you'd do it afterwards if you like."

Francisco gave a polite bow.

'I'm sure your ambush technique rivals your father's hospitality and generosity."

Eoghan smiled, for he interpreted that as a compliment. "We have some of the best bowmen on the island. Watch how they shatter the heads of our enemies as if they were jugs of water."

Francisco smiled again and invited Eoghan to lead the way.

Hidden amidst a thick tangle of bushes that rustled softly in the gentle breeze sat Francisco, Pedro and Eoghan. The air was thick with the musky scent of livestock and the earthy aroma of damp soil and fresh vegetation. Francisco and Pedro covered their mouths, for it was all they could do to suppress their coughing. In the distance, birds sang melodic tunes, and distant sheep bleats echoed through the peaceful landscape.

Cattle dotted the rolling hills, their deep brown hides glistening in the warm sun as they leisurely grazed on the bountiful grass provided by the wet climate. The herders seemed half-heartedly attempting to direct the cows in a specific direction, but their efforts were met with little enthusiasm from both man and beast. Eoghan gestured towards the various cows, expertly reciting their prices as Francisco and Pedro struggled to feign interest in his seemingly unending list.

"And we are here to steal them," Eoghan said when his list finally ended.

Such recklessness jarred Francisco and Pedro out of their stupor.

"But surely they'll know who came and stole their cattle?" Francisco said as he tried to keep his whisper within the bush.

"Yes," smiled Eoghan. "But can they get them back?"

Francisco and Pedro looked at each other and wondered how they had ever ended up in this predicament—from being captains of one of the mightiest ships ever to sail the seas to sitting in a bush as petty cattle rustlers. Their thoughts were disrupted by the huge grin on Eoghan's face.

"We don't kill anyone if you don't have to. All we are here to do is steal the cattle. If we leave the herders alive, they'll remember your kindness, and it makes it so much easier to bribe them to defect to our side should anything happen to their lordly masters."

Francisco smiled as if he had been unwittingly dragged into a children's game and could not insult the host.

"But that only applies to the Irish herders," Eoghan continued. "We kill all the English settlers, no matter where we meet them."

Francisco pointed towards the cattle.

"Then let us go steal some cows."

Crouched low in the bushes, they waited patiently until the main body of cows had passed. The clanging of armour and grunts of the Galloglass escort accompanied the slow-moving herd as the herdsmen lazily drove them forward. In a swift and co-ordinated movement, Eoghan and his men emerged from the cover of the woods, arrows notched and aimed at each head of the escort.

The Galloglass constable stepped forward.

"You still haven't learned, have you, Eoghan?"

Eoghan sneered.

"Neither have you, roaming so near O'Rourke fields. I have given you so many chances, yet you still don't fear us."

The constable shook his head and laughed.

"Your biggest mistake is that you do not know your place. If you brazenly come and steal the cattle of the Earl of Clanricard, then you know he will come and take them back. You'll be lucky if he doesn't tell the governor, and they invade and oust you from your lands."

It was Eoghan's turn to laugh.

"What do I care for such empty threats? You call yourselves Galloglass but do not even defend your master's property. The Earl of Clanricard is exactly what his name says he is, an earl. An earl is the puppet of the queen, a limp, impotent man who can't stand up for himself without his master's permission. But we now have men from the king of Spain."

Eoghan proudly extended his hand to introduce Francisco and Pedro, much to their dismay.

"Look, we now have the best advisors the Spanish king can provide. Soon, we'll be the most powerful clan and kings of Ireland once again."

Eoghan expected the constable to shudder in fear. But his foolish, loose tongue only brought rebuke.

"Stealing cows is a child's game. You could even say it was tradition," said the Galloglass. "But cavorting with the enemy is something entirely different. Listen to me, boy, when I tell you to get these men off your land. They may make promises and teach you how to wield a gun, but they will only bring about your demise."

"You're old and try to pass off your cowardice as wisdom. But I'll play your game one last time. I'll steal your cattle but grant you your freedom. But expect little mercy when we come conquering with the guns of the king of Spain."

The constable shook his head once more.

"Can I go now? If I leave now, I could be in my master's fort by sundown. You can have our axes and swords, and we'll set off."

Francisco and Pedro shook their heads at such a quaint arrangement. But soon, Eoghan was herding his newly acquired cattle towards Castle Nua, and the constable had set off in the other direction.

The O'Rourke was waiting for his son when he arrived home.

"So how did our Spanish guests acquit themselves?" he asked.

"I think they are more men of the sea. They did not seem too familiar with cattle rustling, but they'll learn. Let me put it this way, they will soon earn their keep or be guests of Governor Bingham."

CHAPTER 12

THE LURE OF HOME

The O'Rourke did not have to wait long for a reaction to his son's daring raid, for a month later he received a letter sealed with the crest of the Earl of Clanricard. He sat, broke the seal and read. With a deep frown etched on his weathered face, the patriarch summoned his two sons, Eoghan and Brian Óg, to the castle.

As they entered the great hall, the golden light momentarily streamed through the stained-glass windows, making the most of its moments before being obscured by a cloud. It cast shadows across the stone walls, illuminating the tapestries depicting the history of the O'Rourkes, which concentrated on the period when they were the high kings of Ireland all those hundreds of years ago. The servants had even laid fresh hay upon the floor so they could spill their ale without fear of causing either a hazard or an odour. The air was tense as the two sons crossed the floor, waiting for their father's words. Pacing the floor, their father waved the letter dramatically in front of them. Eoghan gulped, for he did not know whether his father's snarls were for him or the letter's author.

"The earl, in his arrogance, thinks he can threaten us," the O'Rourke said, "but he is nothing without Bingham. The high kings of old would never put up with such pathetic threats."

"What did he say?" asked Eoghan. He beamed, knowing he was off the hook.

"He says he wants his cattle back, plus compensation, plus an agreement undersigned by Bingham that we'll not do it again, and if we do, we incur set penalties."

"I know the only place for that letter, Father."

Eoghan leapt from his seat, snatched the letter from his father's hand, and threw it on the fire. The O'Rourke slapped his son on the shoulders.

"We'll make an O'Rourke of you yet. Send our spies to Galway and our messengers to our allies. We must hide our Spanish friends and write again to the king of Spain. We will tell him his men are safe with us, and he should send an army to rescue them."

He turned to his boys, his eyes alight.

"When the king comes with his men, he will see how I have stood head and shoulders above the other clans of Ireland. He will see I am the biggest rebel in Ireland and laud me. Once more, just like our ancestors, we will be the high kings of Ireland."

The O'Rourke's index finger soared to the heights of the extent of his arm. His two boys jumped for joy and ran to embrace him.

"Get off me, the both of you. We have no time to congratulate ourselves. We must be prepared for war!"

The two sons were ecstatic. Their eyes sparkled with a mix of excitement and nervousness. The thrill of proper war filled their stomachs with butterflies, and their hands tingled at the thought of wielding an axe in anger. This was their chance for vengeance as so far, they had done nothing but witness the slow but steady encroachment of the crown and its allies onto their father's land. The occasional show of force from Governor Bingham was nothing compared to what they were about to face. Their father's tales of past glories and victories as O'Rourke warriors fuelled their desire to prove themselves on the battlefield. It was time for them to carve their own path to glory and honour, following in the footsteps of their legendary family name.

The O'Rourke was determined to hide the presence of so many Spanish Armada survivors, so he scattered them among villages for coign and livery. Francisco and Pedro were lodged in a small village near Baile Nua. They found themselves under the protection of Shea Óg O'Rourke, an ambitious middle-aged chieftain. The village was a desolate and barren place, battered by relentless winds that seemed to come straight from the depths of a frozen hell, which felt much worse than the fiery hell their Spanish priests seemed to love telling tales of. It felt like a world away from the warm embrace of Spain, almost as if they had been transported to the stormy islands of Scotland but without any escape route.

Despite being tasked with keeping a low profile and remaining hidden unless summoned by the O'Rourke to train his men, Shea Óg refused to let Francisco and Pedro hide away. He would invite them to dine with him in the bustling village square every night, eager to hear their stories from Spain, the sea, or the battles of the Spanish Armada. Pedro was a master storyteller, his words flowing effortlessly as he regaled the crowd with thrilling tales, his Irish now much improved and whatever shortfalls there were, were supplemented by Francisco. But as each night passed, Francisco grew increasingly anxious as their audience seemed to multiply before their very eyes. The flickering firelight cast shadows on the rapt faces of their listeners, who hung onto every word with bated breath.

Shea Óg was a gracious host and showered his guests with care and attention, for he saw their welfare and wellbeing as a way to ingratiate himself with the O'Rourke. He outfitted them in traditional clothes to help them blend in with the locals and provided them with thick blanket coats to protect them against the harsh cold to which they were not accustomed.

However, what caught Shea Óg's eye more than anything was his daughter, who seemed to linger in the background whenever her father came to attend to his guests. Her presence did not go unnoticed by Francisco, and Shea Óg was determined to stir his interest.

"She's a beauty, isn't she?" he said, referring to his doe-eyed daughter. "I've had all kinds of dowry offers for her, cattle by the hundreds. But I've always said to her, 'I'll look after you and keep you for that man you think is special.'"

Francisco tried to edge away, for he felt himself being cornered.

"You are a good man, Shea Óg, a good father, and you have been kind to me and my friend. I'm sure you'll find some worthy Irish prince for your daughter. She is not for me, for I am a married man."

Shea Óg edged into Francisco's personal space.

"A marriage in Spain means nothing here," he said, winking. "We've got plenty of laws to get you out of that. Now, what if she doesn't want an Irish prince? What if she wants something different?"

Francisco scowled, knowing he had to be firmer with his host.

"You should set a good example and tell her not to tread on the sacred vows. Does she not listen to her father? Does she know nothing of duty?"

Shea Óg laughed.

"You know nothing of young girls today. They set their eyes on something exotic, some man from a faraway land that gets their imagination running, and there's just no telling them."

Francisco smiled and tried to edge away.

"It is better, if she were to marry, that it would be to a man she was familiar with and not one planning to leave at his first opportunity."

But Shea Óg was not to be put off.

"Sure, if you had a pretty young thing warming your bed, you'd be far more inclined to stay."

"Unfortunately, I am a servant to the O'Rourke and am at his disposal. I could not make any compromising promises interfering with my obligations."

Shea Óg slapped him on the shoulder.

"Don't be so afraid, man! I'll sort everything out with the O'Rourke. She'd be happy to sneak into your bed and tell no tales until she has the O'Rourke's permission."

Francisco wriggled out of the corner Shea Óg trapped him in.

"She's a beautiful girl who will make some Irish lord a lovely wife. But my vow to the O'Rourke is like that of a priest."

Shea Óg winked at him.

"Oh, I know what that's like. Don't worry, I'll sort it. I'll even get a nice one for your friend."

"No, don't—"

But Francisco's protests fell upon empty air, for Shea Óg was gone.

Several weeks later, Francisco and Pedro were summoned back to Baile Nua, where the threat of the Earl of Clanricard hung over the castle like a dark cloud. They entered the great hall, and the air was thick with tension and uncertainty. Each person braced themselves for what was to come.

The elders, their hair streaked with grey and faces marked by battles past, were tense and wary. But the young soldiers, unacquainted with the horrors of war and still full of youthful energy, seemed almost giddy with excitement.

The only one who seemed undaunted was the O'Rourke, reclining in his chair with a proud smile as if he alone held the power to defeat their enemies. His right-hand man, Dermot O'Rourke, bowed before him.

"What news do you have for me, Dermot? Are my allies ready to grasp the sword again and send the English home?"

Dermot twitched.

"No, lord. We still await a response from most."

"What does 'from most' mean?"

Dermot's twitch became more pronounced.

"We have only heard from the Maguire, lord."

"And what did he say?"

"'Tell us when you are in real peril not of your own creation, and we will consider coming to your aid.'"

The O'Rourke gripped the handles of his chair and gritted his teeth. He threw himself out of the seat and paced the floor.

"What is that supposed to mean? Will they wait for our greatest moment of peril and then split the spoils with Bingham? Why do you force me into having obligations to such unreliable people?"

"Lord, your allies believe you brought this instance upon yourself, and if they defend your provocations, the crown will come for them next. The O'Neill and O'Donnell wars of succession still rage without any sign of resolution. Without them, no one else will stand with you."

The O'Rourke's blood boiled. "How are we supposed to gain our freedom if we can only react and not provoke? It allows our common enemy the advantage of attack, and we are reduced to bickering about who caused what while they take us apart one by one."

Eoghan stepped forward from the crowd.

"But, Father, it only makes your argument to the king of Spain more convincing that you are the leader of the Gaelic world if you are the only one to stand up to the English."

The O'Rourke snarled at the thought of his only potential ally being so far away.

"Sure, they'd all know that if they bothered to listen. Still, if they must see a sacrifice to shake them out of their stupor, so be it. Yet, we must still prepare. How are our Spanish guests getting along?"

"They clamour to go home yet offer little in the field. They seem to know little of our ways of war."

"Don't you go catching the fever of despair, son. Once we have enough muskets, they will come into their own by hook or by crook. Now, let us talk less and drink more. The day of destiny will soon be upon us."

The servants brought in food, and Francisco saw his opportunity for the O'Rourke sat alone. Francisco tried to sidle up to the O'Rourke but was stopped by the guards. A nod from their master allowed him through.

Francisco bowed.

"What is it?" said the O'Rourke.

"I beg your pardon, but I feel compelled to ask for the benefit of my compatriots—"

"You must get a lot of time to talk to your king with all that verbiage."

"Sorry, lord. When will the first ship set sail for Spain with my compatriots on board?"

"Have you not listened to a word we've said, or do I need to get you a translator?"

"No, lord." Francisco edged away, for his credit with the O'Rourke rapidly declined.

"We are facing a crisis here, and all our supposed allies will not come and support us. Now you approach us in our hour of need when we helped you survive, and you want to arrange safe passage back to Spain?"

"No, lord. I only asked after the previous arrangement we made."

"We arranged that you repay us for risking our lives to save yours. I have seen none of you placing yourselves in harm's way for us, so why would I value your lives over those of my people and spend my energy saving you?"

"Sorry, lord."

Francisco slunk off and rejoined Pedro in the shadows of the hall.

"Did he listen?" asked Pedro.

Francisco shook his head.

"I fear we are stuck here for good."

CHAPTER 13

A PROMISING SITUATION

S everal weeks passed, and the court of the O'Rourke clan braced themselves, knowing it wouldn't be long before the Earl of Clanricard made good on his threatening letter. The Galloglass, who had previously surrendered their earl's prized cattle to Eoghan O'Rourke without resistance, was fiercely determined to reclaim their master's herd. With fiery determination blazing in their eyes, they would either drive the cattle back or meet their end with their heads in a noose.

Eoghan O'Rourke took a band of men to scout out the size of the force that had invaded his father's lands. They quickly ascertained that the Earl's men did not have enough men for a full-scale invasion or to secure the land they passed through. However, they were hell-bent on a campaign of revenge destruction.

Eoghan nearly choked as he was forced to follow his father's instructions. He provided enough bait to ensure the invaders followed him and led them straight to the herd so he could spare the people from their vengeance. Once the invaders had their herd, they turned and headed back to Galway. Eoghan followed at a distance, for he was under strict instructions not to antagonise them.

Francisco and Pedro received a summons to Baile Nua. As they entered the dimly lit hall filled with smoke fumes, they found the O'Rourke slumped in his ornate chair, surrounded by a dishevelled array of papers that covered the table before him. The scent of ale hung heavy in the room as if the O'Rourke was seeking solace and courage from its bitterness. However, even with each swig he took from his mug, the weight of responsibility only grew heavier on his shoulders. It was clear that whatever troubles lay within those papers were not so easily washed away by drink.

"Do you know anything about affairs of state?" the O'Rourke mumbled over the lip of his mug. I would give my left arm to be rid of this turbulent mess."

He looked at the walls and the images of his great ancestors from hundreds of years ago. They stared down at him, only adding to the burden on his shoulders. He raised his mug to salute them. "But I suppose that goes hand in hand with being the O'Rourke."

Francisco suppressed the irritation building inside him and stepped forward and bowed.

"What troubles you? I may not have advised the king, but I have run his ships and had many dealings with his admiralty. Egos and the lengths some men will go to change little from court to court."

The O'Rourke gave a wry smile.

"You are in a land where justice is dispensed through the axe. The biggest liars and thieves are those in the crown's courts or her Dublin Council. They wish me to take a sheriff and come under Governor Bingham of Connacht. It is the equivalent of throwing me into a pack of wild dogs."

Francisco could see the promises of escape evaporate before his eyes. He had to keep the dream alive, if not for himself, then for the men.

"What advice do you wish me to give you, Señor O'Rourke?" Francisco said. "You have already answered your own question. To comply is to die."

A lethargic finger acknowledged Francisco's response.

"You are right. You may not be the bad apple your comrades wish to expel from the basket after all."

Francisco sensed a brief window of opportunity.

"If you are after encouragement, then the actions of my king may supply it. Do not think a mere storm has beaten him. Even as his ships limp back, he is plotting his next move. You would do well to position yourself high in his thoughts as the leader of the Irish rebels and the only one to return his men to him."

The energy returned to the O'Rourke.

"You have an eye for an opportunity and know when to make your play and to say it in terms of what the other person wants. That is good. None of my sons has this talent. If only I could send you instead of me to Dublin to meet the council. But I need someone to watch over my sons while I am gone so they do not undo all my good work. If you act as my eyes and ears while I am away and I get a good opportunity, I will help your men return home."

Francisco bowed to leave.

"I take you, lord, as a man of your word."

"Do not take me for a man of my word. Take me for what I am: a man of action. This very day, my priests will write a letter to your king, and it will be sent via a merchant ship to the shores of your kingdom. If your men can bring themselves to do me a service while we wait for your king's reply, we'll all be victorious."

This was music to Francisco's ears, the big chance he had been waiting for. However, his mind was clouded with doubt until he dismissed it. He had little choice.

"Consider me your servant, Señor O'Rourke."

"Then you are to be at the disposal of my son Eoghan, but ignore his musings on war, for they are based on the daydreams of the mind and I want the finest army in all of Ireland. Can you do that for me?"

"Rest assured, lord. Your able men will back up any assertions you may make in the court in Dublin and those of the king of Spain. Write your letter and assert yourself freely."

The O'Rourke smiled as he dismissed Francisco.

As the sun set behind the castle towers, Francisco emerged from its shadowy depths to find Eoghan perched on a stone wall, surrounded by his loyal men. The wind tousled their hair and carried the distant sounds of swords clashing and horses neighing, a reminder of the preparations for the potential war. Eoghan bounded off the wall with a graceful leap and strode towards Francisco, his eyes alight with anticipation of their meeting. It was as if he had been anxiously awaiting Francisco's arrival.

"When does my father leave for Dublin? Is It before the morrow?" said Eoghan.

He hovered behind Francisco's shoulders as if he were a fly. Such was Francisco's new elevation of status, and he thought he could walk off Eoghan's questioning.

"Why don't you go in and ask him yourself? He still sat in his seat when I left."

"When my father leaves, I have work for you."

"I'm sure you do, but please settle any instructions with your father before he leaves, for he has given me tasks to attend to."

Eoghan scowled at Francisco's back, for he did not like his new-found confidence.

CHAPTER 14

THE PANGS OF BEING COMPROMISED

A month later, the two brothers, Eoghan and his younger sibling, Brian Óg, stood at the gates of Baile Nua, their eyes following the movements of their father and his advisors as they loaded bags onto carts and mounted their horses. It was as if they were waiting for their father to leave, eager to be alone in the quiet stillness of their family's lands. The scent of freshly cut hay mingled with the sharp tang of horse sweat. As the O'Rourke approached on his powerful steed, he seemed to loom over his sons like a mountain descending from the sky. Their father's presence always demanded respect and commanded attention, even from his own children.

"Your father is about to enter tense negotiations with the heathens, which could affect the very existence of the clan. Under no circumstances are you to raid outside our borders nor engage the enemy if they come onto our lands. If anything happens to me or they decide to imprison me, Eoghan, you shall be the O'Rourke in my absence. Make any decisions you see fit, but I pray they are sensible. Treat our Spanish guests well, for they give us leverage with both monarchies. Have you listened to what I've said, Eoghan?"

"Of course, Father. What makes you think I'm not listening to you?"

"That stupid grin on your face swiftly followed by what I think you will do as soon as my back is turned. Let this responsibility I'm giving you be a chance for you to learn and grow up, for one day, your father may not return from such a meeting."

"Then our enemies would feel the wrath of the O'Rourkes."

"That is, if they do not devour you first. Now goodbye and look after your brother."

Brian Óg and Eoghan stood, watched their father leave the castle, and waited for the gate to close behind them. Eoghan was overcome with glee and slapped his brother on the shoulder.

"Fetch the men and bring them to the great hall. Then we can begin."

Francisco and Pedro were imprisoned in the cramped musty servants' quarters. The tiny room was barely lit by a single weak lantern that cast deep shadows on the walls but sucked the light from the souls of those trapped within it. Francisco's nerves quickly went as the dark shadows and the claustrophobic room returned him to the trauma of his imprisonment on the admiral's ship. Pedro could only crouch in the corner as his friend howled at the walls.

Francisco brushed past him.

"I hope whatever you have been up to, your father would approve of it."

"He will soon see the wisdom of his sons' ways. Come before you are spotted. Weak minds surround us, susceptible to the queen's coin. Hurry now. We have no time to waste."

They arrived in the great hall to a group of youthful faces, their beards barely sprouted, their knuckles not even cracked from holding the shaft of an axe in the cold piercing wind, their faces white but only broken by pimples rather than scars. They all gazed upon Francisco and Pedro with wonder as if they were rare creatures they only read about in books, if they ever glanced at them, or were passed along in folk tales.

Eoghan invited the Spaniards to the front of the hall and draped his arm over Francisco's shoulder to show that he was his. Francisco shook him off, for he knew Eoghan would not have him killed in his father's absence. Anyway, he had been assigned to talk sense into the boy and for the first time, he realised the magnitude of the task he had taken on. Eoghan paused and considered admonishing Francisco, but this was neither the time nor the place, for it would take the shine off his prize. Instead, Eoghan threw open his arms to call for his youthful audience to lend him their ears.

"Rebels of Connacht, for too long have you been on the run from our cruel oppressor, the heretic queen, and her instrument of evil, Governor Bingham. The Spanish came to our shores, but too many of our cowardly elders set upon them for their own gain or to placate the English. But now, we have officers of the Spanish army to train us how to fight and to drive our enemies back into the sea." Eoghan reached back, grabbed Francisco by the elbow, and pulled him forward.

"Here, my father saved this great captain from the storms, and the captain is so grateful he has agreed to help us."

A roar and a raising of mugs stirred in Francisco an embarrassment that hid his anger at being used so. But with all those expectant, youthful faces staring at him, he knew he was cornered.

"Men of Ireland, I bring you greetings from the King of Spain."

The roar his greeting brought forth told him he had set off on the right track.

"With the blessing of God and the one true faith, we'll defeat the heretical queen."

The rafters shook from the roar of the hall.

"Once we send the men from the armada home, the king will see what good allies you are and send a mighty army."

The cheering stopped, and the youths murmured amongst themselves. Eoghan pulled Francisco back by the elbow.

"They don't want to hear how you plan to abandon them. Too many times have they been promised an army, only for a handful of men to land on an obscure beach and then be slaughtered."

Francisco pulled his elbow back.

"They should have considered that before they robbed and slaughtered my men as they lay on the beaches and sold the rest to their supposed enemy."

"Remember where you are," said Eoghan, his words angry but measured. "You could be dead in a ditch in a bog in Ireland and nobody in Spain would be any the wiser."

Francisco stared at his host and saw the burning of youthful zeal in his eyes. He decided on an appropriate ending for his speech.

"But the king has sent me to make you the most powerful army Ireland has ever seen. All under the leadership of Eoghan O'Rourke."

He reached back and lifted Eoghan's arm to acknowledge the cheers. But few cheers came, only a scathing look from Eoghan and more murmurings from the crowd. It was Eoghan's turn to take back his arm.

"Forgive my Spanish friend. Something must have got lost in translation. The clans of Connacht and Leinster will rise and throw off the oppressors' yoke."

The cheers returned, and Francisco tried to slip back into the shadows. But Eoghan grabbed his arm.

"You have much to learn, my friend."

"Is this what your father would have wanted when he is away negotiating with the crown?"

"Prove your worth on the training ground, for you know nothing of Irish politics. If you don't, you and your men are just useless mouths to feed."

Francisco nodded and held in his anger at being threatened by such a disrespectful youth. He signalled to Pedro to join him and retire, leaving Eoghan to drink with his youthful allies.

CHAPTER 15
CONSIGNED TO MUD

T hrough wind, rain, and shine, Francisco, Pedro, and their Irish hosts took to the fields with the intention of becoming an army that could sweep the English off the battlefield. The young Irishmen beamed and puffed their chests out as they floated in a dream world of fame and glory and how they thought combat would be. Francisco and Pedro tried to look busy and hide their thoughts on how the training progressed. They had to humour their hosts until the day a Spanish vessel came to take them home.

Eoghan led the communication between the Spanish trainers and their Irish hosts with a mixture of Irish and Spanish he had picked up from his father. He tried to coerce Francisco into spending his every waking hour training the men which by and large was successful. But despite all of Francisco's efforts, it soon transpired that these youths had neither the intention nor the discipline to learn the formations or the battle tactics of the Spanish continental armies. Soon, Francisco and Pedro were reduced to sitting uselessly on one side, once more watching the manoeuvres of cattle rustlers and the clashes of armoured Galloglass while the guns recovered from the wrecks of the Armada lay idle.

The idleness of both Spaniards and guns soon caught Eoghan's attention as he came to observe the training. Francisco's knee shook as he sat, for the scowl on Eoghan's face betrayed that he was losing patience with him. He prayed for the return of the O'Rourke before the loss of patience reached its nadir. But his eyes remained firmly on the sparring, for the least he could do was show an interest.

Eoghan's jaw stiffened as another Spanish-inspired formation fell apart. He locked over to his Spanish trainers, who looked sheepishly away. Eoghan's hand formed a fist. This would not do. It was time to set an example.

Brotherly rivalry flourished like a twisted flower in the mud. Eoghan and Brian Óg often sparred with each other, for there was a certain reluctance among the other youths to give them a rigorous examination of their fighting skills. Eoghan especially had a fragile ego, and no one wished to incur his wrath by knocking him to the ground. It was time to pick the flower from the mud.

"Brother, pick up your axe. It is time to show how an O'Rourke fights."

Francisco saw the glint in Brian Óg's eye and how his hand darted to his axe. Pedro put his arm across Francisco to stop him from intervening, for he knew this fight was coming. Brian Óg gripped the shaft of his axe and nodded to his entourage. He turned on his heels and slammed the shaft down towards Eoghan's head. Eoghan laughed as he dodged the blow.

"How come you are always my greatest rival?" he said to his brother before swinging the butt of his six-foot axe shaft low, forcing his brother to block.

"The only advantage you have over me, brother," Brian Óg said before swinging his axe towards his brother's shoulder, "is age. But that won't last long."

Eoghan parried, but the blade still grazed his shoulder. They both stopped, and Eoghan put his fingers to his shoulder. His face reddened when blood trickled down them.

"If you have to fight," Francisco cried from the circle of men surrounding the brothers, "use sticks, not axes. I don't want to tell your father you killed each other in a training fight."

But Eoghan's blood was up. He threw his brother back with his axe shaft and rained blows down upon him until Brian Óg could barely raise his axe to defend himself. Eoghan lunged forward, and Brian Óg skipped back. Eoghan thrust out his foot and dragged his heel down his brother's shin. Brian Óg collapsed on the ground. Eoghan raised his six-foot Galloglass axe above his brother's head to complete the subjugation. But a rider broke through the nearby woods and interrupted the smugness of his victory.

"Lord, lord, I have news of your father."

Eoghan extended his hand downward to help his brother up before he turned to the dismounted messenger.

"Well, out with it, man. Everyone will know about it soon enough."

"The lord deputy has detained your father. He will be held until he agrees to the lord deputy's terms and takes a sheriff unto these lands."

Eoghan flung his axe into the mud.

"Well, that changes everything. Eoghan stood with his hand on his hip as he paused to think. His other hand went to his chin to steady it, for it was visibly shaking. Francisco moved towards him, but Pedro stopped him again.

"He must decide," Pedro whispered.

Eoghan filled his lungs and puffed out his chest to look authoritative.

"Brian Óg, you shall stay here and protect our lands. I will join the rebels of Mayo and stir up enough trouble so the lord deputy is forced to release our father. Francisco, despite your performance over the past couple of days, circumstances have granted you a reprieve. Take the men you have seen which you consider most suited and train them to use your guns. And can someone get me a bandage for my shoulder, or will this shirt be ruined?"

Eoghan prepared to leave for Baile Nua, his head a swirl of fury while his heart beat with excitement. But he had not left the training grounds before another messenger arrived.

"Lord, lord, I have a message from the archbishop of Armagh."

Eoghan took the letter from the messenger and read it while he walked. He threw the letter in the mud and strode back towards the castle. Brian Óg saw the letter and, always wanting to be involved in the political affairs of the clan, ran and retrieved it before it became illegible by sinking into a puddle of mud. He devoured what he could read and ran after his brother.

"But Eoghan, such Spanish ships could have soldiers and guns."

Francisco and all the other Spanish soldiers at the training grounds heard Brian Óg mention Spanish ships and saw how Eoghan discarded the letter without telling anyone its contents. Thinking he was trying to deceive them, they ran after Eoghan. The MacDonnell Galloglass deemed the sons of their master to be under threat and ran after the Spaniards. Eoghan heard the shouts behind him and took to his heels. The more he ran, the more Brian Óg shouted about the Spanish ships, and the more the Spanish soldiers thought Eoghan was trying to trick them into staying. Eoghan tripped and raised his arm to shield himself from the oncoming Spaniards. His brother towered over him, determined to fight off the Spanish, who were not far behind. The Galloglass tried to get between the Spaniards and the son of their master, but Spanish blood was up, and fists and feet flew. Francisco caught up with Eoghan and Brian Óg but was apprehended by their Galloglass bodyguards.

"Stop this madness," Francisco said as the Galloglass pushed him back. "We are all supposed to be allies. Just tell us what the letter said."

But everything seemed to stop when a scream was heard from behind them, and they turned to see a MacDonnell Galloglass pull his dagger out from the stomach of one of the unarmed Spanish soldiers.

Everyone froze and watched the man fall to his knees whilst attempting to hold back the blood gushing from his stomach. Francisco rushed at Eoghan only to be thrown back by his guards.

"Is this all we are to you? Tools to be bartered, used, and disposed of when you are finished?"

Eoghan had turned entirely white, and the ability to construct sentences had abandoned him. His guards looked for guidance, and Eoghan came to his senses when one of them touched his scabbard.

"Do not harm our guests," Eoghan said. "Apprehend that man and send him to the Brehon on charges of murder."

The Galloglass was set upon by his comrades and carried away.

Francisco dragged his hand through his hair. He emitted a string of Spanish curses and turned to see his own men had congregated together in defensive groups, and the Irish were surrounding them. He turned once more to Eoghan, hoping to make him see sense.

"Is this what it is to be, Eoghan?" Francisco said. "You slaughter defenceless men in the woods because they asked you to keep your father's promise to set them free? You may think you can hide our bodies by burying us in the woods, but word will get back to the Spanish king, and he will curse you. Those wise Irish clans that choose to side with him will set upon you and get his revenge. Is this what you want to tell your father you did in his absence?"

Eoghan slapped himself in the face with the palms of his hands. It was not supposed to go like this. He heaved a sigh and tried to compose himself. He tried to suppress the swirl of feelings in his head and turned to address Francisco like the son of a chieftain should.

"My man will be put on trial and will pay for his actions," Eoghan said. "An O'Rourke always keeps his word. You will arrange your men in groups and they will be smuggled onto the Spanish ships. However, you must choose who is going to stay. Then you will come with me to Connacht. Let us hear no more of this sorry tale."

Francisco scowled and cursed but signalled to his men to follow Eoghan, for he knew they would all be killed if they resisted. Their comrade was now dead, and they had no wish to join him. They lifted his body upon their shoulders and carried him back to the castle as his blood dripped down their shirts.

CHAPTER 16

FREEDOM LIES WITH THE SEA SHELLS

T he next day dawned, casting a dim light over the assembly gathered in the shadow of Baile Nua's towering walls. No amount of sweet birdsong could break down the walls of ill feeling that had been erected the day before. The Spaniards were sombre and quiet, still mourning the loss of their comrade who had been buried deep in the forest the night before by a select few. The MacDonnell clan kept the rest of them under watchful guard, but they were at least treated to a bountiful dinner thanks to Eoghan O'Rourke's orders.

Eoghan needed to regain the good favour of the Spanish, his allies, to impress the young rebels of Connacht who looked up to him as a leader. Losing their admiration was not an option after all he had done to gain it. Francisco stood at the forefront of his fellow Spaniards, representing them with a heavy heart and wary mind. The thought lingered in the back of his head that their hosts could turn on them at any moment, slaughter them and hand their bodies over to the English for a meagre reward. He pushed those unsettling feelings down, knowing that showing doubt or mistrust towards Eoghan would only give the impulsive young man second thoughts about their alliance. The tension was palpable, but as the O'Rourke's eyes and ears, it fell upon him to break the silence.

"So where are we going today?" he said.

Eoghan cleared his throat, for he knew he had to sound authoritative.

"As I said yesterday, an O'Rourke always keeps his word. We are going to meet the Spanish ships along the coastline. I'll warn you, though, it is an arduous journey through some dangerous lands with people more than willing to turn on you and sell you out to the English."

Francisco smiled and nodded to his men to reassure those who could not speak Irish.

"Well, I'm grateful at least that you wish to keep my head on top of my shoulders. Is this all there is going? When do we set off?"

Francisco looked around him and, by his best estimates, reckoned there were not more than five hundred men in total.

"First, we must split into smaller groups and arrange a rendezvous point to reassemble by the coast. Then, we'll signal the Spanish ships and see how many men they can take on board. Have you decided who is going to stay?"

"I will stay, as will a few others. However, we must first resolve how your plan is going to work. Will my men be armed? They must be able to defend themselves. Why are they being broken up? It will be hard to persuade them to accept these terms given what happened just yesterday."

Eoghan glared at Francisco, for he did not like to be questioned.

"These are the terms of the O'Rourke. Your men can accept them or roam the woods and bogs and make their own way back to Spain. If I release a gang of armed Spaniards into the countryside, Bingham will invade us immediately. Our mutually beneficial alliance must be built on trust."

"You say you will send my men to the coast, but how do I know you'll not murder them in the woods?"

Eoghan grinned.

"You don't. Hence, trust."

Francisco rubbed his chin.

"If that is what it is to be, then so be it. Men, split into groups of ten, and we head towards the coast."

The men complained, but Francisco ordered them to split into groups anyway. Francisco signalled to Pedro to join him, for he assumed he was in his group along with Eoghan.

"No, not him," Eoghan said. "We need to split up the leaders in case something happens. Let him lead another group."

Pedro came and embraced Francisco.

"Good luck, and I hope they have cleared up the bodies on the beach."

"So do I my friend, so do I."

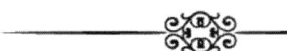

Francisco, Eoghan, Brian Óg, and some MacDonnell Galloglass made their way to the beach where they were supposed to meet the Spanish galleon. Eoghan strode ahead of him and had no wish to engage Francisco in conversation. It was as if he did not want to be here, and he considered the mission to be folly. Francisco scowled at Eoghan's hypocrisy of travelling with his brother, and that only made him more mistrustful of him. However, they quickly made their way across fields and wood, rivers and hills, and soon they had sight of the sea.

They stood atop a small, grassy hill as the sun descended below the horizon, casting an orange and pink glow over the land. The shadows of the surrounding woods seemed to stretch out away from them, robbing them of protection should they need to hide.

A majestic Spanish galleon danced upon the choppy waves on the distant horizon, its sails billowing in the wind. The Spanish soldiers were rooted to the spot, mesmerised. Each ripple in the sails inflated their hope. Francisco stuffed his trembling hand into his pocket to rub his St. Christopher medal and fought the tears welling in his eyes.

"You have sent them for me," whispered Francisco, his eyes locked onto the Spanish ship. His thumb and index finger were pressed on either side of the medal. In his mind's eye, his wife's hand extended across the water to give him the medal. He smiled and basked in the brief, warm glow of his heart.

Eoghan glared at him, for he could estimate Francisco's dreaming from the twitches on his face.

"Don't forget, this ship is not for you. You bartered your service so your men could escape on this ship. But do not despair. When your ship comes, you will board it a glorious hero."

Francisco did not look away from the ship for he did not want to give away his emotions. He dreamt of wading out to the small rowing boats to be brought to the ship and leaving this spoilt brat to his inevitable fate. But he must pray hard and live in the moment to keep his dream alive. He squeezed hard on the medal hoping its abrasive edges would return him to his senses.

"Everyone must hide until I give the signal," he said as he marched along the beach and directed rogue Spaniards to hide behind the dunes.

But they had none of it, for they no longer trusted him. They pushed back at his soldiers, and scuffles broke out. The Irish backed away, refusing to draw their weapons, for the accidental death of the Spanish soldier was still prominent in their minds

The boats from the ship out in the bay rowed towards the shore, their oars having picked up pace to cut through the now choppy waves and leaving a trail of frothy white foam in their wake. The Spaniards waded out into the water to hasten their rescue. They threw their arms in the air and shouted prayers of thanks to their comrades. Feeling his power slip away, Eoghan threw his hands in the air in defeat. The boats reached the bay and stopped where the water was waist-high. All the remaining Spaniards on the beach rushed into the water together, overpowering a small boat and its passengers with sheer numbers and determination. Those who had once been rescuers were now thrashing in the water, desperately fighting against drowning. Francisco scanned the waves to see if he knew those who could be rescued.

Suddenly, an arrow shot through the air and struck one Spaniard as he first wetted his feet in the water. Eoghan's eyes darted around the shore, trying to pinpoint where the deadly projectile had come from. The sheriff's men stormed out from behind the dunes and raced towards the beach, intent on catching anyone vulnerable.

"RUN!"

Amidst the chaos and carnage, the remaining beach-bound Spanish soldiers scrambled towards the rescue boats, desperately trying to escape the wretched island. The English soldiers waded into the sea, determined to stop anyone escaping back to the ship. With oars as weapons, the Spanish sailors defended their boats ruthlessly, knocking aside any attackers and sending them crashing into the churning sea below. The air filled with shouts and screams mingled with the sounds of clashing weapons and splintering wood, the severing of limbs, and the waves became blood-red.

The English horsemen swept along the dunes to drive anyone hiding there onto the beach. Those unlucky enough to be in their path were cut down. Those who survived merely added to the panic and mayhem as whatever Irish ranks had drawn up broke and fled towards the woods at the south end of the beach. It was becoming a massacre.

Francisco's body tensed, and he froze, his feet rooted to the sand on the edge of the beach. The chaos of battle raged around him as he stood helplessly, his heart aching for his men who their enemies were cutting down. His muscles ached from the lingering effects of the abuse he had suffered when in jail. He was the eyes and ears of the O'Rourke and senior commander of the Spanish on shore, but in that moment, he felt powerless against the onslaught. Eoghan grabbed his arm in a desperate attempt to pull him away from the danger. Francisco's mind raced with fear, anger, and determination as he tried to find a way to turn the tide of the brutal fight.

"We've been ambushed," Eoghan said as he pulled Francisco's elbow. "We must leave now, or we're all dead on this beach."

Francisco shook him off.

"If you'd armed us, we'd have a chance."

"This is no time for recriminations. We'll look for the traitor afterwards. We need to get off this beach."

Francisco remained motionless, his eyes locked on the onslaught across the sandy expanse. Eoghan raised his axe and roared for his men to retreat. Francisco's hand absently grabbed a discarded sword, its metal glinting in the sunlight. His mind raced with thoughts of charging down the beach and rallying his outnumbered troops for one last stand. But then he felt a sudden tug on his arm as a group of his loyal men ran up to him, their faces etched with fear. They firmly held him back, their voices pleading for him to reconsider.

"You must help us escape."

"I wish to die with my men," Francisco said as he wrestled with the imprisoning hands upon him.

"We are your men now and we have no wish to die this day. Lead us to safety or always be damned for abandoning your men."

Francisco felt in his pocket for his medal. It felt cold and slimy now, for water and blood had soaked his breeches. He thought back to his trial, where he was accused of cowardice for not taking his place on the battle line. Had he earned his verdict by his inaction now? His wife and family flashed before his eyes, his hopes now dashed of sailing back to them. He felt the hilt of the sword in his other hand. He felt the eyes of his men wishing to flee and the shouts of Eoghan telling him to retreat. He took out the medal and saw the smiling face of a conniving Irishman grinning at the success of his act of treachery. It was no longer the face of the Spanish St. Christopher, his protector upon the seas. He threw the medal in the sand.

"Damn you and all your temptations and false hope. You let me dream and then stole it away from before my eyes."

His men pushed him after Eoghan. Francisco bit his lip and took to his heels. The light rapidly faded to cover their tracks.

CHAPTER 17
THE RELUCTANT ADVENTURER

It was a treacherous journey back to Baile Nua for Francisco and his men, as they had to trek through rugged terrain and constantly evade the patrols of the ruthless governor of Connacht. They quickly got separated from Eoghan and his bodyguards. They had to rely on the protection of a handful of Eoghan's Galloglass they came across on the way, who luckily recognised Francisco.

Francisco's feet were like rocks dragging his unworthy body through wood and field, bog and stream. His heart was hollow, for the place where once had sat his belief in God and the memories of his family now felt like it had been carved out of his chest. Once that section of his heart touched the open air, it was cast down onto the beach to get trampled by the feet of the sheriff's men and the hooves of their horses to get washed away in the blood of his men and into the hollowness of his heart had been cast rocks of guilt and despair.

The woods around him felt like a prison, mocking him with their untamed beauty while he wallowed in self-hatred. Was this his deserved fate, to be hunted down for his mistakes? Why did God see fit to let him live? Indeed, he was a coward because he did not try to save his men. He was unfit to be a ship's captain, unfit to serve the king, and he deserved to be in these woods with these savages to be hunted down and killed. God had forsaken him, and he must have become a tool of the devil to cause the deaths of so many of the men under him. He stumbled forward and wished for God or whoever else to take their wrath out on him and punish him. Make every step a torture for what he had done to his own men.

But despair filled the mouths and minds of the men he still commanded, and he had to uplift them. They told their tales of the comrades they saw fall and their despair at being trapped on this godforsaken island. With a sharp intake of breath, Francisco realised he was still a captain, and he could not tell his own tale of woe. If he could not be a captain, at least he could act like one. He listened to the men's stories and put his arm around them. He promised them better times, but only if they made it back to Baile Nua. They rallied around him, and he saw that his words had given them at least a modicum of hope.

Finally, after several days of cautious travel, they reached the gates.

Despite the exhaustion that weighed heavily on his shoulders, Francisco announced himself confidently at the gates, and after a tense exchange with the guards, they were granted entry. As he made his way through the crowded courtyard, filled with survivors from the ongoing conflict, Francisco's heart sank once more as he noticed the dwindling numbers of his fellow Spaniards and the absence of his close friend Pedro. Disheartened, he continued his search until a familiar face caught his eye and approached him.

"I see you got off the beach," said Calum as he looked Francisco up and down to see if he was injured. "Eoghan O'Rourke wants to see you in the great hall."

But Francisco had no time for the whims of Eoghan O'Rourke. He gripped Calum's forearm.

"Have you seen Pedro?"

"Some of your comrades lie on the beach, some drowned in the water, but a few made it onto the ship. Pray it is the latter, for I have not seen him here."

Francisco grimaced and made his way to the keep.

Francisco was escorted to the grand hall by a group of guards, their armour gleaming in the torchlight as they marched in unison. Gone was the air of authority and gravitas that usually surrounded the O'Rourke family, for the room now buzzed with the nervous energy of young men who had had their first meeting with failure. Eoghan, the eldest son, slumped in his father's ornate chair with his legs carelessly thrown over one arm. His younger brother perched on the steps leading up to the chair, surrounded by their loyal followers who were all indulging in wine and boasting about their recent exploits on the beach. Upon catching sight of Francisco, Eoghan sprang up from his seat. He gave a curt smile.

"There he is, our brave Spanish trainer. I have fulfilled my promise to you, for I said I would bring your men to the beach but gave no promise of success. Now it is time for you to fulfil your promise to me."

Francis bowed as he held in his anger at how they could drink and make merry after such a failure.

"I did promise your father, and I intend to keep my word. It is best if we wait here in the safety of the castle until he returns. We cannot predict the consequences of our trip to the beach, and we will need his guidance on how to handle it properly."

Eoghan took measured strides towards Francisco with his finger wagging.

"Excuse me, Spanish gentleman, but you made your promise to the O'Rourke and not my father in a personal capacity. Therefore, as the acting O'Rourke, you made that promise to me, and I intend that you fulfil it."

Francisco froze and glanced around for support.

"If you do not intend to fulfil it," Eoghan said, " then I will have to free my people of the risk of protecting yours. What is it to be?"

Francisco sighed. This was a trap he did not want to snap around his remaining comrades.

"Tell me your plan."

Eoghan began to pace the raised platform that underpinned his father's seat.

"The governor is on a war footing and will no doubt come to Breifne to seek revenge. However, rebellion ferments in the west with the Burkes and their various allies. We should go west and join them and bring the revolt back to Breifne."

"We should stay here and defend your father's lands if need be," said Francisco. "Better still, we could stand idly by if Bingham rides through your lands, deny any knowledge of the incident at the beach, and direct him to your father's talks in Dublin. That is the best path to peace."

Eoghan skipped off the platform and began to circle Francisco.

"Why would your king put you in charge of such a powerful ship if you are unwilling to fight? I am starting to think that some of your comrades were right about what they said about you. Maybe they left you behind as one of their worst captains they were happy to sacrifice for you would not fight."

Francisco scrunched his hand into a fist and bowed his head to hide his scarlet cheeks.

"It is a matter of knowing when to fight rather than fighting at every opportunity."

"And your opportunity is now. You need to earn your keep, or I will consider protecting you and your colleagues a risk not worth taking."

Francisco's jaw clenched.

"Tell me your plan, and I will lead whatever men you provide me with. We can take the ones of mine that are fit and healthy, but remember, for every one of my men found by the English dead or alive, many of your people will hang."

"I knew you would see it my way. We leave in a week."

Francisco returned to Shea Óg's village with the sun providing a warm glow as it set behind him. Pedro was nowhere to be found, and the only places he could think of as relatively safe where Pedro knew to go were the castle and the village.

The air was thick with the smell of burning wood and the distant sound of laughter from the villagers' homes. As Francisco approached the gathering of the villagers around the roaring fire, he could not help but feel a sense of despair. They were without a care in the world while its burden seemed to lay on him.

The sparks that flew up in plumes of smoke, reaching towards the darkening sky, were the only glimmer of hope on this dismal night.

Francisco joined Calum by the fire, his eyes scanning the dimly lit faces of those sat around the flames for any sign of Pedro. But alas, there was none. It seemed as though he had been taken by either the devil or the deep blue sea, leaving Francisco with a heavy heart and a sense of loneliness that anchored him to this earth. Francisco took to his bed as soon as it was polite to leave.

A week passed, and as the first rays of sunlight pierced through the hut windows, Francisco was awoken by the bleating of goats and a chill that seemed to seep into his bones. Morning prayers were now a distant thought. He only considered his bodily needs and what he had to do to survive that day. He longed to wash away the grime and sweat that clung to his body, but he seldom had the luxury of time to do so. The rough fabric of his clothes scratched at his skin, reminding him of the uncomfortable nights spent in his cramped prison cell. Despite his search for water, he could only find small pots and vessels left over from the night before, their contents now cold and uninviting.

"There's no time for that," said Calum as he stood in the doorway. "You have a long march ahead of you, and no matter how clean you get this morning, the bogs of Connacht will put the bugs and dirt straight back on you."

Francisco cursed and began to think the church was wrong all along and the realm of the devil was cold, for this would be the perfect place to torture him and men like him from the sunny climes.

"Have you heard anything from my friend Pedro? How many of my comrades made it back from the beach?"

Calum scowled like a beast dragged from its hibernation.

"Don't ask me things I don't know at this hour of the morning. I feel the same chill, have the same parched mouth and the same aching belly as you. The only person who can give you such answers is the acting O'Rourke, but even you do not want to meet him for fear of the price he will ask for his answers. All you can do is pray his father returns before he drags you off on some other folly."

"He should consider me his conduit to the king of Spain and treat me accordingly," said Francisco.

"All your status sank out in Sligo Bay, and you have little left to barter with than your life and your unsuitable military experience. Let's see if you can impress the little lord with your sword."

Calum threw Francisco a sword, and Francisco did little to shelter his feelings.

"Come on," said Calum. "There is plenty more disappointment where that came from. But now you need to catch up with your new master."

CHAPTER 18
THE EXPEDITION BEGINS

F rancisco and Calum arrived back in the courtyard of Baile Nua Castle to meet the rest of Eoghan's assembled expedition to Connacht. The group was a mix of eager youths with fresh faces, few scars, full heads of hair, and seasoned veterans who carried their age and experience like a heavy weight on their shoulders and only sparse hair on their heads. Some wore smiles, excited for the adventure ahead, while others trudged along with weariness in their steps, perhaps feeling like they were being forced into this journey by the foolishness of those who smiled.

Eoghan sparred in the yard with some of the other youths, and he wore the biggest smile of all. When he spotted Francisco among the crowd, he rained down blows upon his partner until they finally admitted defeat. Eoghan beamed, hoping Francisco was impressed with his abilities. As he walked towards Francisco, sweat glistening on his brow and chest from the exertion, he felt a sense of accomplishment and pride swell within him after his victory.

"Greetings, my Spanish friend. Today, we set out to begin liberating this island for the glory of God, the O'Rourkes, and all that serve either or, preferably, both."

Francisco frowned in the face of such foolishness.

"The devil can take this island, for you lead us into folly before your father returns. However, I will come with you, if only to guide you so your father may set eyes on his son again."

Eoghan turned to see the reaction of anyone who was listening. But all nearby turned their heads.

"Don't be so pessimistic, old man, or I may leave you behind. Since you would be a burden by being a useless mouth to feed and be worth a pretty penny or two from the English sheriff, I fear you would not be a burden for long."

Francisco grunted for he knew this was all the sense he would get from the young man.

"I agreed to go, so let us leave and stop toying with me. We have many enemies, so let us concentrate on them."

Eoghan smiled as he brushed past him.

They were soon out in the woods and bogs of Connacht, and to Francisco, they all looked the same cold hell. It was worse now he could associate it with the bad memories of escaping from the destruction of the Armada, being captured and the massacre at the beach. Thoughts of his wife, family, and return to Spain faded into no more than a distant dream.

He had some reluctant companions among the Spanish soldiers and sailors who were so cocky when they volunteered him in the hall of the castle to help the O'Rourke while they made their escape. But the massacre on the beach meshed with the damp bog underfoot, and all hope drained from them as they marched forward, dull-eyed and slovenly.

They seemingly marched for days, by light sticking to woods, forest and bogs lest the governor discover them before they had the chance to unite with their fellow rebels. They pressed on by night for the first couple of nights for the enthusiasm of the young rebels of Connacht who found their way to Baile Nua had convinced Eoghan that the whole province was up in arms, and they would have to travel barely a night and a day to find themselves in a cauldron of rebellion. However, several nights and days passed, and Eoghan and his ill-disciplined rabble feared every horseman on the horizon lest they be a scout of the English army. They were soon alone and friendless in the middle of Connacht with only the eyes of wolves and bandits for company. Eoghan left his men in hiding while he climbed a hill in a poorly disguised pretence that he knew where he was going. Francisco, by now, had grown tired of his charge's follies and wished to return to the relative safety of the castle. The only way to do that was by persuasion, and he needed to get his young master alone so he could decide without losing face. He climbed the hill after Eoghan. He found the Irishman straining his eyes to see beyond the horizon.

"There is no shame in admitting the young rebels lied," Francisco said as he stood beside him. "If you get the men home safely, they will forgive you."

Eoghan did not look at him and sought to strain his eyes further on the horizon.

"I will not better my father's negotiating position by sitting in a castle like a coward. The only way we'll be free is by fighting."

"The only way you will help your father's negotiating position is by not causing needless trouble. Order your men home, and we'll not speak of this again."

But his wise words could not penetrate Eoghan's ears. He was searching for hope.

"Look. There. Smoke on the horizon. I knew there was rebellion. If there is to be no fighting, then what use are you? I may as well take the reward from the English rather than shelter and feed you. Now rally your men, for we march towards the smoke."

Francisco looked to see if he could draw any conclusions from the tiny plumes of smoke and tried to think of something persuasive to end this folly, but by the time he turned to address his master, he was gone. He sighed for he knew he was in for a march into the unknown.

CHAPTER 19
FOLLIES AND FAILURES

The light began to fade along with Francisco's hopes. He went back and rallied his men from behind bushes and trees in the wood and set them on the road to follow their master. He cursed, for Eoghan had taken a horse and ridden far ahead towards the smoke, abandoning his men to trail in his wake as best they could. The fires in the distance were more abundant now, and there was no sign of his youthful master. Night fell, and he gathered the men together and camped for the night in a clearing in the woods. He allowed his men the luxury of lighting fires, for the night sky was already filled with smoke, and a little more would make no difference. Besides, the heat would ward off the devil of the cold and warm the spirits of the already disheartened men. Brendan MacDonnell, the constable of the MacDonnell Galloglass, flopped beside him, the clinking of his chain mail stealing any element of surprise. He slapped Francisco on the thigh.

"What follies have you brought us out here to fulfil, oh peace-loving captain?"

Brendan grinned like a man who would stab Francisco in the back at the first opportunity. He was a veteran of many a fight for his O'Rourke masters and had the scars on his face to prove it. But Francisco had to keep on his good side, for he had few friends among the Irish.

"I would gladly relinquish command to you if it were in my power," Francisco said as he stared into the fire. "But I am forced to follow this foolish boy. I can only spend my night in prayer and contemplation for all the good that will do me. If I cannot persuade the boy, hopefully the Lord, if he is still listening, will work through me or someone else and make him see sense."

"That's why we call you peace lover," Brendan said as he broke into a grin and shrugged. "Why spend the evening before battle sharpening your blades when you can say a few prayers instead? I don't understand why your king would put you in charge of a mighty fighting ship when all you want to do is stay in your cabin and pray?"

Francisco did not share his companion's sense of humour.

"The devil and his pangs of cold on my feet give me enough trouble tonight. State your business or leave me in peace until first light."

Brendan leaned in to whisper.

"The men are unhappy with this folly. They have no wish to leave their wives and children undefended and to put their lives at risk for no gain. Order them to return home if there is no sign of the young master by midday tomorrow."

Francisco held the constable in a fixed gaze.

"You are supposed to be your master's finest men, his protectors. Why would you look to abandon him and enter into subterfuge in doing so?"

Brendan grinned.

"We also think like you do, peace lover. Whatever we do out here will undermine our true master as he negotiates in the viper's den of Dublin. If you can save me and my men without us losing face, you will have gained an ally in the O'Rourke court for you and your comrades. Take it from me. You need them."

Brendan grinned once more, lifted himself up and wandered back to join his men by their campfires.

Francisco was left to ponder how the snare tightened around him.

As the first rays of sunlight peeked over the horizon, the camp stirred from its slumber, its occupants already on high alert. Brendan made his way through the maze of tents. The soft grass beneath his feet muffled his footsteps. He found Francisco's tent and watched as Francisco splashed water onto his face from a nearby bucket, the droplets sparkling in the early morning light.

"Remember what I said last night," said Brendan. "You need friends."

Francisco glanced at him. Brendan's face was streaked with dirt and sweat. As Francisco continued washing the grime from his skin, he barked orders to his men. He wanted to find his young master as quickly as possible and get their group moving again. The camp was in a frenzy as they packed up their tents and belongings, eager to continue their journey. With everything loaded onto their horses, they settled down and waited anxiously for the scouts to return with news of their missing leader.

The sun hung low in the sky, casting a yellow glow over the landscape. Francisco took a moment to shield his eyes from the brightness and estimate the time of day. His breath appeared as a thin mist in the chilly air. Brendan stood behind him, shrouded in shadows, but made his presence known with a gentle cough.

"It is almost time to give the order," he said as his finger pointed to the sun's position in the sky.

"I will make sure to tell our young master how eager you were to abandon him," Francisco said.

Brendan slapped him on the back.

"Now, that's not what friends do for each other, is it? Especially those who are stuck in a foreign land."

Francisco sighed and reached for his water bottle to wet his throat before he shouted his orders at the men. They could take their chances when they returned to Breifne because, for all they knew, their young master was already dead. He drank to drown any guilt he felt, for he was still a soldier plotting to abandon one of his men. He raised his hand to point towards Breifne, but a voice interrupted him before he could extend his finger.

"Captain, the young O'Rourke returns."

A man pointed to the edge of a nearby wood, and Eoghan rode out from it alone. Francisco's heart leapt at the reprieve while his honour and his shoulders slumped as his life was needlessly in danger once more. Eoghan pulled up his horse in the middle of the camp and leapt off. His face lit up.

"The army of the O'Flahertys and the Burkes lies just beyond that yonder hill. They have called all the men out from their subservient clans, and they plan a march on Galway."

Eoghan shook as he could barely contain his excitement in his young body.

"What would you have us do?" said Francisco, trying to hide his disappointment. "We barely have the clothes on our backs and the butt of stale bread in our pockets. Surely, it is not enough to sustain us on a long campaign in such a landscape. Are your friends going to feed us?"

But he could not bring enough sobriety to his master to make him think straight.

"We shall live off the land as heroes of old." Eoghan raised his sword above his head. "Are you with me, men? Let us burn the English out of Connacht and return to our homes as the champions of our people."

The men cheered, and Brendan spat as he glared at Francisco. Both men knew they could not get away.

The ground squelched beneath their feet with every step as they marched through dense forests, swiftly followed by soggy bogs. The scent of damp earth and decaying leaves hung heavy in the air, which caught in Francisco's lungs, making him cough almost constantly. But still, he trudged on, consumed by melancholy and guilt but determined to do his duty.

Eoghan led the way like an excited child, constantly pointing out towards a distant mountain that he claimed was the land of the O'Flahertys—a place where the English would not dare to tread. Brendan caught up with Francisco, who walked with his head down in deep contemplation. His mind raced with thoughts of how he could possibly escape his predicament and whether he could even remember the way back home. Brendan bowed his head to mimic Francisco so that he caught his attention.

"Hello, peace lover," Brendan said. "You had your opportunity for one brief moment to save us. Now, here we are." He swung his arm around him to emphasise the hidden dangers lurking in such a beautiful landscape.

Francisco shook his head and laughed.

"You walked all this way just to needle me? Is that for your own entertainment, oh he of the scarred face that owes his living to his six-foot axe? Why do you want to retreat so much when you thrive on tales of honour and your battle prowess?"

Brendan gave a toothy grin.

"I may be adept at telling a tall tale to please the women or up my price if the odds are against me, but I am no fool. The only thing that waits for me in these barren mountains is a bullet or the tip of a sword. A Galloglass may seek glory and reward, but occasionally, he is grateful when someone provides him with an excuse that may help him save face."

Francisco grimaced as his head flooded with the obligation of duty, the verdict of his trial, his time in prison and standing on the edge of the beach watching his men get slaughtered. He would not fall foul of the actions that cast him into those holes again.

"If you help my men and me, the excuse will be provided. The sooner the boy's father returns, the better it will be for all of us."

But their planning was interrupted by the cry of a scout.

"The O'Flahertys are just ahead!"

All heads turned to see the scout point towards a gap between two hills. Eoghan's excited young companions ran behind him toward the gap. Francisco turned to Brendan.

"You will excuse me if I do not follow the exuberance of youth. One set of rabble tends to look like another in this godforsaken land."

Brendan grinned.

"You never know. They may have some handsome, well-attired Galloglass escorting them."

It was Francisco's turn to smile.

"We should be blessed to have such fortune."

"I may have lost my looks, but still have my brains. It is time for the Galloglass to come into their own," and Brendan waved goodbye to Francisco as he walked away.

Brendan and his men formed a strong, protective line at the rear of the column as they entered the narrow passage between the two looming hills. The rocky ground crunched beneath their boots, and their heightened alertness enhanced the noise and sensation of the rocks on the soles of their feet. As they advanced, their heads swivelled from side to side, scanning for any potential threats. Suddenly, upon the tops of both hills emerged two formidable rows of men, the sun glinting off their guns.

"FIRE!"

With a bang as loud as thunder and two wisps of smoke that rose to join the clouds in the sky, a hail of bullets descended on Eoghan and his men. The young rebels from Breifne and Connacht were mown down like wheat before a scythe, their blood staining the hillsides as they fell for the musket men could barely miss such was the mass of men. The rebels were easy pickings for the English shot trapped as they were between the slopes of the hills, the bodies of their dead comrades and falling over each other in their desperation to escape. The shot could not reload fast enough to ensnare all in their trap.

Amongst the falling bodies Eoghan's horse bucked. Eoghan was thrown into a pile of his former men. Without a pause for thought, Francisco ran towards him through the smoke and grabbed his flailing arm. He pulled his young master through the mud, for he thought he was unconscious but alive. The shot reloaded, and the body of a man fell upon Eoghan and broke Francisco's grip. His arm fell limply to the ground. Francisco felt a sharp pain in his shoulder and was then overwhelmed by the smell of burning flesh. A hand gripped his other shoulder, and a familiar voice came.

"Come on," Brendan said. "He is gone, and so will you be if you do not run."

Francisco looked over his shoulder as if asking for sympathy. He did not get any.

"You got lucky. That's just a scratch. My men will bandage that up for you. Let's hope you did not burn up all your luck. Now, let's go."

They took to their heels and ran back to Breifne, while Eoghan's former scout went to Galway to collect his reward.

CHAPTER 20

RAIN, WIND AND TRAITORS

F rancisco's new friendship based on affinity through the experience of war began to pay immediate dividends. Brendan allowed him and other Spanish stragglers to shelter behind the shields of his Galloglass as Eoghan's army disintegrated. Half fled into the countryside to make their way back to the villages of their clans while the O'Rourkes attempted to gather together to fight off any pursuers that wished to chase them all the way back to Breifne. The Earl of Clanricard's men were eager to escort them off their master's land but less enthusiastic to fight a pitched battle with them. They harassed them at a distance, picking off stragglers whilst herding them back to their own lands. The mood of the O'Rourkes was mournful, for as foolish as Eoghan was, he was still popular with the soldiers.

They arrived back in Baile Nua with their tails between their legs, and Brendan sent whatever men had the discipline to remain under his command home to see their families. Only Francisco and the Spanish survivors remained with him.

"Have you nowhere to go?"

But the forlorn looks of the bedraggled Spanish drew no sympathy from Brendan.

"Go back to the villages the O'Rourke assigned you to. Eat and make what merriment you can, for when the O'Rourke returns, there will be hell to pay.

You'll only get the briefest respite from the repercussions of Eoghan O'Rourke's foolishness."

Francisco bowed his head and waved Brendan goodbye. He could see the weariness in Brendan's eyes, and there would be no reasoning with him tonight.

Three other Spaniards needing a hiding place had been placed with Francisco in the village of Shea Óg O'Rourke. They crossed over the last of the rolling hills before the village came into sight. The evening fires were lit, and the villagers seemed unaware of what misfortunes would befall them. Francisco stopped the men before they came into earshot of the village.

"Whatever you do, men, don't tell them about the defeat," said Francisco. "Let us eat, make merry, and have one last night before the news spreads. We must still find a sympathetic ear to smuggle us back to Spain. Our best hope is still the O'Rourke, should he return."

The men nodded, and they continued towards the village. When they arrived, they went their separate ways to the huts allocated to them by Shea Óg. Francisco braced himself as he approached the hut bedside that of Shea Óg. The memories of Pedro came back to haunt him, and how he did not know if he was dead or if he had just abandoned him to his fate. Then he saw Máiréad O'Rourke helping to prepare the food for the evening. She smiled coyly at him. He sighed and went into his hut to change his clothes.

There soon came a knock on the doorpost, and Francisco looked up to see Shea Óg leaning on it, grinning at him.

"So how's our mighty warrior from across the seas? You scampered back pretty quickly from Connacht, but I won't spoil any of the stories of your bravery that you may wish to tell my daughter, who's prepared a special meal for you. We can save the disclosure of any embellishments to your deeds until after the wedding night."

Francisco shuddered at the thought of a wedding.

"I have not become any less married since I returned from Connacht."

Shea Óg grinned.

"Oh, I think you have. Once that ship left Sligo Bay, so did your chances of returning to Spain. So, consider yourself divorced. I'll be a good father-in-law to you. I won't be too demanding."

Francisco tried to ignore him.

"Have you heard anything of the return of the O'Rourke?"

"No news yet, but it will probably be bad, and that is hardly a prediction. He can't see to accept the truth, this lord of ours. That is not to mention his foolish son. How is he, by the way? He was the one who led you on this folly into Connacht, wasn't he?"

Francisco sighed as he contemplated the best answer to give. He looked at Shea Óg's quizzical face and decided on the truth. He would find out soon enough anyway, and lying would only jeopardise his welcome. He hung his head, if not in remorse, then for show.

"He is dead."

A small smirk grew on the side of Shea Óg's lip. Francisco did not know how to react. Was this a trap? Did Shea Óg want Eoghan dead for his own sinister reasons? At last, Shea Óg lifted himself from the doorpost.

"Ah, don't worry yourself. It was inevitable that he would get himself killed one day. He had all the foolishness of his father in his bones and none of the sense. What we have to worry about is the mess he left behind. Tell me what happened before we go to the fireside and you make up stories to impress my daughter."

Francisco shook off the last comment.

"We got ambushed and cut to pieces by the English shot. I tried to save the boy, but he was shot from under me as I tried to drag him away. I suspect the scout lured us into an ambush. It all seemed too perfect, and the boy fell straight into it."

The grin refused to leave Shea Óg's face.

"Rain, wind and traitors. That's all you can expect from any raid into Connacht. Any other aspirations are just folly."

Shea Óg walked into the hut and slapped Francisco on the back.

"Come let us eat and make merry, for the story of your failure doomed my comments of the failure of the O'Rourke into a prediction. My daughter will seem all the more attractive in the flicker of the firelight now that you need friends. The governor of Connacht will find the bodies of Spaniards on the battlefield and come searching for their comrades. Any hope of rescue from the sea will be cut off. You may as well hide out here in the back of beyond until the heat dies down. You can fill the womb of my daughter with half-Spanish children to pass the time. Now come on and get your best glib on you. She is waiting for you."

"Let me change, and then I will join you."

"Don't be too long, or I will have to come and fetch you."

Francisco cursed when Shea Óg had gone. He thought of his wife and children waiting for him in Bilbao.

"Forgive me, my love, but I must do what I must to survive to get home to you. If I don't do it for myself, then I do it for my men to protect them."

He blessed himself more out of habit than conviction and took his place by the fire.

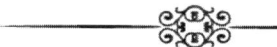

Francisco watched as his men made merry and sang and danced to traditional Spanish songs to entertain their hosts. Neither Francisco nor Shea Óg breathed a word about the calamity in Connacht, for Francisco did not want to ruin the night for his men, and Shea Óg did not want to sully the prize of his daughter. Máiréad came and presented Francisco with the food she had especially prepared for him, and he smiled and thanked her, for he had no wish to insult his host by telling her it was barely better than the food he got on his ship.

At the dinner that night, Calum noticed how Máiréad had singled out Francisco for special treatment and that Shea Óg was always trying to put them together. He saw that Francisco was polite and tolerated the advances of

Máiréad. He also noticed Shea Óg's son had sat near them and had his ear cocked in their direction. Calum waited for his opportunity, for with all the ale Shea Óg was forcing down his throat, he would soon need to relieve himself. Francisco soon had to go behind the huts.

As Francisco opened his bladder, he received a thunderous slap on the back.

"How goes it?"

Calum grinned as Francisco stared down at his soiled hands and stained breeches.

"That's an old Irish traditional greeting," Calum said before leaning in to whisper. "So is the fact that the man who marries a daughter is beholden to the father if that man is of higher rank. By the looks of it, Shea Óg wants to make you his dog."

Francisco wiped his hands on the back of his breeches.

"Another Irish tradition," Calum pointed to Francisco's wet backside.

"I have had enough of your Irish traditions," spat Francisco. "I would have rather taken my chances in the ship's prison if I knew I would be subject to all of these 'traditions' along with the devil of the cold."

"Well, the only way out I can see for you is with the blessing of the O'Rourke."

"Then I have no time to waste. If I stay here, I will be married by the morning."

"Do you have any friends in Baile Nua?"

"Brendan of the Galloglass will take me in."

"Let us set off now, for we have no time to waste."

They slipped in and out of the huts and then into the woods to provide cover for their escape. Shea Óg's son soon got suspicious when they did not return and when to tell his father.

"No one insults my daughter so," Shea Óg growled. "Do not embarrass your sister and tell of her prospective husband's deeds. We will travel to the O'Rourke as soon as he returns, and if we do not return with a husband, we'll return with his head."

CHAPTER 21
A FATHER'S REVENGE

As the moon rose high in the sky, Francisco and Calum journeyed through the dark and treacherous lands of Breifne. They moved swiftly, their feet barely making a sound on the rugged terrain. By midday, they had reached Baile Nua. Francisco's voice echoed through the stillness of the castle as he called out to the guards at the barred door, assuring them that Brendan would let them in. The heavy gates creaked loudly as they swung open, and they stepped into the courtyard. The walls were made of sturdy stone, weathered by time and battles fought long ago. But even in walls so sturdy, the men were nervous and paranoid in fear of the wrath of Bingham. Brendan's face was stoic and determined as he stood before them, his features as sharp and unyielding as the slabs of rock that dotted the bogs of Connacht.

"What has you back here so quick?" Brendan said. "It does not bode well for the clan to have a Spanish captain creeping around with so many spies about."

Francisco gave Brendan the warmest smile he could.

"Through no actions of my own-"

"That's not a good start," Brendan interrupted.

"I have fallen out with my host and need a hiding place until the O'Rourke can resolve our grievance. Would you know of such a place?"

Brendan grinned.

"You must be desperate to place yourself in a Galloglass debt. I know of such a place but bear no responsibility should Shea Óg come to seek you out."

Francisco gave a mock bow.

"As the king of Spain's representative in Briefne, I thank you for your kindness."

"Don't get carried away now, peace lover. You haven't seen it yet. I will arrange for someone to guide you and Calum there, and Calum will fetch you when the O'Rourke returns."

Francisco reached out and grabbed his hand.

"A thousand thank yous from the bottom of my heart."

"There may be rather fewer thank yous when you return, but you will be dry and fed nonetheless."

Brendan signalled to one of his men and whispered in his ear. The man signalled for Francisco and Callum to follow.

Francisco went into hiding and it was over a month before Calum returned to bring him to Baile Nua. The weather had turned considerably colder as it was now the beginning of winter. They once more knocked on the gates of Baile Nua and asked for Brendan. He eventually came to the gate, his mood surly.

"How was your accommodation? How many thank yous do I get now?"

"The thank yous diminished by the day, especially when the cold wind blew down your rickety door. It was the worst place I have stayed without the fear of a trial hanging over my head."

Brendan managed a wry smile.

"At least you found it more comfortable than sharing a bed with Shea Óg's daughter. But no matter. The O'Rourke has returned from Dublin and does not bear good tidings for any of his Spanish guests."

"I take it he no longer seeks the favours of the Spanish king?" said Francisco as he raised an eyebrow at his chilly reception.

"Speak to him yourself. But I warn you, Shea Óg has beaten you here and has not a kind word to say about you. I have yet to mention the debacle in Connacht, but I'm sure Shea Óg has. The O'Rourke will summon you soon enough to unleash his anger, but let's just say for now, the O'Rourke mourns his son."

Francisco placed his hand on Brendan's shoulder.

"I have ridden the waves off the coasts of Scotland, driven by your devil of the cold. Yet, here I still stand. I will speak to your master as the representative of the Spanish king and am confident I will meet you after in this same courtyard a free man."

"I'm glad you feel so confident. My men will escort you in, and I'll provide some refreshments for your friend here."

Francisco turned to Calum and shook his hand.

"We may have had our differences in the past, but you have been good to me since we got to know each other. I especially thank you for delivering me to your master's door."

Calum smiled.

"I fear fate has different paths for us. I must go and defend my family, and you are destined to serve the O'Rourke. Goodbye, my friend, and if I do not see you again, I hope you get your wish and return to Spain."

"So do I, my friend, so do I."

Francisco embraced him and turned and went into the castle.

With a heavy hand on his shoulder, Francisco was led through the grand hall, the scent of burning wood and ale filling his nostrils. His heart pounded as he was brought to stand at the back of the room, surrounded by opulent tapestries and flickering candles.

At the front of the hall, seated upon a throne-like chair, sat the O'Rourke. His face contorted in a storm of anger as words he did not want to hear settled in his ears. The constables stood before their lord, recounting the tale of his son's reckless journey into Connacht. To his right sat Brian Óg, favoured by his father above all others, elevated in his father's esteem by the death of his brother. On the periphery, Shea Óg stood with grim determination etched on his features. The constables spoke quickly and urgently, for they dared not hold back their accounts. They knew all too well the O'Rourke's infamous temper and feared its consequences. Suddenly, a hush fell over the hall as the O'Rourke's piercing gaze landed on Francisco.

"Bring him forth. Let him linger in the shadows no more."

The O'Rourke stood and waved his men forward. The constables who had stood in prominence before all took to the wings as Francisco stood alone before the O'Rourke. Francisco noticed out of the corner of his eye Shea Óg smirking as he leaned on a pillar. The O'Rourke flopped down into his seat, resigned to hear another morbid tale.

"Tell me then, oh Spanish captain, of your role in this debacle. I have heard so many trying to place the blame on others, but my ears still burn for the truth."

Francisco took a breath, and the O'Rourke leaned forward.

"I'm sure you have heard many stories of your son's foolishness."

"That is something he would have grown out of if allowed. That is why I asked a wise head like you to look after him."

Francisco gulped, steadied his voice, and blocked out the images of his previous trial that flashed before him in his mind's eye.

"Unfortunately, we were deceived by traitors and ambushed. The enemy surrounded us on three sides, and even your son's bravery could not surmount the odds. I saw him thrown from his horse, and as the bodies of his men fell around him, bombarded by the enemy's shot, I grabbed him, but before I could haul him to his feet, he had been riddled through with lead. The enemy was closing in around us, so I had to abandon your son's body. I got this for my efforts."

Francisco lifted his jacket and showed his still bandaged shoulder. The O'Rourke sat silent, smouldering in his chair. Francisco decided to continue.

"Please forgive me for my contribution to the catastrophe, but if I had not abandoned your boy, I would not stand before you today. But in my opinion, it is better for you that the English don't find a dead Spanish captain on the battlefield."

The O'Rourke bent over to hide his face and gripped the top of his nose between his fingers.

"That is the most honest explanation I have heard all day, and I thank you for it," the O'Rourke said as he battled to control the emotion in his voice. "I was off on my own fool's errand to the Irish Council in Dublin. They surrounded me like the shot that surrounded my son and fired volley after volley into my sides to try and break my will and give up on Breifne. But I managed to escape with only their lies on a piece of paper I was supposed to keep. But I fear now that all my efforts have been in vain, for my son has undone what little good I achieved or time I bought. I have sent word to our allies to heed our call should Bingham attack us, but I think it will fall on deaf ears as it did the last time."

Brendan stood forward and shook his fist.

"The MacDonnells will stand with you. Breifne will not fall."

The O'Rourke managed but a faint smile.

"I fear we will be severely tested in the coming months. We must find out what our spies in Galway think."

"I will send word to them at once," said Dermot O'Rourke as he stood forward and bowed before his master.

"Then we should all go our separate ways and prepare," said the O'Rourke.

The men of the clan turned to leave. Francisco looked around him. His hands shook, for he could hardly believe his luck. Was that it? Where was his punishment for his part in the folly? Shea Óg raised his hand.

"What about my grievance with the Spanish captain about how he disrespected my daughter?"

"I did no such thing," said Francisco.

The O'Rourke was about to leave but turned around to face Francisco.

"This man says you disrespected his daughter and abused his hospitality. Is this so?"

"He wants me to marry his daughter, and I declined. I told him I was a married man, and he refused to respect me. He then tried to force the subject, so I left and came here."

The O'Rourke turned to Shea Óg.

"This man told me the most truth today and tried to save my son. Therefore, I am inclined to believe him. If you still bear a grudge, go to the Brehon and have a price put on any grievance you can prove. Then I will pay it. Swallow your pride and differences, for we will soon have a bigger foe to fight."

Francisco nodded and took leave while Shea Óg still stood mouth agape. Francisco went to find Brendan to see if he could arrange better lodgings than last time.

Shea Óg walked out to the courtyard and spat.

"No one disrespects my daughter like that and makes me look a fool in front of the O'Rourke."

He called his men to him and whispered in his secretary's ear.

"See that note is sent discreetly to the Earl of Clanricard."

The man nodded, and the deed was done.

CHAPTER 22
A FATHER'S PROMISE

T hree long months dragged on, the tension niggling at the already fragile Francisco as he spent his days in the grandiose court of the O'Rourke. It was at these junctures of stresses and strains that he realised the actual effect his imprisonment had upon him. He tried to pray to renew his faith in God and his belief that he would get another chance to return to Spain. But every time he bent down, his knee would hurt, or his mind would be blank, and he would lose interest in the prayer halfway through. The best he could manage was a short prayer of gratitude that his shoulder was improving.

News of Eoghan's untimely death had spread like wildfire, leaving a void in leadership that threatened to further destabilise the already volatile region. The downfall of the Burkes had swiftly followed the defeat of Eoghan, and now the governor of Connacht could turn his full attention to Breifne.

Rumours quickly swirled throughout Galway and beyond, claiming that the Earl of Clanricard had declared the O'Rourke's teenage son Teigue O'Rourke as the rightful heir to the Kingdom of Breifne under English law. This news enraged the O'Rourke, who had disowned his own son after his wife left him because of his rebellious ways and the boy was much younger than his bastard son Brian Óg, his chosen heir. The earl's ambitious claim only added fuel to an already blazing fire.

To counter this threat, the O'Rourke summoned representatives from adjacent clans and those from Ulster, along with their Brehons, who were willing to brave the treacherous winter journey to Baile Nua. Despite attempts from the governor of Connacht to discourage attendance, word spread, and the villages surrounding Baile Nua were made available for lodgings for any guests who wished to attend.

One such guest was Desmond MacCabe, representing the adjoining Maguire clan. He arrived secretly in the dead of night and was given lodgings in the village of Shea Óg. He sat on his horse, drenched from the shower that greeted him on the Breifne border, escorted by two Galloglass bodyguards while his horseboy knocked on their host's door. Moments later, Shea Óg opened the door. He straightened his shirt so he would look presentable.

"You must be the Maguires, my lovely neighbours from beyond the hills," he said. "It'll be an expensive trip for you, for I'll be seeking compensation for all the cattle raids and losses I have suffered because of you."

Desmond got off his horse and nodded to his host.

"Hello, Shea Óg. The Maguire would surely listen if you could ever substantiate any of your claims. We expect some good hospitality from you as you'll want us to be good neighbours. The north reverberates with rumours of the impending invasion of West Breifne."

"Ah, don't mind that. The O'Rourke is always picking a fight with someone. We've been here forever and will be here until the end of time."

"Don't jinx yourself. Now, can I have a meal for my men and me? We will not trouble you for long as I need to report back to the Maguire."

Shea Óg snarled as he tried to estimate how long was long. He begrudgingly returned to being a host.

"The boy can sleep in the nearby huts with the horses and the Galloglass. You'll be in here with me."

Desmond took his bag from the horse boy and followed Shea Óg into his house. Desmond looked around the hut without trying to guess the origins of some of the odours. More than Shea Óg and his most precious cows were in occupation here. Shea Óg pointed to a seat covered by a blanket.

"Now, why don't you wrap yourself up by the fire? I'm sure only the dogs have sat on the blanket and no other horrid beasties."

Desmond scowled at him but sat, threw the blanket over his shoulders and was given a bowl of soup.

"Now I'm not one to listen to gossip, nor spread rumours about a man," said Shea Óg. "But we've heard down here you've fallen out with the young Maguire and were wondering why he sent you and not anyone else he does favour?"

Desmond grimaced at Shea Óg's words, which distracted him from his soup.

"I served his father well, and he appreciates that. I have also fought with the O'Rourke many times and remain acquainted. Why would the young Maguire chop and change now when he is only settling in with his father not long in the grave?"

"Maybe because he does not expect the O'Rourke to be there much longer?"

Desmond exaggerated his final slurps and handed Shea Óg his empty bowl.

"I'll thank you for the food but not the mischief. If he does fall, I'd advise you to pledge to the Maguire, for he's the only one who'll protect you. Now show me to my bed, for we have to leave early in the morning."

The warm, savoury scent of roasting beef wafted through the hall of the O'Rourke as Desmond made his way inside. Nervous murmurs filled the air as delegates and nobility from various clans gathered, their eyes darting around in anticipation. The tension was as thick in the air as the gravy for the beef being stirred in giant pots suspended over the mature embers of the fires. The Galloglass lined up on the surrounding walls did nothing to alleviate the tension. They merely enhanced it, just as the pies of cow's innards would enhance the gravy when that part of the meal was finally served.

Desmond strode confidently through a path cleared for them with Shea Óg by his side, bowing deeply before the O'Rourke and his son as they were formally announced. Then, they were escorted to join a group of onlookers along one side of the path, eagerly awaiting what was to come.

"There's not many here, are there?" said Shea Óg as he smirked. "Even some of the nobles kept away for fear of being ousted when the English come."

When the last of the guests were announced, the cleared path melted away, and the crowd became one.

"Excuse me," Desmond said to Shea Óg as he stepped away. "I have the business of the Maguire to attend to, no matter the turnout."

Desmond scanned the crowd, searching for familiar faces. He recognised only a handful and even fewer that he deemed important enough to approach. The chieftains had all taken a cautious approach, sending less senior men as representatives to the O'Rourke, both to protect their own lives and to avoid offending the governor of Connacht and giving legitimacy to the O'Rourke. Finding someone who believed Brian O'Rourke would survive the year was no easy task. Any attempts at discussing this matter were met with the sound of the O'Rourke slamming the butt of his ceremonial staff on the floor, silencing any dissent. Finally, the O'Rourke took centre stage at the top of the hall, commanding attention and respect from all in attendance.

"Good evening all, noblemen of the O'Rourkes, dignitaries of the clans of Ireland and the representatives of the esteemed Brehon lawmakers. I welcome you all to my humble abode. As you can see, I can afford to line my walls with the most experienced Galloglass, the finest tapestries showing the long history of the O'Rourkes, and with the feast I have laid out before you, to fill the stomachs of my esteemed guests with the finest food. All of this, despite the rumours of my impending doom."

The O'Rourke's arms circled the room so no one could miss what he had mentioned. Eyes followed his arms, and polite clapping rippled through the hall.

"As you may have heard, I recently lost a son. God rest his soul. But I have been blessed by God with bountiful loins and other sons of equal ability. So I have called you all together this evening not to mourn the passing of one but to celebrate the ascension of another. So I raise a mug and ask you to salute my new successor, Brian Óg O'Rourke."

"Brian Óg O'Rourke," the guests chorused back and raised their mugs in unison.

"Now, don't let me keep you from your beef and ale any longer. I will come around and greet each one of you personally."

The room rang with the pounding of mugs on tables as the servants circulated, filling the mugs of all in the hall.

The O'Rourke worked his way around the room, dispensing kind words for the representatives of the other clans and words of encouragement for those of his own. Brian Óg trailed in his wake, and the O'Rourke ensured he introduced him to everyone whether they knew him or not. At last, they came to Desmond, who had Shea Óg hovering behind him. The O'Rourke had reserved a healthy slap on the back for Desmond.

"What are you doing here, me 'ol mucker? I thought you had been retired out to the lakes and were enjoying the fishing?"

"Well, I've come out of retirement just to see you," Desmond said. "Now, how did you manage to get yourself in so much trouble?"

"If I told you and it got around, nobody would ever have children again." They both laughed until the O'Rourke's face stiffened, and he took a more serious tone. "I'm under pressure from all sides, and few of my kinsmen have turned out today. I fear my other son will come from Galway with an army to try and assert himself. If the governor comes, can I rely on the axes of Fermanagh?"

Desmond looked at his friend and had never seen these pleading eyes before.

"The new Maguire is young and bedding in, so you never know what he'll do. But the best I would expect is a raid into Sligo, for we are not strong enough to engage in a sustained war with the governor of Connacht."

The O'Rourke looked to the heavens.

"Is there none of my clan allies that will stand by me?"

"You can always come and stay on the islands with me. Hide out there like the old days until the heat is off before going home again."

The O'Rourke looked into the distance.

"I fear there is no more 'old days', and this ousting will be it. Drink and enjoy your meal. I must venture forth until I can find an ally that will stand by me."

The O'Rourke slapped Desmond on the back again and moved on to the next dignitary.

CHAPTER 23
A FOREIGNER'S PLEDGE

As winter's icy grip loosened, Francisco quickly realized why these months were not considered part of the fighting season. He was besieged in Baile Nua by the wind and the rain. The constant howl of the wind through the arrow slits and the thrashing of the rain against the walls made Francisco's yearning for home and his family a weight around his neck. Everything was so much more bearable when he just considered himself the damned and could not remember a better life.

The O'Rourke prowled the corridors and the great hall, cursing and damning his supposed allies, for all had seemingly abandoned him in the darkness of the winter. He could not even train his men or boys to replace those who got killed. Every time they stepped out into the courtyard, their chain mail seemed to get waterlogged, and colds and flu would then ensue and multiply, and soon, the whole castle would be sick. The Spaniards seemed to be constantly banished, for they were the carriers of most of the winter ills.

One winter's morning, the O'Rourke ran into Francisco, who was crouched in a corner, whispering with his men. Francisco signalled for his men to rise when he saw the O'Rourke coming.

"Here we are all together," the O'Rourke, snarled, the whispering fueling his paranoia, "me a hostage to fortune and you a hostage to the rain. I hope you will not repay us by leaving your bodies littered all over the battlefield and bring down further wrath upon your generous hosts?"

Francisco scowled and dismissed his men, for it was his duty to shield them from the O'Rourke's temper and preserve their remaining fragile morale. But from the look on the O'Rourke's face, Francisco thought it best to change the subject.

"Have you made a plan to escape, lord? Should it come to that?"

The O'Rourke looked horrified at such a thought and continued to stride down the corridor, for he needed to do something to absorb his restless energy. Francisco hurried to keep up with him for it was rare to get the opportunity to speak to the O'Rourke alone these days.

"You could find sanctuary with the king of Spain," Francisco said to the O'Rourke's back. "You would have no better advocates for your cause than those you risked your life and your lands to rescue whilst others slaughtered their Spanish brethren, despite being the subjects of their most powerful ally".

The O'Rourke juddered to a halt, his body as ridged as any Galloglass axe staff. He gritted his teeth and looked Francisco in the eye.

"The O'Rourkes were once kings of Ireland and have never been thrown off their lands. We have survived much worse than this before."

Francisco knew he had to find a way around this immovable rock or he and his men were as good as dead.

"I would never suggest that you abandon your people. You could go to Spain, raise an army and could be the king of Ireland once again."

A smile cracked on the O'Rourke's face, the first seen there for many a day. He slapped Francisco on the shoulder.

"We shall see what the spring brings, but we will plan for my Spanish advocates to come with me if we need to seek the king's aid. Can you write to your master to arrange a ship?"

Francisco pondered what the reaction in Spain might be to receiving a letter from a coward and a fugitive. But washed up on the Irish shores were so many bodies of men with their reputations still intact, he felt sure he could use their signatures and no one would be the wiser.

"I will write it if you can get it smuggled to Spain."

"Ah sure, that's as easy as tying it to a little bird."

The O'Rourke beamed and made a bird shape with his hands and made it fly in the direction of Spain. There was the possibility of escape after all.

Several weeks later, messengers came from the borders of Breifne to Baile Nua. Swiftly afterwards, the O'Rourke called his constables and nobles together. Long gone was the smell of roasted beef that would waft in when the O'Rourke wished to show off his greatness and generosity. Gone were the eager faces of youth wishing to clash swords in anger for the first time, and gone were the representatives of the allies of the O'Rourke. In their place were the hardened faces of seasoned Galloglass and the quivering faces of youths who realised this battle may be their only shot at glory but would more likely end in their death.

The worry had even taken its toll on the O'Rourke. He still wore the same garb of authority but it had become ill-fitting, a little too large, his shoulders did not fill out the frame as they once did and the chest was a little shallower. His hair was now completely grey, whereas the year before, it was merely salt and pepper. As he waited for the inevitable, his laps of the castle sapped his energy, and he lifted himself out of his chair with a listlessness unfamiliar to all who had gathered to listen.

"It has finally happened."

His voice was more a croak than the booming roar of old.

"But much worse than we feared. The Earl of Clanricard and my son from the wife who abandoned me approach from the south, Bingham invades from Sligo, and the lord deputy's men invade from the east. I had sent forth messengers to all our allies, but because we face such a force, I fear they will not heed our call. I do not intend to be besieged in this castle and wait for them to starve me out. I am going to take to the forests and resist from there. Their coalition will break during harvest time, and we can emerge from the forests and take our lands back. Who is with me to fight like the O'Rourkes of old?"

Brendan stood forward, his chest puffed out as if he was the last defender of MacDonnell Galloglass pride.

"We won't let you down, lord. You have been good to us and always been generous with your rewards. We'll stand by you."

The room held an eerie silence as the other prominent men looked at each other to see who would step forward.

"You will always have the support of the king of Spain for the kindness in taking in his men."

Francisco stepped forward and he gave those who stood behind him an accusatory look, daring them to similarly pledge allegiance to their lord.

"I will stand with you, lord," said one man who followed him.

"So will I," said another.

Soon, all the prominent men of Breifne stepped forward, albeit mostly out of guilt or to avoid appearing a coward in front of their peers.

"Good," said the O'Rourke. "Then let us pack our things before nightfall, for if we dither until morning, we will be trapped."

The O'Rourke exited the room, and his men did the same. Plots and intrigue were thick upon their lips. Brendan wore the face of a man who had been asked to arrange his own funeral. He called Francisco over and lowered his head to indicate the exchange was to be in hushed tones.

"It was a brave thing you did today. Somebody had to persuade the waverers. But they will have gone before the week is out. Stick with me and we'll make our escape into Maguire country. We can hide out on the lakes. There are far more unpleasant places to be on this island to watch spring unfurl."

"I would like that," said Francisco. "But let us see if we can make a fight of it before we have to go and hide."

CHAPTER 24
THE FOREST

T he O'Rourke took to the forests and lived like a bandit with Francisco, Brendan and his Galloglass. The chieftains of the clan who stayed loyal to him put up a token resistance, but the force that invaded from three sides was overwhelming. Some chieftains submitted early to have their lands spared, and the others took to the forest to be with their leader. Baile Nua fell without a fight and the Earl of Clanricard and the governor of Connacht installed the fourteen-year-old Teigue O'Rourke as the new O'Rourke.

Food soon ran low as the harvest had been poor, and they had made little provision for a long war. The peasants soon turned on their former lord as the loyal soldiers threatened to steal their crops. They pointed towards the forests, and the earl swept through their hiding places and cleared them out. One by one, the rebel chieftains either surrendered or fled.

Brian O'Rourke was left in the northern forests with his Galloglass and a contingent of Spanish. His numbers were much reduced, and only a hardcore of loyalists remained with him. When they were not evading mounted patrols and scavenging for food, they were trying to take weapons off the dead, for every time they lost a man, they lost his equipment, too. Francisco attached himself to the O'Rourke with the lure of escaping to Spain. He acted as his advisor and sounding board, for he knew he was a dead man if he was parted from the O'Rourke. The reward for a Spanish officer was as much as a farmer could make in over a year.

It was time to eat on an incredibly bleak day, for all the O'Rourke heard was tales of defections or men he had lost to the English sword. His hand juddered as he stoked the fire beneath the rabbit on the spit. He stared blankly, trying to figure out how it had all come to this. His son Brian Óg ran through the camp, covered in large globules of mud, with the blood splatter of others across his face.

"Father, Father, it is over."

He collapsed onto his knees. His chain mail had become a burden covered in dried mud and blood. He threw it off and caught his breath. The O'Rourke threw down his stick and went to his son. Brian Óg placed his hand in the extended hand of his father.

"I am sorry, Father, but I lost most of my men. They came at us from all sides with bows. All we could do was run. They seemed familiar with the forest. I can only assume that some of your former minions have turned on you."

The O'Rourke collapsed into himself as if overwhelmed by stomach pain. He staggered back but then saw his son's horrified face. He remembered he had to be the O'Rourke and stood up with a new resolve.

"We are the O'Rourkes, the former kings of Ireland. They will not make us into a shire and minions of the queen. I will seek help from our allies, even if I have to go all the way to the king of Spain."

He helped his son up from his knees and placed his hands on his shoulders.

"You must stay here and rally the men. There must still be resistance when I am gone. Once Bingham knows I am gone, he will relent and return to his province. Then it is up to you, for the memory of your ancestors, for the memory of your brother, to defend the family honour, the family name, the family lands."

Brian Óg clasped his father by the hand and looked straight into his eyes.

"It is a heavy burden you place upon these young shoulders, but I will prove myself worthy of your faith. Go forth and bring back an army, and I will make sure there is something worth returning for."

The O'Rourke embraced his son until tears invaded his eyes and threatened to embarrass him in front of his men. He let go of the embrace and stood and looked his son in the eye with as much pride as he could muster. The O'Rourke slapped his son on the shoulder and turned to leave.

"Brendan, come with me to Fermanagh and pick only a handful of your best men, for we are travelling light. Francisco, bring two of your men with you, for if we go to Spain, I hope my cause will be well represented. We leave as soon as we gather our things."

The O'Rourke went to his tent to collect his belongings. However, before he could get there, an arrow whizzed past his head and lodged itself in a tree.

"They are upon us!" Brian Óg raised his sword and cried out to rally his men. "Drive them away. Save the O'Rourke!"

The men of the camp charged towards the arrows. Brendan signalled to two of his men and they went to protect the O'Rourke.

"We must leave now, lord, or they may capture you."

The O'Rourke dug into his bags, trying to decide what to bring.

"There is no time for that. We are well within arrow range. The next could be through your head."

The O'Rourke cursed and threw down his things.

"To the horses then. Get Francisco and your men, and we'll leave."

Arrows came thick and fast, for Brian Óg had yet to find their source. The O'Rourke made it to the horses, and then he, Francisco, Brendan, and two Galloglass mounted up and rode as fast as they could towards Fermanagh.

CHAPTER 25
THE COURT OF THE MAGUIRE

Their horses pounded through the dense forest, hooves echoing off the trees. Despite their weariness, they rode on, determined to reach Maguire country as quickly as possible. The O'Rourke finally halted his horse and dismounted, his muscles aching from the long journey. He walked a short distance away, ensuring they were alone in this unfamiliar land. Taking a moment to catch his breath, he rubbed at his temples with his thumb and index finger, trying to ease the tension that had built up during their frantic ride.

"What is wrong, lord?" Brendan said. "We must not rest until we get to Enniskillen, for if we are pursued, they will care little for borders."

The O'Rourke turned to him, his face a fit of rage.

"Can I not mourn for one son as I have condemned my other to death to save myself?"

"You don't know that, lord. You can still save him if we can rally the Maguires to our cause. Get on your horse, for no salvation will be found for anyone standing out here in the cold."

The O'Rourke turned his back, for he was ashamed of his tears.

"Look, lord. Francisco holds your horse for you. Let us ride while there is still daylight, for the robbers and bandits will come when the night descends."

The O'Rourke stormed past him, ashamed of his display of emotion and thinking it made him look weak in front of the men.

They rode towards the towering gates of Enniskillen, their horses' hooves kicking up mud as the last rays of sunlight disappeared behind the low rolling hills. The river splashed and gurgled alongside the castle, the perfect invitation to tired and dirty men. But the O'Rourke had a job to do, and he had to summon the last of his energies to appear as the O'Rourke to his Maguire neighbours and impress them enough to shelter him despite the dangers that pursued him.

The fortress loomed above them, its stone walls and fortified towers even more intimidating to weary men. As they drew closer, they could make out the intricate carvings and symbols etched into the massive wooden doors, hinting at the rich history and legends within them. The O'Rourke's voice echoed through the quiet evening air as he called out to the guards stationed atop the gate tower.

"I am the O'Rourke, and I call upon my neighbour to shelter me and provide hospitality as per the terms of our treaty and the traditional friendship between our clans."

Several perplexed faces appeared on top of the walls to see if this claimant could be who they claimed to be. Francisco twitched on the back of his horse, both at his unease of riding in the traditional Irish way without stirrups and at why, after all the O'Rourke's bragging, they did not fling the gates open for him. The men on the ramparts called their constable, who peered over the wall at the O'Rourke in disbelief of his claims.

"Your master will not be pleased with the hospitality you show to one of the most important clan leaders in all of Ireland," said the O'Rourke as he shook his fist up at the rampart.

"If you're so important, why are you calling here at twilight?" said the constable. "How do we know you are not in league with the English, and this is a ploy to get us to open the gates?"

"Let me assure you it is no ploy, and you humiliate your master by forcing him to apologise to me for you casting such insults down from your walls. Open the gates, for I grow cold out here."

"Let me consult my master, for I do not want to place him in peril because you claim insult."

The O'Rourke waved him away.

"Do as you must and pray it does not earn you a flogging."

The minutes dragged as the O'Rourke took out his temper on the men on the walls. But eventually, the scraping sound on the other side signalled the removal of the door bar. A handsome, well-dressed young man appeared with a smile of greeting on his face.

"Welcome, oh exalted leader of the O'Rourkes. I apologise for making you wait out here in the cold, but it is not every day we find a stranger at our gates claiming to be the O'Rourke. As I'm sure you understand, our men had to be certain."

"No, I do not," the O'Rourke growled. "My fame as a rebel spreads far to the north and even across the seas. Your men should have recognised me immediately and flung open the gates for me."

The young man bowed.

"I can only apologise and hope the feast we are preparing for you makes up for it and is worthy of a man of your stature."

"I am famished, so it is the least you could do. Now, what is your name, boy, so I know who formally invites me in?"

The young man bowed again.

"I must apologise again, for our hospitality has not been up to the standard our master expects. My name is Donnacha and I am the advisor to the Maguire."

"You are a bit young to have gained wisdom, but you may make up for it with intellect. Please invite me in, show me to a bath and bring me to your master."

Donnacha extended his arm in invitation.

"This way, please."

Donnacha invited the O'Rourke into the great hall where Hugh Maguire and his advisors waited for him. The O'Rourke smelt fresh, having bathed and donned clothes given to him by the Maguire as his own garments were being washed. He nodded at Donnacha, who bowed in deference. The veins of the O'Rourke surged with confidence. He was at last being shown the respect he deserved.

He had not met the new Maguire but knew he was young. He heard he had replaced all his advisors with younger men. The O'Rourke was well used to the cut and thrust of diplomacy and inter-clan politics and would easily bully them into doing what he wanted. He would soon ride back to West Breifne at the head of an army. He saw his old comrade Desmond standing beside the Maguire and knew he had an ally. But he would save all that until after he had eaten.

"Please sit," and Donnacha extended his hand.

The O'Rourke sat, picked up his fork and plunged it into the side of roast venison. But the smell of mud and dirt interrupted the waft of the meat. He looked beside him and there sat Francisco and Brendan, sullen and still stinking of the road. But that did not dent the contentment of the O'Rourke. He placed the contents of his fork in his mouth. They cooked the venison to perfection.

"I am sorry to disturb your meal," said the Maguire, "but time is of the essence. We received this."

Donnacha came and placed a letter in front of the O'Rourke. It bore the seal of Bingham, the governor of Connacht.

The O'Rourke glanced at it but did not pause from shovelling food in his mouth.

"Since when did you take orders from him?"

The Maguire sat forward. His unwanted guest would not disrespect him.

"The Maguire takes orders from no one. However, we must consider the threats contained in it. Three armies have invaded your land, and we could not hold all of them off if they turned their attention northwards. But we are still your ally even though they prohibited us from sheltering you."

The O'Rourke scowled at having his enjoyment of the food spoiled. He put down his fork and gave the Maguire his full attention.

"Then what are you to do with me? I see you didn't waste any bath water on my men. Is this because we are to be cast out onto the road again, and there is little point in them cleaning themselves?"

The Maguire sat back in his chair. It was his turn to scowl in this tense exchange.

"Bingham has also offered a substantial bounty on your head if you care to read the letter. Given the reward is offered on a dead or alive basis, there are few places of refuge for you."

The O'Rourke picked up his fork again and stuffed some food into his cheeks, fearing his meal would be cut short.

"So you will not throw me out the gate, for if you did, I would be straight into the arms of the bounty hunters, and no leader wants to unleash such chaos on their lands. So what is to be done with me? Will you take the reward for yourself while you fatten me like a prize bull?"

The Maguire sat forward at this perceived insult to his hospitality.

Your old comrade, Desmond, will take you to the islands. When it is safe, we will smuggle you into Tirconnell."

The O'Rourke threw his fork down and spat out his food.

"Your father would never have treated me like this. He always honoured the treaties he made. If there were only one reliable man in all of the north, it was Cúchonnacht Maguire."

Hugh Maguire stood up and slammed his fists on the table.

"Do not come here and wave my father's good name in front of me to gain an advantage. The only service that will bring you is to wear out your welcome. You and your foolish sons brought the English upon yourselves. That is why none of your allies will come to your aid. You even endanger me by brazenly bringing a Spanish captain into my halls. I, too, have sheltered the Spanish, but I do not parade them around in front of the lord deputy and the governor of Connacht and dare them to do something about it. My hospitality ends when this meal does. I suggest you leave for Tirconnell at your first opportunity. Goodbye, and I hope it is in better circumstances next time we meet."

The Maguire stormed out with Donnacha in his wake. The O'Rourke and his entourage sat mouths agape. Desmond remained seated opposite them and shrugged.

"Sure, you may as well finish your meal. I've only fish to offer you on my island."

Francisco and Brendan looked at each other, and neither needed a second invitation.

CHAPTER 26

PRIDE AND ITS SLIPPERY SLIDE

"**M**y pigs that would drag their snouts through the mud and shit of my yard had more pride than you," said the O'Rourke. "How can you eat his food when he has thrown us out into the woods?"

Francisco and Brendan threw down their utensils and scowled at the O'Rourke.

"We have been faithful to you, lord," said Francisco. "Would you deny your men the last chance of a decent meal?"

The O'Rourke flipped his plate and stood to leave as his meal dripped from the table onto the floor.

"Decent? Decent!? I'm surprised you don't choke on the last meal of condemned men. By what he said, I would not be surprised if Bingham himself was outside those doors waiting to hang us in the yard."

Desmond stood and walked over to the O'Rourke.

"What is a young man with little experience to do when the most wanted man in Ireland comes knocking on his door seeking sanctuary? He couldn't handle you."

The O'Rourke's anger deflated as his ego inflated.

"You should have told him who I was before I arrived. Surely you talk about me in the court as the greatest rebel alive?"

"Oh, but you are too much to live up to for those with little experience," said Desmond. "He hears the stories, and yet he cowers under the weight of your shadow. Give him a chance to get used to you being here and to see that the English army is not about to arrive at his door, and he'll soon warm to you."

"Well, it had better be quick, for my son's sake."

"Now, don't dilly-dally," said Desmond to Francisco and Brendan. "Fill your pockets with whatever food you wish to take for the ferryman awaits."

The O'Rourke sneered as Francisco and Brendan took as much food as they could carry.

"We're not beggars," he said. "What will the Maguire think of me if my men stuff their pockets with food?"

"He shall think them good warriors taking their opportunity," said Desmond. "Now take the food he has left out so we can leave while there is still light."

The O'Rourke begrudgingly nodded his approval. The Maguire's servants gave them some bags and Brendan and Francisco packed enough for the O'Rourke as they both knew that hunger would eventually eat his pride.

They made their way to Desmond's boat, the sound of rushing water and creaking wood filling their ears as they neared the Enniskillen quays. The O'Rourke's eyes narrowed at the sight of the vessel, a mixture of resentment and suspicion evident in his gaze.

"Are you caught up in some plot to drown me?"

Desmond smirked at what his friend had become.

"It is no plot to have you travel the lakes in the boat of the common man. Sure, if we had a procession for you, the governor would spot you a mile away and wait at the end. You'll have to get used to the sodden ground and the fern now that you're a fugitive."

"What about my men? How will they all fit in there?" said the O'Rourke, drawing derogatory circles in the air above the boat.

"They won't all fit on my island either. Decide who you will take and send the rest to Tirconnell or back to West Breifne to help your son. All you need to do is get to Tirconnell, and you can hire some Scottish Redshanks there, and you'll be back in West Breifne in no time."

Francisco broke into a sweat on the windswept quayside. Was this his journey's end? It was all down to whether or not the O'Rourke would choose him to continue the journey. He remembered Desmond from the beach and feared if he was left behind, he would end up as a slave to the Maguire trying to train his savages.

The O'Rourke pondered his decision.

"Lord, you need a bodyguard and an advisor," said Brendan as he stood forward on the quay. "Send your bodyguards to your son and take Francisco and me. We can get you safely to the house of O'Donnell."

The O'Rourke stroked his chin.

"So be it. Let's get this boat journey over with."

Donnacha quietly excused himself from the company of his master and quickly donned a weathered hood and cloak. He stole down the winding streets of the bustling Enniskillen town, careful to avoid detection as he navigated through the crowds and makeshift huts that lined the roads. Finally, he reached the outskirts of town, where a small alehouse stood alone on the edge of a muddy road. As he approached, a one-armed man covered in grime lifted a tankard to his lips and nodded at Donnacha with a friendly smile. Inviting him to sit down, the man gestured towards an empty stool at his table.

"Drink?" said the man. He grinned to show it was he who had Donnacha wrapped around his little finger and he was not beholden to him, even though they sat in the middle of Maguire territory.

"I cannot stay," said Donnacha. "The arrival of the O'Rourke has my master all in a tizzy. He wants to ride straight down to West Breifne to liberate it from your brethren, and it strains every sinew in me to persuade him not to."

The man raised his mug and saluted him.

"He's lucky he has someone with such sense to advise him."

"Don't make fun of me when I am here under duress, Captain Williamson."

The captain lifted his jacket to show his dagger.

"Just to let you know you are not safe even here and not to take liberties with me. Sit down so I may see if you were followed."

Donnacha nodded, sat, and scowled at his host in a timid attempt at defiance.

"You do your young master a service by sitting down and talking with me," said the captain. "Someday, he may even realise it. Now, tell me, where is the rebel O'Rourke?"

Donnacha leaned forward so his words would not be taken in the wind.

"He was sent on his way with the minimum of hospitality so he would not suspect. He is on the lake and is staying on an island. You should apprehend him there and do with him what you wish as long as you do not bring the Maguires into it."

The captain threw up his remaining hand.

"What's the good in telling me that? They will easily lose me on the lake."

Donnacha squeezed his hand into a fist, for the murky bog of this plot was dragging him under.

"I will give you one of my best men, Aonghas O'Braoin, loyal to Connor Roe but trusted by the Maguire. He will be your guide, but should his collusion be discovered, he must kill whoever may disclose it."

The captain grinned and slipped Donnacha a bag of coins.

"That's for your trouble, and if we successfully catch the O'Rourke, Governor Bingham will make sure that Connor Roe is declared sheriff."

Donnacha pocketed the money and got up to leave.

"It was a pleasure doing business with you," said the captain. "It is good to have this back door to the Maguire."

"As long as he never finds out about it," said Donnacha, "and my head remains on its shoulders."

The Captain grinned.

"Send your men to the quayside, and I will meet them there. Once the scourge of the O'Rourke is gone, we'll all be the happier."

Donnacha nodded and disappeared back into the street.

CHAPTER 27
THE PERILS OF THE DARK

Francisco and Brendan dangled their feet over the jagged rocks of Desmond's island, the tips of their toes barely touching the cool, clear water below. The sun was setting in a blaze of oranges and pinks, casting a warm glow over the small patch of land that felt like their own private paradise. They had crossed to the other side to escape from the incessant complaining of the O'Rourke, but on this tiny island dotted with sparse trees, there was no escaping his booming voice. It was as if the island itself could not bear to be separated from the chaos of the mainland.

"You should make your little islands into jails," said Francisco. "Your prisoners would soon break from the wind off the lake and the constant rain with little shelter.

"It's funny you should say that," said Brendan as he slapped him on the knee. "Some of my favourite incarcerations have been on islands."

Francisco's face fell.

"Have we been tricked?"

"No," said Brendan, trying not to laugh. "Desmond has come here to retire. But some of the other islands over there are jails."

Brendan pointed to the multitude of islands in the lake. But Francisco did not care. They all looked like frozen hellholes to him.

"Why would Desmond want to retire out onto this island? Surely if he wants to die, it would be easier and more honourable to die in battle rather than freeze to death in a shack on an island in the middle of a freezing lake?"

"The Maguire gives islands out as a reward. You can build crannógs on them or use them as a place of sanctuary."

Francisco crossed his arms and pulled a face.

"Now you are just pulling my leg. He is a prisoner on this island and has tricked us into coming here. The O'Rourke will be furious when he finds out."

"He won't have to wait long. Look." Brendan pointed out onto the lake.

"Are those boats?" said Francisco. "Are they coming for us?"

"I'm not going to wait to find out. There's a huge bounty on the O'Rourke's head and a pretty penny for yours too. Come on."

He slapped Francisco on the shoulder, and they ran back to Desmond's hut.

The O'Rourke stood outside Desmond's hut, swearing blue murder at his host.

"What do you mean I have to sleep outside? I am the O'Rourke, not some damn horse boy. My ancestors were the kings of Ireland. Do you want me to freeze to death on your wretched little island? The Maguire must think little of you if this is your reward for years of service."

"Now, calm down," said Desmond. "You're shouting so loud they'll hear you on the mainland."

"And so they should! Does the Maguire know you are mistreating me so?"

"I am doing no such thing. My manservant Arthur here has been fishing all day so that he could prepare you a meal."

A skinny, meek man emerged from the shadows and bowed his head. The O'Rourke only grunted in reply.

Brendan ran down with Francisco to the O'Rourke and halted before him.

"Well, the good news is, lord, you'll not be staying long."

"And the bad news?"

"The bounty hunters have taken to the lake."

The O'Rourke went for his sword. He held the tip in front of Desmond's face.

"Is this the Maguire's doing, or are you perhaps angling for a better island?"

Desmond gritted his teeth as he reminded himself of his past friendship with the O'Rourke.

"I suggest you remove the blade from my face, for I am your best chance of living. The price on your head is so high it could have been anyone. It was definitely not the Maguire, for he is too young and idealistic. If I had to put money on it then Donnacha, Connor Roe Maguire or a combination of the two would be my bet. But the longer we argue, the closer they get. I suggest we get in the boat and head for Tirconnell. But it all starts with you putting down your sword."

The O'Rourke growled but lowered his weapon.

"Forgive me, friend, but Irish politics make you paranoid."

"With good reason," said Desmond. "But you still need to recognise your friends."

"Then I must trust you as being mine. The O'Rourke may be vulnerable, but his people need him alive."

"Stop pontificating and get in the boat."

The O'Rourke scowled but picked up his bags and ran towards the boat.

CHAPTER 28
THE DEAD OF NIGHT

C aptain Williamson commanded a fleet of three boats. He filled them with his own men and those of Aonghas O'Braoin who served as their guides, with only the faint glimmer of moonlight reflecting off the lake's surface to show them the way. The men paddled silently through the calm waters, their eyes adjusting to the dim light as they searched for any signs of movement or danger. The stillness of the lake was only disturbed by the gentle lapping sound of waves against the sides of their boats, the hooting of distant owls and the occasional howl of a wolf.

"How can you tell one island from another?" said the captain. Straining his eyes to make out the protruding blobs from the lake merely amplified his frustration.

Aonghas grinned back from the bow.

"We're water babies, see. Born and grew up on the lakes. I'm well acquainted with Desmond's island, be it bathed in shadow or illuminated in the moonlight. Donnacha always told me one day he would send me to assassinate Desmond on his island, so I have spent many days and nights scoping it out. I'll get a handy bonus by bringing back his head."

"As long as you don't get distracted from the mission, I don't care what deals you have done on the side. Now, will the island be well defended?"

"I almost would have felt guilty before slaying an old man and his cook, especially because Desmond was a great warrior once. But the O'Rourke will have some bodyguards that will prove an obstacle. Nothing that cannot be surmounted by us retaining the element of surprise."

Aonghas crept up to the top of the boat and thrust his finger into the darkness.

"It's that island over there. Caress the waters, boys. Don't make a sound. The less noise, the less work your axe will have to do."

The oars glided through the water, creating ripples that spread out in perfect circles behind the boat. In the distance, an island lay before them, its silhouette crowned by towering trees on top of a small hill. A low-lying headland with gentle slopes and rocky outcrops extended outward like a welcoming arm into the tranquil waters. The captain crawled up to the bow, his eyes fixed on the mysterious island ahead.

"Can you see anyone on shore?" he said.

"No, and if they are not expecting us, I wouldn't think they would be looking out for us. Desmond's house is on the other side of the island, and he cannot see out onto the main lake from it."

"Then we may have our element of surprise."

The captain slapped Aonghas on the back. Aonghas gave him a pithy look.

"I did say no noise."

"Sorry."

"Pull up the oars," said Aonghas.

With a swift hand gesture, Aonghas commanded the other boats to prepare to land. One man from each vessel shed his heavy armour, swords and axes, before gracefully slipping over the side of the boat and diving into the cool waters. They swam towards the shore with strong, determined strokes, their muscles rippling beneath the surface. As they reached the rocky coast, they hoisted themselves up and peered up the hill, scanning for any signs of danger. Satisfied, they gave another signal to their comrades in the boats before returning to take hold of ropes and guide them safely to land. The men disembarked, climbed to the top of the modest headland and reassembled behind Aonghas.

"The house is on the other side of the hill. You are to climb to just below the brow and resist the urge to look over until I signal to attack."

The men nodded in silent understanding and split into preassigned groups, their dark forms blending seamlessly into the night. Each step was taken with calculated precision as they climbed up the hill and through the sparse trees, making sure not to disturb any twigs or leaves that might give away their presence. Aonghas retained a select few, their eyes trained on the target ahead. In front of them stood Captain Williamson and his armed men, their weapons glinting threateningly in the moonlight.

"If we cut them off from their boat, there is no escape," said Aonghas. " I suggest we split the remaining men in two. One group circle to the harbour to block their escape. The rest of us will do a frontal assault. No one will take Desmond's head from me. Do you want to join the frontal assault?"

"I thought you'd never ask," said Captain Williamson.

They crouched low in the dense bushes, their breaths coming in quick, shallow gasps. The flames of a crackling fire illuminated the night sky, casting dancing shadows across the trodden grass around the surrounds of the house. Beyond the glowing embers, a sleek boat was moored in a sheltered cove, gently bobbing with the rhythm of the waves. The scent of smoke and fish lingered in the air.

"Where is everyone?" whispered the captain in Aonghas's ear.

"The boat is tied, so they must be in the house. If we charge them now, they will be trapped. What would you have me do, captain?"

"Collect our reward in the easiest way possible."

Aonghas steeled himself.

"LET'S GET THEM, MEN!"

With a mighty roar, Aonghas lifted his massive axe and charged towards the house, his men following closely behind. They descended from the shallow hill like a stampede of wild animals, their eyes blazing with determination as they surrounded the boat in the harbour, effectively trapping it. The air was filled with their fierce battle cries as they closed in on the house, ready to tear it apart with brute force. Their charge turned into a cautious trot and then a slow walk, their anticipation-fueled excitement now replaced with wary apprehension.

Aonghas's men reached the house first, peering through windows with sharpened eyes filled with bloodlust and anticipation of victory. A strange silence fell over them. Not a single creature stirred within the confined space except for a few birds fluttering nervously in their cages.

"There's no one here," said the bravest, willing to endure Aonghas's wrath.

"By God's breath, I damn them to hell," said Aonghas. "Search the house and prepare the boats. They can only have gone to the mainland."

CHAPTER 29
RELIVING THE PAST

T he boat glided smoothly through the dark waters, guided only by the
faint twinkle of starlight reflecting off the surface. Francisco braced
against the wind as he took one of the oars and Brendan the other. His dream of
returning home was as far away as ever. He hoped and prayed the direction he
was instructed to take would be to row downriver. For downriver lay the sea, and
the sea would mean a port that could hold a Spanish ship to bring him home.

"Over there," said Desmond, pointing to a small rocky shore. "Pull up over
there."

Francisco's prayer died in his mouth. It was as if he prayed to an empty sky,
as if this island was not part of the earth God watched over. He swallowed hard,
hoping he could quickly move on. But he still had not got used to disappointment.

They rowed as gently as possible to avoid getting caught in the reeds or
excessively shallow parts of the lake. They reached their destination on the
north shore of Lower Lough Erne, a peaceful and secluded spot nestled among
towering trees and rocky cliffs.

The air was heavy with the smell of damp earth and decaying leaves, as if
nature was trying to repel Francisco from her shores. The moon cast a dim glow
upon the landscape, creating shadows that danced eerily across the shoreline.
They disembarked the boat into knee-high murky water filled with hidden

stones and boulders. Francisco winced as he scraped his feet on the jagged edges of unseen rocks.

"Pull the boat onto the shore," said Desmond as he stood up in the boat and pointed to the spot he selected. "I still need to get home after I leave you in Tirconnell."

Francisco looked at Brendan, who returned his scepticism. It would be a kindness to lose the boat, to put Desmond's delusions to rest and make him choose somewhere more hospitable to retire to. But they still needed him, for he was the only person who knew the way to Tirconnell. They made sure his boat was well hidden in some bushes.

"We need some horses," said Desmond. "My manservant Arthur will fetch some for us. In the meantime, we'll camp here for the night."

Desmond walked towards the edge of a wood overhanging the lake to despatch Arthur and to look for somewhere dry and sheltered to rest.

"What about the bounty hunters on the lake?" said the O'Rourke to Desmond's back.

"They'll never find us here the way we weaved through the little islands on the lake. We'll have to be careful on the road to Donegal Castle. It is wild country between here and there."

Francisco followed in Desmond's wake, waiting for instruction.

"Here will do," Desmond said, pointing to a sheltered spot beneath an oak tree. "Hopefully, it will only be a few hours until Arthur returns."

Desmond went to fetch his bags from the boat, and Francisco and Brendan gathered firewood. The O'Rourke looked out onto the lake to ensure they were not being followed.

"No fires," and Desmond put his foot through Francisco's and Brendan's creation. "You light that, and it can be seen for miles. We'll all be dead before the morning."

Desmond's face told there would be no negotiations. Francisco and Brendan lay down beneath the oak tree and pulled what they could use as blankets around themselves. Whatever warmth they could generate was soon eclipsed by the chill of the wind off the lake.

"It's times like this I wish they had hanged me on my ship," said Francisco as his teeth rattled in the cold.

"It's times like this I wish I could have joined you," said Brendan.

Francisco knew now was the only time he may be sure he could get any sleep. His muscles ached, and his bones were weary, but he still could not banish the thought of what a fool he had been to bet everything he had on following the O'Rourke and had not taken his chances against the bounty hunters. All it had got him was shivering in the dark in a cold, damp wood.

As the sun rose the next day, they set off for Tirconnell. They were grateful for the horses that Arthur had provided, but the soft and muddy ground made it difficult to push them too hard for fear of injury. A restless night and their meagre rations from the Maguire being already consumed heightened the tension between the travellers. Their various resentments grated in their tired and hungry state, and Francisco had almost too many to count.

Desmond finally called for a break, signalling for them to dismount and take a well-deserved rest on a nearby hill overlooking Donegal town. The cool breeze and peaceful view provided a brief respite from their journey thus far.

"Don't get comfortable," said Desmond. "The horses need a rest, and their day's work has barely started."

Brendan's stomach grumbled loudly, prompting him to scour the surrounding area for signs of sustenance. Meanwhile, the O'Rourke excused himself to find a private spot to relieve himself. Francisco lingered awkwardly in front of Desmond, trying to suppress his swelling anger as he remembered when he first met him. Desmond squinted as he tried to figure out why Francisco looked at him so.

"Do I know you from somewhere?" said Desmond. "For you sure seem to know me."

Anger pulsated through Francisco's veins. How many of his men was Desmond responsible for killing or enslaving, and he could not even show him the respect of remembering who he was?

"The beach. The beach where the Spanish galleon ran ashore, and you made prisoners of its men. Do you remember me from the beach?" Francisco's voice was taut.

Desmond squinted even harder.

"Whoever you are, you look far better than when you came upon that shore. If you have not realised it already, you have something to be grateful to the O'Rourke for."

"I have already paid a heavy price for life, but I wonder if I was luckier than my men who came ashore that day?" Francisco snarled back at him.

Desmond stroked his beard to mask his cringe and looked the other way.

"We certainly didn't cover ourselves in glory in those days after the Armada landings. Many of your fellow countrymen died, some came to gainful employment with the Irish chieftains and some even set out back to Spain, but God only knows how many made it back. But you should count your blessings the O'Rourke took you in. Many men talk big but have weak hearts. Be grateful for what you've got."

Francisco gritted his teeth, feeling the sharp edges of each one as he bared them in a feral snarl. With fists clenched so tightly, his knuckles turned white, he lunged towards Desmond, ready to pummel him into submission. Desmond stepped back and placed his hand on his belt where Francisco could see its vicinity to his knife. Francisco stopped in his tracks, his cheeks flushed.

"What did you do with those men you brought back from the beach? I escaped, but did you kill my comrades to get your revenge?"

Francisco raised his fists and took another step forward. The tip of a sword danced before Francisco's face. He stopped mid-stride.

"Easy there, fella," said Brendan. "There are things we should all be angry about but things we should be grateful about too. Desmond here is going to get us to Tirconnell, where we'll be safe. Then all debts will be repaid and be in the past. Isn't that right, Desmond?"

Desmond nodded, his face sheer granite.

"I am a great respecter of your nation and your king, Francisco. If you don't understand yet what I did and why, then you have not stood enough in the murky waters of the Irish clans. Tirconnell will be enlightening for you."

The O'Rourke returned, felt the tension and stood between Francisco and Desmond.

"I didn't know my bladder was that big to have missed so much. Why have you turned on each other when you have no shortage of foes to fight?"

Francisco pushed Brendan's blade away.

"For the sake of my freedom, seeing my family once again and Señor O'Rourke, I have no quarrel with you, Desmond," Francisco said through gritted teeth, "for I am in your hands and can only hope my trust in you is well placed so I might live. I promise not to kill you in your sleep, and may God strike me down if I do. The journey makes me irritable, and I long to finish it. Let us make haste to our next destination and hope we are received better than at Enniskillen."

"Well, Desmond?" said the O'Rourke with a raised eyebrow. "Surely you can rest easy now? May we let bygones be bygones?"

Desmond pulled down on his coat as if that would rid him of the built-up tension.

"It has been forgotten already," and Desmond nodded to Francisco.

"So our journey together continues," the O'Rourke said, "What of our reception in Tirconnell? Can I easily hire Redshanks there?"

"The mood in Tirconnell can best be described as incendiary," said Desmond. "They are having one of their many wars of succession. But if we can avoid getting killed or captured, it is the best place in Ireland to hire the Scottish mercenaries you crave to drive the English out of West Breifne."

"Then let us leave our differences here and carry on," said the O'Rourke.

They all nodded, mounted their horses and followed Desmond.

CHAPTER 30
THE PAWN

T he group set off at a brisk pace with the wind in their faces, their horses' hooves thundering against the rocky ground as they headed north. The landscape around them was rugged and untamed, with rolling hills and scattered patches of thick forests. Francisco could barely keep his eyes on the way ahead, for the sustained pressure of the cold wind on his face made unwanted memories of the islands around Scotland and the cold hell of the depths of the storms tumble back into his head. The rolling up and down the hills and the pounding of the hooves did little to relieve Francisco of his daymare.

Desmond kept a watchful eye behind them, knowing they were likely being followed. They avoided other travellers or groups of horsemen, not wanting to risk any unwanted encounters. As they approached Donegal town, Desmond's heart began to race. The O'Donnell patrols could be seen in the distance, their flags waving proudly in the wind. Without warning, a group of horsemen surrounded them, causing Desmond to tense up. He quickly realised these were not friendly faces. He knew none of them. Desmond motioned for the others to stay quiet and let him handle the situation. His mind raced as he tried to devise a plan for getting out of this potentially dangerous encounter unscathed. He rode to the rider he thought was the leader. He gave his most confident smile as if he was meant to be there.

"Is Donnell O'Donnell still the O'Donnell here? I lose count of who's in charge in the inter-clan bloodbath," he said.

"Aye, it may be a mouthful, but that he is," said the riders' leader.

"Well, tell him it is Desmond MacCabe and I am on a very important mission for his ally, Hugh Maguire."

"I hope for your sake he has time for your important mission, for he has an important mission of his own."

Desmond paused, for he did not know if the man was trying to trick him. He hoped he was the only one who could hear his heart thump in his chest.

"What's that?" Desmond croaked, his mouth suddenly gone dry.

"To crush the rebels of Ineen Dubh."

Desmond's heart began to slow, and his shoulders dropped.

"Well, don't let us stop you from killing each other. All we're here for are the Scottish mercenaries."

"You should be so lucky. Maybe you'll get your pick from who's left standing after the civil war."

Desmond paused, then tried to move the conversation along.

"May we pass? I am here on urgent business from the Maguire."

The lead rider scrutinized them.

"You'll find the O'Donnell in the boundaries of the castle. Be warned, he'll have scant time for you if this is all the men you have brought."

"Don't worry, we'll make the conversation worth his while. Now, good day, and may God's blessings be upon you."

"I'll take your blessings, but the day will not be good yet," said the lead rider. "I am under instructions to escort you in. Now follow me."

As they rode up the gentle incline towards the imposing gates of Donegal Castle, the sounds of bagpipes and lively chatter filled the air. A campsite sprawled around the base of the hill, bustling with activity and resonating with the distinct cadence of Scottish accents. The scent of smoke from campfires and cooking food mingled together, warmth and song comforting the tired minds of the travellers. As they reached the crest of the hill, the grandeur of the castle came into view, its stone walls standing tall and proud against the blue sky.

To Desmond and the O'Rourke, this was no mere structure but a symbol of strength and resilience steeped in centuries of history. To Francisco, it was no more than the fortress of a bandit, one who wished to lay terror on the surrounding districts and had no more ambition than thievery and to have his ego stroked. The camp was one of beggars, angry peasants, drunkards and thieves. If he ever got back to the king of Spain, he would have to rehearse the retelling of his tales to ensure they were suitably embellished to retain his head.

Desmond smiled as he looked around the camp.

"There looks like plenty here to go around," he told the lead rider. "I'm sure your master can spare a few."

"Once he comes back with the head of his stepmother, then I'm sure he would be willing to share. But until then, I wouldn't fancy your chances."

"I'll thank you for your opinions, informative as they were. But please, just bring me to your master and leave the diplomacy to me."

The leader of the riders signalled to open the gate.

"Don't say I didn't warn you. He only has eyes for the prize of becoming the O'Donnell. But I don't think sense will stop you from trying."

As they rode through the gates, the group dismounted their horses and took in the sight before them. The once majestic courtyard had now become an extension of the camp below, albeit for the officers of the men outside the protection of the walls. The battlements were marred with charred wood and lingering smoke, evidence of a recent attack.

Francisco cursed his luck, for it seemed he had leapt out of the fire and into a pot of boiling water. In Breifne, at least, they ran away and hid, hoping to emerge on a better day. Here, he could feel the heat of battle, as if an attack could come at any moment. But here it was, clan on clan, with the English nowhere in sight. But why would they need to be? Why risk your own lives when if you leave them alone, they will kill each other, and all you have to do is wait until they are at their weakest and seize victory?

Suddenly, a young man with long brown locks of hair came striding towards them from the tower of the castle. Despite his youthful appearance and lack of battle scars or a beard, he swaggered over as if the master of this whole endeavour.

"Greetings, strangers. You see a gift from my stepmother before you on the castle walls before she fled. She could not face me nor could bear to surrender to me what was rightfully mine. I am the O'Donnell. Are you here to offer your services as hired men?"

Desmond barely had time to breathe before the O'Rourke brushed past him to take control. The O'Rourke thought himself a master of impressing youth. He had two himself. He swelled with pride at how his two boys turned out. Alas, with a pang of regret, for one was already dead and the other in perilous circumstances.

"I am Brian O'Rourke, the greatest rebel in all of Ireland. Come and embrace me."

The O'Rourke grabbed Donnell and embraced him. Donnell's men went for their swords, but their master signalled for caution. He wriggled out of the O'Rourke's embrace and stood back to take in the strangers before him.

"All sorts of rumours have ventured their way up here about you," he said, pointing at the O'Rourke as if he were an old curiosity. "There's a large price on your head."

The O'Rourke winked and opened out his arms.

"See, what did I tell you? The greatest rebel in Ireland."

Donnell smirked.

"The enormous price on your head brings bounty hunters and the attention of the crown. An unwanted distraction from fighting my cunning stepmother and something she can complain to Dublin about. Why do you come calling at my door?"

The O'Rourke, under any other circumstances, would have pulled his sword on such a disrespectful youngster, but his boasts had drawn the attention of the other men in the yard, and Donnell's men had formed a circle around them. He pulled himself closer to Francisco and Brendan for protection.

"I am here to call on the old O'Rourke–O'Donnell alliance," he said with an unfamiliar quiver. "Our clans used to dominate Connacht and can do so once again. All you need to do is lend me some of your Scottish mercenaries. I will retrieve my lands and return them to you with the interest of my men to assist you in the consolidation of Tirconnell. What do you say?"

Donnell eyed him up, maintaining the same smirk.

"I think you're a beggar who's come here with nothing to trade. You have no lands, and no men follow you except an old Galloglass, a really old Galloglass, and a Spaniard. If I were to give you my men, why would I give the lands back to you when I was the one who conquered them?"

The O'Rourke gritted his teeth.

"For you would have to use up so many men to hold those lands, it would be far more profitable for you to have an ally who is grateful to you for life than to be perpetually fighting bandits in the Breifne forests."

"You are not making your offer sound any more appealing to me. However, if you follow me on my expedition to defeat my stepmother and prove yourself, we can discuss you getting some Scottish mercenaries."

The O'Rourke's jaw dropped as he composed the most diplomatic riposte possible.

"This is the only offer you will get," continued Donnell. "Ride with us now or wait in my dungeons for the English to pay your ransom."

The O'Rourke looked to his men, and Francisco and Brendan nodded.

"I'm too old for fighting," said Desmond as he held up his hands. "You don't want the inconvenience of having to haul my fat body around the Tirconnell mountains trying to find a bit of deep earth to bury me in." He beckoned the O'Rourke forward to whispering distance. "I will see what I can arrange here. With this young fool, you will end up either dead or in prison."

"What is it to be, O'Rourke?" said Donnell.

"Those that can fight will fight. Those that are old will stay here."

"And which are you, old man?" said Donnell.

The O'Rourke did not dignify the question with a response but signalled to Francisco and Brendan to mount up.

CHAPTER 31

THE DEVIL OF THE COLD DOES HIS DAMNEDEST

I neen Dubh proved herself to be very illusive and refused to offer battle to Donnell O'Donnell, much to his frustration. The O'Rourke, Francisco, and Brendan were virtual prisoners as Donnell dragged them up one mountain after another, through one valley and the next, for a whole two months in pursuit of her. Finally, Donnell thought he had Ineen Dubh trapped in a valley, and he moved his army in for the kill.

Francisco and Brendan trailed behind a seemingly endless column of horsemen, making their way up the winding hills and through the verdant valleys of the lower Tirconnell mountains. The scent of damp earth and wildflowers filled the air as they rode, accompanied by the distant sound of rushing waters.

Ahead, the O'Rourke rode confidently along the narrow, winding mountain paths, eager to impress the O'Donnell with his charm and wit. The sun threw long shadows across the landscape to compensate for the biting wind stealing its heat. But the riders pressed on without hesitation.

Francisco could not help but feel a twinge of envy for the O'Rourke's unshakable self-assurance. No matter what happened, the O'Rourke seemed to find some well inside him to dip his bucket and rejuvenate his soul. But Francisco had no such reserves for his moods, which were on the precipice of melancholy, only held back by a holey blanket meant to keep in the heat.

"This valley is the mouth of the devil of the cold," said Francisco to Brendan, who rode beside him. "Do not tell me any of your lies that this is supposed to be summer."

Since they left West Breifne, he had not managed to touch any additional clothing except the blanket, and the valley was one long wind tunnel.

"Take me back to Spain with you if you manage to hitch a ride on a passing ship," said Brendan. "Your lands sound like heaven compared to this windswept hell."

Francisco gave a wiry smile.

"My plan to hitch a ride on a ship back to Spain seems to have died a death since we left Breifne. The O'Rourke lured me here on false pretences to this freezing mountain. Now, I only wish he would try to redeem himself and use what little influence he seems to have to get us some proper blankets."

Brendan punched him in the shoulder.

"Stop complaining. You'll soon warm up when someone belts you over the head with their axe and the blood flows down your body."

Francisco smiled.

"Do Galloglass specialise in gallows humour, hence the name?"

Brendan laughed.

"Now you're getting into the spirit of things. You have to laugh when your balls are getting frozen off halfway up a mountain."

"But what I want to know is if my balls will ever get off this mountain. From what the O'Rourke said in Breifne, he would rally his allies, march back into his lands, and throw the English out. Now, we are virtually prisoners halfway up a hill to be sold to the English if our captors lose."

"Don't let your chin drop," said Brendan. "That's Irish politics for you. As soon as these young upstarts take their heads out of their arses, they'll see what's good for them. If they don't unite behind the O'Rourke and defend him, then the English will come and pick them off one by one."

"I thought you wanted me to lift my chin up?" said Francisco. "If my survival depends on any of the young men I've met seeing sense, then I may as well save myself the disappointment and accumulated misery and throw myself off a cliff."

"Ah, come on. Your trip to Ireland can't have been that bad."

"You may be good Catholics and hold the one true God in sufficient reverence, but this is the devil's island, be he the devil of lies and temptation or he of the cold."

"And there was me thinking that you were past all that and used to the life of a soldier. They must have been too nice to you on your big fancy ship. You have regaled me with your sea battle stories where you were all lined up in nice neat rows to fight at agreed times and then go back and recuperate in your tents in the Netherlands before returning to the sea and taking turns to fire upon each other once more. It's not like that here. You must take your chances at the snatches of happiness you get. If we get off this godforsaken mountain, I'll introduce you to some local women, and they'll soon warm you up."

Brendan grinned with a strange pride that he was the one to tell his friend how things really were. Francisco looked away and over the valley and wondered how much blood would be spilt to possess her today. Brendan slapped him on the arm and pointed ahead of them.

"Look, there's some movement up ahead. The answer to your problem of being cold may be about to be resolved. Soon, you can rob the dead."

Brendan roared laughing, for it was the best wind-up for Francisco he had thought of yet. Francisco's head dropped, and he thought of being back in his house in Spain in the luscious warmth, watching his wife make a meal and his children running around in the fields. He soon snapped out of it.

"That damn fool will not listen to a word I say." The O'Rourke threw his free hand in the air and tugged on the reins of his horse with the other. "The boy walks straight into a trap. Oh, I should be blessed to have such stupid enemies as that boy. If so, I'd be back in my castle right now with my son."

Brendan coughed to rid himself of the joviality that possessed him so he could adopt a sufficiently sombre mood to address his master.

"If you think we walk into an ambush, we should move to the rear so we can get back to Donegal Castle should we need to."

"It is dreadful cowardice to contemplate such a thing, but one should know when to die and what to die for, and this is neither. I fear we may need to make our escape if we knew where to go."

"May I suggest we follow the winner of any such confrontation we should find ourselves in but do not participate to antagonise the other side?" Francisco said. "We cannot rule out the possibility of them winning."

The O'Rourke smiled and pointed at Francisco.

"I knew I brought you along for something. It is rumoured that Ineen Dubh and her men hide in these hills, so we must hurry to the rear."

The O'Rourke and his men turned their horses on the narrow path but ran straight into a unit of O'Gallaghers marching behind them.

"Where do you think you're going?" said the O'Gallagher constable. "No one leaves without the explicit permission of the O'Donnell. Now turn around before I set my men on you."

Brendan held his hand above his sword grip and looked to the O'Rourke. The O'Rourke shook his head and signalled for them to turn around.

Their feet pounded against the rocky terrain of Tirconnell as they marched, their path guided only by whispers and rumours from their fellow soldiers. The young O'Donnell was determined to capture his elusive stepmother Ineen Dubh and her hired fighters, but she evaded him like a cunning mountain fox. As they pressed on, the land grew steeper and more treacherous until they found themselves on a narrow path carved into the side of a towering hill. The brow of the hill loomed above them, while the valley below lay deep and forbidding at the bottom of the steep incline beside them. Each step required careful footing and every turn brought them closer to their target, but also deeper into danger.

Francisco rode carefully past the lines of foot soldiers until he was level with the O'Rourke.

"I don't like the look of this," Francisco said. "It is too perfect an ambush spot to go to waste. I have fought enough bandits in northern Spain to know this is a trap."

The O'Rourke gave a little laugh.

"I may be the most wanted man in Ireland but today I am merely a passenger at the whim of another. The O'Donnell constables tell me Ineen Dubh is camped in the next valley and is unaware of our approach. That is why he hurries over the mountain."

"He cannot wait to jump into the trap. I have seen a few such places in my wars for my king that ended up littered with the graves of my comrades."

The O'Rourke could sense Francisco's complaints were serious.

"I know you speak sense, but we are hemmed in here, prisoners of circumstance. What would you have me do? Wait for the possible arrows of Ineen Dubh, or fall back on the swords of the O'Gallaghers who are right behind us?"

As Francisco opened his mouth to respond, a deafening hiss deadlier than a pit of snakes filled the air as a storm of arrows descended upon them. He lunged from his horse, shoving the O'Rourke to the ground and lay on top of him. The impact of the fall sent the O'Rourke's cries of pain echoing through the chaos as his shoulder hit the earth with a sickening thud. Meanwhile, his once loyal steed thrashed and writhed in agony, riddled with deadly arrows that pierced its flesh, severing sinews, muscle and bone. Struggling to catch his breath, the O'Rourke lifted his head and winced in agony as he tried to ease the pain shooting through his shoulder.

"Down," and Francisco grabbed him by the back of his head and forced him down. Before the O'Rourke could protest, another shower of arrows fell. Francisco lay on top of the O'Rourke as two more showers of arrows fell. The sound of bagpipes came from the other side of the hill.

"Get up. We have to run," said Francisco, and he pulled the O'Rourke to his feet. He looked around for Brendan, but all around him were the bodies of dead men and horses and wounded men groaning beneath the horses. The O'Rourke lifted his head, absorbed in his own world.

"I hope you haven't broken my shoulder. I landed on my sword arm. I may need that later."

Francisco slapped him on his good arm and signalled to him to look around. The O'Rourke's jaw dropped. He had woken up to a graveyard. He cradled his bad arm and thrust out his hand.

"Help me up. The Redshanks will be here soon."

The ground trembled beneath them as a deafening growl erupted from the other side of the hill. Without hesitation, Francisco snatched up the O'Rourke, and they plummeted down the steep incline, rocks and debris flying in their wake. With each jarring impact, the O'Rourke's shoulder screamed in agony, tears stinging his eyes. Finally, they skidded to a halt on the valley floor, and the O'Rourke struggled to sit up, his face contorted with excruciating pain.

"If it was not broken before, it certainly is now," he said as he tried to protect his arm by holding it to his chest.

"Look above," said Francisco as he pointed back in the direction they had come from.

They looked up and saw the Redshanks charging down the hill to smash into the remains of Donnell O'Donnell's army.

"We must leave," said Francisco, "before you Irish perform your rob-the-dead ritual."

"Don't try and play the high and mighty with me just because you saved my life."

The O'Rourke raised a grin and thrust out his good hand to be helped up. Francisco grasped it and led him away from the battle in the direction from where they originally came, for he knew no other place to go.

CHAPTER 32
ANY PORT IN A STORM

Men plummeted from the treacherous mountain path, their bodies colliding with jagged rocks, shattering their bones. The Redshanks charged down the hill, trampling over the fallen as they swept towards their target. Their swords sliced through flesh and bone like butter, turning Donnell O'Donnell's once proud resistance into a river of blood that flowed freely down to the bottom of the ravine. Ineen Dubh's army showed no mercy as they relentlessly pursued their enemies, determined to claim victory in a single day. The valley echoed with screams and cries as the remains of Donnell's army fled for their lives, hoping for some reprieve within the walls of their castles.

Francisco and the O'Rourke pushed their bodies to the limit, barely able to keep up with the fleeing troops of south Tirconnell. The O'Rourke gritted his teeth against the searing pain of his shoulder, each step sending a jolt of agony through his body. He was a wounded animal, reliant on instinct alone to make his escape. But the youth of south Tirconnell showed no compassion for their wounded allies. They threw off their armour and weapons as they sprinted past them towards the safety of the woods. They hoped the limping wounded would slow their enemy down, thus aiding their escape.

The O'Rourke's body finally gave out, doubled over in a fit of violent coughing that seemed to tear his already injured lungs apart. Time was running out, and they needed to reach cover before it was too late.

"You don't want to die here, running away from an ambush, do you?" said Francisco, hoping to goad some energy back into the O'Rourke's limbs.

"As I always taught my boys, you've got to know when to run," said the O'Rourke.

He held his head up once he had recovered a little. Sweat poured from his brow,, and his skin had gone sallow. He tried to smile, but his face was just creased with pain. He tried to keep up the facade of being the O'Rourke, for it was the only thing that kept him on his feet. But Francisco knew the face of a man bereft of hope from all his time spent as a ship's captain.

"We must keep running or else we'll die," said Francisco.

He took the O'Rourke's good arm and slung it over his shoulder. They had got but a few yards before the O'Rourke stumbled. Francisco struggled to pick him up, for the O'Rourke seemed to pile on the pounds as hope slipped away. Francisco looked over his shoulder to see the Redshanks still charging towards them.

"Is the O'Rourke to die in a cold bog in Tirconnell?" said Francisco in the O'Rourke's ear.

"The O'Rourke must live," the other croaked back, hauling himself to his feet again. A pair of arrows whizzed past his head, and he fell to his knees once more.

"Come on, get up." Francisco tugged again on the O'Rourke's good arm.

"Look," the O'Rourke said, his voice merely a rasp. He pointed ahead to a group of rocks upon which a man stood on a horse surrounded by Galloglass.

Francisco leaned down to him.

"I can understand that you wish to die with a sword in your hand, but I have not come all this way to commit suicide."

"No. Look." The O'Rourke pointed once more at the man on the horse. Francisco strained his eyes. Could it really be?

"Desmond?"

With a mighty heave, Francisco flung open the creaky door to the herder's hut. The hinges squealed in protest as he burst inside. A mother stood just outside, her body shaking with sobs as she shielded her children from the harsh world beyond. Her tears streamed down her cheeks, leaving glistening trails in their wake. Their clothes were tattered and dirty, evidence of a life of struggle and hardship. The mother's eyes pleaded for help but also held a fierce determination to protect her young ones at all costs.

"Stop your crying," said Desmond, standing beside her. "If we were here to kill you, we would not be having this conversation." He tried to inject kindness into his voice, but the woman's tears did not stop. "Here." He reached into his pocket and pulled out a bag of coins. "Take this. Consider it rent. There will be more where that came from if you show my men where to forage for food safely."

Desmond's burly men gripped the struggling O'Rourke tightly, their calloused hands clamping down on both of his arms as they hustled him through the doorway. The commotion caused by their forceful entrance sent the woman's kitchenware scattering across the floor, clanging and clattering in a chaotic symphony. Pots and pans crashed to the ground, spilling their contents and adding to the mess that now covered the once orderly room. Stools were overturned, the wooden legs scraping against the floor with a harsh grating sound. The woman could only watch helplessly as these rough intruders trampled upon her home.

"If they break anything, we'll pay for it," said Desmond, wishing not to upset the woman more than he had to. "As soon as my men recover, we'll be gone."

The woman wiped away her tears but left the anger.

"If you had asked me, I would have shown you the other entrance around the back that my children and I use as we wait for my lazy husband to fix the door."

Desmond was unsuccessful at hiding his cringe.

"Are you from the battle in the other valley?" she continued. "I don't want the other side coming here and taking revenge on me and my children. My husband and the other men of the clan will be back soon enough and won't take kindly to you killing or abusing us."

Desmond went into the hut, picked up the pots and pans, and set them neatly to one side. He then picked up the stools, brought them outside, and set them down.

"There. You sit there while my wounded are tended to. My men will make a rabbit stew, and there'll be plenty for you and your children. I'll make sure of that. But the sooner my wounded men are seen to, the sooner we'll be gone."

The woman guided her children away and cursed beneath her breath. She walked towards the other herdsmen's families to watch as the Maguires took over the rest of the huts. Desmond shook his head as he walked by and patted one of his men on the chest.

"Watch them all, but especially her," he pointed at the woman's back as she walked away. "But try not to harm anyone. It's a long way back to Fermanagh if a pack of angry herdsmen is pursuing you."

He went into the hut to check on the wellbeing of the O'Rourke. The O'Rourke had been placed on the bed at the back of the room, which was a couple of raised planks of wood, a straw base , a blanket as an undersheet and a blanket over the O'Rourke. Desmond had to hold his nose.

"How can you sit there when the whole of the inside stinks of cows?" he said to Francisco, who had not given up on his vigil by the O'Rourke's side.

"My nose is getting acclimatised to your country, I have been here so long. If you hadn't noticed before, all your enclosed spaces stink of cow."

Desmond laughed.

"There are many true words spoken in jest. How is he?"

"Sleeping now but still alive because of you. He wouldn't even have got to bragging about how much his ransom would be to those bloodthirsty Scots the way they laid into the O'Donnell's retreating men."

"That's good to hear, at least."

Desmond turned around and heard someone enter the hut.

"I have a surprise for you," he said to Francisco as someone stepped out from the shadows behind him.

"Brendan."

Francisco leapt up to embrace him, but Brendan put out a defensive arm to fend him off. Francisco stood back with his arms empty, and Brendan pulled down his shirt.

"I wasn't as quick-witted as you," he said, revealing the bloody bandage across his right shoulder. "I took an arrow and then fell off the side of the road. The next I remember, I was looking up at Desmond's ugly mug."

He slapped Desmond on the shoulder and received a grin in reply.

"So why are you here?" said Francisco to Desmond. "I thought you were too old to fight?"

"I am, but I was sat in Donegal Castle, and the Maguire's Galloglass arrived too late to catch up with the O'Donnells. Call me an old fool, but I couldn't resist marching with the men again. We arrived after the Redshanks loosed their volleys of arrows and waited at the back of the valley to rally any fleeing Maguires. That's when we came across you."

Francisco placed his hand on Desmond's shoulder.

"I, for one, am grateful you did. But what are we going to do after we patch up the men? Surely not go back to the Maguires, what with the bounty hunters there?"

"The best we can hope for is that Ineen Dubh's lust for revenge has been quenched by her victory today. Who knows, with some luck, she may even lend the O'Rourke her Redshanks, for she may be finished with them. I will send men to Donegal Castle and see how the land lies there. Meanwhile, all shall rest and see what fate serves us in the morning."

CHAPTER 33
A SERVING OF RABBIT AND FATE

The men of the Maguire ventured out into the dense woods and murky bogs, their steps rustling through the undergrowth as they searched for prey. Their efforts were rewarded with a bountiful harvest of plump rabbits, their soft fur damp from the morning dew.

Desmond permitted fires to be lit despite the risk of being discovered by other groups of hungry men scattered throughout the mountains after the recent battle. It seemed only natural for the herdsmen to cook along their migration routes, blending in with nature as they sustained themselves. The aroma of boiling rabbit stew wafted through the air, mingling with hints of wild herbs and edible plants gathered from the field and forest floor. Outside the main hut, Desmond sat with Francisco, relishing the hearty meal before them as they picked at steaming rabbit bones. One of the Maguire guards approached them as they ate, breaking their temporary peace.

"The herdsmen's families fled into the night," said the guard.

Desmond did not pause from enjoying the rabbit.

"Then we do not have long here. We must decide on a destination. Are the scouts back from Donegal Castle yet?"

"We see a group of men to the south but cannot tell yet who they are."

"Tell me as soon as you know. Tell the men to be in a constant state of readiness to leave."

The guard nodded and left. The Galloglass physician came out of the hut, mopped his brow, sat down and gratefully accepted his bowl of stew.

"How is he?" said Desmond.

"Resting," said the physician. "He took a heavy blow to his shoulder and arm, but nothing is broken. The bigger blow was to his ego. He needs to rest and recuperate, but he can be moved to somewhere safer to do that."

Desmond returned to his bowl.

"At least that is something. We leave as soon as I settle on a destination."

Francisco finished his bowl and patiently waited to see if there would be seconds. He saw the look of satisfaction on Desmond's face as he dismissed the physician.

"You're enjoying this, aren't you?"

Desmond could not contain his smile.

"It's just like old times."

"Lord, lord," came a cry from the periphery of the camp. "Men approach from Donegal Castle. They are Maguires."

Desmond's eyebrows shot up as he swiftly rose from his seat to greet the unexpected visitors. The previous cold and unwelcoming reception from the Maguire made Francisco suspicious of their true intentions. Along the path, twenty Maguire Galloglass stomped towards them, their boots leaving deep imprints in the muddy ground. Despite the dirt and grime that coated their armour, they seemed relatively fresh and clean compared to the battle-worn soldiers under Desmond's command. Desmond gulped for it was the same number of men as he had.

Desmond's own Galloglass, gathered around their campfires, did not seem fazed by the sudden appearance of their rival clan. They briefly glanced over their shoulders out of curiosity before returning to their meals of stew. Desmond's heart sank as he recognized the leader of the opposing Galloglass. Despite his disappointment, he still courteously extended his hand to the commander before him.

"Welcome to the camp, Aonghas O'Braoin. What news do you bring from Fermanagh?"

Aonghas walked straight past Desmond's outstretched hand and looked upon the stunned faces of Desmond's men.

"I have no news for old men," Aonghas said. "You are retired and no longer work for the Maguire. Who is in charge here?"

He surveyed the men with such a scowl that none dared to speak.

"So no one is in charge?" Aonghas said.

"I was about to tell you..."

"Be quiet, old man. Your friendship with the dead Maguire no longer protects you. You have no authority here."

"The men listen to me," Desmond said as he drew himself up to full height.

Aonghas turned and looked at the men again.

"If any of you men who are sworn to the Maguire wish to volunteer and tell me they follow someone who does not have the blessing of the Maguire, they should step forward. But if you do so, I will deem you in breach of the oath you swore when you were admitted to the MacCabes, and you will be dealt with accordingly."

His voice rang out, daring any of the men to come up and defy him. Time stood still, and in the silence of Aonghas's stare, those he laid eyes upon felt their muscles tense as they readied themselves for action. Francisco could feel the weight of his eyes upon him, his gaze burning into his soul. His hand slowly drifted towards his dagger. Each breath seemed to hang in the air, the only sound of his heart pounding in his ears. He did not want to die this day, in this unknown bog, to rot away with the corpses of the battle. But he may not be given a choice. The scent of sweat and fear filled his nostrils, and he steeled himself for whatever may come next.

Aonghas turned his back on the men, and as no one stepped forward to assault him, the moment seemed to slip away.

"Good," said Aonghas. "Then it is I who is in command. Where is the O'Rourke? Show him to me if you still have him in your possession."

Desmond moved his lips, but Aonghas raised his finger to silence him. One of Desmond's former men opened the door to the hut where the wounded, including the O'Rourke, lay. Aonghas entered the hut and emerged a few moments later.

"It is him. I am under instruction from the Maguire to bring him back to Fermanagh. Men, take any wounded who can survive the journey back to Donegal Castle. Leave the rest and I will arrange for someone to return for them. But pack up all you can. We must leave as soon as possible."

Aonghas walked off, and Desmond followed him. Desmond's face reddened as he struggled for words and courage.

"I must protest. The Maguire sent me on a mission to get the O'Rourke to safety. You have no right to take custody of him."

Aonghas spun around and prodded his finger in Desmond's face.

"I have every right, old man, and you have none. You can leave now, for we have no use for old men who cannot fight and will only eat our valuable food. You can take the Spanish captain with you, for I have no wish to give the English the excuse to hang me."

Aonghas pointed towards Francisco, who rose to his feet when he realised he was being talked about.

"How am I supposed to return to Fermanagh?" said Desmond.

Aonghas smirked.

"How did you get here?" Aonghas pointed towards the hills, the opposite direction from which he had come. "I suggest you start walking. You wouldn't want the humiliation of me having you removed from the camp at sword point, would you?"

Desmond's shoulders slumped, and Aonghas grinned from ear to ear. Desmond signalled to Francisco to join him.

"Where are we going? Why is he doing this?"

"Just walk."

CHAPTER 34
NOMADS

F rancisco glanced over his shoulder and watched the Maguires efficiently dismantle their campsite. In front of him, Desmond meandered aimlessly through the bog, lost in thought, his feet sinking into the murky earth with each step. Francisco quickened his pace, easily striding over to join him. The damp earth squelched beneath his feet, leaving a trail of muddy footprints in his wake.

"Where are we going?"

"I don't know. West? Towards the sea? The woods will be full of beaten men, the valleys with marauding Redshanks. Aonghas knew that banishing us from the camp and the protection of the MacCabe Galloglass was a death sentence. Now we just have to choose whether we die by the axe or of starvation."

Francisco stepped in front of him and grabbed him by both shoulders.

"I have not come this far in your cold and rainy land to die now. If your howling winds could not extinguish the flame of hope in my heart, neither can you. We walk towards the sea. There is always hope for me of a passing Spanish ship, be it a trading vessel or a survivor from the Armada. You can come to Spain with me and be my guest at my house. My wife will serve you the finest home cooking and the best wine. You will never want to leave and wonder why you spent most of your life in rainy, cold Ireland. You lead us to the sea, and I will tell you tales of my homeland that will warm your heart."

Desmond hung his head.

"I'm sorry for what I did to those Spanish sailors who needed our help on the beach that first day I met you. Believe me when I tell you, meeting me was the best thing that could have happened to them. What must you think of us?"

Francisco placed his hand on Desmond's shoulder.

"You are good Catholics who, when you can stop fighting each other, take the fight to the heretic queen."

Desmond smiled.

"You are a good Catholic too, to still think kindly of us, given all that has happened to you."

"Let's not test the boundaries of my tolerance too much with this conversation, for we still have to get out of this bog alive."

Desmond raised a smile.

"Now, in which direction are we going?" said Francisco.

Desmond pointed towards the hills, and they set off and did not look back at the departing Maguires.

Their journey took them through treacherous bogs, dense forests, and rolling fields until they finally reached the valleys of the Donegal mountains. With each step, they navigated their way along the perimeter of a valley, carefully placing their feet on the steep hillsides, mindful of the protruding granite and scattered stones that threatened to trip them up. The ground was slick with mud and patches of tufted grass, making their ascent even more challenging. As they reached the top of the valley, there was no shelter in sight to shield them from view. Desmond's hand pointed at a large herd of cattle slowly making their way towards them, their hooves creating a soft drumbeat against the earth.

"Surely we can walk around them?" said Francisco.

"There's no point in trying. It is one of the herds of the O'Donnell. If it is being driven south, it is to support Ineen Dubh and her reconquest of Tirconnell. We will inevitably run into one of their scouts. Better to walk towards them as a friend than for them to ride us down as if we were stragglers from Donnell O'Donnell's army."

"Speak for yourself," said Francisco.

"Well, if you feel compelled to confess, stand at least blood-splatter distance away from me when they decapitate you."

Francisco smirked.

"We wouldn't want to get your breeches any more dirty than they are now."

"Indeed we wouldn't. Who knows, we may be meeting Ineen Dubh herself soon. I don't want to plead for my life with bloody breeches. She'd never see me pissing myself."

Francisco slapped him on the back.

"Well then, let us go whilst you are still presentable."

Francisco and Desmond stood in the heart of the valley, surrounded by a sea of grazing cows. The air was thick with the pungent scent of sweat and manure, and the sound of heavy breathing and sharpening blades filled their ears. Scruffy men with unkempt hair and bushy beards emerged from between the cows and surrounded them. They brandished swords, spears and daggers, pointing them at their captives.

Francisco's heart raced as he scanned the rugged faces. Desmond stood tall, his eyes darting between the armed men, calculating their next move.

"I am an emissary from the Maguire," he said. "Take me to your leader."

Francisco saw Desmond's leg shake in his breeches but was consoled that the pissing had not started. An old man with flowing white hair and a face as creased as the mountains and valleys of Tirconnell, where he had obviously spent most of his life wandering, emerged from behind the armed herders.

"Which leader do you want to meet?" he said. "The Maguire was the lackey of Donnell O'Donnell."

Desmond paused.

"We are here to speak with Ineen Dubh on behalf of the Maguire. He wishes to make peace with the new ruler of Tirconnell."

Francisco gulped, knowing he was at the mercy of Desmond's guile.

The leader of the herders grinned and removed the piece of grass he was chewing from his mouth.

"A wise choice. For we could have easily arranged for you to meet Donnell O'Donnell by cutting off your heads and throwing your bodies in the next valley with the rest of his men. Now we must work out if delivering you alive to Ineen Dubh is worth more than just delivering your heads."

Desmond raised his hand to speak, and the herdsmen raised their weapons.

"No," came a female voice. "Leave them."

Desmond turned to see it was the woman who he had turfed out of the hut so he could give it to the O'Rourke and the other wounded. Francisco saw Desmond's jowls about to move, so he placed his hand on Desmond's forearm, for he did not see malice in the woman's face.

"They could have killed me and all our families, but this man protected and fed us. Repay his kindness by bringing him to Ineen Dubh and accept what rewards we are given, for you have already been rewarded with the lives of your families."

The leader of the herdsmen signalled for his people to be silent, and then he walked up and eyeballed Desmond. Desmond could smell the foulness of his breath and saw the sizeable gaps between his few remaining teeth.

"You showed my people kindness when most would have killed them or used them to blackmail us. We will grant you your wish. Bring that what it may."

He walked away and signalled for his men to follow him.

"We are going to sit in a valley above Donegal Castle as Ineen Dubh lays waste to the remains of Donnell O'Donnell's men."

"No."

Desmond ran after him.

"It is imperative that I get to Donegal Castle as soon as possible."

"What's your rush? You're too old to fight. The youngsters would quickly make mincemeat of you. Why are you so keen to die?"

"Some of my compatriots, those who would have killed your families, have the O'Rourke as a prisoner and mean to kill him."

"What is that to me? The O'Rourke is nothing but a story as we roam Tirconnell. Why should I care about him?"

"Because if West Breifne falls to the English or they impose one of their sheriffs, the more likely that Tirconnell will suffer the same fate, and the queen will requisition the O'Donnell's herd and probably kill you in the process."

The herdsman turned around and sighed.

"You outsiders all have your reasons to do everything now. No wonder you are at each other's throats all the time. I prefer the simple life and follow the cows. However, if you insist on an early grave, I will repay your kindness to my daughter. You will be fed and my riders will escort you to the camp of Ineen Dubh. After that, it is up to you, for your previous kindness will have been repaid."

"Ineen Dubh will hear about your kindness and wisdom," said Desmond.

"She already knows, she already knows."

CHAPTER 35

LEAVE THE RESCUE MISSIONS TO THE YOUNG AND FOOLISH

The hoofbeats of the horses of Francisco, Desmond, and their escorts echoed through the deserted camp of Ineen Dubh as they rode towards Donegal Castle. They had heard rumours that the fortress had fallen without a single shot being fired as Donnell O'Donnell's army had disintegrated after his defeat and death. As they approached the castle's walls, they could see the same scars and battle damage that had been there months before. But now, there was a palpable sense of triumph instead of an air of defeat and despair. As they rode into the courtyard, they saw soldiers laughing and sharing stories of victory. As they dismounted, they were greeted by a fierce-looking MacSweeney Galloglass constable who stood in front of their horses and eyed them up and down.

"I don't remember you from the battle. Who are you, and where did you come from?"

The constable obviously had been at the battle, for his armour was freshly dented and badly cleaned. The glint in his eye said he had not finished killing his enemies yet.

"We come from Enniskillen and have lost our escort," said Desmond. "We were bringing the O'Rourke northwards for his own safety until another group of Maguires abducted him. We are in fear of the O'Rourke's safety and seek help."

The constable grinned.

"That's an elaborate tale indeed, full of deceptions. Based on your story and what happened yesterday, there are four types of Maguire in Tirconnell. Those you claim are here to protect the O'Rourke, those who have abducted him, and then some who took part in yesterday's battle on the wrong side and are still in the valley because they are dead or those that fled the battle and tell elaborate stories to preserve their lives. You don't look dead, so which of the other three are you?"

Desmond covered his nerves with a scowl.

"We are the type that are emissaries of the Maguire and Ineen Dubh will be very embarrassed that you insulted us so."

The constable signalled to his men and turned once more to Desmond.

"Come down off your horses and surrender your weapons. Once you are unarmed, we can discuss your status."

Desmond and Francisco dismounted and raised their hands.

"We are already unarmed," said Desmond. "If you take me to Ineen Dubh, she will recognise me and reward you for bringing me to her. We are wasting time here. The O'Rourke's life is in danger."

"For all your talk, you could be assassins," said the constable. "Search them, men."

The MacSweeney Galloglass patted down Desmond and Francisco. A sturdy man of around fifty with flowing white hair tucked beneath his morion suddenly paid attention while walking by.

"The O'Rourke? Brian O'Rourke? Who says he is in trouble? He is an old comrade of mine. You," he said as he pointed to the constable. "Who claimed they escorted the O'Rourke?"

The constable looked ashen-faced and stood back and pointed at Desmond.

"It was me, lord," Desmond said, his face alight with this ray of hope. "He won't be alive for much longer if we just stand around and talk. Can you get me in front of Ineen Dubh so that I may organise a rescue?"

"I can do better than that. I can give you the men to carry it out."

The woods and fields of south Tirconnell surrounded Francisco as he rode alongside Eoghan Óg MacSweeney and a fierce band of Galloglass warriors. The sound of hooves thundered through the countryside as they searched for the elusive O'Rourke, their leader's eyes sharp and determined. Desmond, too old to join in the pursuit, had chosen to stay behind, not wishing to engage in battle with other Maguire clans on foreign territory. But Francisco was needed – tasked with identifying the O'Rourke and those Maguires who had been forced into aiding in the kidnapping.

As they scoured the land, the scent of flowers and freshly cut grass filled the air, mixing with the metallic tang of swords and armour generously lubricated with sweat. The men were silent, for they knew their enemy would be formidable, and most had already had their fill of fighting. But their loyalty to Eoghan and their duty to protect their clan pushed them forward, their horses' breaths coming out in hot clouds against the cool Tirconnell air.

Francisco perched uneasily on the back of his horse, his legs straining to stay balanced as, once again, he was forced to ride without stirrups. As the rest of the riders took off at full pace, he was forced to remain at the rear, a rider always assigned to him in case he lost his balance. All he could feel was embarrassment at being relegated to the rear of the group, for fear of falling behind or losing control of his mount. He had managed when he travelled with the O'Rourke, for the O'Rourke's horse was always slow due to his weight. But now, with agile young horsemen, a once proud captain of a mighty Spanish galleon, was reduced to a mere liability on horseback.

Francisco's eyes scanned the horizon as they rode on, taking in the landscape before him. Rolling hills stretched out in all directions, their peaks shrouded in dense forests and cut through by ice-cold streams. It was a beautiful sight, if not for the fact that it seemed he had been unwittingly dragged into a pointless turf war. The O'Rourke's life hung in the balance, and even if they successfully rescued him, would anyone be willing to help them? Francisco couldn't shake off the feeling of isolation and despair, especially when he had to put his trust in a bunch of armed strangers who would cut his throat for a queen's coin.

He sighed heavily, his head dropping with defeat. What good would rescuing the O'Rourke do him? Sure, the O'Rourke had bragged about being the most wanted rebel in Ireland, but that only seemed to make people avoid him or see him as nothing more than a means to collect a bounty. As an officer in the Spanish army, he knew that his word was his bond, and he couldn't turn away from someone in need. But deep down, he couldn't help but wonder how this would bring him any closer to fulfilling his ultimate goal, returning home to Spain.

Determined to catch up with Eoghan Óg, Francisco dug his heels into the sides of his horse and urged it forward. Despite all doubts and uncertainties, he knew he had made a commitment and would see it through to the end.

Eoghan Óg halted when Francisco pulled up and pointed to the hills.

"The Kern say they are just over that hill. They are well armed but travelling slowly because of the number of carts with them."

"We need the O'Rourke alive," said Francisco, "while they would be content with him dead. We cannot approach them out in the open for fear he gets killed in the rescue attempt."

"Why is he so special to you, Spaniard?"

"He is my best and probably only hope of getting home."

"You would get plenty of employment with Ineen Dubh. A far better bet than the O'Rourke these days."

"I would still be trapped and still be a slave."

Eoghan Óg laughed and waved him away.

"Don't be so dramatic. Next, you'll be telling us it was paradise, being rolled from side to side in the storms off Scotland, throwing up all over yourself."

"You ask any of your compatriots who've served under the king of Spain how they've been treated. You'll find none of them will complain about the pay and conditions."

"Ah, but you're all civilised, fighting in the sunshine and taking a day off if it gets a bit muddy or rainy. We've got to make the best of what we've got."

Francisco laughed.

"So you've never served overseas?"

"I've always found plenty of people to kill here profitably. Why turn my nose up at a good thing outside my door?"

"So how do you know the O'Rourke?"

"Plenty of Scottish mercenaries come through my port. The O'Rourke was always on the lookout and came and stayed several times. Hence, I would consider him a friend and risk my own men for him."

"So there is honour here after all?"

Eoghan Óg turned his horse to ride away.

"Of course. You just didn't know what it was."

Francisco ignored Eoghan Óg's grin.

"So, how are we going to get on with saving my master and your friend?"

Eoghan Óg pointed to the horizon.

"The Kern will drive them east so they cannot reach Fermanagh within the day where we cannot attack them. Once they camp, we'll assault at nightfall."

"Will the O'Rourke be safe?"

"I can't guarantee it, but if he is unlucky but lucky, he'll die fighting."

Eoghan Óg grinned again, and Francisco longed for the company of the arrogance of the O'Rourke, his only defence against being a prisoner of the O'Donnells.

As the sun dipped below the horizon, casting a crimson glow over the land, the Maguires sought refuge in a small clearing within the dense woods. They had been on the run all day, constantly pursued by the O'Donnell Kern without ever truly coming face to face with their hunters. But Aonghas O'Braoin was not taking any chances with his prized possession and made sure to take every precaution possible.

Francisco stood at the edge of the woods, his body concealed behind a towering tree as he gazed into the impenetrable darkness ahead. He was tasked with being one of the first to infiltrate the enemy's camp, using his keen eye to distinguish friend from foe. His heart raced as he mentally prepared himself for whatever horrors awaited him on this dangerous mission.

Eoghan Óg, who appeared brave, if not foolhardy, signalled for his chosen men to follow him as they prepared for the attack. The rest of their group remained hidden, awaiting their signal to join in. The air was still and carried only the sounds of the animals of the woods and the faint whiff of smoke.

As the night air grew colder, the Maguire clan huddled beside their fires, their hastily gathered blankets and coats offering little relief from the chill. Despite the warmth of the fire, several men huddled together in a pool of semi-darkness, hoarding what little heat they could. Guards patrolled the perimeter of the camp, their shadows flickering in the light of the roaring flames. The warm glow of the fires offered some illumination, but beyond their reach, the darkness loomed like a predator waiting to strike.

Francisco gripped the sheath of his dagger tightly, trying to calm his nerves as a bead of sweat rolled down the small of his back. He knew this would be a difficult task.

Meanwhile, hidden behind the trees surrounding the camp, the MacSweeney clan prepared for their attack. A rustling in the distance signalled activity in the woods, causing tension among the guards at the edge of the camp. The distant howls of wolves added to the eerie atmosphere but also served to calm the guards' nerves, as it meant there were no imminent threats approaching.

Out of the darkness erupted a fierce explosion, engulfing everything in a blazing inferno. A deafening roar echoed through the air as a stampede of horses trampled over the perimeter guards, crushing their bodies into oblivion with each hoof strike and flaming torches setting fire to anything combustible. The smell of the burning flesh of the Maguires filled the air as the flames continued to rage on, leaving nothing but destruction in their wake.

"AT THEM, MEN," cried Eoghan Óg and he and the MacSweeneys charged out from behind the trees with their axes, scything down anyone in their way. The audacity of the attack swept all before it. Aonghas O'Braoin threw off his blanket and picked up his axe.

"Behead the O'Rourke. Let us not let our brothers' sacrifice be in vain."

With a blood-curdling scream, he charged towards O'Rourke, who struggled to lift himself up in time. Towering over his prey, Aonghas raised his axe high, ready to deliver a fatal blow. But as he swung down with all his might, Brendan, lying wounded nearby, mustered all his strength and stabbed a sturdy stick into Aonghas's side. Though not sharp enough to draw blood, the blow was enough to distract the towering warrior for just a moment. Aonghas was consumed with rage.

"You'll pay for that," said Aonghas, and his axe found Brendan's head instead.

Aonghas turned, and to his horror, where once lay the O'Rourke was only flattened grass. He turned, and ten feet away, Francisco extended his hand to help the O'Rourke up. Aonghas turned to rally his men, but he saw only foes around him.

"RETREAT MEN, RETREAT," Aonghas roared, and his men ran for the woods.

Eoghan Óg signalled for his men to let them go, for he had seen enough bloodshed the past couple of days. He walked over to Francisco and embraced the O'Rourke.

"Come, stay with me, and I will give you shelter."

"Will you help me hire mercenaries to take to West Breifne?" said the O'Rourke in between coughs due to the smoke.

"Let's see how you heal up first, shall we?"

CHAPTER 36
LICKING HIS WOUNDS

The ride back to Donegal Castle did not sit well with the O'Rourke, and its strain caused his health to spiral downwards. Since Eoghan Óg had been summoned to the castle to appear before Ineen Dubh, Francisco assumed responsibility for tending to the welfare of the O'Rourke and ensuring he received proper medical treatment.

"At the bottom of the hill is the camp for the wounded and dying," Eoghan Óg said as he paused before the castle gates. "Go find a physician there. If anyone refuses him immediate attention, tell them I sent you on the orders of Ineen Dubh."

Francisco nodded, and Eoghan Óg's men helped the O'Rourke off his horse and onto the support of Francisco's shoulder. Francisco and the O'Rourke trudged down the hill towards the camp, but they could hardly miss it, for all they had to do was follow the bodies along the roadside and the stink of rotting flesh.

Once they reached the camp, the horror left after the battle of Doire Leathan hit them straight in the face. The desperate pleas and grasping hands of wounded men haunted their every step, their festering wounds reeking of death and neglect. More injured arrived by the cartload dumped unceremoniously at the edge of a growing sea of severed limbs and decaying flesh. Bands of women scoured the makeshift hospital in search of their loved ones, their cries drowned out by the constant moans and groans of agony of the wounded men. Francisco soon noticed the status of the different types of men for nobody wanted the mercenaries intertwined between the sprawling bodies of the native O'Don-nells. That is, except their comrades who seldom came searching, for they still had to fight and earn their wages pursuing the last of Donnell O'Donnell's supporters out of Tirconnell.

With the weight of the O'Rourke upon his shoulder, Francisco caught the attention of one of the women attending the wounded.

"Please, can you help my friend?"

She raised her exhausted-looking blood-spattered face and looked disappointed when she saw the O'Rourke was another of the wounded.

"Look at what I already have to deal with," she said as she pointed to the man sitting groaning in front of her. "If he is not going to die, he'll have to wait."

Francisco furrowed his eyebrows.

"Where are all these men coming from?"

The woman sighed.

"They are still arriving in from the battle of Doire Leathan and all over south Tyrconnell," she said as she turned to bandage the man sitting before her. "Wily Ineen Dubh has a monopoly on all the physicians in Tyrconnell and has gathered them all here. Only the men of those lords who have surrendered are entitled to use her physicians, and the mercenaries have to change allegiance to be accepted in. As she hunts them all down, they slowly surrender, hence the unending arrivals of wounded men."

Francisco pointed at the O'Rourke, who had turned white.

"Can you attend to him? I was sent here by Eoghan Óg MacSweeney on the orders of Ineen Dubh herself."

She took one look at the O'Rourke and shook her head.

"He is beyond my help. You'll need a physician for him. Over there in that tent." She pointed to a large queue of wounded men. "Try there. They should be able to cure him if anyone can."

"Thank you for your kindness," said Francisco as he bowed his head.

"I would mind yourself around here, Spaniard," she replied. "Many a spy or a desperate man is willing to take the reward for giving you up to the English."

"I will be wary," Francisco said, "and thank you for the warning."

Francisco and the O'Rourke set off in the direction she had pointed to.

Francisco arrived at a large tent with only one wall to block the wind. He scowled at those who shouted abuse at him for skipping the queue, but they could do nothing about it as they were too badly injured to stop him. There were several physicians there wrapping limbs in bandages, applying leeches to wounds and severing limbs. No one paid him attention as the woman and boys assisting the physicians scurried around him. He stood beside the physician, who looked the most senior, but the man did not look up from his work. The stench was as if he had descended into the bowels of hell with the accompanying screams of men in pain, which pierced the constant low hum of agony. The physician severed a man's arm at the elbow, for his wound had turned black, and the man had lost the use of his limb. He waved at his assistants to take the man away. The physician turned, took a drink, and mopped his brow. His last patient would never be the once proud warrior he had been days before and never wield an axe again. He would likely become a beggar reliant on charity to live as he went from house to house, or he would lead the short life of a thief in the woods until his former comrades hunted him down.

Francisco saw the troubles etched on the physician's face and saw that there were men here in far worse condition than the O'Rourke, whose most life-threatening condition was depression. But he had to get the physician's attention to ensure the O'Rourke would regain his confidence and be able to get him back to Spain. Francisco tapped him on the shoulder, and the physician picked up his cleaver and spun around.

"Excuse me," said Francisco. "I am sorry to disturb you, but I have someone very important who urgently needs your attention."

Francisco smiled but could barely look the man in the eye.

"I am surrounded by men who urgently need my attention," said the physician. "Who is so important that you barge in and demand I must deal with them now?"

The physician turned to Francisco, his face a peculiar shade of red as anger, stress, and tiredness swirled around it.

"It is the O'Rourke, the lord of West Breifne. You may find a man with worse injuries than him, but none are as important."

The physician laughed and brushed past Francisco.

"Every battlefield is littered with the bodies of lords, chieftains and any type of gentry you may wish to name. The victors ride away with their titles and reputations intact and may be enhanced, and the rest remain in the field or cower until they are hunted down and killed. If this man is as important as you say he is, bring him to the castle and let Ineen Dubh take care of him. Otherwise, get out of my way, or I will have you removed."

Francisco opened his mouth to speak, but the physician had already moved on to his next patient. Francisco realised he had no purchase with the man and turned and went back towards the castle to see if Eoghan Óg MacSweeney could help him.

Francisco leaned against the stone gate of Donegal Castle. His broad shoulders supported the weight of the ailing O'Rourke. He had picked up some mysterious ailment from the hospital camp and could barely walk. The scent of sickness and sweat filled the air as the man groaned in discomfort, his once-robust frame now frail and depleted. The O'Rourke had proved such a burden that Francisco had paid a boy to fetch Eoghan Óg, who came to get them from the camp. Hooves echoed off the stone walls as Eoghan Óg rode on his horse and called for the guards to open the massive gates.

"Open up. I have the O'Rourke here, and he wishes to see Ineen Dubh and the O'Donnell."

A Galloglass constable peered over the wall.

"What side did he get his injuries fighting for?"

"The O'Rourke is one of the most powerful men in Ireland," said Francisco to the constable.

"He doesn't look like that from here," said the constable.

"He calls upon the O'Donnell to honour the treaties and alliances between the two clans. He also asks that he see a physician if the O'Donnell would be so kind as to provide one."

The constable disappeared, and moments later, the gate was opened. He stood before them with several armed Galloglass behind him. The constable pointed to the O'Rourke, moving in and out of consciousness, his head rolling around his shoulders.

"He could be anyone, but since Eoghan Óg MacSweeney will vouch for him, we will believe you. There is no room in the tower for the entire army is camped in the surrounding hills. If he waits in the courtyard, he will be attended to."

They sat beside some barrels, which provided some shelter from the wind.

"Let me see what I can arrange," said Eoghan Óg, and he set off for the tower.

CHAPTER 37
BEING SET STRAIGHT

After several days of questioning and investigation, O'Rourke's identity was confirmed. Now, he sat in the grand hall of the O'Donnell castle, flanked by Francisco and Eoghan Óg MacSweeney on either side.

The room was adorned with tapestries depicting battles and legends of old, while a large fireplace crackled and cast a warm glow over the scene. Some of the tapestries appeared remarkably free of dust or discolouration as if each faction had redecorated when they took over the castle, so it appeared their faction of the clan had the right to rule all along.

Desmond had rejoined them after resting on a nearby farm in the interim. They spoke in hushed tones, planning how best to represent their cause. As they discussed plans and strategies for the upcoming discussions, a sense of camaraderie and determination filled the air. Outside, the sun began to set over the rolling hills of Ireland, casting a golden light through the windows as nature ignored the feuds of men.

A hush fell over the room as Ineen Dubh, accompanied by her husband, entered. He shuffled slowly, bent with the weight of age, and she lovingly helped him into his seat. Their genuine affection was evident as she leaned close to his mouth, listening intently to his whispered words. She straightened up and smoothed her green dress, embroidered with intricate Celtic patterns in shimmering gold thread. With a graceful air of formality and authority, she commanded the attention of all in the room. Despite being likely in her late thirties or early forties, strands of grey streaked through her long brown hair, adding wisdom and maturity to her pleasant features. The occasional crease on her face only served to enhance her beauty and charisma, contradicting the ferocious reputation she had garnered. Standing confidently beside her husband, their hands intertwined with silent strength, Ineen Dubh exuded power and grace. Francisco and the O'Rourke bowed in deference, and then Francisco respectfully stepped back to give the O'Rourke the floor.

"Thank you for seeing me."

The O'Rourke raised his head, but his voice was not the same as that which boomed merely weeks before, and his hand shook behind his leg as if a bout of nerves was the last symptom of his recent ailment.

"I have seen for myself that Tirconnell is in turmoil, and I wish you every success in finally reaching an agreement as the succession to the O'Donnell is settled."

Ineen Dubh smirked.

"My husband is not dead yet. He may be silent, but he still sits attentively by my side."

The O'Rourke bowed again.

"I mean you no insult."

"Did you mean to insult me in the battle of Doire Leathan? My men tell me they saw you running away from the battle afterwards and obtained your injuries then."

"I apologise for any insult I may have caused you. I was coerced. I came with only my man Francisco here, Desmond, a diplomat from the Maguires and a bodyguard who now lies dead. I was easy to manipulate. I came to Tirconnell to hire mercenaries to return and free my own lands from the English. I am not here to get embroiled in any internal O'Donnell feuds."

"That is good to hear, but can anyone vouch for these words? I hear many utterances of surrender, submission and false friendship these days. It is hard to know who to trust. Will the Maguire's man speak up for you?"

Desmond stepped forward and hung his head.

"The Maguire always seeks to honour his alliances."

"Including the one he made with Donnell O'Donnell?"

A bead of sweat rolled down Desmond's forehead.

"The Maguire always seeks to maintain good relations with his O'Donnell and O'Neill neighbours. You can hardly blame him for siding with Donnell when he gave him so much help to become the Maguire."

"If he had asked us, we may have assisted."

Desmond tried to settle the jitters in his stomach.

"I am not here in an official capacity for the Maguire and, therefore, cannot speak for him."

"So then you are an intruder, a spy here to cause trouble?"

"I am here as an old comrade of the O'Rourke to help him in his hour of need."

"Eoghan Óg?" said Ineen Dubh.

Eoghan Óg stepped forward and bowed his head.

"I can also only vouch for him as an old comrade."

Ineen Dubh sat and looked at her husband, who gave a faint nod. She stood once more to give her verdict.

"Irrespective that we found you siding with our enemy in the recent battle, we are prepared to give you the benefit of the doubt and believe your story about your intentions. The O'Donnells keep their promises, so you will be granted sanctuary. Eoghan Óg, will you host your comrade for the duration of his stay, no matter how long that may be?"

Eoghan Óg nodded. The O'Rourke smiled.

"However," continued Ineen Dubh, "my mother and I control the hiring of mercenaries in the north. You will be granted a licence to hire mercenaries from Scotland once and only when I allow it. This should be when all of Tirconnell is united."

Ineen Dubh turned to Francisco, who bowed in front of her.

"Spanish captain, I have heard rumours of English mercenaries hunting you. I have no wish to provide an excuse for the English to come onto my lands. Nor for them to use you as an excuse to impose an English sheriff upon us. Therefore, we will not assist you in returning to Spain nor allow you to roam my lands freely. However, you will be bound to the O'Rourke while he is on our lands as a reward for the loyal service you have provided him. So whatever happens to him happens to you. You may have sanctuary with the O'Rourke as long as he is on our lands."

Francisco went white but held his tongue. Ineen Dubh turned to Desmond.

"As for you, Desmond MacCabe, I suggest you return to your master post-haste, for he may have tasks for you. Do not return to Tirconnell again, giving the impression you represent the Maguire when you do not. Now go before I change my mind."

The O'Rourke opened his mouth to protest, but Eoghan Óg and Desmond pushed him out of the room as Francisco followed. His eyes were full of tears as he saw his dream of returning to Spain once again evaporate before his eyes.

Guided by their armed escorts, they descended the winding steps of the castle tower and emerged into the sunlit courtyard. The ground was hard and uneven beneath their feet, with patches of wild grass peeking out between the cobblestones. In front of them stood three imposing figures on horseback, their MacSweeney armour gleaming in the light. Beside them, a spare mount stamped impatiently, its breath misting in the cool air.

"Is one of you Desmond MacCabe?" said the constable. "If so, this horse is for you courtesy of Ineen Dubh."

Desmond put up his hand and smirked.

"She really lets you know when you're not wanted."

The constable spat.

"She doesn't like being deceived. She's not the most trusting. Now, are you going to ride this horse, or are we going to have to tie you to it?"

Desmond raised his hands in surrender.

"I'm too old to be a prisoner. I have too many aches and pains, never mind the prospect of being tied to a horse. I'm sure you'll spare me a moment to say my goodbyes."

"Don't be too long, for we have better things to be doing than escorting the likes of you off our lands."

Desmond turned to the O'Rourke and extended his arms. The O'Rourke fell into his embrace, still gripped by his illness.,

"Goodbye, my friend," Desmond said, his words slightly muffled by the O'Rourke's collar protruding into his face. "I hope you find what you are looking for."

The O'Rourke slapped him on the back as hard as he could.

"Try not to get yourself killed on the way home." The O'Rourke broke out of the embrace and held Desmond by the shoulders. "And tell the Maguire from me you deserve a far better reward for your retirement than that freezing cold island."

Desmond laughed and turned to Francisco. He hesitated and then held out his hand.

"Surely I deserve better than that," Francisco said and he embraced Desmond.

"I hope God treats you better than Ireland did," Desmond said, "and he gives you the wind on your back to get you home to Spain."

"So do I, my friend, so do I."

Desmond was helped onto the back of the horse. He gave a brief wave before one of the MacSweeney gave his horse a gentle smack and he was through the gates of the castle and gone.

The O'Rourke was granted permission to stay in Donegal Castle until he was fit enough to travel north. He was grateful indeed for the small kindness Ineen Dubh granted him. Unfortunately, he considered it an opportunity to persuade

Ineen Dubh of the merits of giving him mercenaries. He soon began to wear out his welcome. Eoghan Óg MacSweeney, in the meantime, was sent to south Tirconnell to lay siege to the last of the Donnell O'Donnell supporters.

Francisco now had the opportunity to rest, feed himself properly, and catch up with the other happenings in the world. He soon found the ear of a young priest keen to find out about the ways of Spain. It quickly transpired the priest was going to a Jesuit school in Spain, so Francisco wrote letters to his family, which he gave to the priest. The kindness was limited, however, as the priest did not want to be discovered by a Spanish captain on his ship. If he were, the English tolerance for the illegal trade routes would surely vanish. The priest broke it to Francisco as he left and set off for the port without him. Exhausted by the constant cycle of having his hopes raised then dashed, he took to drinking with the soldiers in the camp and this brief comradeship lifted his spirits, if only a little.

The O'Rourke was by now receiving regular medical attention, so he would be fit enough to make the journey to take up residence in Eoghan's castle. He was confined to a simple room in the castle beside the servants' quarters to not draw attention to himself. Weak he may have been, the plots and schemes to raise an army and return to Breifne still buzzed in his head. He summoned Francisco to his room, and Francisco came quickly, his face etched with worry that his greatest hope for getting home had become mortally ill. After being permitted to enter, he opened the door to the O'Rourke's room.

The O'Rourke sat regally in a large, cushioned chair, his rugged face illuminated by the dancing flames of the fire that crackled in front of him. His once wild and unkempt hair had been tamed and combed back, revealing a strong jawline and piercing blue eyes. Despite the makeshift sling for his injured arm, his posture exuded strength and confidence. The heat from the fire warmed not only his old bones but also his spirit, bringing a healthy flush to his cheeks.

"Come and sit," said the O'Rourke, extending his hand towards an empty chair. "We must talk of the goings-on in the world and where next for our mission. Have you heard anything from West Breifne, as you have kept your ear to the ground for news?"

Francisco came and sat but did not look the O'Rourke in the eye, for he had no desire to dash the brittle good spirits his master had constructed and pollute them with his melancholy.

"There is but threadbare news of Breifne," said Francisco. "For all the talk is to what extent Ineen Dubh will exact retribution on her enemies. Whatever room is left for other discussion is about the O'Neill power struggle."

The O'Rourke sighed and threw his good hand in the air.

"So that is it? Breifne will burn for the lords of the north have their noses in their own petty squabbles so they cannot see the bigger picture of one of the last great clans falling to the English. Do they not realise that once I fall, they will come for them next?"

Francisco sighed, for it was as if his master had not learned anything. But it was time for some truth.

"Lord, we both sit here together more as friends than master and servant, for even you will admit that your power has been stripped from you."

The O'Rourke roared with laughter.

"You're one to talk about reality! Once a captain of a mighty Spanish ship having to lower himself to run after an Irish chieftain like an obedient hound. Yes, you can make your point to me about how much I have fallen, how no one wants to know me, and they fear that sheltering me will bring the English down upon them. Then what? Do you feel clever for a few moments? Does it boost your ego ever so slightly to see someone who may have, and I say may have, fallen further than you? Then what? Do you sit and watch while my confidence drains from me and I become a shell of the man I once was? Then what?"

The O'Rourke leaned forward.

"Then your status as the captain of a once mighty Spanish ship is restored. But what happens to that? I'll tell you. Then you become the captain of a Spanish ship with the price of as much money as the Irish farmer sees in a lifetime on your head. Then what happens to the Spanish ship's captain?"

The O'Rourke pulled upon an imaginary rope around his neck and stuck his tongue out as if in the final throws of death. Francisco bowed his head and stared into the fire.

"I will spare the ship's captain the embarrassment of apologising to his protector and pretending the conversation never happened."

Francisco grimaced and looked at the floor.

"I'm sorry. I thought you needed to hear that."

"Well, evidently, I didn't. Now, will you continue your mission for both of our sakes? A civil war is always a great draw for mercenaries, not only from Scotland but also from the other clans. There must be some O'Rourkes about. Seek them out. See if they have any news from West Breifne and if they are available for hire if they do not wish to fight for their clan for free."

"Where will I find these men?"

"In the camps surrounding the town. The bravest ones will be camped beneath the O'Rourke banner." The O'Rourke shrugged. "I would go myself, but we both know how much attention I draw to myself these days. Such is the price on my head."

Francisco rose and squeezed his fist.

"I will return with good news so we can put our failures behind us."

"I have seen nothing to show that my luck has changed. Therefore, come back in good spirits no matter what news you have for me and avoid disappointment."

Francisco nodded and left.

A sharp, insistent knock resounded through the quiet room. The O'Rourke's body tensed as he got out of his chair, muscles ready for action. He carefully moved the cushion from behind the door, its fabric worn and frayed from years of use as a draught excluder. He took a deep breath and stepped back cautiously, keeping a wary eye on the door, ready to defend himself if needed.

"State your name and enter if you be a friend," said the O'Rourke.

A cough came from behind the door.

"It is I, Francisco. I searched until I could bring back some news."

"Then open the door and join me by the fire. If your news brings me down, your company should compensate for it."

Francisco opened the door. He shivered as he shuffled in, the blanket around his shoulders not providing enough solace. The O'Rourke extended his hand to invite him to sit. He leaned forward and gave a reassuring smile to Francisco as if to say there was nothing he could tell him that would be that bad.

"Would you like some soup before you tell me how bad everything is?"

"Do I need to tell you what you already know? Some soup would be nice, though."

The O'Rourke went to the door and poked his head outside. He came back in when he had barked his orders down the stairs. He sat and sighed.

"So, will they fight for me or not?"

"Your son is a bandit in the woods, and they have no desire to join him."

"Would they rally to my cause if I could hire an army of mercenaries?"

"They think you would be dead first. Rumours abound of the price on your head. English spies have been inquiring about your whereabouts. It is no secret that you are here. They fear the price is so high that you will be assassinated or kidnapped soon, so there is no point in risking their lives for a dead man."

The O'Rourke shot out of his seat and made for the door.

"Then my time here is done. I will inform Eoghan Óg that I am ready to go when he is."

CHAPTER 38
BAD TIDINGS

Eoghan Óg MacSweeney provided a small escort for the O'Rourke to aid his escape under the cloak of night but did not join himself as he was otherwise preoccupied in southern Tyrconnell. The group crept out of Donegal Castle, staying within the shadows and avoiding any hint of moonlight. They trod lightly, taking only the mountain paths and the less-travelled tracks as they made their way northwards through Tirconnell. The soft rustle of leaves and branches accompanied their journey, broken only by the occasional sound of horses' hooves on the hardened ground. Suddenly, a scout rode up to the O'Rourke, his horse snorting and shifting anxiously in the dark.

"Lord, we are being followed."

"By how many?"

"It is hard to say. Single riders appear and ride off if they think they have been spotted. Then another scout appears from a different direction, and the pattern repeats."

"How long have they been following us?"

"Certainly since daylight, but more likely since we left Donegal Castle."

The O'Rourke creased his brow and scratched his beard.

"How long until we reach our destination?"

"Less than a day, lord. But if they are after you, we do not want them to know where you are going."

"Then take us somewhere we can ambush them. I would rather die with a sword in my hand than be hunted down in Tirconnell."

The scout paused and then smiled.

"I know just the place."

Francisco lay sprawled on the rough ground, the hard earth pressing against his body. His teeth chattered together, creating a symphony of clacking and grinding that echoed through his head. The cold seeped through his clothes, numbing his skin and leaving him shivering uncontrollably. Every muscle in his body tightened with the effort to stay warm, but it seemed hopeless. He wondered if this would be his final resting place, alone in the unforgiving wilderness.

"Can you not control your mouth?" said the O'Rourke who lay beside him. "I'd get you another blanket if I could, but the enemy is nearly upon us, and I don't want your rattling to give us away."

Francisco edged closer to the O'Rourke so he could whisper.

"Why did you pick a bare hill face upon which to lie before we pounce upon our enemies? How am I supposed to capitalise on the element of surprise when my limbs are frozen so?"

"The cold, the cold, it's always the cold," the O'Rourke sneered. "The luck was not with you when you landed on our shores, that's for sure. How about we make you a grave of granite rocks if you fall today? Then you'll be entombed in the cold forever. You could shake in your grave, rattling the stones, frightening everyone away."

The O'Rourke bulged out his eyes and shook his limbs as if he were the cold ghost of Francisco. But Francisco was having none of it.

"If only you had told me that on the day I stood in the hall and promised to help you for the sake of my men. I should have lied and at least died trying to get back to Spain."

The O'Rourke tutted for Francisco had definitely lost his sense of humour.

"The top of a cold mountain is no place for regrets. The wind goes through you twice as quickly. Now, be quiet. I can see the specks of horsemen on the horizon."

They poked their heads above the rock and observed as horsemen congregated on top of a hill at the head of the valley they were perched above.

"Do you recognise any of them?" asked Francisco.

"They are wearing cloaks, so it is hard to tell. They wander around as if unfamiliar with the landscape, so I would say they are mercenaries."

"Are they going to fall into our trap?"

"One can only hope."

The O'Rourke extended his neck so his head protruded further above the rock.

"What is it?" said Francisco.

"Some are breaking off, but the main body is entering the valley."

"Good. Then let us see what fate holds for us. At least it would get me off this godforsaken rock."

Francisco felt for his weapons placed beside his leg. He had a bow, a weapon he used as a child but a weapon he had become reacquainted with on this devil's island. They fight petty squabbles with the weapons of children, he thought. But he reached for his bow and nocked his first arrow. The O'Rourke slapped his hand against the rock.

"It is nearly time to put your hours of practice to the test."

Francisco's heart thundered in his chest, and his mind raced, calculating the trajectory of his arrow amid the howling winds. He knew he was at a disadvantage, unfamiliar with these harsh conditions. But could he trust his fellow Galloglass soldiers to have his back? Suddenly, a sharp pebble struck his arm. The O'Rourke glared at him and pointed urgently over the hill. Francisco drew his bow and prepared for battle without hesitation as the O'Rourke leapt up.

"AT THEM, MEN!"

A storm of arrows rained down from the hilltop, piercing the air with deadly accuracy. The horses below whinnied and bucked wildly as their riders were mercilessly thrown to the ground. The fleeing warriors on horseback galloped frantically down the valley, desperate to escape the hellish onslaught. O'Rourke lifted his massive axe high above his head with a primal roar.

"FINISH THEM!"

With a fierce, guttural cry, the O'Rourke pushed through the pain in his arm and charged down the hill with reckless abandon, fuelled by a desperate desire for revenge. As he swung his axe wildly, men fell to their knees or onto their backs, helpless against the brutal force of his blows. Blood sprayed from severed limbs and the O'Rourke's face twisted into a sadistic grin as he revelled in the carnage. Nothing could quell his rage, not even the surrendering soldiers who begged for mercy before meeting their gruesome demise under his blade. This was his way of taking out his fury, one life at a time.

"Master."

The blade severed another limb.

"Master."

The O'Rourke wrenched his axe from the head of his foe. A hand grabbed his forearm.

"Master," said Francisco. "I have saved one from your wrath, so we may see who sent him. Come, let the wounded lie in peace and find out who your real enemy is."

The O'Rourke kicked the man who knelt before him in the chest and grunted a curse at him as he fell. The O'Rourke loomed over a quivering wreck of a man whose blood pumped out from his shoulder.

"Give him something to hold in the blood," said the O'Rourke to his men. "Now, who are you, and who sent you? You have until I decide the most apt way to kill you since you pursued me into the mountains." He stood up and stroked his chin. "I think I may cast you from the nearest cliff." He looked at the man and still saw defiance. "What if we tie you to a rock to represent the bounty you would have got for me, and your head would smash on the rocks below all the more violently."

The man's eyes darted around in their sockets.

"You'll let me go if I tell you?"

"If you tell me where I'd find them, I'd even give you a piece of stale bread for your journey."

"I'm a Burke from Clanricard, sent by the earl to bring you back to Galway. A one-armed English captain leads us called Williamson. He can get us a reward for our efforts from the crown and the governor of Connacht."

The O'Rourke bent down into the man's personal space to eyeball him.

"Tell me about this one-armed captain?"

"He is a bounty hunter who mainly chases down and kills Irish soldiers from the Dutch wars returning home to their clans. He is a priest hunter, too."

"Tell me, are you a good Catholic man, or have you fallen for the coin and prospects of the queen's heathen religion?"

"A good Catholic, lord."

"Then how can you work for that man?" The O'Rourke swung his axe clean through the neck of the man knelt before him. He wiped the blood from the axe onto the man's coat.

"Search around and make sure we are not being followed. Then let's get to our final destination. I'm famished."

CHAPTER 39
THE CRASH OF WAVES

Finally free from the constant paranoia of being followed, they pressed on with their journey until they reached the rugged north coast of Tirconnell. The wind here was relentless, whipping off the sea in great gusts that cut through layers of clothing and froze bones to the core. Francisco pulled his blanket tightly around him, but it offered little protection against the biting cold. The coastal landscape spread out before them, a wild and untamed beauty that commanded respect and awe. White-capped waves crashed against rocky cliffs, sending sprays of salty water into the air.

The wind whipped through Francisco's hair, carrying with it the unmistakable tang of salt and seaweed. It was a reminder of the ocean's untamed power, like the devils of the deep offering a small taste of their fury. Standing on the shore, Francisco felt like a tiny boat being tossed about by the mountainous waves of a colossal storm. The roar of the ocean echoed in his ears, drowning out all other sounds and filling him with a sense of both exhilaration and fear.

"There it is."

The scout's outstretched arm pointed to their new residence, a grand Irish castle that stood tall and proud. Its grey walls were solid granite, jutting out on the peninsula like a rocky island in the sea. Surrounding it on three sides were sheer cliffs, overlooking the tumultuous waters of the Atlantic Ocean below. The dense woods had been cleared away, leaving only one approach road leading to the castle gates. As they drew closer, Francisco could see someone riding out to greet them, a precaution, as any visitors could be seen from miles away in this open terrain. The chief scout rode forward to speak with their escort, who signalled for the gates to open. Francisco couldn't help but shiver at the sight of the castle, its exposed position reminding him of the harsh mountains they had just crossed to arrive here. The wind whipped through his hair and stung his face, making him yearn for the shelter of the castle walls.

They rode into the courtyard, and the MacSweeney constable that Eoghan Óg MacSweeney had left in charge came out and embraced the O'Rourke.

"Greetings, my friend," said the constable. "We rarely get such esteemed visitors this far up in the northern wilderness."

The constable looked over the O'Rourke's shoulder at his entourage and stopped his gaze at Francisco.

"That one there with his sun-licked skin may not like it here much."

The O'Rourke laughed.

"He didn't like it in Breifne much either, when he cares to admit it. He asks God every night why he was cursed so to land here and be trapped with us. He doesn't care to admit that either."

The O'Rourke turned and winked at Francisco.

"But he has been a loyal servant to me and is a talented trainer of men, being the captain of a galleon that washed up upon our shores. Give him somewhere warm to rest while we stay briefly as I raise men to bring back to Breifne."

The constable looked away from the O'Rourke.

"Sorry, lord. My master gave me explicit instructions to lay out every hospitality to you, but any plans to return to Breifne are to be placed on hold until he returns."

The O'Rourke's face exploded into a fiery red.

"Am I to be a caged bird when I am really the wolfhound that roams the forest?"

The constable blinked to compose himself, then smiled and extended his arm to invite them into the castle tower.

"I can offer you a good bed, plenty of food and ale and maybe a tour of the islands, but that is all. Your men will be lodged on the castle's lands, for you must all remain hidden until my master instructs me otherwise. Now, will you come and eat with me?"

"I think that is the best offer I am going to get," the O'Rourke begrudgingly said.

Francisco cautiously settled into his new home in the shadow of the imposing MacSweeney castle that loomed over the rugged Irish landscape. The O'Rourke insisted Francisco was housed with a local family who were not subject to the usual coign and livery demands and had been given a generous subsidy by Eoghan Óg MacSweeney to care for their foreign guest properly. But he could not escape the watchful eye of MacSweeney's men, who were instructed not to let him out of their sight.

The O'Rourke was housed in the castle as an honoured guest. As part of his accommodations, Francisco was allowed to dine with the O'Rourke whenever he pleased. The O'Rourke even had free range of the castle's kitchens if Francisco needed any sustenance. It was all part of Eoghan Óg MacSweeney's plan to keep the O'Rourke content and under his watchful eye.

However, several months later, when O'Rourke's belly was full and his wounds healed, he wasted no time getting to know everyone in the castle by first name. He calculated who could be useful to him, who could be bought with bribes, and who remained loyal to the MacSweeney. He procured himself a pen and some paper, desperate to stay connected to his son back in Breifne and gather information about the ongoing war.

However, unbeknownst to the O'Rourke, all his messengers were double agents. Agents of Eoghan Óg collected his letters, and once Eoghan Óg's constable had read them, they never made it further south than Donegal Castle, where they were read on behalf of Ineen Dubh. Some were destroyed, but some were altered or dispatched to Breifne only to return via Donegal Castle again.

The O'Rourke may have suspected what was happening, but he never knew for definite and kept writing.

It had been six long, gruelling months since Eoghan Óg MacSweeney left the castle with his loyal soldiers. Their ranks were now diminished, but their spirits were high as they returned victorious, bloodied and bruised from crushing the enemies of Ineen Dubh. They could see the banners flying high as they approached the castle gates, welcoming them back as heroes. But Eoghan Óg's mind was burdened with another mission requiring all his strength and bravery. The scouts had spotted him marching north from miles away, and the castle had been prepared for his arrival, with guards standing at attention and weapons ready.

The sun shone down on the northern landscape, creating a blinding gleam that reflected off the polished armour of the Galloglass warriors standing in neat lines to greet their triumphant leader. His figure cast a long shadow across the ground as he rode majestically past them. The wispy clouds dotted the sky, and they were at the mercy of the strong winds, constantly shifting and obscuring the sun's faint warmth from reaching the exposed headland.

Francisco stood among them, dressed in a Spanish captain's uniform salvaged from a recent shipwreck just miles from the coast. The original owner of the uniform had not survived his wounds, but some of his men did and now served as drill sergeants for the MacSweeney clan. Francisco, too, had taken on this role since joining their ranks. These Spanish soldiers, still wearing their uniforms despite their new allegiance, were seen as an act of defiance by the local Irish. Those who aided and abetted them had a high price on their heads, making it all the more dangerous for Francisco and his comrades to parade about openly.

With a newfound confidence, the O'Rourke pushed his way through the crowd of constables guarding the castle and made his way to the front. He stood tall, arms stretched wide in a welcoming gesture, head slightly tilted with a warm smile as he eagerly awaited Eoghan Óg's return. His eyes sparkled with anticipation as he prepared to greet his friend.

"Eoghan Óg, may I be the first to salute your glorious victory upon your return home."

MacSweeney glanced from side to side to see if any of his men were forthcoming to save him from the embarrassment of having to be greeted home by the O'Rourke. None were. Eoghan Óg gingerly dismounted and allowed the arms of the O'Rourke to envelope him as he gave the O'Rourke a weak pat on the back.

"We have to talk," Eoghan Óg said in the O'Rourke's ear.

The O'Rourke released him and stood beaming before him.

"Of course we do. We have the liberation of Ireland to discuss."

MacSweeney looked away.

"I must go and speak to my men. We shall talk later. Yes?"

"I look forward to it." Nothing was going to knock the smile off the O'Rourke's face today.

The returning men broke ranks and greeted their families or whoever was waiting to greet them. Eoghan Óg signalled to his constables to join him in a huddle.

"Why are those Spaniards dressed in army uniforms?" said Eoghan Óg. "They will get us all lynched."

"It was the O'Rourke's idea," said one. "He said it would be a show of strength upon your return."

Eoghan Óg ground his teeth.

"I will speak to him. In the meantime, arrange a feast to celebrate our victory."

Fires danced and flickered in the castle courtyard as the moon rose high in the dark sky. The warm glow illuminated the faces of the revellers gathered around, their voices raised in song and laughter. The smell of roasting venison wafted through the air, mingling with the rich scent of ale and the cool night breeze. After years of strife and conflict, peace seemed finally settled upon Tirconnell. The men rejoiced in their victories and toasted their fallen comrades, for they knew their sacrifices had not been in vain. Ineen Dubh and her husband now reigned unchallenged over Tirconnell after years of bitter infighting.

The O'Rourke was eager for updates on Breifne, but no one seemed to have any news about what was happening there. It seemed that few in Tirconnell were concerned with events outside their own territory. He shifted the topic of conversation to the availability of Scottish mercenaries and learned that they would soon return home as their fighting season had nearly ended. He searched for Eoghan Óg, and set out for the grand hall at the top of the tower.

MacSweeney sat at the head of the long, wooden table, surrounded by his constables. A large slab of venison lay before him, its savoury aroma filling the room. His deep voice boomed through the hall as he laughed and joked with his constables, their swords and armour glinting in the firelight. But when the O'Rourke stepped into the room, Eoghan Óg's jovial expression melted away. The reinvigorated O'Rourke made eye contact with Eoghan Óg and strode purposefully towards him. In a show of respect, Eoghan Óg set down his mug of ale and raised his hands in greeting to his guest.

"My friend, why do you come in here with such haste? Tonight, we feast, and tomorrow, we can do business."

The O'Rourke smiled and placed his hand on top of MacSweeney's shoulder.

"Of course, I am here to celebrate. You have won an excellent victory, and I raise my mug to salute its endurance. But a father's needs compel me to talk business, for I have not heard from my son in a long while and wondered if you had any news to bring me?"

Eoghan Óg, in turn, put his arm around the O'Rourke's shoulder.

"If you compel me to talk now and deprive my men of my company, then we shall. Let us go to my private room for our conversation, which is not for public consumption."

They walked down the stairs, escorted by MacSweeney's guards until they were alone in MacSweeney's private room. Eoghan Óg turned his back and looked out the window.

"I have nothing to bring you but grave news."

"But if you bring me news at least I can act upon it. I have written many times to my son but never received a single letter back from him. Do you have any news of him?"

MacSweeney turned around and began to pace the room, lowering his gaze as he did not wish to look the O'Rourke in the eye.

"Governor Bingham is in complete control of West Breifne. Rumour has it he is even beginning to sell the land to English settlers. Your son Teigue is the puppet O'Rourke, and a sheriff has been imposed on your lands. Your son Brian Óg was last heard of roaming the forests by the border with the Maguire."

The O'Rourke turned to the window to hide his grimace. He held his face and dragged his palms down his cheek. Once he had regained a modicum of composure, he whirled around to Eoghan Óg.

"Is my son seeking aid from the Maguire?"

MacSweeney's face twitched, for he intensely disliked the task Ineen Dubh had given him to contain his old comrade.

"The Maguire is barely out of boyhood and has yet to find his feet. The Maguires do not have the strength to intercede and fear if they become embroiled in a war, they will be swallowed up next."

"Then Ineen Dubh must act," the O'Rourke said firmly.

Eoghan Óg bowed his head.

"She has told me I need to keep you under control. You must remain hidden here, for the English are still after you, and the price on your head has only increased after your ambush all those months ago confirmed that you are still alive and active."

"AM I TO BE A CAGED BIRD WHEN I AM A WOLF OF THE FOREST?"

The O'Rourke's cheeks burned with fury, but something in his eyes gave way, and he spun into melancholy and thought he was powerless.

"I'm afraid so," Eoghan Óg said calmly but firmly. "Once the civil wars of the north are resolved, Ineen Dubh will consider allowing you to hire mercenaries."

"No one tells me what to do, not even the queen herself!"

The O'Rourke flung open the door and stormed out.

"Do not do anything that would make me put you under guard," Mac-Sweeney called after him down the corridor. But he was already gone.

CHAPTER 40

PROMISES WORTH A PRETTY PENNY

As the warm days of summer slowly melted away, the O'Rourke found himself idling away his time in the peaceful tranquillity of Donegal Castle. His days were spent hunched over a desk, carefully crafting letters to the chieftains of the north, seeking their support and allegiance. The ink flowed freely from his quill as he poured out his hopes and plans for securing Breifne, ending the ongoing civil wars in the O'Donnell and O'Neill clans and expelling the English for good. But unbeknownst to him, most of these letters ended up crumpled and tossed into the fire. For Ineen Dubh, stirring up trouble was the last thing on her mind. She had to return Tirconnell to her former strength and secure an alliance with the new O'Neill.

Francisco filled his days with vigorous training sessions for the Galloglass warriors, teaching them Spanish ways of war, musketry, honing their skills and preparing them for battle. In his free time, he would join the local fishermen on their expeditions in the vast Atlantic Ocean, learning their ways and sharing stories of his homeland. As one of the few Spaniards trapped in this foreign land, he sought comfort and camaraderie with those he felt were closest in character to his fellow countrymen. He tried to bribe a few of them to take him back to Spain, but Eoghan Óg had driven the fear of God into them, so none of them would help him. Francisco's dreams of his wife and children seemed as distant as ever.

Meanwhile, the MacSweeneys remained vigilant in protecting their castle and territory from potential spies. Their patrols scoured the dense woods surrounding the stronghold, ever watchful for any signs of intrusion or betrayal. Despite Eoghan Óg MacSweeney's desire for loyalty, not everyone was as devoted to him as he had hoped. Some of the O'Rourke's sympathisers believed that he had been unjustly treated and made themselves known to him. The O'Rourke eagerly bent their ears, seeking support for his cause. However, his access to funds was limited, with most of his wealth tied up in property and cattle back in Breifne and his credit sources non-existent. Desperate and running low on options, he resorted to dealing in promises, hoping to buy time until he could secure more resources. But as time passed, the value of his promises dwindled, and the price on his head became increasingly enticing.

Feeling the pressure mounting, the O'Rourke began to pester Eoghan Óg MacSweeney for assistance in pleading his case at Donegal Castle with Ineen Dubh. At first, Eoghan would brush him off or actively avoid him when he became too persistent. Left with no other choice, the O'Rourke turned to making grandiose promises in hushed corners to anyone who would listen. One such person was the captain of a ship that frequented the seas between Tirconnell and the Scottish Isles, offering potential aid in the O'Rourke's plight.

The O'Rourke's reputation preceded him, enhanced by the whisperings of one of the constables he had befriended. The constable's wife belonged to the O'Rourke clan, so he was sympathetic to their struggles. Out of a sense of duty and kinship, it was arranged that the constable and his friend Francisco escort the O'Rourke to Rathmullan, one of the main O'Donnell ports in north Tirconnell, where most of the mercenaries from Scotland landed. Together, they made their way through winding streets until they reached a large alehouse, known to be frequented by both sailors and mercenaries.

The smell of stale ale and sweat filled the air as they entered, mingling with raucous laughter and rowdy chatter. The atmosphere was charged with excitement and danger, making it clear that this was not a place for the faint of heart. But for the O'Rourke, it felt like home, where he could drink, fight, and forget about his troubles for a little while.

"He's over there," the constable said, pointing to a large man in a tattered coat wiping the froth of ale from his beard whilst laughing with some of his seafaring comrades. The O'Rourke walked straight over to him and stood between the sea captain and his men, barely saying hello.

"I am here to talk business," said the O'Rourke, looking the captain straight in the eye. "Are you open to a proposition?"

"Aye, I'm always open to that," the captain said. "Sit, and my men will make themselves scarce."

The men did just that, grumbling that their drinking session had been interrupted.

"Do you know who I am?" said the O'Rourke as he opened an expensive bottle of wine imported from Spain that he had taken from MacSweeney's cellar.

The man was a native of the Scottish Islands who was far more concerned with the price he could get for his goods or the payment he could get for transporting mercenaries. He greedily eyed the bottle of wine whilst forgetting to watch for the intentions of who was serving it.

"Well, you must be very important to get a bottle of wine like that."

"I am, and I've got plenty more where that came from."

The O'Rourke poured the captain a generous mug of wine.

"There'll be plenty more to go around, for I am here to do business."

The captain took a large swig of wine and held up the mug to admire its contents once a suitable sample swirled on his tongue.

"I'm in the business of hiring mercenaries, as many as an enterprising captain can bring me. Whoever can supply me with the men I need would indeed become rich."

The captain looked up to catch the glint in the O'Rourke's eye. It was the perfect image to catch the captain's greed.

"You know that Ineen Dubh and her mother monopolise hiring mercenaries? The Scottish lords only deal with her, for they trust her and know they'll get paid."

"That's why I pay more. But I'd take all the risk off you. All you need to do is transport them over here, tell them what I offer and where to find me, and they would get a handsome fee and have no risk of ruining their business with the O'Donnells."

"So, you'd pay me a fee for introducing you to the leader of the mercenaries with no blowback on me?"

"Exactly."

The captain leaned backwards.

"But to do all that properly would create some expenses."

The captain rubbed his thumb and forefinger together and grinned at the O'Rourke.

The O'Rourke nodded.

"I can see to those."

"But, I need some of those expenses in advance. There'd be nothing like a gift of wine or ale that they could drink on the boat on the trip over with me in their ear telling them how great you are."

The O'Rourke reached into his pocket and discreetly handed the captain a bag of coins. The captain rolled the bag in the palm of his hand.

"They drink a lot."

The O'Rourke searched his pockets and gave whatever other coins he could find. He grimaced as he handed them over.

"Their pay will come as a generous share of the loot generated from me taking back my lands. I have a lot of scores to settle, and I mean a lot."

He leaned forward to the captain.

"When can I have my mercenaries?"

"Give me a couple of months. I need to speak to them on their islands, and then they have to gather their men. Don't worry. You can find me here most weeks. I have to go back and forth, for you know yourself, business still has to go on."

"Indeed I do."

The O'Rourke beamed and stuck out his hand.

"So here's to our bargain?"

The captain gave him a stiff but firm handshake.

"Now don't let me down?" the O'Rourke said.

The captain just grinned.

The passing of the winter months felt like an eternity for Francisco and the O'Rourke. Francisco's emotions were in constant turmoil, swinging from excitement to anxiousness as he saw the hiring of mercenaries as his ticket home. In his mind, each day that passed without news of their arrival dragged on painfully slowly. He remained haunted by thoughts of his family, and the idea that his wife thought him dead and had remarried began to enter his mind.

Meanwhile, the O'Rourke would tirelessly pace back and forth in the castle, his mind consumed with thoughts of his secret plot. He knew Ineen Dubh would disapprove, but how could she stop him once he had his army? The idea of facing her wrath in Tirconnell was a distant concern compared to his burning desire to escape. But why would she fight an enemy who wanted to leave? The O'Rourke questioned himself, yet he couldn't shake the determination fuelling his mission. Despite his impatience, he resisted the urge to venture out to the port of Rathmullan and draw attention to himself or his plans. Instead, he remained confined in his room, pacing and waiting for any news.

As the O'Rourke paced the courtyard one spring day, he felt something in his pocket. He grabbed downwards and caught himself a little wrist. He lifted the arm and found the face of a brown-haired boy at the end of it, his face tangled in pain.

"Let me go, let me go," said the boy as he kicked out his feet.

But the O'Rourke held him far enough away so the boy's flailing feet did not connect with anything.

"You're lucky I did not reach for my dagger when I felt you stealing from me," said the O'Rourke.

"You're the one in luck, for I placed a letter from the Scottish captain in your pocket."

The O'Rourke felt his pocket and sure enough there was a freshly placed letter. The O'Rourke felt his other pocket and pulled out an increasingly rare coin lodged there. He put the boy down and handed him the coin.

"For your troubles."

"I hope yours aren't just beginning," said the boy as he ran off before he could collect a clip around the ear for being cheeky.

The O'Rourke hurried into his room in the tower with his hand firmly jammed in his pocket to protect his precious letter. He slammed the room door closed, ripped past the seal of the Scottish MacSweeney clan, and devoured the contents.

The sun had barely peeked over the horizon, casting a warm glow over the dew-covered grass as Francisco and the O'Rourke made their way down to the stables. The crisp morning air carried the scent of hay and fresh manure, mingling with the earthy tang of sweat and leather. The horses whinnied and stamped their feet eagerly in their stalls, anticipating the day ahead. Francisco ran his hand along his horse's sleek coat, feeling the powerful muscles beneath.

"Where might you be going?" said the master of the horse as he led some horses out for an early morning run.

"I've been told the hunting is good in them yonder hills," said the O'Rourke, pointing in the opposite direction to Rathmullan. "I thought we'd go there to entertain ourselves."

"Well, good luck with that and don't get up to any mischief that would draw attention to yourselves."

The O'Rourke turned and grinned to Francisco.

"I was wondering where the spirit of my dead father had gone."

CHAPTER 41
DOWN WITH THE DOGS

A s soon as they were out of sight, Francisco and the O'Rourke turned their horses around and rode at breakneck speed towards Rathmullan. The wind whipped through their hair and clothes, carrying a sense of freedom and rebellion. The O'Rourke was elated, feeling like a child who had escaped from his chores to bask in the carefree joy of being alive. Francisco, on the other hand, was more cautious and calculated. He could not help but see the folly in this plan, and he could understand where the O'Rourke's deceased son Eoghan got his reckless streak from. On the other hand, this might be his only chance to return to Spain.

Still, it did not occur to Francisco that he may die that day. For all the O'Rourke's misfortunes, he was still well respected amongst the clans whose heads had not already been turned by the size of his bounty. They were careful as they rode, avoiding any large bodies of men and hiding when they saw men on horseback. Having to hide in the cold of north Tirconnell had made them paranoid, and the O'Rourke considered this his last chance.

Finally stopping atop a hill overlooking Lough Swilly, they caught their breath and surveyed their surroundings. The shimmering water below seemed to stretch for eternity, reflecting the golden rays of sunlight beaming down from above. The air was crisp and clean, carrying a faint scent of saltwater.

"Look," said the O'Rourke, sitting erect on his horse. "The captain has repaid our faith. Those ships have to be his carrying over the mercenaries, for it is the exact time he said it would be."

Francisco strained his eyes to estimate the size of the small fleet.

"They are not conventional ships that I would expect on the ocean, but at least a thousand warriors should be on board."

The O'Rourke was not for deflating.

"One thousand is not enough, but a good start. Once I march south through the valleys, men will flock to join me, and by the time we reach West Breifne, I think I could double that. Then I will bring the war to Bingham."

He beamed at Francisco, but his zest did not set Francisco's heart alight.

"Well, I hope the captain bought enough wine to have the Scottish chieftains predisposed to you before you meet them."

But no amount of pessimism could dampen the O'Rourke's mood.

"Today is a good day. I can feel it in my bones. Let us ride down so we may be on the shore to greet them when they get off their ships."

They rode to the outskirts of the village and tied up their horses. Francisco glanced over his shoulder.

"There are not many soldiers here nor men to unload the boats. You would think Ineen Dubh would be here to greet the mercenaries as they disembark?"

"It is not for me to question the movements of Ineen Dubh," said the O'Rourke as he waved Francisco's concerns away. "They will have me to greet them, and if the captain has done his job, then that will be sufficient. Let us stand on the docks to help our new friends off the boats."

The O'Rourke stood legs astride and hands on hips as the boats from Scotland threw their ropes ashore so they could moor. His smile was not for containing.

"Excuse me, lord," came a voice from behind them. "The MacSweeny would like a word with you."

Francisco and the O'Rourke turned around to see a constable from Castle Doe and three armed Galloglass standing behind them.

"I just have to meet the ship's captain on the lead boat that I have some business with," said the O'Rourke. His hand trembled as he pointed out onto the lough.

"He's not asking."

The constable put his hand on the hilt of the sword tied around his waist. The O'Rourke's head dropped, for he knew protesting was pointless. They were led to the alehouse by the docks, where the O'Rourke had met the captain before. The constable led the way, and the three guards stood behind them to ensure they did not run away.

"Where is he then?" said the O'Rourke with a sigh as he entered the building.

MacSweeney sat hunched over, his face illuminated by the flickering flames of the fire. Their reflection danced in his eyes as he sat alone, deep in thought. Across from him was an empty seat waiting to be filled. He motioned for the O'Rourke to sit. The O'Rourke obeyed, wary of potentially losing his only remaining ally in Tirconnell. He settled onto the chair, feeling the warmth of the fire against his back and the tension between them.

"How long have you known?" said the O'Rourke.

"From when your bag of coins rested in the captain's hand."

The O'Rourke scowled.

"Don't look at me like that," said MacSweeney. "The man is a cousin of mine. How do you think he got such a lucrative trade route? You must be getting desperate if you would forget that such a prominent man would not be enmeshed in the status quo."

"Well, more fool me then. So I wasted the last of my money on mercenaries that never would be mine?"

"Think yourself lucky that the last of your money did not land you in more mischief than you are already in."

"So what is to be done with me?"

Eoghan leaned forward.

"I have always been your friend and have always defended you. I have done more than you will ever know to defend you. Ineen Dubh never trusted you since you sided with Donnell O'Donnell."

"I didn't. I was coerced," the O'Rourke protested.

"No matter. She never saw it that way. I had to persuade her to allow you to stay in Tirconnell and allow me to shelter you."

MacSweeney paused and contemplated the result of telling the whole truth.

"She wanted to hand you over to the crown as she considered you more trouble than you were worth."

"Are you trying to clear your conscience before you carry out your role as executioner?"

MacSweeney shot back in his seat.

"No, it is not like that at all. You may have tested the limits of our friendship with your antics over the past couple of months, culminating in today's, but I am still a man of my word." MacSweeney sat up straight. "I think we would both agree that your time here is done. Yes?"

The O'Rourke hesitated and then nodded.

"I have used up much credit with Ineen Dubh to be allowed to deal with you myself. Once you are off the dock, she will greet the mercenaries. By the way, they were always intended for her."

The O'Rourke's head dropped.

"Let's face it," MacSweeney continued, "you're just rotting in my frozen old castle waiting to be assassinated. The O'Rourkes are forgotten about in the turmoil of the north."

The O'Rourke nodded again.

"But I believe in the Gaelic order," MacSweeney continued, "and that the O'Rourke clan should be restored."

The O'Rourke sat up, and a faint smile came across his face. Maybe he would survive the day after all.

"You paid my cousin to transport something across the ocean to Scotland, and you will get your money's worth. When the mercenaries have disembarked, I will arrange for you to go to Castle Sween so you can plead your case for mercenaries directly with the men of the islands."

Elation overcame the O'Rourke and he grabbed MacSweeney's hand with both of his.

"Thank you, thank you. The O'Rourke thanks you, his clan thanks you."

MacSweeney tried to suppress his smile.

"I have not finished yet."

He clicked his fingers and his men entered. Four fine specimens of Irish wolfhounds tugged on their chains. The dogs bounced on their paws, and their agile frames showed they were in the prime of life.

"I know you have fallen on hard times," said MacSweeney, "and you cannot appear as a beggar with no money in front of my clansmen. Therefore, I give you these four dogs as a gift, and you are free to give them to whomever you choose so you may get your mercenaries."

The O'Rourke strode over to inspect the dogs, giving each one a robust pat on the head before moving on to the next one.

"I cannot thank you enough," said the O'Rourke, fighting back the tears in his eyes.

"You can thank me by getting on the boat and not returning without your army. But if you do, do not cause trouble for Ineen Dubh, for she has shown you much kindness in the circumstances."

The O'Rourke nodded, hurried back to his seat, and held out his hand.

"Let me thank you again."

MacSweeney waved him away.

"There is no time for that. Get on the boat to evade the bounty hunters and make a clean getaway."

MacSweeney signalled to his men, and they stood behind the O'Rourke to indicate it was time to go.

"Thank you again," said the O'Rourke as he was ushered out of the room.

MacSweeney cringed as his friend left.

Francisco perched anxiously on a rickety cart, flanked by guards armed to the teeth. Despite the cool breeze wafting from the lough, a single bead of sweat glistened on his forehead, evidence of his mounting unease. His eyes followed the ragtag band of mercenaries as they noisily disembarked from the ship, boasting and joking about the riches they would plunder and bring home on the return journey. They marched past Francisco, barely sparing him a glance as they set up camp outside the small town. But his mind was consumed with worry. Was the O'Rourke truly negotiating fair terms for their services? Or was this all just an elaborate trap?

The imposing figure of the O'Rourke emerged from the building, surrounded by his entourage and flanked by his fierce guard dogs. He boldly waved to Francisco, a smug expression playing on his face as he made his grand exit.

"Pick up your things," said the O'Rourke, "we're leaving."

Francisco slung his heavy bags over his shoulder and sprinted after the O'Rourke.

"Where are we going?"

"Scotland, to acquire some mercenaries."

Francisco looked at the mercenaries marching past them in the opposite direction and tried to figure out what had just happened in the house. In the distance, he saw Ineen Dubh appear surrounded by guards. She embraced the mercenaries' leaders. Francisco scurried after the O'Rourke, for he knew something was badly awry.

The MacSweeney Galloglass constable spurred his horse on, racing towards the small harbour several miles away. As he crested a rolling hill, the shimmering waters of Lough Swilly came into view, stretching out as far as the eye could see. A lone house sat atop a nearby hill, providing a commanding vantage point over the lough. The constable quickly tethered his horse and made his way inside the house.

Upon entering, the smell of freshly cooked fish and ale filled his nostrils. An eclectic group of fishermen and traders sat at various tables, their laughter and chatter filling the air. In one corner, a group of rugged journeymen and hired swords traded stories and coins over their drinks.

Amidst the noise and chaos, the constable's keen eyes searched for his contact. In a dimly lit corner, he spotted the man he had come to meet. Ignoring the man's obvious annoyance at being disturbed, the constable boldly sat beside him, ready to conduct his business.

"He has left. Gone to Scotland."

"What for?"

"To hire his own mercenaries."

"Where?"

"Castle Sween."

Captain Williamson put his remaining hand in his pocket and pulled out a bag of coins.

"For your troubles. Plenty more where that came from for valuable information."

The constable took the bag and discreetly put it in his pocket. He nodded and left.

CHAPTER 42

ROUGH SEAS, NEW BEGINNINGS

This was no grand, majestic vessel as Francisco had known. Instead, it bobbed and lurched on the choppy waves, sending most of its passengers' stomachs up into their throats. The transport ship was a rickety children's toy compared to the sturdy Spanish galleons that braved the open ocean.

As he steadied himself against the swaying walls, Francisco couldn't help but study the captain's weathered face. Despite his grey hair and deep creases, he looked more like a man in his fifties than his thirties. The harsh life at sea had clearly taken its toll on him, but he still barked orders at his men with the zeal of a younger man.

But nothing could dampen the spirit of the O'Rourke and his new lease of life. Francisco watched as he tended to his four dogs, trying to soothe them amidst the chaos. Those dogs were the last riches he had.

"Hang onto the ropes," said the captain through the roaring wind and lashing rain. "We'll be in the shelter of the islands soon enough."

Francisco sheltered at the bow of the boat and wrapped his hands around some secured rope. He fought off the memories of the storms of the Spanish Armada.

Soon enough, the captain proved himself right, and they sailed along the relatively calm but still choppy waters between the islands and the shore up the

Sound of Jura. The captain came to speak to the O'Rourke and Francisco as he had never made his peace with them.

"I'm sorry about what happened, but really, it was the best thing for you," said the captain to blank, seasick faces. With no reply forthcoming, he thought some advice would make a suitable peace offering. "No matter, those stormy seas are behind you. The MacSween is a cranky old soul with no favourable disposition to Hugh O'Neill in the north. The walls of his castle were built on the hundreds of years of his clan waging war as mercenaries in Ireland. Still, he trusts no one but Ineen Dubh, who wants to keep control of the supply of mercenaries all to herself and an excellent job she does of it as well. You want to spend as little time as possible here and go to Edinburgh to meet the king, the real power in Scotland."

The O'Rourke scowled.

"What sort of advice is that from a man who just tricked us?"

"It is the best advice you will get, mark my words," said the captain. "I am the man who just saved you and gave you a second chance. As soon as you inhale the stale air of the castle hall, you'll be trying to thank me. But I'll have already taken to the waves."

"Absconding with my money, more like. Strike a bargain with me to transport my new army to Ireland and note I said a bargain, be it for me to judge it good value."

"As soon as I see you marching down the glens at the head of your force, I'll be there with the lowest offer."

"So you're not that confident of my success?"

"On the contrary. I need to see how many men you have so I can assemble the ships. But enough of the future. Look to the present," and the captain pointed to the ever-nearing shoreline.

The imposing walls of Castle Sween towered over the lough, casting a dark shadow over the choppy waters. The sailors expertly threw their ropes to the shore, securing their ship in place. A small jetty jutted out from the rocky shore, its wooden planks leading to a set of ancient stone stairs carved into the cliffs.

Clearly, this was not the bustling harbour from which the MacSween clan had departed on their journey to Ireland.

The relentless waves crashed against the weathered jetty, their force threatening to break through the wooden planks and swallow them whole. Nowhere was free from the spray.

"Now get on the jetty, and we'll say our goodbyes," said the captain.

"Are you not going to wait for me just in case something goes wrong?" said the O'Rourke.

"I won't wait for you, just as the tide will not wait for me. Your destiny is up them stairs, not on my ship."

The captain pointed the way to Castle Sween.

"Look forward. There is nothing behind you until you walk forward. Now get up them stairs."

The O'Rourke checked the leather leads of his powerful hunting dogs, ensuring they were securely attached to their collars. He gave them a few gentle pats on their sleek heads before turning to the imposing captain standing nearby. The man nodded once towards the stairs, indicating it was time to make their ascent. Francisco, a strong and weathered hand at the helm of many a sea voyage, offered his support by placing a firm hand on the O'Rourke's arm and guiding him up the steep steps with practised ease. As they climbed, the sounds of distant waves crashing against the ship's hull grew louder, sending a shiver down Francisco's spine.

The worn stone steps carved into the cliffs which led to the castle were at a steep incline, clearly designed to favour the defender from above and exhaust any potential attackers attempting to scale them. The O'Rourke huffed and wheezed his way up, his injuries and ailments from Tirconnell draining his strength. Francisco patiently assisted him and took the reins of two dogs who eagerly pulled at their leashes. As they climbed higher, guards emerged from the castle walls, alerted by the arrival of the boat and these unexpected guests. Once they learned the identity of their guests, they hurried down to offer assistance. The steps were slick with seawater and rain, making each step treacherous. The O'Rourke slipped and fell to his knees several times but worked out a way to climb up supported on one side by Francisco and with one hand on the rock-face on the other. But finally, they reached the top and were directed straight to the great hall, for the MacSween was known for his wariness of strangers.

As they set foot in the hall, a thick cloud of acrid smoke engulfed them, stinging their nostrils and burning their eyes. The gusts of wind howling down the chimney only added to the chaos, sending the smoke billowing out in all directions until it reached the ceiling. At the far end of the room sat an elderly man, hunched over in a creaky chair with his twisted nose and white wispy hair portraying menace to the eye of any beholder. His twisted mouth curled into a cruel sneer as he surveyed the intruders with a glint of malice in his eyes.

"Who is it that comes to my castle uninvited? I know I am supposed to extend the hospitality of the islands to you, but if all you bring is a dark cloud of misery and death, then I will cast you back into the sea. State your name before I set my dogs upon thee."

The O'Rourke bowed and signalled for Francisco to do the same.

"I am the great O'Rourke, lord of West Breifne, and am here to share my riches with you."

The MacSween looked him up and down.

"You may be great where you come from, but I have never heard of you, which means you're not great here. All you look like sharing are the raindrops from your soaking coats, and I've got plenty of rain, thank you very much. Now tell me why I should not throw you off the cliffs and back into the sea?"

One of the MacSween's advisors leaned down and whispered in his ear. The O'Rourke looked at Francisco and gulped.

"My man informs me you are here to hire mercenaries. Why did you not go through Ineen Dubh with whom I have a perfectly good arrangement? Are you spies? Have you come to seek proof that I defy my king? If so, I have some especially jagged rocks on the other side of my castle walls, especially for spies. We could hang you out of a basket over the sea from the walls and get the truth out of you before the sun goes down even though it be late in the day."

The O'Rourke bowed again.

"I am not here to insult or to spy but to do business with the great lord of the mercenaries. I have both seen and heard of your men's prowess on the battlefields of Ireland and mean to hire you to assist in regaining my lands."

MacSween sat forward and cocked his right ear in the O'Rourke's direction.

"I am old and a little hard of hearing, so let me repeat what you just said."

The O'Rourke bowed once again.

"If it pleases you, lord."

"You are in a land dispute with…"

"The governor of Connacht, a province in my land."

"I am slightly deaf, not a half-wit."

"Sorry, lord. No insult intended."

The O'Rourke looked to the floor, and MacSween sat back in his chair.

"So you come to me with no lands and presumably no money to recruit my men on the promise that if they defeat the English governor, they will get some cattle?"

Francisco noticed the beads of sweat on the O'Rourke's forehead. But nothing would stop him from pleading his case.

"There is much glory to gain alongside an abundance of wealth. Your men could retire to their islands and never have to be mercenaries again. Such is the wealth on offer."

"Says he of the empty pockets. Unfortunately for you, the king of Scotland has decreed that the clans of the islands should stop sending men and arms to Ireland, and I am considering obeying it. Hugh O'Neill had the gall to murder one of our relatives, and Ineen Dubh has requested that we deal only with her. Therefore, you can climb down the steps you came up and wait for a boat back to Ireland or go to Edinburgh. I care not what you do as long as you leave my castle."

Francisco could see the anger welling up in O'Rourke's neck veins, so he stood in front of him and pushed him away.

"The only thing anger will get us is killed. Come on, let us leave."

They were escorted into the courtyard, their dogs wandering in front of them, and then stopped by the captain of the guards.

"Which way do you wish to go?" the captain said. "To the left is the gate to the sea, and in front is the way to Edinburgh. Which way?"

The O'Rourke looked at Francisco.

"Edinburgh is this way," the O'Rourke said, pointing to the main gate. "I see no point in returning home empty-handed."

"Then Spain is that way for me," said Francisco.

"I can give you horses," said the captain in the O'Rourke's ear. "The Irish have many sympathisers in Edinburgh, and if you contact my friend, he will arrange an audience with the king."

The captain slipped a note into the O'Rourke's pocket.

"How do I know this is not a trap?"

"You don't. But neither do you have a choice."

The captain watched the O'Rourke leave. The MacSween hobbled up behind him and slipped a letter into his pocket.

"See the one-armed man gets this," said the MacSween. "I may as well get something from my day being so rudely interrupted."

CHAPTER 43

ONCE UPON A DRINK IN AN EDINBURGH TAVERN

For days on end, Francisco and the O'Rourke traversed the vast expanse of Scotland, their loyal dogs faithfully running alongside them. As they rode through unfamiliar territory, they were forced to make frequent stops at various farmsteads for directions, as the captain of the guard had neglected to provide them with a map. With no provisions to sustain them, nor money in their pockets, they relied on entertaining their hosts with tales of their homeland – Ireland, Spain, and even the infamous Spanish Armada – in exchange for their generosity. Once they had the Firth of Forth to their left, their spirits rose, and horse and dog alike bounded over the wet turf with a spring in their stride. They reached the outskirts of the town that lay in the shadow of the castle perched on top of a hill with sheer cliffs on three sides.

"This must be Edinburgh, according to all I have heard. What a perfect place for a castle," the O'Rourke said as he shielded his eyes to admire the building.

At last, something comparable to Spain, but Francisco kept his thoughts to himself. The O'Rourke held out the note the constable gave him at Castle Sween.

"Look, it says there is a tavern in the shadow of the castle that takes in Irish travellers. Owned by an O'Neill, no less. Apparently, plenty of Irish sympathisers there can provide assistance and access to the king."

Francisco shrugged.

"We have nowhere else to go, so why not go there?"

They trudged along looking for the tavern, for the streets were a sea of mud lubricated by the frequent showers. Multi-storey houses lined each side of the road, an alien sight to the O'Rourke, who stared at the occupants and passers-by, wondering what wealth they had accumulated to live in such grand dwellings. Dublin, Galway and maybe a few other towns had such houses, but this city seemed to have them in abundance. The streets smelt of bread, and the street carts were filled with abundant goods imported from the continent, especially from France and Spain. Both their stomachs rumbled – Francisco's for food he remembered from years ago and the O'Rourke's for food he had never tasted.

"This must be it."

The O'Rourke pointed to a mud-splattered sign, and in the top right-hand corner was the recognisable edge of the Irish harp symbol. The clothes and state of the men falling out the door and the songs of the clans they sang confirmed it. Francisco nodded and braced himself in case of trouble. They entered the door, and the first thing that hit them was the musty smell of unwashed men. The O'Rourke hesitated and hovered by the bar, deciding whether to introduce himself, for he had no money to buy food or drink. A hand rested on his shoulder.

"Don't worry, you're safe here. We've been waiting for the man with four dogs."

The man smiled, and the O'Rourke gave a nervous grin.

"I'm Diarmuid O'Neill. I'm a friend. If you look at that table over there, they are also your friends, and they are expecting you."

The O'Rourke followed Diarmuid's finger to a shadowy table where several bearded, long-haired men grinned and raised their mugs. The O'Rourke followed Diarmuid over to the table. A large man stood up, putting his arm around the O'Rourke's shoulders.

"A thousand welcomes to the most wanted man in Ireland," he said in his thick Irish accent. "Sit and drink. Eat your fill, and then we'll talk, but not here."

The O'Rourke's grin gained some confidence, and he invited Francisco to sit with his new friends.

They stayed for several hours questioning the men about how they knew they were coming and ultimately decided they could trust them. Diarmuid guided them under the cover of nightfall through the maze-like backstreets of Edinburgh to what seemed like a safe house. The shadows seemed to dance and shift as they made their way towards an inconspicuous two-storey house, its windows tightly shut and curtains drawn. The surrounding houses seemed to huddle together in the darkness as if seeking protection from the unknown dangers lurking in the shadows.

"You will be safe here, and we can talk," Diarmuid said. "There'll be guards on the door. Good loyal lads."

"Thank you, my friend. I will remember you when I speak to the king."

Diarmuid ushered them into the old stone house, its walls damp and cold from the winter air. He carefully lit candles throughout the room, casting a flickering glow on the ancient furnishings. With a practised hand, he started a fire in the hearth, the crackling flames providing warmth and light. From a wooden cupboard, he retrieved some blankets and handed them out to his grateful guests.

"You'll need these until the place warms up. But you'll probably need them after as well. They're clean. Nothing but the best for the O'Rourke."

The O'Rourke and Francisco huddled close together, their blankets pulled tightly around their bodies to ward off the chill of the night. Diarmuid bent down to add a few logs to the small, flickering fire. Crackling wood filled the air as he straightened up and turned away to retrieve two mugs of ale. He returned with the mugs carefully balanced, steam rising from their frothy tops.

"Now I think we can have that talk," he said.

But when he checked, both the O'Rourke and Francisco were fast asleep.

"May as well have these myself, then," and he sat beside the fire.

A long six months later, the first rays of sunlight filtered through the window of the safe house, rousing the O'Rourke from his slumber. He had been disappointed many times, and Diarmuid's friendship had grated upon him, for all he seemed to offer were the dark shadows of the alehouse and the musty smells of the safe house. But today was supposed to be the fruition of his long wait. At last, Diarmuid came through with an audience with the king.

The Irish merchants in Edinburgh had generously pooled their resources to provide him with attire befitting his meeting. As the O'Rourke gazed upon his new clothes in the mirror, a renewed confidence coursed through his veins. Diarmuid meticulously smoothed down the shoulders of his jacket, glancing briefly at Francisco, who stood off to the side, looking forlorn and neglected amidst all the preparations.

"Don't worry, we have you sorted, too," Diarmuid said, nodding towards Francisco. "We'll introduce you to the Spanish ambassador, and he'll see about getting you sent home."

Francisco smiled, and his hands shook as he clasped them in thankful prayer.

"Thank you! Thank you! I always knew you would see me right, Señor O'Rourke."

"Stick with me, and that I will," said the O'Rourke, not lifting his gaze from himself in the mirror.

Francisco ignored the O'Rourke's self-absorption and thought of his own passage back to Spain. Meanwhile, O'Rourke started pacing back and forth, practising his speech while he waited for his evening appointment with the king.

As the sun began to set, the promised reception of the O'Rourke with the king of Scotland was finally upon them. The O'Rourke and his entourage settled into their temporary residence at the bustling tavern, greeted by an array of handshakes and praise from lowly and well-to-do Irish settlers who had made Edinburgh their home. Francisco couldn't help but notice how every boastful tale the O'Rourke had told about himself had made its way to Scotland, each taken as truth and earning him even more admiration. It was precisely what the O'Rourke needed, a boost to his already inflated ego before he faced the intimidating prospect of meeting with the king.

With a determined stride and rosy cheeks, the O'Rourke set off to scale the steep hill that led to the towering castle. His loyal supporters cheered and waved as he walked through the bustling streets, their voices carrying words of encouragement and good luck. But as they reached the foot of the hill, they slowly peeled away, disappearing down narrow alleyways at the sight of the king's intimidating guard on top of the castle walls. Soon, only Francisco, Diarmuid O'Neill, and a few young Irish noblemen remained by his side, warily escorting him to the castle gates.

He stood tall and confident and knocked on the massive wooden doors. Behind him, Francisco and Diarmuid held the fierce hunting dogs on tight leashes.

"Who stands beneath the king's walls with a mob at his back?" a captain shouted from the ramparts.

The O'Rourke gave a disgruntled look over his shoulder at Diarmuid. He was expecting the gates to be flung open for him. The O'Rourke shook his head and put it down to an incompetent captain on the walls, whom nobody had informed of his arrival.

"It is the O'Rourke, a friend and ally of the king, having come all the way from Ireland. I seek an audience with him. I was assured it was arranged, and I would be well received."

The captain's head disappeared and reappeared a few minutes later.

"Whoever told you that planted a lie in your ear. No one gave us notification of such an appointment. If you think marching through his majesty's streets with a mob causing an affray would make the king think you are a friend, then you are gravely mistaken."

"Look behind me," said the O'Rourke, throwing his arms into empty space. "Where is the mob? Where is this affray you speak of? All that is before you is a friend with a gift for the king."

The O'Rourke stared up at the ramparts, trying to suppress the twitches on his face. The head of the captain darted in and out of view several times as he obviously consulted some unseen person.

"What is your gift to the king?" the captain asked as he came into view again.

"The hunting dogs my friends are holding behind me," and the O'Rourke pointed back to Francisco, Diarmuid and the dogs. The captain leaned down on the ramparts as he squinted and assessed the dogs. One gave an untimely bark and tugged on his leash.

"Those dogs look like they could be set upon my men, meaning they can be used as weapons." The captain straightened up and scowled. "If you are a friend of the king as you claim, remove yourself from the gates and refrain from causing any more disorder. If you fail, I will set the king's horsemen upon you."

Before the O'Rourke could protest, Diarmuid hooked his arm.

"Come. Let us not die this day before the king's gate. I have another way."

The O'Rourke let himself be dragged away, for he knew he should be out of earshot to hear Diarmuid's plan. Diarmuid slung his arm across the O'Rourke's shoulder and pulled him near so he would not be overheard. When he was out of earshot, the O'Rourke felt safe protesting.

"I hope this new plan is better than your old one. There was no audience with the king arranged today as you promised. Have I waited for six months just to be humiliated like this?" he snarled.

"I was assured by your supporters in the clans from the islands that he agreed to see you," Diarmuid protested. "Nevertheless, I have a back-up plan. In a week, the king hears petitions from anyone in his lands who may have a dispute that needs to be resolved. It is open to anyone, so you can queue up and be heard. You can bring your dogs for the king as the people often bring him gifts to show their gratitude. I can get you past the gates and to be seen."

The O'Rourke ground his teeth and made a fist, hoping such actions would absorb his frustrations. Was this another lie out of Diarmuid's mouth? What had he to gain by such deceptions? But he deduced that if he had come this far, he might as well try for what other choice did he have?

He pulled his coat down and curled his lip.

"If I have to be a beggar and enter by the beggar's entrance, then so be it. But the O'Rourke will not forget this slight."

Diarmuid smiled nervously and patted him on the shoulder.

"Come, I know where to get a good drink while we wait."

CHAPTER 44

A COURTLY DANCE

A week later, Francisco and the O'Rourke found themselves at the end of a long, winding queue in the grand hall of Edinburgh Castle. It was the time allotted by the king to hear the grievances of his people so anyone could queue and wait their turn to ask for the king's justice. Francisco and the O'Rourke shuffled along at the back of the queue and looked at the ground to compose themselves and hide from prying eyes that may call them out as imposters who should not be there. The smell of sweat and nerves lingered in the air as people jostled for position, eager to have their voices heard by the king. In the hall, the clan chieftain stood beside the courtier, the merchant, and the southern lord. All represented the wide range of factions the king had to juggle and draw together to keep happy.

As they neared the front, the O'Rourke's previous anxieties returned with a vengeance. He had been told in the taverns that he would be greeted as one of the significant chieftains of Ireland, but instead, he found himself standing behind local Scots with land disputes and cattle rustling allegations. The O'Rourke registered his name and grievance with a clerk who walked along the line, carefully noting each petitioner's concerns. This information would be passed on to the king, who needed to understand the core of each issue before meeting with the petitioner. The O'Rourke swallowed his pride and gave only the barest of information, eager to get through this process as quickly as possible and not be rejected on some administrative detail.

He stood shuffling in the queue, clenching his teeth, listening to the farmers telling stories of missing cows, kidnapped daughters, absent fathers, and people accused of witchcraft or blasphemy. He felt increasingly out of place, comparing these petty struggles for justice and fairness against his own turmoil of fighting for the freedom of Breifne and, ultimately, of Ireland.

The O'Rourke peeked over the shoulders of those before him to size up the king. King James VI of Scotland slumped on his throne, the heavy crown atop his head threatening to tumble off with each careless movement. His eyes, usually sharp and observant, now appeared dull and listless as he gazed out at the grand hall filled with scruffy petitioners vying for his attention. He inwardly cringed as he feared having to feign interest in another story about a fluctuating number of sheep resident on the hill of God-knows-where and why he had to do something about it.

The king's fingers absent-mindedly tapped against the armrest of his throne, a habit he had acquired during long, tedious meetings such as this. The rich velvet of his robe pooled around his feet, the intricate embroidery catching the light and shimmering like stars in the night sky.

Despite the lavish surroundings, an air of restlessness hung heavy in the chamber as if even the very walls yearned for excitement and adventure. The king let out a heavy sigh as only he could, longing for something to break the monotony of his royal duties and bring a spark back to his weary heart.

The O'Rourke finally came to the front of the line and squeezed the tension from his fists. He twitched as he went over the speech he hoped would refill the king with the passion for rebellion. The King's secretary stepped forward.

"Sire, may I introduce the one who calls himself the O'Rourke? He is a chieftain from somewhere in the middle of Ireland. I cannot say where for he did not have the foresight to bring a map."

The O'Rourke seethed with anger as the secretary continued to treat him disrespectfully. His jaw tightened, and his breath came out in short, controlled bursts. Every fibre of his being wanted to throttle the impudent man, but he knew it would do him no good. Baile Nua, it was not. As he turned his head, he caught sight of a well-dressed, one-armed man grinning in his direction. It was the English captain. His enemies had arrived before him and were already making their moves. But before him sat the king himself, offering both a grand opportunity and potential finality. The O'Rourke took a deep breath and lowered himself into a deep, respectful bow, ready to seize this crucial moment.

"My name is Brian O'Rourke, chieftain of the O'Rourke clan. We are one of Ireland's greatest clans, having been previously high kings of Ireland. I come to you as Ireland's greatest rebel."

There were cheers from a certain section of the crowd, and the king looked around to see who was the most boisterous. The movers and shakers of the court did neither. The highland chieftains, the O'Rourke's most likely supporters, remained silent and looked uninterested. The king smiled, for he noted that the O'Rourke had support from the rabble but not amongst the factions of court. That would make him easier to control. But one man moved and shook his finger as he stood forward from the king's advisors.

"Can this man make up his mind what he is?" The English ambassador Robert Bowes stood defiantly in the middle of the hall and pointed an accusatory bony finger at the O'Rourke. His clothes bore an air of respectability, but his mouth contained the poison of a snake. "Not only do we not know where he is from, he also claims to be a king and a rebel. How can one be both? From the state of him, he looks far more like a rebel than one fit enough to converse with you man-to-man, sire. If he is the greatest rebel in Ireland, it means he is a criminal, and he seeks refuge from the laws of your neighbour, the queen of England. There is a handsome price upon that rebel's head, so whatever he asks for, the queen will double it to prevent him from creating mischief. May I suggest the queen would extend many favours to whoever handed over this criminal?"

"Who are you to suggest who is a criminal in our lands?" came a voice from the crowd of onlookers.

Robert bowed deeply in front of the king.

"Forgive me, sire, if I was over-enthusiastic in defending your reputation as a just and wise monarch who sees the upholding of the law in other territories as an example to his own."

"I will extend the man the same courtesy I have to any other petitioner today," said the king, "and let him say his piece before I pass judgment."

"Of course, Your Majesty," and Robert bowed again and melted back into the crowd. "But do not forget that merely a week ago, your men wisely turned him away from your gates for causing an affray."

The king frowned at being interrupted. Robert bowed once more and stepped back to give the O'Rourke the floor.

"Come forth and speak your piece," and the king waved the O'Rourke forward.

If Robert had meant to knock the O'Rourke's confidence, he had succeeded, for the O'Rourke hid his shaking hand behind his back. The O'Rourke tried to bow as low as Robert and almost succeeded until his back twitched, and he jolted upright.

"Thank you for allowing me to continue, Your Majesty." The O'Rourke ran through what he wanted to say in his head until he was ready to speak. "Scotland and Ireland have shared a long heritage completely apart from the state that calls itself England. Indeed, the sounds of Scottish accents are common in the north of Ireland, and we have adopted many of your mannerisms and colloquial flourishes. In the not-too-distant past, it was even a serious topic of discussion that the kingdom of Ireland pledge our allegiance to the king of Scotland."

"Is the rebel of the shadows and bushes here to claim he speaks for Ireland?" said Robert. He raised an eyebrow to the king and smirked at the O'Rourke. "It is more ridiculous than someone posturing in clothes caked in mud in this great court and claiming they speak for the highland clans."

The O'Rourke snarled as he began to lose his cool.

"I know the lords of the north of Ireland, and they would switch their allegiance to you without hesitation if they knew they had your protection."

Robert prowled around the court in the free space beneath the king's seat. He bowed and extended his arm with a flourish as if asking some respectable young lady to dance.

"And so it begins, the merry dance of the Irish chieftains. First, I am your friend, and we jig arm-in-arm, then I remember an old grudge when we are enemies, and we clash swords, then we dance arm-in-arm once more until the queen places gold in the pocket of one, and they slit the throat of the other."

Robert stopped swaying from side to side.

"Is this a serious proposition by this known liar and murderer? Sire, do not be deceived by his deceitful words for who knows what could happen were your judgement to become tarnished by them."

Robert skipped behind the O'Rourke.

"But let us not be poor hosts and let him have his say. If he is right, you could double the size of your kingdom. You would have the troublesome, unruly clans to the north in the highlands and, for fairness' sake, let us say the equally unruly Irish clans across the sea. Sire, you could be in an eternal loop touring your kingdom, resolving blood feuds and land disputes, and as soon as you took down your tents, they would be at each other's throats again. But let that not interrupt the fairy tales of the past. This wanted man has to tell you that Scotland and Ireland are really all one big people, and everything would be fine and dandy if you ruled them all, irrespective of who actually rules Ireland. It would do us good to have some amusement after all the tales of strife and murder we heard today from the other clans."

The king's lip curled upwards as he gripped the arms of his chair.

"Please finish your pleading, O'Rourke, before the English ambassador sucks all the air out of the room."

The O'Rourke bowed again.

"Thank you for allowing me to continue. Now, my ancestors, for as long as time is recorded, have always gone to the Scottish islands to hire men—"

"Sorry to interrupt," said Robert, "but I have a question. Why is it always Scottish blood they wish to spill to resolve an Irish blood feud?"

"Please refrain from interrupting me," said the O'Rourke, a little red-faced. "The king has given me permission to speak, and I wish to take advantage of that."

"I am so sorry. I do not mean to be rude. I am unfamiliar with the code of the bandits of the woods of Ireland. However, in a respectable court such as that of the powerful and just king of Scotland, he has advisors to assist him in deciding.

We must translate petitions into something the king can understand and relate to. He cannot relate to someone who slits the throats of the representatives of legitimate monarchs or preys on innocent farmers to rob them of their livelihood and justify that by some unwritten fantasy that they own all the land. But please continue. May I beg to be so presumptuous, but you still have the king's ear."

The O'Rourke folded his arms, cast aside all the eloquent flourishes and tales of the past, and decided to get straight to it. If the king did not control the English ambassador, he would not get to the crux of the matter before the king tired.

"Sire, I am here to hire mercenaries and seek your permission. I have brought these four beautiful wolfhounds from the lands of Ireland as a gift for you."

The O'Rourke waved to Francisco, who brought the dogs forward so the king could inspect them. The king finally broke into a smile.

"They are fine beasts indeed. I assume they are already trained as hunting dogs and friendly enough for my men to take them?"

The O'Rourke smiled.

"Only the best for the king of Scotland."

The English ambassador could not allow the goodwill of the gift to settle.

"Those highland chieftains had better make sure this beggar has some money in his pockets before he asks them to shed blood for him," said Robert. "My men inform me that he came with little baggage besides those dogs."

"I will not be insulted by the accusations of being a beggar," said the O'Rourke, who finally snapped and cast a finger in the English ambassador's direction.

Robert grinned, knowing he had finally got under the O'Rourke's skin. He bowed in front of the king once more.

"Please forgive me, sire, and let our guest continue his pleadings to leave mere pennies on the table when requesting the finest feast."

Francisco, now empty-handed, stepped backwards to the front of the on-lookers to observe what happened next. A hand hooked his elbow, and his eyebrows raised when he heard Spanish spoken in his ear.

"The Spanish ambassador wishes to speak with you when your Irish companion has finished his pleadings with the king."

He turned around to see who whispered in his ear, but all he could see were the pale faces and red beards of the Scottish looking at the proceedings.

"How many mercenaries would you be looking for?" said the king.

"As many as you can spare," the O'Rourke said as he smiled at them getting down to business. "But two thousand would do for starters."

The O'Rourke grinned at Robert. The king sat up but did not give away his thoughts through expression.

"I will consider your request and summon you when I have decided."

"That is a wise choice, sire," said Robert. "The amount of Scottish blood to be spilt to carry out a war with the kingdom you wish to unite under one monarchy should the dearly beloved Queen Elizabeth pass away needs consideration indeed. Allow me to offer my services to supply any information you may require to make that decision. I especially have information about the character of the man in whose hands it is proposed we place the fate of so many Scottish lives, indeed the fate of the Scottish throne."

"I'm sure I will not have to ask for your opinion, for you will freely give it," said the king. "However, O'Rourke, a term of my considering your request is that you stay within the confines of Edinburgh until I have reached a decision."

"I most certainly will, and your people have made me feel very welcome."

The O'Rourke bowed once again and slipped back into the crowd. He beamed from ear to ear and went to find Francisco.

CHAPTER 45

AMONGST FRIENDS

F rancisco trailed behind the O'Rourke as they made their way out of the grand hall, his mind racing to decipher the success of the meeting. As they exited the hall with purposeful strides, it was clear that the O'Rourke's thoughts aligned with his confident gait. Francisco was more conflicted, for success would only send him back to Ireland.

"Psst, hey, come here."

Hidden in the shadows, a mysterious figure beckoned Francisco to follow him. His voice was low and husky, barely audible. Francisco could not see the man's face, but something about his demeanour compelled him to take a chance and follow.

"I will meet you at the tavern later, Señor O'Rourke," he said towards the O'Rourke's back and interpreted the casual wave over the O'Rourke's shoulder as permission to leave.

The man's hand waved impatiently, beckoning Francisco through the dimly lit corridor. Francisco felt for the dagger that should have been secured in his belt but remembered with disappointment that all weapons had been confiscated upon entering the hall. The man shook his head disapprovingly at Francisco's tense and aggressive stance. He opened the door to a nearby room and gestured for Francisco to enter. Tentatively, Francisco peeked around the corner and was met with the warm, beaming smile of a well-dressed middle-aged man from his homeland. His heart swelled with a sense of familiarity and comfort in this strange place.

"Greetings, my friend. I am Juan de Villamediana, the Spanish ambassador to the king of Scotland. We heard a Spanish officer was advising the O'Rourke so we were curious to meet him."

Francisco's eyes welled up with tears as he ran towards the man and embraced him tightly.

"It is so good to meet my fellow countrymen. You do not know how good it is to see you."

Juan patted him on the back and held him for as long as he considered it not rude to break the embrace.

"Are you a survivor of the Armada?"

"My ship sank off the coast of Ireland, and I have had to make my way there ever since. The O'Rourke has been a good friend to the king, protecting his subjects by taking us in until the English governor invaded his lands. He saved many a Spaniard's life."

"I will have my men watch over him. Are there any other survivors with you?"

"No, I am alone. Some men were left in the land of the O'Rourkes to fend for themselves. Others the O'Rourke helped escape to a ship off the coast of Ireland."

"I have heard that such a ship returned to Spain."

Francisco tugged on Juan's sleeve as the tears welled up in his eyes.

"Do you know who survived? I am looking for my friend Pedro."

Juan stepped back from such raw emotion.

"I only know that some men made it back to Spain, but I don't know any details."

"Could you find out for me?"

"First things first. Please sit, for I need to ask you some questions about your experiences."

"Of course."

Francisco looked behind him and settled into an adjacent chair. His nervous smile indicated his eagerness to please. Juan gave him a kind look, for he knew time was short but did not want to apply unnecessary pressure.

"The king has been petitioned numerous times to send an army to Ireland. What do you know of our prospective Irish allies and their military capabilities?"

Francisco's heart raced with anticipation. His tongue caught between his teeth in an attempt to contain his excitement. He knew that whatever answer he gave here could shape the course of his entire life.

"I have lived with, advised and trained the men of the O'Rourke. I have spent time with the Maguires and lived amongst the O'Donnells for nearly a year. I would be most valuable to the king to stand at his side and advise him which petitioner is a charlatan and which is not. But back in Spain," said Francisco, smiling. "He would be hard-pressed to find anyone with more experience."

Juan nodded and smiled.

"I will write to the king and tell him of you but request that you stay at the side of the O'Rourke."

Francisco's head dropped.

"What if the Scottish king grants him his wish for his mercenaries, and he has to return to Ireland at the head of an army? What would the king do with me then? All I have striven for is to return to my homeland and see my family. I have more than done my duty."

"What is your name so I may mention it in the correspondence to our king?"

Francisco swallowed hard. To give his name may be to give away his identity. He did not know if all the records of his trial and conviction made it back to Spain or had ended up at the bottom of the ocean. But if he lied to the king God may curse him to forever remain at the side of the O'Rourke.

"I am Francisco Butero, captain of the *San Pedro* in what was once the king's great and glorious fleet. As you see, I have been down on my luck but hope to revive my circumstances by serving our God-fearing king."

Juan raised his eyebrows.

"A captain no less. To survive in such a hostile land for so long is indeed an achievement. The king will be especially interested in that."

At least the ambassador had not recognised Francisco's name. That was something, at least. But he had to probe more to see what potentially awaited him when he returned home.

"Were the survivors of the Armada treated as heroes?"

The ambassador's voice changed as if he was slightly embarrassed.

"Those who made it home were greeted with due reverence by their families, but some of those who had not performed so well were left to the king's wrath. Rest assured, you have served your master well and will be handsomely rewarded."

But Francisco was not so sure. Some survivors knew who he was and what he had been convicted of. He would never escape the king's wrath, but maybe he could impress him with his knowledge of the Irish.

"I wish to return home as soon as possible," said Francisco. "Please make any necessary arrangements and offer my services to the king."

Juan nodded and showed Francisco to the door.

"It will be done, but for now your mission continues. Be the eyes and ears of the king until recalled."

A small smile tugged at the corners of Francisco's mouth as he nodded. His heart swelled, and a renewed hope filled his chest, relieving the dense fog of doubt and despair weighing him down. It was a glimmer of light in the darkness, a ray of sunshine after a long nightmare. It gave him the strength to keep going.

CHAPTER 46
THE DAGGER STRIKES

For several nights, the renowned O'Rourke held court in the bustling tavern, drawing in all the Irish of Edinburgh to partake in his company. The air bounced with the scent of ale and wine, and those under their influence danced and swayed out into the streets, spilling their merriment onto the cobbled pathways. Bards-in-exile lifted their voices in traditional songs of old, while poets wove tales of myths and heroes from distant lands. The O'Rourke revelled in the lively atmosphere, feeling like he had been transported back to his glory days in Bailie Nua. As he sang, his laughter echoed through the establishment until his voice grew hoarse. He embraced everyone within reach, shaking hands and sharing hugs with genuine warmth. And when his belly could hold no more ale and food, he attempted to fill it even further, unable to resist the temptation of this joyous gathering.

The ragtag group of men who gathered around him were a mix of exiles from Ireland. Their faces were weathered and weary from years of seditious activities. Alongside them were merchants and battle-hardened warriors returning from service in the wars of Europe, where they had fought as mercenaries for the Spanish king. As word spread, more and more people flocked to see the infamous O'Rourke, eager to pledge their loyalty and offerings to him. Some offered their swords, others their ships or money to his cause.

Francisco joined the celebrations for a different set of reasons, causes of similar joy, no doubt, but reasons he felt no compulsion to reveal to his friend or his hosts. He had repaid any debt he felt towards the O'Rourke, bringing him to the brink of his greatest success.

On the third night of celebrations, he slumped down onto his chair, barely able to mouth the words of the refrain the room had sung for what seemed like forever. The O'Rourke sat beside him and slapped his knee.

"This is it. I can feel it." The O'Rourke gritted his teeth and shook his arms to relieve his frustration. "I have all the swords in the room. Who knows how many other Irishmen there are dotted around Scotland who would be willing to fight for my cause?"

"You certainly have found your audience." Francisco raised his mug to salute him.

"You can return with me and train the men. We can have the most glorious army in Ireland," said the O'Rourke. He turned to Francisco, his eyes the size of small plates. "We can write to your king to send his men and finish the English. You can return home a hero unless you find some young Irish girl to settle down with."

Francisco chinked mugs.

"Let us not let our imaginations run away and enjoy the here and now. No matter where we end up, we'll have to endure some hardship to get there."

"Pah! You Spaniards don't know how to have fun."

"It is true," said Francisco. "How can we think of having fun when our teeth rattle in our mouths because your countries are so cold?"

The O'Rourke slapped him on the shoulder.

"Nothing a thick blanket and a woman to warm your bed wouldn't cure. Why don't you take your pick? Many a young woman would like to be seen with you. You may be a bit old, but the Mediterranean charm makes up for some of it."

Francisco playfully pushed him away.

"Save your jesting for your new drinking friends. Now, did you have something serious to say when you came over here?"

The O'Rourke flashed his teeth.

"The king wants to see us tomorrow." The O'Rourke butted Francisco's mug with his. "So lay off the ale. You've got to be at your best."

"I'll be saying nothing. You should heed your own advice." Francisco pointed at the O'Rourke's mug.

"Sure the hangover will just remind me of the seriousness of the occasion. A bit of ale in me will do me a world of good when I have to make speeches to this lot. When I get granted mercenaries, they will soon realise they must leave their families for a while."

"I wouldn't overestimate the king's generosity," said Francisco. His brow knitted to ensure the barely sober O'Rourke knew this was a warning. "He is an ambitious man and it does not necessarily serve his ambition to have you marauding around Ireland at the head of a Scottish army."

"If you're going to be a misery guts, why don't you spend your evening on your knees in prayer? I'm sure our hosts can point you in the direction of a church. In the meantime, I'll drink your share."

Francisco knew he would not wipe the grin off the O'Rourke's face, and now was not the time for warnings.

"Look, the bard is about to finish the song, so you can go and request the next one."

The O'Rourke pricked up his ears.

"You're right. My, you have settled well. Drink your ale, and don't be so miserable."

With that, the O'Rourke was gone, elbowing his way through the crowd to the bard.

The next day the O'Rourke was administered a bucket of water in the face, purely for medicinal purposes.

"What... what are you doing to me?"

His arms clawed at the air, but broken fingernails, no matter how sharp, would not defeat this enemy. Only gravity would.

"The day has come to meet the king," said Francisco as he lowered the by-now-empty bucket. "We have to prepare no matter how much of a formality you think this will be."

"I may be wet but I am not a fool," said the O'Rourke as he threw off his blankets to sit up in his bed. "I may have been robbed of my kingdom, youth and ability to wake up after a night's drinking without a sore head, but I know how to greet a king. Now get me some bread and water and a bucket to wash. You are cast in the role of my assistant today, oh captain of the high seas. If we succeed, you will have an abundance of riches with which to replace your ship."

Francisco laughed.

"I will leave the pot for the washing water to boil extra long, for hopefully, the sting of it on your face will sober you up."

The O'Rourke quickly got dressed and secured his scabbard to his belt.

"So, have you prepared an adaptable speech for the king today? Come what may?" said Francisco.

"The time for pleading is over," said the O'Rourke. "He decides what he decides, and I live with the consequences."

The O'Rourke sat and ate, and Francisco kept everyone else away so he could have some time alone with his thoughts. But such efforts were to disappoint Francisco, for the O'Rourke was no more sensible than before. The O'Rourke threw down his napkin.

"Right, I am finished. Assemble the men. For now, we go to the castle."

The O'Rourke stood in the doorway of the tavern and faced outwards to his cheering supporters outside. Francisco lifted the O'Rourke's heavy outer coat and symbolically placed it upon his shoulders.

"First to the castle, then to the shores of Ireland," the O'Rourke called out to his supporters. They cheered and raised their weapons or mugs or threw their hats in the air.

"Follow me, men."

With an air of confidence and determination, the O'Rourke strode out of the tavern, followed closely by his loyal companions Francisco and Diarmuid. The bustling streets seemed to quiet in reverence as they passed by, the crowds parting and encircling them like a protective shield. Eyes turned, and heads craned to glimpse the O'Rourke marching towards the castle gates, surrounded by a fierce and well-armed mob. Every inch of him exuded power and authority as he approached the gate, his dagger striking it with a resounding thud that echoed through the city streets.

"Open up. It is the O'Rourke, and I have an appointment to see the king."

The constable on duty at the gate tower stuck his head over the top of the wall.

"Disperse your mob and surrender your weapons, or you will not gain entry, and we will set the king's horsemen upon you."

The O'Rourke snarled at such aggression.

"We come in peace, and this is merely a demonstration for the king of the strength of feeling of his people for supporting their Irish brethren."

The constable's demeanour did not change.

"The king devotes much of his time to listening directly to his people and does not need a mob on his doorstep to know what they want. Now disperse your mob before we declare you hostile."

The O'Rourke shook his head and smiled but turned to his supporters.

"Children of Ireland, I must go and see the king, but I must do so relatively alone at his request. Please disperse and reassemble at the O'Neill Tavern this evening so I can update you on what happened today, and we can celebrate and plan our return home. Do not worry about me, for the king is our friend and ally and would not call me here if it was not so. Here is to the liberation of the O'Rourkes and the other clans of Ireland."

The O'Rourke held aloft his dagger, and the crowd held up whatever weapons they had and saluted their own clans. They began to drift away to the refrains of the numerous songs to the past they shared the night before. A few minutes later, the O'Rourke, Francisco and Diarmuid stood alone beneath the gate.

"Well?" called the O'Rourke to the guards. "I am as alone as a man of my standing will get."

The constable tutted and ordered the gate to be opened. He climbed down the stairs and stood with his guards on the other side of the gate.

"Surrender all your weapons to my men, or you will not gain entry to the castle."

The O'Rourke reached for his dagger and held it out by the tip.

"Is your master going to let you volunteer to come to Ireland with me? It'll make you a rich man."

The constable glared at him.

"I am happy in service to my king right where I am. Now, is that all your weapons? We have no wish to be unfriendly and search you, but you should fear the king's wrath if you lie to the king's men."

The O'Rourke looked to his two companions. Diarmuid threw his eyes to the heavens and took a concealed dagger from the small of his back. The constable stood directly in front of the O'Rourke.

"Is that everything?"

It was the O'Rourke's turn to throw his eyes to the heavens and take a concealed dagger from his boot.

"Can we go now?" he said.

"Let us proceed," said the constable as he indicated the way. "I wish to delay you no further."

The constable walked in front and his men behind. They entered the doorway of the main tower and waited for permission to enter the great hall.

Francisco caught sight of the ambassador's agent he had met the week or so before, crouched down behind a pillar near the entrance. The man's face was tense, and his eyes darted around nervously. He signalled for Francisco to follow him again, but this time with more urgency. Francisco scowled and pointed towards the back of the O'Rourke's head, wanting to stay focused on the task. But the man gestured to him with even more fervour, his hand slicing through the air like a blade. Frustrated, Francisco pointed back at the O'Rourke, trying to clarify that he needed to keep his attention on their target. The man stepped forward and waved his hand as if it were a paddle, desperately trying to get Francisco's attention. With a sigh, Francisco stepped away from the group to admonish the man and prevent him from causing any distractions during this crucial moment.

"Now."

The guards turned their gleaming axes and swords towards Diarmuid and the O'Rourke, their muscles tensed and ready to strike. Diarmuid's hands trembled as he reached for something hidden in his garments, desperation and fear etched on his face. The constable's sword pierced through his chest with a sickening thud, causing Diarmuid to crumple to the floor in a pool of blood. The O'Rourke's face went ashen as he threw up his hands in surrender. Francisco moved towards the O'Rourke, but the ambassador's agent grabbed his arm.

"Come this way if you want to live."

CHAPTER 47
DEMONS OF THE SEA

The man's grip was firm as he dragged Francisco into a dark, musty room. His jaw was tense, burdened with the weight of a truth about to spill out. But Francisco waved him away, his mind racing, his heart thumping. He crept towards the door and cautiously pressed his eye to the small crack, only to be met with the intimidating figure of a one-armed man standing before the O'Rourke.

"I hereby arrest you under the authority of Queen Elizabeth." said Captain Williamson, "with the co-operation of the king of Scotland. You are charged with treason and will stand trial in her majesty's courts in London." Captain Williamson grinned and pressed his face towards the O'Rourke. "I have followed you across Ireland and Scotland, waiting for this moment, and it feels better than I imagined it would." He leant back with a satisfied grin. "Throw him in jail until we are ready to leave."

Francisco turned to the man with a crown of beady sweat and a face as white as any man's who was born in a bog.

"Did we walk into an ambush?" Francisco snarled. "Did you know about this all along?"

Francisco squeezed his knuckles white as his face reddened.

"We couldn't save him," said the ambassador's agent as he cowered before Francisco's anger. "He was always doomed. The Scottish king has aspirations to succeed to the throne of England so he could not be seen to be aiding Irish rebels. Why did you come here believing any different, for it is well known?"

Francisco dropped and turned his head.

"Maybe it was a convenient way to be rid of him by those who did not want him around."

"I would think that is along the right track, señor. The ambassador used up much of his political credit to plead for your life with the king. The Scottish king still wants friendly relations with Spain, and the ambassador convinced him it would not look good to publicly execute the captain of a Spanish warship. The Scottish king relented but fears once the English captain finds out you are here he will come after you as well. We have prepared a ship to take you to the Netherlands and then to Spain. But you must hurry."

But Francisco's feet were glued to the floor.

"What about my friend? I cannot leave him to die after all we have been through."

"Forget your friend. He is already dead. The ambassador has neither the will nor the means to release him. Now come before the guards come searching for you."

Francisco felt paralysed, unable to move even a muscle. His mind was consumed with thoughts of the O'Rourke, a man who had saved him countless times. But in this moment, all he could think about was the foolishness of Eoghan O'Rourke's charge into the ambush that had been prepared for him. The memory flooded his senses and overwhelmed any other thoughts that tried to surface. Now was not the time for foolishness. It was the time to survive.

"Lead the way," said Francisco.

Francisco arrived at the docks with a few hours of daylight remaining and was ushered through the chaotic hustle and bustle by a man who seemed to know his way around. Passing by stacks of crates and barrels, they finally reached a small merchant ship that was being loaded with various goods for export to the Netherlands. The captain of the ship, a grizzled and portly figure, emerged from the vessel and made his way down the wooden plank onto the dock. The pungent smell of saltwater clung to him like a second skin. He greeted Francisco with a firm handshake before turning to inspect his precious cargo.

"She may not look like much compared to the monster you once command-ed, but she is fast and light and would outrun most ships we could encounter on our way."

"As long as she does not get stopped nor rock too much, I will be satisfied. My sea legs were robbed from me in a dream in an Irish bog."

The captain slapped him on the shoulders.

"It will all come flooding back to you and I don't mean that literally. I don't want to curse your ship."

"All I seek now is a quiet life," said Francisco. "To sit on your deck, read a book, think of reuniting with my family or watch the clouds go by overhead. Such things are what heaven is made of for a man like me."

"Well, I'm sure I can arrange some clouds."

One porter ran up to the captain.

"Scottish soldiers are coming. They are looking for the companion of the Irish rebel."

The captain's face dropped.

"Load the ship and cast off. We need to get out of here."

Francisco was bundled onto the ship as roughly as any piece of cargo. The ambassador's man disappeared into the crowd of bustling sailors and cargo handlers on the docks. A band of heavily armed men charged down the docks towards them as Francisco's ship slowly pulled away from the shore. The wood-en planks creaked underfoot as the ship cut through the water, leaving a flurry of activity and shouts from the soldiers on land. Francisco could feel the salty ocean breeze on his face and hear the seagulls crying above him. He inhaled deeply through his nostrils and closed his eyes. He embraced the start of his journey back home.

Francisco was given little time to find his sea legs, for the storms started not long after they had put out to sea. They sailed for a couple of days, hugging the English coast, but they could not land, seek shelter or turn back because of the cargo they held. Francisco felt guilty as he felt the eyes of the pale, seasick men judging and cursing him. He considered throwing himself overboard, which would relieve everyone of their burden. Since he went missing in Ireland, there was a chance he may be declared a hero and save his family the humiliation of welcoming back a convicted man. But Francisco took to his knees once more and prayed. It felt hollow and contrived, but he persisted anyway.

The time had come to leave the English coast and brave the North Sea, for the English sea patrols had become more frequent. Francisco climbed out of the hull and onto the deck. He knew these seas well but never like this. It was if the demons of the Scottish sea had flown south to finally swallow him up. He looked through the crashing waves that battered the sides of the boat and tossed it about as if it were a toy sailing across a little pond. The swirling collision of the kaleidoscope of grey hell above his head was a familiar sight too. He tried to pick out the coastline for he was sure he recognised this section of the sea. It was especially meaningful to him as he thought it was the very point where he left the line to repair his ship which had set him on this wretched path.

"CURSE YOU DEMONS OF THE SEA THAT TORMENT ME. YOU MAY HAVE DRAGGED ME THROUGH SEVEN SHADES OF HELL BUT YOU WILL NEVER BREAK ME!"

But there was a prolonged crack overhead, and something indeed broke. A beam of wood fell from the mast, and Francisco's head was one of the objects that broke its fall. Francisco fell to the deck and lay there as the chaos of the ship and the sea became one.

CHAPTER 48
SNARING THE PREY

"I demand to see the king. I demand to see the king," the O'Rourke roared over his shoulder as he struggled in a throng of guards. Captain Williamson followed behind with a sword in his remaining hand, beaming at the thrill of bagging his prize.

"Who are you, an Englishman, to arrest me on Scottish soil?"

"I am just an agent of her majesty taking a criminal back for trial in the proper jurisdiction," said the captain as he smirked at his prisoner. "You are no great lover of the law and proper jurisdiction, as will soon be established in your trial."

The O'Rourke struggled as much as he could, but Williamson's men had a firm grip on him.

"I am here in Scotland as a diplomat for my clan," cried the O'Rourke, "and I therefore demand immunity from these charges."

Williamson waved him away.

"I could read you out the warrant the king himself signed for your arrest, but I won't bore you with the details. I hope you have a few friends in London willing to lend you substantial amounts of money for lawyers of the quality to stand in front of her majesty. They don't come cheap, you know."

"We should settle our differences here and now. Me and you in the courtyard in front of the king."

Captain Williamson laughed.

"Do you think the king will consider you a brave man if you challenge a one-armed man to a duel? But to earn your reprieve, you have to also win. No, I am an agent of her majesty, and she pays me to bring men like you to justice. Not in a street brawl but in a court of law for all to see. Now stop inconveniencing my men with your struggling and go peacefully. You need to keep your wits for your defence."

The guards threw him into a cell beneath the castle, where his demands to see the king went unanswered.

For months on end, the O'Rourke was left to his own thoughts and fears in his secluded cell. Outside, the king's men worked tirelessly to suppress any protests over his controversial arrest. But not all could be controlled. When word of the O'Rourke's incarceration reached the streets, the fury of his supporters boiled over into rioting and destruction. In reprisal, the once bustling O'Neill's tavern now lay in ruins. Its walls crumbled from the flames that had engulfed it by order of the king. As for the O'Rourke himself, he remained silent and still, numb to the chaos erupting around him.

Finally, once the disquiet had died down and the memory of the O'Rourke had begun to fade, Captain Williamson and his soldiers arrived to forcibly remove the O'Rourke from his cell. With rough hands, they dragged him out and tossed him into a carriage that was sealed shut and covered with heavy canvas. It was a long journey to the docks where he was loaded onto a ship bound for London.

A week later, exhausted and disoriented, the O'Rourke found himself imprisoned in the infamous Tower of London. His bed consisted of nothing but piles of damp straw, and the only view he had was of dark stone walls rising endlessly above him with a narrow slit of light he could never reach.

Captain Williamson descended the steps to the dark, musty cells, a sinister grin plastered across his face. He peered down through the sliding window in the prison door at O'Rourke, hunched on the damp straw and determinedly avoiding eye contact with the captain. The air was thick with the stench of sweat, fear, and despair. O'Rourke's ragged breaths echoed off the cold stone walls, laboured but defiant. But despite the oppressive atmosphere, he refused to give Captain Williamson the satisfaction of acknowledging his presence. Captain Williamson unlocked the door and stood towering on the threshold.

"I chased you all over Ireland," said Captain Williamson. "You were the proudest of the proud. Now look at you. Pathetic."

The O'Rourke turned around on his knees and faced the wall.

"We asked amongst the Irish merchants and the gentry who had settled in London if any of them were prepared to stump up for your defence or asked if they knew anyone who would. Do you know what their answers were?"

The O'Rourke looked downwards and muttered some curses to the floor.

"No, you don't know? Neither do we, for none of them replied. But do not concern yourself. The queen wants justice to be done and seen to be done, so she shall appoint a lawyer for your defence. At her own expense to boot."

A guttural growl came from the back of the cell.

"I'll speak in my own defence."

"What was that? Sorry. I couldn't hear you?" The captain cupped an ear towards the cell.

"I'll speak in my own defence."

"What? Sorry?"

The O'Rourke turned around, his face a blaze of red.

"I'll speak in my own defence, God damn you, I'll speak in my own defence."

Captain Williamson laughed.

"As you wish. Be it on your own head. But I doubt you will know the intricacies of court behaviour or be able to weave your way through the twists and turns of the law."

"It doesn't matter. I'm a dead man anyway."

"What was that?"

"Leave me until you return with a trial date."

"That is why I am here. It begins next week." The captain turned to one of his men. "Throw in the quill and paper." He turned back to the O'Rourke.

"To work on your defence. Never let it be said you were treated unfairly." He laughed and slammed the door shut.

CHAPTER 49
DEJA VU

A sudden chill cascaded over Francisco's face, jolting him awake. He strained to lift his head, but it felt as though a heavy weight was pressing down on it, smothering him in a thick layer of numbness. His limbs refused to obey his commands, trapped in the claustrophobic tunnel of pain and disorientation. Through the haze, he could hear muffled voices as if they were shouting through layers of water. Desperately, he tried to move, but his body was unresponsive – as if his orders were bouncing off a solid wall in his brain. Slowly, feeling returned to his hands, bringing a tingling sensation. As he flexed his pins and needles-possessed fingers, he became aware of the cold water and gritty sand beneath them. Memories of a living nightmare flooded back and he couldn't help but sob bitter tears that mixed with the cool water beneath his face.

But then, something changed. Voices in the distance. Friend or foe? Francisco did not know. The voices grew clearer and more distinct, mingled with an overwhelming surge of energy coursing through his body. Did he need to run? Did he have the power to defend himself? He pushed himself up from the ground with all his might, only to collapse back down in defeat. But determination fuelled him as he lifted himself once more, this time managing to raise his head off the ground. Then, he heard those voices speaking Spanish. They spoke Spanish! Relief washed over him as he realised he was no longer alone in this foreign land. A curious face peered down at him from below a morion helmet before everything went black again.

As Francisco opened his eyes, he first noticed the thick thatch above him. The sturdy construction of the roof could be felt in the heat radiating off it. He focused on moving his fingers, feeling the coarse texture of the blanket beneath him and its tightly woven edges. With great effort, he slowly raised his head to see a guard with a shining morion helmet rising from his seat nearby. The metal glinted in the sunlight, casting shadows on the surrounding walls.

"Tell the captain he is awake."

Francisco strained to lift his head, but the weight of exhaustion pulled him back down. He could hear a flurry of voices around him, their words blending like a symphony of chirping birds. Amongst the noise, he was grateful for the familiar sound of Spanish, like a soothing melody in the chaos.

As the captain strode into the room, his authoritative presence gripped all. He motioned for the guard to vacate his seat, and with a screech, the chair was dragged across the rough floor. With great effort, he placed it in front of Francisco so that their eyes could meet, though Francisco's head barely lifted to acknowledge him.

"Who are you?" said the captain. "How do we know you are not an English spy?"

Francisco smiled at the roof.

"You do not know my joy to be surrounded by Spanish voices."

The captain leaned forward.

"I cannot vouch for the truth in that, but even English spies are capable of flattery. Why should we nurse you back to health when you could be a spy?"

"Please tell me where I am, for my answer is long and it could aid in the storytelling."

"This is the Netherlands, the Spanish Netherlands."

Francisco raised his head and struck his pillow. It was not home, but it was definitely a sanctuary on the way home.

"I set sail from Edinburgh on a merchant ship. Are the crew here? Did anyone else survive?"

"Roberto?" the captain said to the guard at the door.

"A few survived, captain, but most washed up on shore dead."

The captain turned to Francisco.

"You are the only one alive and awake to tell the tale. And to top it all off, you speak Spanish. Can you see why we would be suspicious of you?"

"I can understand your caution. Does the war still continue?"

"The war with the English? It drags on, and we are in a stalemate. They bombard us now with their spies. Hence our suspicion of a Spanish speaker being shipwrecked and coming from the direction of the English sea."

"I have a letter of passage signed by the Spanish ambassador to the king of Scotland. He can vouch for me."

"Alas, we found nothing in your pockets. You had no bag that washed up beside you, and the ship sank to the bottom of the sea. We only have your word and do not know if you are good for it."

"I am a survivor of the Armada. I had to hide out in Ireland for a couple of years and then went to Scotland to help the Irish chieftain who protected me hire mercenaries to return to Ireland to retake his lands. Unfortunately, he was given up by traitors, and I fled under the protection of the ambassador. I got caught in a storm and ended up here."

"That sounds like a story I would like to hear in full one day, but were you that traitor who gave the Irish rebel up?"

"No."

Francisco tried to hide the insult he felt, but he barely had the strength to talk, let alone hide his feelings.

"That man was my friend, and it broke my heart when I could not stay and defend him."

"Then you must give us something to persuade us that you are not a spy."

Francisco remembered the letter that should have gone from the ambassador back to Spain to plead the case for the annulment of his previous conviction. He had to pray it had arrived.

"I am Francisco Butero, the captain of the San Pedro, who took part in the Armada and sank off the coast of Ireland. My name should be in the king's records. I can give you any evidence you wish to support that."

The captain smiled and then rose to leave.

"Then I salute you, captain, and will believe you until we receive an answer from the king's clerks. In the meantime, I hope you enjoy the hospitality of the Spanish army."

"Thank you. I am just glad to be here."

CHAPTER 50

REACQUAINTANCE WITH CHAINS

Francisco lay in the army field hospital for what seemed like an eternity, slowly recovering from his injuries. The guards addressed him as Captain Butero, a title that stroked his ego and reminded him of his role in the navy. The doctors tended to the severe gash on his head, marvelling at how lucky he was to have survived such a wound. They told him he had lost a considerable amount of blood while floating unconscious in the water.

For the first week, Francisco could barely move, confined to his bed as he healed. But gradually, with the help of the guard, he began to walk around the tent until he could do so on his own by the end of the second week. As several months went by, he regained strength and mobility. He spent more time outside with the guards, joining in their laughter and lively conversations. With each passing day, Francisco's tales of his adventures in Ireland became more animated, his voice growing stronger with each retelling.

Basking in the warm glow of the blue Dutch skies, Francisco sat outside on a wooden bench. The sun's rays beat down on his skin, causing him to shield his eyes from the harsh light. He watched as the captain returned with two guards trailing behind him, their shadows looming over Francisco's seated form. The captain's powerful presence blocked the sun, creating a darkened spot in Francisco's vision. Francisco squinted against the brightness, trying to make out the captain's expression as he towered above him.

"Good morning, Captain Butero. I hope you have been enjoying the hospitality of the Spanish army?"

Francisco smiled.

"Your men have been very good company, and the food wasn't that bad either."

The captain grimaced.

"I have some good news and some bad news."

Francisco sighed.

"Well, it makes a change from my life being just bad news. Please continue."

"The good news is that you will return to Spain on the next tide."

Francisco sat up and smiled.

"So soon? What bad news could possibly follow that?"

The captain gulped, for he had become friendly with Francisco and cringed at the thought of giving him such bad news.

"You were sentenced to hang by the leader of the Armada. You are to return to Spain for trial, with the sentence to be carried out if you are found guilty."

Francisco fell off the back of the bench, choking on his words. He had to be helped back into a seated position.

"But what about all I have done for the king? The Spanish ambassador sent the king a letter to plead for him to reconsider."

The captain was not for moving.

"Save that for the court. Men, seize him."

The guards restrained the once-proud Francisco and clamped heavy iron shackles around his wrists and ankles. His skin was now pale and bruised, his eyes sunken and distant. He was thrown in with the other prisoners into a cart cage, all headed towards the same fate across the seas to Spain. The stench of sweat and fear overwhelmed Francisco's battered senses, only broken by the occasional moan or cry of despair from those trapped in the cramped confines of the cart cage. Francisco closed his eyes. He thought of his family, he thought of Pedro, he thought of God. Surely one of them would intervene to save him?

Francisco was roughly bundled onto another ship, its wooden deck slick with seawater and salt spray. The smell of fish and sweat lingered in the air as he was thrown into the dark, dank jail below deck. The rough waves rocked the ship back and forth, tossing him around like a rag doll. Despite his restraints, he could feel his stomach churning and threatening to heave.

Francisco drifted towards Spain and his impending doom on a sea of pain. The manacles chaffed, his muscles cramped up, and the howls of his fellow prisoners reverberated in his ears. The images of his time in the cell of the admiral's ship came flooding back, along with the memories of the jailer trying to torment him. He took to his knees to pray, but his knees were no longer the same, and soon he had to sit, for the pain was too much to bear. He tried to settle himself down by counting the time it took to travel to Spain, for he knew the journey from the Netherlands well. But trauma seeped through every crack as the waters did when the admiral's ship struck rocks and broke in two off the coast of Ireland. He tried to think of his family, but they became a distant, unreachable memory. He tried to sleep, but that was when the trauma found his mind at its most defenceless. He took to prayer. His words were hollow, but the exercise distracted his mind enough for him to pass the time.

Francisco had lost track of the days when the ship finally juddered to a halt. Francisco was dragged from his slumber and shoved onto the ship's deck. He shielded his eyes from the bright sunlight and stumbled off the ship, looking every bit the condemned man that he was. Slowly, his vision cleared, and he took in the skyline of the bustling port, his eyes tracing familiar landmarks that he had sketched countless times in his mind.

"I return to Bilbao, a destitute criminal. What if my family have come down to greet me?"

Tears blurred his vision, a thick haze of self-pity clouding his thoughts. He had endured so much and should have been welcomed home as a hero, but now he had to endure this. In the distance, he saw faint shadows moving in the harsh sunlight, their identities shrouded by its brightness. Fear gripped him as he anticipated the arrival of his family, hoping they wouldn't see him in chains and view him as a failure. But no one came except for more guards, their armour glinting in the unforgiving light.

"Am I to stay in Bilbao? Can I see my family?" he said to the guards.

They marched him across the pier and threw him into a covered prison wagon. His hands scraped on the uneven wooden floor. He looked puzzled at his captors as they locked the cell door.

"It's Madrid for you. The king wants to see you."

Francisco's heart leapt. The king wished to see him. Maybe it was for his wise counsel? He looked at his filthy, bloody hands and his sleeves that had turned to rags. There could be only one outcome.

CHAPTER 51
A TANGLED WEB

From the slit of a small window, the O'Rourke peered down at the mighty river Thames. The bustling city sprawled before him, its grandeur and chaos a stark contrast to the quiet countryside he was used to. Below, the docks were alive with activity. Ships of all shapes and sizes sailed leisurely up the river, carrying precious goods and hardworking fishermen. Women scrubbed clothes and other items along the shore in the cool water. As he looked out at this scene, the O'Rourke let out a heavy sigh that seemed to weigh down his entire body. His hand trembled as he brought it up to rub the bridge of his nose, lost in thoughts of his uncertain future.

A dull thud echoed through the stone walls as a knock came on the heavy wooden door. The sound was sharp and insistent, like a warning. He was allowed out of his dark, cramped cell to meet with potential legal counsel for the first time since his trial date had been set. These lawyers would be paid anonymously by his few supporters within the exiled Irish community in London who could afford their services. It had taken them a long time to persuade the O'Rourke to accept their help and legal representation as he had proved very mistrustful. As the door opened, a young assistant hurried in, his footsteps echoing off the cold, damp floor.

"I am here to present you with a selection of clothes you may wish to wear for your trial. Shall I usher the servants in and have them lay the clothes on your bed?"

"Will the queen be at my trial?"

The boy looked confused and irritated at being delayed in completing his task.

"I have no idea, lord. Shall I lay your clothes on your bed?"

"I need to know who I am supposed to impress before I pick my clothes?"

"I know nothing of trials or who will be in attendance besides yourself. I only know about clothes. May I lay them on the bed?"

"If you must. And tell my legal counsel to hurry up if you see him."

"I think he is already here, lord. Shall I send him up?"

"Yes, yes, and don't dilly-dally about it either."

The boy left, and the O'Rourke was left to stare at what was left behind on the bed. He was at least allowed the dignity of selecting his own clothes.

A sharp knock jolted the door, followed by the entrance of a tall, skinny man. His long nose and pointed chin were accentuated by a neatly trimmed beard that matched the colour of his dark, bushy eyebrows. He entered the room with a stack of leather-bound notebooks tucked tightly under his arm, his posture rigid and proper as if he were carrying something of utmost importance.

"And who may you be?"

The man put down his books and stuck out his hand.

"Ardgal MacAodhgáin of the Brehon family, the MacAodhgáins. I'm from the Munster branch of the family and used extensively by the Irish merchants for they place little trust in the locals."

"Then I have something in common with your previous employers. Sit and let us talk, for we have little time to prepare."

Ardgal perched on the end of the chair with his notebook resting in his lap.

"What do they mean to do to me?" said the O'Rourke. "Do they really mean to put me on trial? Surely this is some cruel jest designed to insult me?"

Ardgal paused as he calculated how much O'Rourke knew about his predicament. Out of politeness, he decided upon very little and would use this basis to steer his explanation.

"They mean to try you for treason and to hang you if they find you guilty."

The O'Rourke laughed.

"It is no joke," said Ardgal who did not even twitch as the O'Rourke laughed.

"Well, how can they do that? I am a foreigner. How can I be a traitor in a land that is not my own?"

"They will pose some complicated legal arguments to state why their court is the correct venue to try you in. If you could restrain yourself in these sections and let me pose my legal arguments, I will see if, at the very least, they would deport you to stand trial in Ireland."

"Oh, I would so much prefer an Irish rope to squeeze the life out of me than an English one."

Ardgal frowned.

"Try to be respectful in the court. They have your life in their hands."

The O'Rourke held Ardgal firmly in his gaze.

"I have been fighting with the English with my words and my fists since the day I was born, and you will not stop me now."

Ardgal reeled back and shook his head.

"You will get plenty of opportunity to defend yourself, but please let me lead. If you go in there angry, flailing insults, then they will skip the parts where you will get to defend yourself and move straight to sentencing."

The O'Rourke growled and raised his nose in the air.

"I expect any English court to be rigged, for that is the only way they can get me."

"Well then, you look at me as the man to get you a fair trial, and once I have created that platform upon which you can speak, then you can go out and express yourself as the O'Rourke."

The O'Rourke offered his hand to Ardgal.

"That is the most sensible thing you have said all day."

CHAPTER 52

THE SUBSTANCE OF SEVERAL TREASONS

The notorious O'Rourke was brought to the court by a formidable wall of armed guards. Their weapons glinted in the torchlight, poised and ready for any sign of trouble. As he was led to his seat at the front of the court, all eyes were on him and whispers rippled through the crowd at the sight of the savage from Ireland. Behind him, his escort stood tall and vigilant, prepared to absorb and annihilate any potential threat.

News had spread throughout London of the barbarous Irish warlord who was being put on trial for mercilessly slaughtering English soldiers and other heinous crimes. The galleries behind the O'Rourke slowly filled up with a mix of fascination and morbid curiosity. Whispered conversations and malicious rumours swirled through the crowds as they eagerly awaited the start of the trial.

It seemed someone had taken it upon themselves to spread even more venomous lies about the O'Rourke's actions, inciting a mob from the docks and slums of London to demand his execution. The mob had marched its way from the docks and, on the way to the trial, attacked any known Irish street seller, shopkeeper, or merchant they found. The street outside the court reeked with the stench of rotting fruit confiscated at the door and carelessly thrown onto the streets and alleys.

As he waited for his trial to begin, the O'Rourke idly passed the time by biting his nails. This was always the worst part for him, the tense lull before the inevitable clash of axes in battle.

The judges strode into the room, their long robes swishing behind them. Their faces were as solid as granite, and they placed their books on the table before them. The guards behind the O'Rourke commanded him to stand, and he did so with a grumble. Squinting, he studied the faces of the judges as they took their seats. He didn't recognise any of them. Where were his peers? Shouldn't those who understand his world and actions be the ones to judge him? Murmurs and rumours swirled around the packed courtroom, eyes drilling into the O'Rourke's back. But he refused to let their judgement break his focus on the matter at hand, determined to defend himself against whatever accusations lay ahead.

The lead judge glowered down from his raised platform, his piercing gaze fixed upon the O'Rourke. His black robes stretched tightly over his broad frame, and his beard was neatly trimmed. He exuded an air of authority and power. As he looked down at the O'Rourke with disdain, the crowd fell silent, holding their breath in anticipation for the trial to start.

"You are the said Brian O'Rourke, the subject of the trial today?"

"I prefer to be addressed by my official title, the O'Rourke, as I am the head of that traditional Irish clan if it is all the same to you." Ardgal glared at him. "Lord." The O'Rourke inserted the last word to please his legal counsel but to no avail.

Ardgal stood up.

"He is the said defendant, lords. Please allow him some leeway, for he is unfamiliar with the decorum of the court."

The lead judge looked unimpressed.

"He has certainly stirred up the animosity of the people, so we would advise that he contemplate any provocative statements he may wish to make, and if he must, please ensure these comments have merit."

"He has permitted me to speak on his behalf today, lords."

Ardgal sat down.

"Good," said the lead judge. "Now we can proceed."

"Excuse me."

The O'Rourke rose to address the judges.

"What is it?" the lead judge growled. "We are about to get started."

"Is the queen coming?"

The lead judge looked perplexed.

"What?"

A ripple of laughter came from the galleries. A hint of red spread on the cheeks of the O'Rourke.

"Is the queen coming? Should you not wait for her?"

More audible laughter came from the galleries.

"Why would the queen be coming?" the lead judge said as he threw his hands in the air. "Is this man drunk? Counsel, I hope you haven't let this man have one too many ales before coming to this court?"

Ardgal went to stand up but had barely left his seat before the glare of the O'Rourke sat him down again.

"I am not drunk, and I am offended that you insinuate I am. I am the O'Rourke, the leader of the O'Rourke clan, one of the most powerful clans in Ireland. Indeed we have many a high king of old Ireland in our lineage. The queen may be your sovereign, but she is not mine. I am an independent chieftain and should be afforded the respect of a foreign leader."

The O'Rourke warmed to his subject.

"If the king of France came to your shores, would you storm where he is staying and put him on trial for treason against another monarch? There are also three kingdoms established on these fair isles. They be England, where I am now stood a prisoner, Scotland, from where I was abducted, and Ireland, a kingdom I am adjacent to and, when discussing the jurisdiction of this court, not part of. I am very familiar with these matters, for often, when I enjoyed my freedom and served my people, I would go to Dublin to negotiate with the kingdom of Ireland on an equal footing. Therefore, as the leader of an independent state, I ask you, where is the queen? Only the monarch should try another sovereign leader, not this sham I see before me."

The O'Rourke sat down to the jeers of the gallery. The judge slammed his fist on his desk.

"I must have silence. Guards, ensure the galleries keep the peace. I do not want this defendant to inspire a riot with his defiance."

The guards moved to the walkways beside the galleries and tried to quell the jeers but with no success until the judge once more slammed his fist on his desk. The judge took advantage of the lull to move the case on, for he did not know how brief it would be.

"These are complex legal matters you bring up."

"Getting hung, drawn and quartered is complex for me too," said the O'Rourke to the laughter of the gallery.

"I'm glad you can find a funny side to it. We will deal with the jurisdiction, but to clear up the simplest matter, the queen is not coming and will not be persuaded to come."

"These proceedings are a sham, for I am being tried as a common criminal. It is whoever signed the warrant for my arrest and those who abducted me that should be here in my place to stand trial for kidnap."

"You do yourself no good to say the queen should be in the dock with you."

"Then she should employ better lawyers to think of more apt charges than treason."

The judge's hand clawed the air as he regained his composure.

"That is all to do with jurisdiction. These questions will be covered during the duration of this court case. However, we must begin this trial now that we have sorted the issues of the defendant's guest list. Please, clerk. For the benefit of the court, read out the charges levelled at the defendant."

The clerk rose from his seat, his back hunched slightly under the weight of a large ledger in his hands. He gingerly placed the bulky ledger on the table, cringing at the loud creak. He cleared his throat.

"On the request of her majesty the queen, the charges brought against Brian O'Rourke of West Breifne are:

One: that said Brian O'Rourke in July 1586 sought the deprivation and overthrow of her realm in Ireland;

Two: in August 1586, he procured the assistance of Alexander and Donald MacDonald to raise forces against the queen;

Three: that he caused her majesty's name to be set upon an image of a woman which he caused to be set upon a horse's tail and to be drawn through the mire and then set upon by his Galloglass with their axes to hew, cut and mangle, the while uttering traitorous, rebellious and most wicked speeches against her majesty;

Four: that the said Brian O'Rourke protected and aided the escape of ship-wrecked survivors of the Spanish Armada, in direct contradiction of the instruction by her majesty to hand any survivors over to her representatives in Ireland;

Five: that the said Brian O'Rourke did continuously breach the peace and cause affray upon the lands that surrounded his;

Six: that during the course of these raids, he was responsible for the deaths of her majesty's soldiers;

Seven: that in the course of these raids, caused extensive damage and destruction through pillaging and arson;

Eight: that Brian O'Rourke went to Scotland to recruit mercenaries to continue his reign of terror on the queen's lands in Ireland."

The clerk sat back down with an audible sigh, his duty done.

The judge glared at the galleries to suppress any murmurings at the reading of the charges.

"So now we have heard the substance of several treasons, what do you plead to these charges?"

The O'Rourke stood up slowly.

"I do not recognise the jurisdiction of this court, so thereby have no comment."

The judge shook his head.

"Clerk, put it down as not guilty and let's move on." The judge turned to the O'Rourke again. "Given that you now know the charges, how would you like to be tried?"

"May I have a week to consider the charges and consult with my lawyer?"

The judge shook his head.

"The charges are well known to you, and you met with your lawyer beforehand and had plenty of time to discuss them. Judging by today's actions outside, any delay would carry the serious risk of causing an affray. Therefore, the trial proceeds today."

The O'Rourke grimaced and ground his teeth.

"I am a prince in my lands and a descendant of the high kings of Ireland. Therefore, only the queen can sit and judge me, for she is a fellow monarch."

The judge laughed.

"You do yourself no good by trying to distract the court with such ridiculous notions. You will be tried by a jury of your peers."

"You are not my peers."

"Then I fear today you will be disappointed to learn who your peers are. Let us proceed with the trial."

"May I please interject here as the O'Rourke's legal representative?"

Ardgal stood up and moved between the judges and the O'Rourke for this felt like the place the O'Rourke would be least likely to interrupt him. But the O'Rourke called him back and demanded his ear.

"What are you going to say?"

"I am going to undermine their case based on their use of the law."

"I am the O'Rourke. Their laws do not apply to me."

"The rope they hang you with will squeeze whatever neck is placed within it without prejudice. Let me do my job, and you can finish them off afterwards. All of what I will say pertains to your argument."

"I have put my faith in so many since I left my beloved Breifne, but been rewarded by so few."

"You know my family and how much importance it places on being seen as the pre-eminent Brehon family in all of Ireland?"

"I do."

"Well, imagine the esteem I would give to my relatives if I successfully defended the O'Rourke of all people in London of all places."

The O'Rourke sat back with a smug smile.

"You may proceed."

Ardgal straightened his doublet and stood before the judges.

"Indulge me, learned gentlemen, to return to a subject we merely skirted over in the opening of the proceedings, for I deem it to be the essence of the case."

The judges were unmoved, but Ardgal continued anyway.

"May I take you esteemed gentlemen, and you onlookers in the gallery, to the thirty-fifth year of the prestigious reign of Henry VIII? An act was passed that concerned itself with the trial of treasons carried out in his majesty's dominions. It then went on to define these said dominions as being 'done, perpetrated or committed by any person or persons out of this realm of England'. A somewhat ambiguous text whose interpretation revolves around the interpretation and placement of the word 'out'.

"However, this was repealed by the treason acts of Philip and Mary, which states 'all trials thereafter to be had, awarded, or made for any treason shall be had and used only according to the due order and course of the common laws of this realm and not otherwise'. As you well know, Ireland is a separate kingdom with its own laws. So how can you try my client here today?"

"I am familiar with the law," said the judge. "What is the point you are trying to make?"

"None of the alleged offences took place in England."

The judge slammed his quill upon the table.

"Why do you try to slow down the court with such irrelevancies? It is a well-established precedent that he can be put on trial here in England."

"Humour me, since we are here bargaining for a man's life. What are your legal justifications for putting him on trial in London? The kingdom of Ireland has its own laws and courts. Indeed, all the charges were compiled in Ireland. Surely it would make more sense to put him on trial there?"

The judge took a slow, deep breath and sifted through his notes. He gave a faint grin when he found what he was looking for.

"Let me bring you back to the case of the Catholic agitator, John Story. He both supported a rebellion in northern England and encouraged the Spanish to invade. He was put on trial for treachery for acts outside England and executed. All of this was justified through his trial and the precedent set. Therefore, we can put your client on trial."

The judge smiled, and Ardgal turned to face the O'Rourke and paused. He stuck his index finger in the air.

"The only thing in common in both cases is that the crown sent its agents into another country, kidnapped their victims and put them on trial for treachery. Two wrongs do not make a right. However, there are glaring differences. John Story claimed he was a Spanish subject, albeit at least he was born in England, and some of what he was accused of in his lifetime occurred in England.

"My client was not born in England, committed no crime in England, nor is he a subject of the crown."

Ardgal spun and raised an accusatory finger towards the judges and turned to the gallery to see if his point could generate some support. He received a smattering of boos.

"Let me remind you," said the judge, "you are not the star of a penny play down by the docks, a pompous sycophant pirouetting for the applause of the crowd. This is a serious business.

"The court, in its seriousness, has deemed that the medieval principle of 'the laws of England bind as well those of Ireland as England when they refer to both'. As to the question of which law will apply to the case, the treason law of 35 Henry VIII will apply because your client is not a subject of the realm of Ireland, rather he is a subject to the queen against whom this treason has been committed.

"Now, may we continue the trial?"

"Excuse me, your honour," said Ardgal, "but we must first settle the law before the case can be presented. Let me take you back to 1584 when the Irish Council wished to execute the Catholic archbishop of Cashel under the very same law, which, for the record, is the treason law 35 Henry VIII. These alleged offences were committed on the continent, again not in England. They asked its law officers for a judicial ruling about the applicability of the said act to the case. The legal judgement was that the 'statute is not confirmed nor established in this realm'. Indeed, no English legislation has been effective without either confirmation by the Irish parliament or proclamation by the monarchy. Can the court confirm that either of the parties have confirmed the application of this law to Ireland?"

The judge sighed.

"As a subject to the crown, your client is going on trial today. I note your request that her majesty deems the law applicable, but the court deems this as implied as the crown has agreed on the charges."

"But my client is not a subject of the crown."

The judge's head went down as he again sifted through his notes.

"Because he says it so, does not make it so. Because he signs it so, makes it so. Let me remind you where your client confirmed he was a subject of the queen. In 1542, the Irish parliament declared Henry VIII as king of Ireland, notwithstanding that the Irish lords retained their regalian rights which your client is so fond of referring to.

"However, in 1577 your client entered into an agreement with Sir Nicholas Malby that recognised the sovereignty of the crown and merely a year after, your esteemed client became 'Sir' Brian O'Rourke. What more confirmation of acceptance of the sovereignty of the crown do you need to have than the adaptation of the word 'sir' to his name? Well, if you want more, in 1585 he surrendered his lands to the crown and was regranted them back. That is two treaties your client signed that state he is a subject of the crown. What more evidence of submitting to the crown and acceptance of his status as a subject do you need, or do you wish to argue some more?"

The O'Rourke leapt out of his chair and threw his finger at the judge.

"They had a proverbial knife to my throat. What was I supposed to do?"

The judge laughed.

"So your plea to the court is the queen forced you to accept one of the largest grants of land in Ireland and ensure your children would inherit it, and in all of this, you claim she took advantage of you?"

The judge raised his eyebrow, and the O'Rourke's face turned purple.

"We all wish the queen would take advantage of us too. Now the court has ruled on jurisdiction. May we present the evidence against the defendant?"

The clerk returned and placed his ledger on the bench.

"We have several depositions from Sir Richard Bingham, the governor of Connacht, within whose province the defendant's land falls. Unfortunately, he cannot attend the court, as he is on the queen's duty. We also have written depositions from multiple witnesses, but all are too afraid to attend due to intimidation from the supporters of the defendant."

The O'Rourke leaned over to Ardgal.

"Am I ever going to get out of this flotsam and jetsam of a case?"

Ardgal grimaced.

"You'd be lucky to get out of here with your life."

CHAPTER 53

ONE LAST CONFESSION

The O'Rourke paced the floor of his cell and pieced together the shattered remains of his life. Bereft of energy, he sat in the corner in a heap dressed in rags, dirt and lice. His beard stank. Or was it his armpits? Or was it just all of him? He did not know. He was just trying to rally enough spirit to care. He had no visitors except for the guards, who took pleasure in blaming him for the destruction caused by his trial. They would come specifically to taunt him with new stories.

Ardgal was long gone. After the O'Rourke had been sentenced, the mob incited by the tall tales told at the trial went on the rampage, destroying the homes and businesses of anyone associated with Ireland and the rebels. The much exaggerated crimes of the O'Rourke had driven them into a vengeful frenzy, and many of the mobs ended up outside Ardgal's premises. Once they burned down Ardgal's premises and home, he fled back to the relative safety of Ireland.

The O'Rourke sat alone. He had the thoughts in his head and the occasional visit of a jackdaw to the window of his cell for company. He could not tell how long he had been there. By all accounts, it had been a week, but the O'Rourke had no wish to care as he knew at any moment he could be killed. Be it hung as per his sentence or murdered in his cell, all he knew was he would soon face death. It depended on how it would look in the politics of Ireland, an ever-moving subject he now knew nothing about. However, which way, he knew it would be cruel and humiliating. No better way to put down the savages of Ireland. He contemplated his life, where he went wrong, how the court case was a fix, and when they would carry out the sentence.

A knock came upon the cell door. He raised his head in curiosity. The guards were usually not so polite. The door creaked open. A single hand gripped the rim of the door, and Captain Williamson stood in the doorway grinning.

"Look at the mighty O'Rourke. How pathetic have you become? You called so much for the queen to attend your trial, saying only she could judge you. But look at you now. The only thing you are high king of is the lice."

The O'Rourke glared at him momentarily and then looked up at the narrow slit of light from the window above his head, hoping for the more pleasant company of the jackdaw.

"If you are not here to murder me in my cell, please leave. I'd rather spend my last days lording over the lice than looking at your ugly mug and stump of a hand."

The insults of a condemned man did little to lessen Williamson's grin.

"I am here to tell you your lice will no longer have a master after tomorrow. It is the eve of your death, and I am here to offer you some form of redemption for your multitude of crimes and sins."

The O'Rourke glanced up at Williamson.

"Tell me what it is, for I fear I will not be rid of you until you torment me with whatever wicked plan inspires that smirk on your face."

Williamson's grin only grew as he turned to invite someone into the cell.

"Really?!" the O'Rourke spat. "Is this my final humiliation?"

Archbishop Miler Macgrath of Cashel sneered at the O'Rourke and gloated over the pitiful condition of his former critic. A man in his sixties, he stood in his traditional white robes with only the hem muddied by the street. His hands were clasped together in prayer in case the robes did not signify his holiness enough. His goatee beard and moustache had a base of black hair being subsumed into a sea of white but styled and groomed so the bottom formed a point. His eyes narrowed, and his lips curled into a cruel grin as if in the back of his mind, he was listing slights he believed the O'Rourke had committed against him. He smirked as he calculated his revenge.

"No, my son," Miler said. "I am here to absolve you of your sins."

The O'Rourke burst out laughing.

"I got to hand it to you, Williamson. You really know how to humiliate me. You could not get a normal priest to hear my last confession. You have sent him, the abomination who turned away from being a bishop in the one true faith to being an archbishop, and a most corrupt one at that, in the queen's blasphemous religion."

"You are not in the court now. The only crowd you have to play up to is God and all his angels," Captain Williamson said, his smirk only growing larger. "That is, unless you are happy your destination is hell?"

The O'Rourke shook his head and then turned to look at the slit of light above his head to see if his jackdaw had returned. If he had any control of his circumstances left, he wished to deny his tormentors the pleasure of his attention. But they were persistent if nothing else.

"Now, you have not long left upon this earth," Miler sneered. "Confess your sins, and if you wish to see your son prosper, convert to the queen's faith. We'll tell your son and all of Ireland what a good example you set today."

The O'Rourke thrust his arms towards the heavens and laughed.

"I suppose it is ironic that the most notorious priest in Ireland should offer to absolve the sins of the most famous rebel in Ireland. But for heaven's sake, just gouge my eyes out, cut off my ears and throw them to the dogs. I wish to be in the silent solitude of prayer to the one true God when my life expires. I will curse you, Miler, until you cut my tongue out, and I cannot curse anymore, or I have taken my last breath. Do with me what you will. I am the O'Rourke, the last descendant of the high kings of Ireland and the biggest rebel in Ireland. You will not take that away from me. Hang me, you cowards, and let my death forever weigh down upon your souls."

"If you wish to damn your soul for the sin of pride, then so be it," Milar said as he turned to leave. "I have far more of our countrymen to convert who wish to live in the glory of the queen."

"Tell the guards what you want for your last meal," Captain Williamson sneered. "But I would not advise you to eat it. Many of the guards have relatives who have died in the wars in your savage land."

He turned and left the O'Rourke to nurture what shreds of dignity he had regained that day.

CHAPTER 54
THE FOUR CORNERS OF IRELAND

The executioner led the O'Rourke to the doorway where he could see the scaffold from which he was to be hung. A large crowd gathered in the square. The mood was seethingly feral. The O'Rourke looked pale and sickly, his hair and beard unkempt. They had stripped him of anything that could convey his former status and reduced him to rags. He looked like a common criminal, a street thief or a murderer. Gone was any of the O'Rourke's bravado and vibrancy that so entertained the court during his trial in what seemed a lifetime ago. He just concentrated his energies on dying with dignity and giving nothing to his enemies.

"Sorry, your worship," the executioner said as he grinned and pointed to the scaffolding. "The queen won't be coming to place the noose around your neck today. You just have a commoner like me who has that privilege. But look, they have prepared the rope with one of your peers, especially for you, oh, the high king of Ireland."

The O'Rourke watched as a terrified man dressed in rags and pleading for his life was placed in the noose. They hauled him high, and he kicked his legs in a last-gasp effort to set himself free. But he quickly turned crimson and then hung still. They left him swinging in the wind for a few minutes. But they did not cut him down and let him fall to the ground in front of the gathered crowd. They carefully lowered him, loosened the rope around his neck and reset the noose.

"Now it's your turn," said the executioner. "A freshly greased rope compliments of one of your peers."

The O'Rourke tried to hide his shudders. He knew they would try to torment him so they could report back to his people that they finally broke him. But he would not give them that pleasure. Still, the executioner could see him wince and gave him a smug grin.

"Do you know what the worst part of my job is?"

The O'Rourke just looked at him, too exhausted physically and emotionally to raise any anger into a glare. The grin subsided a little when the executioner did not get a reply.

"It is when the rotten fruit bounces off your head and fragments hit me. Most undignified."

That did raise something of a glare from the O'Rourke.

"Oh, how terrible for you."

"We'll see how bad now, for it is your time."

The executioner shoved the O'Rourke in the back and onto the path cleared through the crowd. The first fragments of cabbage struck his face.

The O'Rourke received a quick kick to the back of his knees, and he fell upon the raised platform. His outstretched manacled hands failed to break his fall.

"Get him up," Captain Williamson sneered.

The O'Rourke heard slow, methodical footsteps behind him echoing on the scaffold boards.

"People of London," Captain Williamson said as he threw his remaining arm out to the crowd. "Here lies an enemy of the queen, an enemy of the people of England and a spreader of papist lies. I give you Brian O'Rourke, who calls himself the high king of Ireland. But all I see is a common criminal who can only call himself high king of the head lice. He is not so high and mighty now, is he?"

A chorus of boos rang around the square, and a volley of rotten fruit rained down on the O'Rourke and in his general vicinity. The O'Rourke raised his head once the barrage was over. He lifted himself to his knees and turned towards the voice while being struck on the jaw with a cabbage.

"Williamson, you demon. You are lucky God only took one of your arms. Have you come to torment me one final time?"

Captain Williamson threw his head back and laughed.

"You could not be more wrong. The fact that you have been found guilty justifies my calling you a devil. However, before you depart this sacred earth, upon which you have done so much to inflict pain, death and chaos, I am going to give you one last chance to redeem your soul."

Captain Williamson walked forward to the front of the platform and stood before the baying crowd.

"Accept the faith of our queen and at least go to hell with an unblemished soul. I doubt even the almighty could forgive the plethora of your sins."

Miler Magrath stood out of view of the crowd in his ceremonial robes, ready to hear the O'Rourke's final confession if he faltered in fear of the noose. The O'Rourke glared at Captain Williamson.

"My answer is the same as yesterday. I was born a Catholic, and I will die a Catholic. Now send me off to judgment before my God, for I tire of listening to you."

"If you have no wish to unburden yourself of sin, then we shall damn you to hell. It makes no difference to us. The queen's justice will be done. Men, place his head in the noose and sharpen your knives. The sentence of being hung, drawn and quartered will be carried out. His body parts will be sent to the corners of Ireland as a warning to any who would choose to rebel." He turned once more to the O'Rourke. "Do you have any final words?"

"Oh, stop with your bluster and just get on with it." The O'Rourke closed his eyes to pray and felt the noose tighten around his neck.

CHAPTER 55
AN AUDIENCE WITH THE KING

Francisco observed the young men diligently going through their drills from his perch high above the courtyard. With a benevolent smile, he watched as determination etched itself onto their faces, all eager to seize their opportunity to impress their masters. He saw the decisive thrust of swords into sacks tied to posts, the satisfaction on their faces at mastering their tutor's instructions, and the grace and ease in their movements when everything worked in perfect tandem. But he also noticed the struggle, the grimaces, the beads of sweat on furrowed brows, the laboured movements as if their bodies were caked in mud. Then he looked towards the edges, where some stood with confident smiles, new and inexperienced but filled with self-assurance. Beside them were others whose faces contorted with fear, lacking the confidence of their peers.

Francisco had seen these expressions many times before as he forged raw young men into ship's crews for king and country. Not all of them would make it, and not all of them deserved to, having been criminals press-ganged into the navy or taken up with the seedier elements once they joined either through bitterness, coercion or fear. But Francisco had moulded them all and tried to keep them all alive, sometimes despite his orders. But here he was once more, clean-shaven and in a fresh captain's uniform, once more to face the king's justice.

He remembered when he was young and married his wife, wearing such a uniform. Her beauty was undeniable, a mesmerizing sight that took the breath away. Like a waterfall of chestnut tresses, her hair cascaded down her back in waves, catching the light and shimmering with every movement. She looked ethereal in her flowing white gown, a vision of grace and radiance. He wondered if she still looked the same and if she had given up on him and remarried. Did he really deserve her after all he had done? Surely she could never forgive him for the disgrace he had brought to the family name by being sentenced to hang. He pondered some more about his family. By how much would his children have grown since he was gone? Would they remember him? Would they still want him as their father?

A knock came at the door, and the daydreams fell apart.

"Come in."

A young sergeant stood there, all shakes and stutters, what Francisco recognised as a man compelled to carry out orders against the grain of his moral disposition. Francisco did not want to see suffering on anyone's face that day as he had only recently accepted his fate with the help of a priest.

"Is the tribunal ready for me?" Francisco said. "Don't worry yourself with your orders. Our mind weaves a complex web when we are afflicted by doubt. You will not be called to be the aggressor this day. I go quietly to my fate. If my king does not want to hear how I have served him in Ireland, no matter how many times I prayed that he would, then I am at peace with that and will pester God no more to do favours for a sinner."

"But you are wrong, captain. Your prayers were answered. It is not the tribunal that awaits you. It is the king."

Francisco felt his stomach shrink into a ball of pain.

"Have I no recourse to plead my case?" said Francisco, his voice reduced to a dry croak.

The young man lowered his head to whisper into Francisco's ear.

"It is not my place to question the king. Come along now, and do not make a fuss. Either way, your fate is sealed. You said you would cause no trouble."

"And I shall keep my word."

Francisco lowered his head and followed the young man.

Francisco was escorted through the grand corridors of the castle, his footsteps echoing off the marble floors as he made his way to his audience with the king. The opulence of the castle was unparalleled, dazzling even compared to what he had seen in Ireland. Every surface was adorned with vibrant tapestries depicting scenes of battle and celebration, and ornate weapons and armour were displayed proudly on the walls. Everything seemed so perfect, so wondrous, as he advanced through the bowels of the building to see the most powerful man in the world. Francisco could not help but feel like a drowned rat stuffed into a uniform about to be trapped in a room with the ship's cat. The king must truly be blessed to possess such wealth and luxury to have all of this at his command. He, in contrast, did not even own the clothes he wore.

"Don't idle," said the sergeant as Francisco lingered beneath the tapestries to celebrate the king's navy. "The king does not have the spare time to be wasted by the likes of you."

With trembling hands, Francisco released the corner of the silky cloth from between his index finger and thumb. As he followed the sergeant, his boots echoed against the marble floor of the grand hallway, each step leading him closer to fate. They approached the elaborately carved doors into the king's hall, with intricate designs of feathers and angels dancing across their surfaces. In a moment of respite, Francisco traced his fingers along the delicate etchings, marvelling at their beauty and losing himself in the details. He rejoiced in feeling as if his senses would soon be shorn and he would be no more than a spirit floating, wondering if he would meet God's judgement. Memories flooded back to him, all those times waiting outside halls in Ireland and Scotland, hoping for just a glimmer of recognition or a chance to plead his case, only to be rejected. But now, as he stood on the brink of uncertainty, strangely enough, he felt at ease. He held no expectations, only a resigned acceptance of whatever may come next. He would answer the king's questions with honesty and humility, then bow his head in gratitude for the opportunity to serve before meeting his unavoidable fate. The door creaked open before them, ushering Francisco into his final audience with the king.

Francisco's steps faltered as he approached the grand hall. His heart raced as he was suddenly overcome with nerves. Francisco instinctively lowered his head.

"Move. Your king has summoned you," said the guard before pushing Francisco in the back. Francisco stumbled forward. He never felt so vulnerable, so diminished, so alone.

This hall was unlike the halls in Ireland or even Scotland. It demanded to be admired. The walls were adorned with priceless paintings, each brush stroke capturing the glory and conquests of the Spanish crown and their armies and navies in meticulous detail. Instead of bearded men vanquishing an animal or directing a rabble of cow herders into battle, vast pictures of King Philip dominated the walls. In one, he was on a bucking horse as his armies in the background conquered Europe. In another, he ate with his courtiers in a scene obviously based on the Last Supper. In others, he merely looked regal or holy as he stared down at all that gazed upon him.

On other walls hung huge tapestries, hand-woven from the finest silks and threads, from every corner and corridor. Their intricate designs told tales of courage and honour that stirred the hearts of all who saw them. None of them looked old or tattered or like they had recently been put up due to a change in leader.

As he walked through the grand hall, armoured suits stood tall and formidable in alcoves along the walls. Each suit gleamed in the dim light with a fierce splendour, bearing engravings and embellishments that showcased the incredible skill of the craftsmen who had forged them. These were not just mere suits of armour but symbols of strength and triumph over enemies vanquished. The O'Rourke could have filled his hall with all the suits of armour alone. Such was the difference in size and grandeur.

The king sat at the end of this vast chasm of opulence. A formidable wall of guards flanked the throne, their stern faces adding to Francisco's growing sense of unease. As he walked with head bowed, he could not help but steal glances at the king, a man almost considered a living deity so close in flesh and blood. It was hard to focus on the king, for he seemed small, given the splendour of his massive throne and the draped flags of his royal armies on the wall behind him. The king's head appeared to be supported by his neck ruff rather than the ruff being a decorative appendage. His face was pale and pointed, long and thin, as if he was sickly and did not see much sunlight. His hair and beard were immaculately trimmed, but that did little to negate his sickly appearance. This must all have been the effects of spending so much of his life in prayer.

The regal figure sat uncomfortably on his ornate throne, the weight of his robes seeming to burden him even further. The vibrant red and gold collars of his jacket stood out sharply against his pale skin, adding an unnecessary stiffness to his already rigid posture. A heavy set of rosary beads was tightly wound around his right fist, resting on the arm of his throne. Francisco's shoulders slumped. Was he asking for divine forgiveness for condemning one of his loyal servants to death?

A courtier broke into Francisco's right-hand vision, snapping him out of his awe at laying eyes on the king.

"Your majesty, this is the captain who survived the Armada and spent several years amongst the natives of Ireland. He was also found guilty of cowardice by the admiral of your great Armada, amongst other charges, and was set to be executed. However, be it divine intervention or the work of the devil, he was saved by a storm, unlike many of his men. So by fortune or ill will, he stands before you today."

The king waved his hand, and two groups of courtiers came from either side of the room and gathered a safe distance away from Francisco. Francisco raised his head but did not recognise any of the faces. He bowed his head once more and waited for the pronouncement of his sentence. When no words came, he looked up to see the king engrossed in his notes.

"Your record was quite good until the Armada," the king said, looking over the top of his papers.

Francisco bowed his head lower.

"I have always tried to serve you to the best of my ability, sire."

"Hmmm, then you saw fit to abandon the line just as it was about to face the English onslaught?"

Francisco felt the king's eyes on the top of his head, leaving him with a crown of sweat.

"My ship would have been a hindrance to the manoeuvrability of the fleet. It was better to do repairs than be a burden, sire."

"The admiral did not think so," the king growled.

"I begged to differ with the admiral and said so at my trial, sire," Francisco said, his voice starting to shudder.

"Are you saying my admiral was wrong?"

The king sounded animated.

"It was no slight on you, sire," Francisco said, struggling to get his words out. "I did what I believed was in the best interests of you, the fleet and of Spain."

Francisco lowered his gaze once more. By now, his face was red, and sweat rolled down his forehead and cheeks and dripped on the floor. The king flung his papers down in a fit of pique.

"No one should desert the line, for they answer to their commanders just as I answer to God." The king sat back in his chair and tried to curb his temper. "So why should I not send you to be executed right now?" said the king.

Francisco kept his eyes firmly on the floor and tried not to stutter.

"You should carry out my sentence, sire, for I am truly sorry for what I have done. I only ever meant to protect your men and your ship. But I shall not waste your precious time with my excuses, for I am at your mercy. However, let me first divulge my knowledge of the Irish so it may assist you should you ever decide to give them aid. Then I will have performed my duty to you, sire, and my country, and will gladly go and receive my sentence which your servants deemed fit to give me."

The king took a deep breath in through his nose and pondered.

"Do not presume your sentence is already set. I have learned a lot about your time in Ireland. I received many letters from the Irish asking me to send large armies to their aid. The devil and the deep blue sea have robbed me of most I have sent. It is like the heretic queen is protected by the devil himself. You have met many of their chieftains, as they call themselves. What was your impression of the Irish when you stayed amongst them?"

"They were savages but good Catholics, sire. They would always vigorously defend their faith against the blasphemies of the heretical English."

The king paused to consider what Francisco had said.

"Can they fight?"

"They like nothing better. They would turn upon themselves if they didn't have the queen as their enemy."

The king hesitated, for many of his advisors said an army in Ireland could be difficult to supply, and there was a risk of it being isolated.

"Then, if I went to assist them, they could turn upon me?"

"Nothing guides them more than the light of God. They would see your arrival as a divine crusade. If you put yourself forward as a defender of the faith, they would flock behind you."

The king squeezed his rosary beads between his fingers as he wrestled his conflicting thoughts about what to do with his wayward captain. He shut his eyes and prayed while Francisco did not remove his gaze from the floor. The king drummed his fingers on the end of his armrest to signify he had reached his decision.

"I think God had a mission for you, and you are before me fulfilling it. Therefore, I deem it unwise to carry out the sentence that dangles above your head. You have done me good service in your time in Ireland so let that be deemed the punishment for your crimes. I hereby pardon you from any offences you may have committed in the past."

Francisco's body trembled with emotion, his limbs unable to support him any longer as he sank to his knees. His head bowed low in a gesture of profound gratitude, and tears streamed down his cheeks as he found himself overwhelmed by the king's generosity and kindness.

"Thank you, sire, thank you."

"Now go and work with my advisors on the best way to provide aid to the Irish. You have much service yet to give."

"Thank you, sire. I will serve you well until the day I die."

The king's captain took a firm grip on Francisco's elbow and guided him to the side of the grand hall, where a group of elegant courtiers waited patiently. The ornately decorated windows let in a cool breeze that brushed against Francisco's clammy hands, causing him to break out in a cold sweat. A gentle tap on his shoulder startled him as he stepped towards the window to catch his breath. Turning around, he was met with the warm smile of a man dressed in the regal garb of a bishop, his head tilted slightly in curiosity.

"My name is Edmund Magauran, the archbishop of Armagh and the main liaison between the Irish lords of the north and the king of Spain. I would like to thank you on my own behalf and theirs, for you have done our cause no end of good by speaking up for us today."

A faint, weary smile tugged at the corners of Francisco's mouth as it struggled to break through the exhaustion that weighed heavy on his mind. It was a fleeting moment before the overwhelming weariness overtook him once again, draining all traces of emotion from his expression.

"I did it all for my friend Señor O'Rourke. Without his help, I would not be here today. I said what I thought he would want me to say."

The archbishop furrowed his brow and placed his hand on Francisco's forearm.

"But do you believe it to be true?"

"Every word. A man who thinks he is inevitably for the rope will tell the truth."

"Well, bless you for doing that," and the archbishop placed his hand on Francisco's shoulder.

Francisco became anxious and grabbed the archbishop's forearm.

"What about Señor O'Rourke? The last I saw of him, he was being dragged away by English soldiers."

The archbishop dropped his head.

"Alas, they put on a show trial for him in London and then hung him. I do not want to say what they did next, for I fear you are of fragile mind."

Francisco's shoulders shook as he buried his face in his hands and wept. He could feel the weight of sadness pressing down on him, making it hard to breathe. Suddenly, a comforting hand was placed on his other shoulder, causing Francisco to look up through his tears.

"Pedro?" Francisco's hands fell from his face, and his head spun like he was in a dream.

Pedro gave him a warm smile.

"It is I, my friend."

Francisco enveloped him in a warm, tight embrace, his arms squeezing with all his strength. Then, with a sudden release, he stepped back and gazed at him with curious intensity.

"How did you get here?"

Pedro placed his hand on Francisco's shoulder and proudly smiled.

"Some of the men made it off that godforsaken beach, thanks to you. When we heard you had been recaptured in the Netherlands, we petitioned the king to pardon you."

Francisco's heart swelled with joy.

"You saved my life."

"It was only a fraction of the payment for saving ours. Come, your family waits for you. You are to stay in Madrid and have been given a house by the king so you can stay near and act as an advisor about Ireland."

Francisco stumbled backwards, his arms flailing for balance. In a swift move, he was caught by the Irish-in-exile courtiers who had gathered around the archbishop, their strong arms holding him steady.

"Come," said Pedro. "All the bad times are in the past. Come and celebrate your return with your family and friends."

Francisco steadied himself as thoughts flashed uncontrollably through his mind. His family, how God saved him, his hardships in Ireland, being shipwrecked. He finally settled on the O'Rourke. He could have easily been on the same scaffold with his friend. He wiped away one last tear.

"The O'Rourke would never turn down a feast."

Francisco looked down the stairs below, and out from the shadows stepped his wife. This time, Pedro had to catch him to stop him from collapsing. His wife smiled up at him. She appeared much older now, with her grey hair floating behind her on the breeze from the courtyard. Her face was etched with wrinkles, probably from worrying about him. But now, at this moment, she was the most beautiful woman in the world to Francisco. Just like she had been on their wedding day. A young man stepped out from behind his wife and gave a nervous smile towards him. His boy had begun to embrace manhood.

With shaky steps and a supportive hand from Pedro, he descended the stairs as his wife waited below with open arms. His heart thumped in his chest so loud that he looked at Pedro to see if he could hear it. Each step connected with the stairs as if he was floating in a dream. After all that had happened, he was here in the king's palace, his honour restored, and he was about to be reunited with his family. As his foot touched the floor at the bottom of the stairs, he fell into his wife's embrace.

CHAPTER 56
HISTORICAL NOTE

This story, set mainly in Ireland from 1588 to 1591, is a mash-up between the real stories of Francisco de Cuellar, a Spanish captain who was shipwrecked on the Irish coast, and Brian O'Rourke, one of the last leaders of the O'Rourke clan. The O'Rourkes were based around the modern Irish county of Leitrim. It is not a straight retelling of either story: I have taken the general concept of de Cuellar's story, which at is the beginning and end of this book, and the O'Rourke's story is the middle. I chose these stories as it acts as a sort of prequel to the events in the Exiles series. The politics of this story have to play out to set up *Exiles*.

Writing about Irish clans is difficult. It is quite an obscure subject matter. In my day, they were barely covered in the school Irish history curriculum, only a mere sidenote in any of the Irish history museums, and the castles were poorly signposted and in ill repair. There is also little imagery left from the time, and what is left is barely recognised outside academic circles or the small number of history fans of the period. Added to that, the multitude of clans, the obscurity or sameness of the names, and the fact that the clans turned against each other on a regular basis, can all make for a confusing read. Therefore, I have tried to make it as clear and as linear as possible.

It is also difficult to get a decent map of the period that contains all the elements I want. Hence, I have had to create them myself from a multitude of sources, including present-day maps, for the details.

That leads to the dilemma of history versus entertainment, which is the main reason I mashed together the two stories. The de Cuellar story has a good beginning and end, but the middle sags slightly. The story of the O'Rourke is good, but there is little detail in the historical records. Therefore, the main milestones in the story are historical, but the details are fiction.

There were several facts I did change, however, so the story flowed more easily while still remaining within the general story and the mood at the time. The O'Rourke did not meet the king of Scotland, nor did he travel to Edinburgh as far as I know. However, the best way to dramatise the situation was to have him meet the king and have all the political pressures in Scotland at the time play out in front of the king. Doing it as it happened would have meant introducing a load of short-term new characters and switching between Edinburgh and Glasgow, which would have made the story much clunkier. The legal arguments made in the court are the actual arguments they debated according to the historical sources. On the other hand, De Cuellar met the king of Spain.

Overall, I think the book is a decent representation of the period and stays relatively true to the underlying stories while being mainly fiction.

C R Dempsey, June 2024

If you enjoyed this book, please join my mailing list for release updates and offers.

<u>Books I used as historical sources:</u>

The Annals of the four masters.

Sixteenth Century Ireland – Colm Lennon

Tyrone's rebellion – Hiram Morgan

Elizabeth's Irish Wars – Cyril Falls

The Nine Years War 1593-1603 – James O'Neill

ATLANTIC OCEAN

TIRCONNELL

RIVER ERN

DONNELL
O'DONNELL

LOUGH
MELVIN

TADHG ÓG
MAC CLANCY

LOWER
LOUGH
ERNE

FERMANAGH

DONOUGH
O'CONNOR SLIGO

SLIGO

SIR HUGH
MAGUIRE

BAILE
NUA

UPPER
LOUGH MAC NEAN

LOUGH
GILL

BRIAN
O'ROURKE

UPPER
LOUGH
ERNE

ÍOCHTAR
CONNACHT

DRUMAHAIR
CASTLE

WEST
BRIEFNE

SIR JOHN
O'REILLY

COLLOONEY
CASTLE

RIVER
UNSHIN

EAST
BRIEFNE

RIVER
OWENMORE

LOUGH
ARROW

LOUGH
ALLEN

BRIAN
MAC DERMOT

LOUGH
KEY

WEST BRIEFNE

1580s

LEITRIM
CASTLE

LOUGH
EIDIN

MOYLURG

RIVER
SHANNON

CASTLE
TOWN
LORDSHIP
PRINCIPAL LORD/CLAN
HILLS   WOODS

MAGHERY
CONNACHT

ANNALY

ABOUT AUTHOR

If you enjoyed this book, please join my mailing list for release updates and offers. https://landing.mailerlite.com/webforms/landing/i1l1n2

C R Dempsey is the author of the 'Exiles' series, set in Elizabethan Ireland. He has plans for many more, and he needs to find the time to write them. History has always fascinated him, and historical fiction was an obvious outlet for his accumulated knowledge. C R spends lots of time working on his books, mainly in the twilight hours of the morning. C R wishes he spent more time writing and less time jumping down the rabbit hole of excessive research.

C R Dempsey lives in London with his wife and cat. He was born in Dublin but has lived most of his adult life in London.

C R can be found at:

https://www.crdempseybooks.com/,

https://www.facebook.com/crdempsey,

https://www.instagram.com/crdempsey/,
Twitter: @dempsey_cr

ALSO BY

If you enjoyed this book please would you leave a review on the retailer where you bought it.

To read more books in the *Exiles* series click on the QR codes below to be brought to your favourite online ebook store.

Bad Blood
□□□□ *"A new piece of Irish historical fiction that pulls you in through its protagonist, and is full of plenty of action," - Reedsy Discovery*
□□□□ *"To say this book is rich with action, adventure, and deep meaty history is putting it mildly," – The Historical Fiction Company*
□ □ □ □ □ *"a tale that is filled with twists, including stab-bings-in-the-back, and one that puts readers on the edge of their seats," – The Book Commentary*

Acknowledgments

Thank you to all my family and friends and all of those who helped to create this book.

Special thanks to Mena (endless patience and support)

   Thank you also for the professional support of:

   Book cover: Dominic Forbes

   Editing: Robin Seavill

Both these individuals can be found on www.Reedsey.com

Printed in Great Britain
by Amazon

49791171R00178